ZIGGURAT:
How Ur Gave Birth

a novel by

Kenneth Briggs
in collaboration with
Janet Briggs

Chora House Press
Langhorne, PA

Also by
Ken & Janet Briggs

YIN AND YANG COME HOME:
A Picture Book of Being There

ACKNOWLEDGMENT

We wish to thank those who have helped us in the preparation of the manuscript for *Ziggurat* with their critiques and suggestions; Suzanne Newton, Bill Appel and Irene Thornberg. Duke University deserves credit for nourishing our aspirations with various workshops and their excellent library facilities. The discourse on death by Ut-Napishtim on pages 258-259 is taken from the translation of S.M. Dalley, *Myths of Mesopotamia* and the cuneiform quotations from *The Epic of Gilgamesh* on the back of the jacket were hand copied by R. Campbell Thompson.

First printing June 1998

ISBN 0-9661945

LCCN...97-94731

Editing, design and printing services provided by About Books, Inc., 425 Cedar Street, POB 1500, Buena Vista, CO 81211.

Every relationship to the archetype,...works because it releases in us a mightier voice than our own. He who speaks in primordial images speaks with a thousand voices; he enthralls and overpowers,.... He transmutes our personal destiny into the destiny of mankind, thereby evoking in us all those beneficent forces that ever and anon have enabled mankind to find a refuge from every peril and to outlive the longest night.

Jung, C.G., "On the Relation of Analytical Psychology to Poetry" *Collected Works*,

CHAPTER ONE

He must have passed by the city that day. If there was a special reason for this inspection it might have been a concern that Nannar-Sin was hiding in the underworld, leaving the city at the mercy of Utu's fiery darts. He must have dropped a pebble on His way. How else could we explain what was to transpire, not just in the next year and a half, but for as far as you can see?

Gart would understand about such a pebble. Only yesterday he had tossed a clod out into the west basin and watched the expanding ripples extinguish themselves on the shore, except the sector of each arc that went out through the water gate and into the channel of the Euphrates. He had thought about those fading traces of his effort and wondered if they were still present in some form when the water reached the sea.

Of course, Nannar-Sin would never desert Ur, his most treasured fief, although certain persons in high places were beginning to wonder. No, Nannar was simply resting and completing his plans to put Utu in his proper place very soon, if ever so briefly.

Gart knew little of high places, as yet, and such concerns were merely beginning to organize in his thinking. He was no longer a boy, but his persistent optimism and ambition may have blurred any sense of the city's drift.

This noon his ambitions dozed with him and the animals at his feet as he perched in the shade. Soon he was dreaming. As his slumber deepened, darkness enveloped him and he experienced a transient pleasure, relaxing as the smooth, cool mud sucked him downward. But now a sense of oppression as suffocation gradually crowded in upon him. His heart began to race as water began to trickle into his nostrils.

"No! Eber-Sin. NO. NEVER." The voice roared up out of his belly and exploded against his skull in a brilliant burst of pain.

Gart grabbed the support pole with one hand to keep from falling over backward into the pen. Gingerly he touched his bruised forehead with his other hand. What a rude awakening! He shifted on his uncomfortable corner seat. It was so hot! He had been dead tired already by mid-morning. What had he been dreaming?

His good cheer and excitement over the events of this morning had gradually evaporated as he worked under the broiling sun. As he had mused about the unexpected invitation, he had a strong sense that "the critter" was around, somewhere. That wasn't necessarily good news, though. What if it had come to warn him to get out of here, to save his life? That would mean giving up his whole project. He had experienced a certain sense of foreboding hovering over the yards. It hadn't faded in the four months since they had found the old man beaten to death. In fact – Gart squinted out into the brilliant sunlight — it was hardly fifteen paces from here that they had found him.

Why would anyone want to do such a senseless thing to the poor old fellow? Was someone or something out there trying to send a message to me? he thought, or did they think the old Akkadian still owned the business? Gart had finished buying him out two years ago but the old fellow continued to hang around and help out. It was the only life he had known.

Oh, there had been all sorts of stories, even huge monsters said to slip into the city through the water gate at night to steal into the yards to seize their supper, devouring cattle and sheep without a trace and crushing anyone who saw them. Gart gave little credence to these stories, especially since his chief source was Jeme, who relished telling the wildest tales and mixing them with more plausible ones about rich and powerful persons, not named, who coveted the land on which the yards were built. There was no direct evidence for this either, although another trader had been beaten under circumstances that were never explained and another one had left the city. Business had surged for Gart, a blessing that made him increasingly uneasy.

Was anyone really after his little plot of land and his business, or had someone just beaten the old man out of mindless resentment of all outsiders, or of jealousy toward someone who was making it when they weren't? If so, Gart was a good candidate for the same treatment. Everything had been going so well for him in the last year, ever since he had married Leah. Had he finally gotten in too deep, living too high — and so far from home?

As his headache faded, he was beginning to recall flashes of his dream. The mud he had been sinking into seemed to be in the pond near his home village. As this impression became clearer, his initial tinge of longing and loneliness mixed with distress and a mounting anger at himself. Something treacherous inside had dulled him to sleep and sucked him back into the mire of doubts he thought he had overruled. What are you doing here, Gart? That uncomfortable question was back. Well, he was here — and he was staying. To cut and run would be abhorrent, murder or no murder.

He hopped down from his seat, ready to engage the real world once more, but that real world smacked him with a wave of dizziness and a bath of searing heat. He soon jumped back up onto his perch in the shade.

He peered out from under the dusty palm frond canopy. He barely managed to blow away the drop of sweat as it left the tip of his nose. The shade helped a little. He had spent the morning building it. Even the dozing animals must be questioning, as he was, why anyone would chose to live in this oven of bricks.

He must wait, but he could not. The brightly lit yards out there were torpid, motionless, but he sensed something alive in that endless moment. Something had changed. Soon the sun would be going down behind the walls. What could disclose itself during these torrid days?

This week was the height of summer and this was the hottest part of the day. Here in the city everything was concentrated; power, wealth, even heat. But if other people could stand it, so could he. He shifted himself down the poles to the corner of the pen, moving his head and eyes around and up to search the darkest corner under the awning. Perhaps he could see again those pointy ears and sharp white teeth. A cold prickle ran up his spine. He had sensed a slight movement out in the yard. Was he expecting something to grab him in broad daylight? Silly, he could see nothing out there but heat waves.

Back under the canopy there was, at least, some relief for his eyes. Maybe if he squinted a little he could see "the critter." Naah, not likely. The only time he had been aware of the — whatever it was — it had come on its own terms. There had to be excitement like when he was picked for officer training, or two years ago when he finally bought out the old Akkadian at such a favorable price. There was also the time he had finally talked Brother Shem-ki into giving him a steady share of the temple business, and now again this morning. He had not seen a clear picture of this visitation, like the other times, but he had experienced a strong sense that it was around somewhere while Mahn-so-ni was speaking to him.

"There's going to be an important political meeting at the hall this evening, Gart. I would consider it a personal favor to me if you could come. You know where the Council Hall is, don't you?" the councilman had said.

"Yes, near the north gate, about two streets in," Gart had replied.

Now, squeeze the eyes once more. Umn...no, yes! There was something – two little white things hanging down! Those could be teeth. The corner seemed darker now. The ears must be up above, on the reed awning. Eyes would be hard to see. Could this be his animal spirit friend, guide — whatever it was?

"Brrrrzzt.... Brrrrzzzt.... Brrrrzzzzt." The intermittent sound was subdued but, because of the surrounding silence, clear and unmistakable. Those were tiny wasps' nests up in the corner of this stockyard pen and not the teeth of any critter, imaginary or otherwise.

"Brrrrzzzt....Brrrzzt....Brrrzzt. The wasps continued their complaining. Gart stirred. He couldn't concentrate. The slightest movement out in the yard and his eyes would jerk away. Coward! he raged at himself. What monster would be out on a day like this? Don't you know that evil comes from the dark?

"Gaarrrt.... Gaarrrt."

Gart looked down with a start at the four old ewes lying in the shade at his feet. His head brushed the dry and dusty palm fronds of the roof of the shelter. The sound was definitely bleating but also very much like his name. He could see no sign that his sheep were talking. Their breathing was deep and rapid. It was too hot for them to stir.

"Gaaaarrrt... Gaa…a…rrt."

There it was again! He stooped a bit, peeking under the edge of the roof of the shelter in the direction of the sound. There they were, two familiar figures, but out of their usual setting. The two young men, bare-chested and bare-headed, were approaching through the maze of livestock pens and shelters. Approaching? Stalking, in its most exaggerated and comical version, was more like it. This he would expect of Orson who was leading the way, hands cupped around his mouth. He was evidently the source of the bleats. It did look strange to see Kre-eg, the taller, sharp-nosed one, joining in, following Orson's lead for once.

"Which one of you sheep are in charge here?" asked Orson. Both of the visitors kept their gaze fixed on the ewes although Gart's body was in no way concealed by the spindly wooden posts that supported the shelter.

"Oh, you are, ma'am?" Orson continued to address the old ewe. "Have you seen a slightly confused looking young lieutenant of the Civil Guard wandering around here? Oh! There you are, Gart. I didn't recognize you in the crowd."

"All right, you jokers!" Gart climbed out of the pen and its shade to join them. "What the hell are you two town boys doing down here in the stockyards?"

"Why, seeking the pleasure of your company of course!" said Kre-eg. "Nice place you have here." He gave a loud sniff, nose elevated as he surveyed the maze of pens, dung heaps and racks of drying hides.

"Well, I admit, it doesn't smell like a brewery." Gart delivered what he considered to be a token counterattack by referring to Kre-eg's family's business.

Gart was tempted to believe they had come to seek the pleasure of his company, but he would not be in any hurry to let his guard down. He had only known these men for the three months since they started officer's training, and he still felt like an outsider and a little suspicious of the whole Civil Guard program and his own motives for joining. In the eight years since he had come to live in the city of Ur he had made few friends except for courting his recent bride and the necessary attention to her family.

Even in dealing with the animals he bought and sold he deliberately stayed aloof. It was better that way. He wanted none of the pain he saw in his father when he had to butcher his own sheep.

"Come on now, you two," said Gart. "This is out of your territory, especially you Kre-eg. How come you're out here?"

"Kre-eg had to come down to my boss' warehouse to arrange for another shipment of barley for his father. Nam-Ku and his brewery account for about half of our business these days." Orson paused to wipe his brow.

"It was so damned hot in that warehouse I thought I would pass out." Kre-eg picked up the story. "Ors seemed too confused to write up the bill, so I thought I had better get him out of there."

"Yes, and…?" said Gart, still questioning their motives.

"We decided that our only hope to cool off was to go jump in the river. Ors mentioned it wasn't very far to where you worked so we thought maybe we should take you along to guard our clothes and kill snakes," said Kre-eg, ducking his head under the roof as he swung his long legs into the pen.

"That was right bright of you, Lieutenant," said Gart. He noticed that both he and Orson were showing off each other's new military titles. "You may also have saved my life, too.

"Let's head for the water."

"Which water? Do we go outside the walls to the river or the canal, or will one of the harbor basins do?" asked Orson.

"We can try the west basin," said Gart. "The river can change six feet over night. If it's lower than yesterday I don't think we would want to swim in the basin, but we might be able to go out the river gate. Let me check the animals' water and I'll be ready." Gart poured the contents of a large leather water bag into two small pottery troughs.

"I'll just take this along to the river," he said, shouldering the empty bag.

The three young men lowered their heads and squinted as they climbed the gate of poles at the western edge of the stockyards.

Just then, the silence was broken by muffled squawks and flapping noises. Three vultures appeared above the southeast city wall and flew a short distance before they banked and glided back out of sight near the spot where they had appeared. Whatever had disturbed them was evidently less fearsome than the heat.

Gart peered down the dusty street in the direction of the harbor. Visions of many tempting pools of the past were suddenly before him, a succession of boyhood swimming scenes, usually with the whole pack of cousins and friends. In those days, his belonging was automatic, unquestioned.

In a few minutes they were at the west harbor basin. But there would be no swimming here. The basin with its mooring posts and scattered sheds was as deserted as the alleys they had just left. The waters had receded, leaving a large margin of mud banks strewn with a few battered old reed skiffs and one or two small boats hollowed from logs. A pair of gulls landed to inspect the piles of garbage and fish entrails. It should be easy, though, to walk the solid mud bank out through the river gate and down to the river.

"Well — I don't know about this." Kre-eg shaded his eyes and surveyed the mud banks.

"It's no problem," said Gart. "That mud will hold us. We can walkout the river gate." As he spoke, he felt again the seductive pull of his dream, still fresh.

"Yes, but what will we find out there besides the river?" Kre-eg asked. "It's dangerous outside that wall. They say there are a lot of drifters going through the garbage heaps. Some of them wouldn't hesitate to stick a knife into you."

"I thought you were just joking when you said you needed me to watch your clothes and kill snakes," said Gart. "I'm not sure it's any safer here, inside the walls."

"I guess I'm just a born city dweller," Kre-eg said as they made their way along the mud at the basin's edge. "The walls — we just think of them as protecting us."

"I had forgotten," Orson said. "You are the only one of us here from an old family. My family has moved back and forth every few years from our village. Gart comes from the sand hills where the air is pure — if the sand don't blow. Your family must have been here forever."

"Well, actually," Kre-eg hesitated. "I guess my grandfathers were the first ones to come here."

"Really? From where?" Orson asked.

Nosy cuss, that Orson, Kre-eg was thinking, but why should I be so touchy? It sure won't make any difference to these two.

"Out east — Elam, or someplace like that." His voice trailed off toward the end of his answer as he shifted his gaze back to the mud bank.

Just as they reached the gate, a thin layer of water advanced rapidly over the dry mud of their path.

"Hey, what's this?" Orson asked.

Gart turned to face him just in time to see their tracks in the mud disappear beneath the rising water. They could hear a low rumble to the west and then some men shouting.

"But it's blue sky up there," Orson protested. "It never rains here in the summer."

"Maybe not," Gart said. "But look through the gate to the west. That sky looks.... Hey, come on out here!" Gart was through the gate, gazing at the western sky. It was changing with amazing rapidity. Once again, Gart felt like he had burst into a different world. As the others joined him they felt a short blast of hot wind and watched, fascinated, as the murky haze of sand and dust boiled upward to meet the descending sun, now a bearable but glowering red disc. Lower down, the storm clouds themselves crept south: tan, red, a tinge of purple, a band of black. Sheet lightning flashed to the south, a flicker, two flickers to the north. A dust funnel danced along the ridge across the river.

Out of the enveloping quiet Orson tried to speak.

"Oh my, all this for our swimming part...for us?" His voice faded, faltered, the thrust of his joking words a puff in the face of the storm. The three fell silent, their exchange of glances affirming the impressiveness of the moment.

Finally, Orson tried again, his tone hushed. "Do you feel as small as I do?"

His companions nodded mute assent.

Several dugout canoes came gliding through the reeds, their crews standing and poling rapidly.

"Hey, you fellows, better head for high ground. There must be a real gully washer up river. The old gal is really on a surge," one of the men shouted to the trio, who were now ankle deep in water.

"Let's go!" said Gart. Even wading with the current, the going was getting difficult as the mud softened beneath them.

"When this surge passes the currents out of this basin could be pretty – "

"Dangerous." Gart finished Orson's warning as the three of them headed up the bank out of the water, which was now knee deep.

"Hah!" Kre-eg snorted with disdain, although he did not argue the matter. "You married men better get home to your wives."

Gart and Orson did not reply. They trudged on for several minutes until they reached the corner where their ways would part.

"That's right, we'll do that," said Gart. "However — I did have something planned for this evening. Would the two of you want to come with me?"

Orson stopped abruptly and straightened up. "Oh, a little deal on? What's this?"

"Oh, nothing really." Gart felt a trifle flustered. "It's just a meeting. You know Mahn-so-ni, don't you? Well, he mentioned they would like to have some new blood. Younger guys."

"Yes, I know Mahn-so-ni. What kind of a meeting is this?" Orson looked perplexed.

"Well, it's kind of a neighborhood meeting, an organizing meeting you might say," Gart hurried through his explanation.

"Why, Gart, you wouldn't be thinking about messing around in politics, would you? My, my, wouldn't Papa have been proud of you if he had known you were coming out for councilman or something! That would put you one up on him, a pillar in the big city instead of a village headman.

"Pillar," Kre-eg repeated, half to himself.

By now, Gart was feeling flustered and vulnerable.

"Ah come on, get off my back, Kre-eg," he muttered, his face hot.

"That Mahn-so-ni is pretty sharp," said Orson. "He probably has a job all picked out for you."

"I'm not volunteering for anything I don't understand, and what do I know about city politics?" Gart snapped, irritated.

"It's perfectly respectable to go to a public meeting."

"Oh, yes, perfectly respectable," said Kre-eg with a big grin.

Respectable or not, Gart felt like a small bug whose hiding place had just been discovered. He squirmed. He feared his cheeks were glowing. He mumbled his last remark about respectability. That was followed by an extended pause. Kre-eg was obviously enjoying Gart's embarrassment.

"Right! Perfectly respectable," Orson said. He was thinking, we better let the poor guy off the hook.

Gart was thankful when Orson motioned for them to resume their walk.

"New blood, eh?" Kre-eg had picked up the theme. "They had better get started. We may see our first battle duty right here in the city. Let me tell you, if the City Council doesn't get off their assembled fifty fat butts and do something, this place is going to break apart, and very soon."

"Say, you are serious!" said Orson. "I didn't realize you went in for that, Kre-eg."

"And just what should the city fathers do, good sir?" Gart asked, much relieved and surprised by this turn in Kre-eg's conversation.

"Hell, how would I know? They are supposed to come up with the answers, and all they do is sit around and pick their teeth. I don't pretend to know how to run this city. Most of this riffraff slipping into town.... I don't know what you could do with them. It is getting serious."

Nodding agreement and without further comment, Gart started down the narrow alley between the single-story, mud-brick and reed-wattle buildings; a mixture of shops and homes. "Well, Kre-eg, are you coming or not?" he tossed over his shoulder.

"I don't know if I want to get involved," Kre-eg answered, "but why don't you drop by my parents' house on your way to Orson's? I'll think about it."

Both automatically assumed Orson's availability and cooperation.

"It sure has been a lot of fun, swimming with you fellows," was all he said.

As the three parted company Gart was already reviewing his words of invitation with some surprise. They had sprung from his lips almost unrecognized by him. They were as unexpected as the sudden appearance of his friends. In spite of that, this seemed like a powerful day — and it wasn't over yet.

As Kre-eg made his way home he muttered under his breath and drifted from one side of the narrow street to the other. I hate it! he thought. Why couldn't I just say *yes* or *no* to Gart? Am I afraid that he is just someone else trying to lead me around?

Gart paused at the foot of the stairs, looking up through the open door of the tiny second floor apartment, theirs as long as they paid the rent. He made no sound but she must have sensed his presence as Leah appeared promptly on the landing. Her lively, dark eyes and smiling composure drew him swiftly up the rickety stairs. She reached up to embrace him but did not linger there.

He tried to tell her about the storm across the river as she set out their evening meal, but words alone sounded flat. The awe he had felt was receding, but inside himself — the roiling clouds.... What could they portend?

He drew up his stool and hunched down over the low table as he hurried through the simple meal of bread, gruel and onions, daring to meet the eyes of his new bride only briefly. He felt compelled to break away from their gentle tug, two-thirds teasing, one-third reproach. He was a very lucky man to have made such a marriage, but damn, she could fluster him, and she knew it. This was not the red-faced fluster he had felt that afternoon but more of a squeeze, flutter, squish, flutter just behind the lower end of his breast bone.

Damn! He hated to be flustered. So, why did he keep looking back at her? If he was going to get anywhere, he couldn't sit at home every night holding hands with his wife. Not that she had ever asked him to. Damn! Damn!

Leah was as soft in body contour as she was in her gestures. She disquieted him every bit as much as Kre-eg did, but in such a gentle way. She was a mystery to be savored, but Kre-eg was a puzzle to be solved, Gart instructed himself. Should he tell her more about the business of the evening? He had described it to Leah almost as sparsely as he had to his friends, but Leah had not grilled him as Orson and Kre-eg had.

Leah almost laughed at her husband's confused smile and curt nod as he backed out the door, but she thought better of it. Instead she followed him out to the landing and watched him stride out of the courtyard gate. Turning, she carefully surveyed her new world.

She lingered by the door. It was still very hot inside. With the door closed she would soon need a lamp if she was to work. There was little sea breeze through the two tiny windows high on the east wall, just enough to bring a whiff of urine and rotting vegetables from the alley at the rear of the building. Still there was something there that drew her indoors. The newly whitewashed walls, the smooth clay finish of the floor, the soothing symmetry of the surfaces, the strange rectangularity of the spaces, the smell of new wicker work. Each object, every one of the sparse furnishings, was known to her personally. As she entered she turned back to see the top of the ziggurat above the roofs, its serene shape and symmetry drawing her eyes, drawing her out and up. How strange that drawing feeling was, and stronger now. Lately she had seemed more and more tied to the apartment and her loom. As her output of cloth increased and her designs improved it seemed that her relationship with her father was somehow becoming contaminated by his compliments and encouragement. His tailoring business was doing almost too well now — thanks, in part, to her production.

She looked over her tiny realm once more. Slowly a burdensome sadness perfused her body. Would this be enough as time went by? If children came.... Well, maybe this could be all right.

"Is this all there is to being grown up?" she whispered to herself.

The house of Nam-Ku, banker and brewer, was located in the northwest quarter not far from the temple compound, as befitted a man of his means. Gart presumed he would have a chance to see inside, at least for a moment. He had heard that the building had belonged to one of the fifty families until about twenty years ago when Nam-Ku had included it in a deal to pay off the owner's large debts. As the storm had passed around the city, there was still a little daylight when he approached the house.

On this street most of the buildings were of two stories. The houses were wider as were the streets. Although there was some variation, most of the walls had plaster in good repair and many had been whitewashed recently. Nam-Ku's house, like most, turned a blank wall to the street except for a row of slender vertical apertures high on the building just below where the flat roof must lie. Each slender window was bisected by a single wooden bar, also vertical. The total effect was to make friendly what would otherwise have been a foreboding, massive block of masonry. There was, of course, an entryway at street level. The outer doors were open.

As soon as he entered the doorway, Gart could see a servant, who arose from his perch on the rim of a small pool immediately inside the courtyard. The court and the pool of baked and burnished brick must have been built purely for decorative or religious purposes. Such grand houses would have another courtyard for hearth and housekeeping farther back.

The servant, a hulking, surly looking fellow with numerous old and fresh scars on arms and face, went to summon Kre-eg. Gart had just begun to look around when he heard voices through the hallway that must lead to the second court.

"Certainly. Why do you even hesitate?" The message, carried on a strident tone, bounced off of the wall of the little hallway, just as two men came into view.

"Father wanted to meet you, Gart." Kre-eg directed the formal introduction with style and ease as they each murmured the proper responses. This did not interfere with Gart or Nam-Ku as each vigorously inspected the other.

Nam-Ku was a stocky, middle-aged man, slightly shorter than his son but wider of frame and much fleshier. His broad and prominent forehead and the forward thrust of his neck served notice of an ongoing strong and willful principle.

"I was just telling my boy here," Nam-Ku began, "that tonight's meeting comes at a very good time. Last week was Kre-eg's twenty seventh birthday and I told him, 'If you are ever going to be a pillar of this community, it's time to burn some brick'."

Pillar, thought Gart. Hadn't he heard that expression already that day?

"Kre-eg tells me, Gart, that your business is coming right along and that you have some property inside the walls. That's hard to come by any more and must be especially pleasing to you, as I understand you are from out of the city."

"Well — uh — just barely outside the city," said Gart, puzzled by this remark. "My people have always done all of their business here, buying and selling with lots of time spent here in Ur." He felt a rising tide of irritation, not so much at the question as at his own rush to explain himself to this second generation Elamite.

"Property inside the walls." Why should Nam-Ku know about that?

"Uh — Kre-eg, no more foot dragging. Are we understanding each other?" Nam-Ku's voice was still low but the confidential tone was gone.

Gart turned his head just in time to see the look exchanged between father and son as the older man turned to leave the court. In that dead-level gaze there was no trace of humor.

Kre-eg indicated his readiness to go solely by an elevation of an eyebrow. They headed for Orson's apartment without further comment.

The one-story buildings of Orson's quarter contained a greater variety of reed-wattle, thatch-roofed and mud-brick, flat-roofed dwellings. Most were whitewashed and better maintained than those in Gart's neighborhood.

Kre-eg rapped sharply as they went through the doorway but didn't break his stride until they were in the middle of the small apartment.

"Hi, Sari, Ors. What the hell goes on here? Is the honeymoon over, or did you just decide to open it up to the public?"

Sari looked up from her work at the shelf where she was stacking the supper dishes. She smiled in her slow, unruffled way. She seemed a good partner for Orson, slow of pace, open-faced and bland.

"If you fellows are going out to save our city or something tonight, you should be on your way rather than hanging around teasing me," she said. "Please leave the door open. There is still a little light that I can use for spinning." Having settled that matter, Sari seated herself on a cushion against the back wall and smiled as she waited for them to clear the tiny room. Duly dismissed, the three men streamed out of the apartment chuckling among themselves. As they started down the street Gart's backward glance caught Sari seated there inside the open door, framed by evening light inside the darkening room. Her head was already nodding slightly, in cadence with her busy hand spindle.

As they went along, the number of people in the street increased. The supper hour was now over and the three broke rank frequently to let other people pass. Within two blocks the streets had narrowed to the degree that the three of them could not walk abreast. The doorways and street corners were occupied by surly looking young men, alone or in pairs, but there was also an occasional thin and tattered child or old man. They heard little conversation. Gart began to feel uneasy. This is silly, he thought. He had frequently walked this street alone in the daytime. It had not occurred to him to bring a weapon. So far as he could see, his companions were unarmed also. After all, there was no specific threat. Those walls — narrowing. Why did his chest — even his head — feel so much pressure? What was happening to him?

"Oooh, that's a pretty one!" The voice came from a knot of six or eight scruffy-looking young men with whom they nearly collided as they rounded a corner.

"I think it's my necklace they are talking about," said Kre-eg as they tried to thread their way through the loiterers.

Kre-eg was wearing a necklace that consisted of a metal chain and several attractive stones of lapis lazuli. Such adornment was common among both men and women of means.

"Wouldn't that look nice on me?" The scruffy-looking spokesman had fallen into stride with them. His companions were slipping ahead of them, blocking their intended path.

Gart could see the gleam of bronze. At least one had a knife. Perhaps they all did. As he scanned the array of faces confronting them he was struck by the variety: insolent, dull, anxious, but now that one over there behind the others, those lusterless eyes, dark and feral, taking it all in with out comment. Suddenly he was aware more of his own reaction than of their accosters or of any plan of escape. Hot, fluid forces surged within his body. He could feel fangs and claws sprouting, feel bony plates crunch and hackles rise, even taste the blood!

As the spokesman reached to touch the necklace, Kre-eg twisted his body and raised one arm slightly to fend him off.

"O.K., fellow, leave the necklace alone. I have plenty of tokens here in my bag." Kre-eg looked down steadily into the youth's eyes, his voice smooth, his words measured. He turned, reaching across his body toward the bag on the left side of his belt.

"CHARGE!" he screamed.

Kre-eg had suddenly driven his sharp and bony elbow into the lower breast bone of the young man. That unfortunate fellow now slowly folded up, his head lolling backward, an expression of amazement on his face.

All remaining parties jumped to the pursuit. Gart and Orson's position gave them an advantage and they were soon ten paces ahead of the pack and only twice that distance behind Kre-eg. Gart spotting a broken brick on the street, scooped it up and, in a leaping pirouette, hurled it behind him. It must have found a mark. The curses and pounding of footsteps quickly faded behind them.

"CHARGE!" Orson bellowed in Gart's ear as they raced toward where they had seen Kre-eg turn a corner. Now they saw him peering around a building, grinning at them.

"Thanks a lot for the warning, Commander," said Orson with as much sarcasm as he could muster while catching his breath. "Didn't you see that knife?"

"Sure, I saw three knives."

"You *are* crazy," Orson gasped, his ample frame still bent over, hands on knees.

"Oh, stop whining, Ors. It was a squeeze, but you made it didn't you?" said Kre-eg, dismissing the matter lightly with an upward jerk of his shoulders.

"Should we notify the watch captain?" Gart asked.

"Forget that," said Orson. "They aren't set up to handle this sort of thing. The most they would do is call out the backup watch officer,"

"And — so?" asked Kre-eg.

"Tonight, that's me," said Orson. "I may call you next."

"In that case, do forget it." said Kre-eg. "Gart, is this the place we are looking for?" He pointed across the street at the open door of a large, single-story building whose smooth brick face presented no other feature to the street.

No one was at the door. After checking the nearby streets, they filed into the entryway. This opened directly into a large, poorly illuminated room.

Half a dozen middle-aged men were sitting and standing about the edges of the room as they conversed in low voices. They recognized no one.

They collected three of the wicker stools from the large cluster in the front of the room and sat, leaning against the back wall of the building. Gart now inspected the room in detail. This was the assembly hall of the City Council of Ur. He had never been here before.

The walls were so thick the heat of the day barely reached the inside surface, which was now providing them with a comfortable back rest.

He closed his eyes, but his mind was immediately flooded with vivid scenes, not just of the escape of moments ago, but of the entire series of events of the day leading up to the three of them sitting here waiting for Mahn-so-ni. His eyes popped open and sought a more restful scene in the shadows cast by the palm log rafters of the ceiling. This was a one-story building, but the ceiling was high, perhaps twice a man's height.

"Are you sure your big time friend is going to show up? You do have the right day don't you? I'm getting antsy," Kre-eg said. He got up abruptly and walked to the entrance but soon returned.

"Some more people are coming," he said. "I hate to be early, and I am still not sure I want to be here."

"Oh relax, lean back and catch your breath. This isn't so bad. It's almost cool, and there aren't any flies. What more could you ask?" Orson replied.

Gart smiled. Soon his eyes closed, but again he could not relax. He could still feel the aftermath of his vivid killer instinct reaction.

After a few minutes he could hear Mahn-so-ni's pleasant, baritone voice through the inner door to the right of the entryway. The speaker entered briskly and shortly they could see his gray hair crowning a high, smooth forehead. His eyes moved rapidly from group to group as he greeted all in turn, arriving finally at Gart and his friends who were lingering near the entryway. "Gart! It's good to see you here." He seemed genuinely pleased. His eyes turned searchingly and fully into Orson's and Kre-eg's faces. His eyebrows arched.

"This is Kre-eg-el-Sheh and this is Orson-til-Chah: fellow officers with me in the Civil Guard," Gart responded.

As Mahn-so-ni questioned Orson and Kre-eg concerning their work and business connections, Gart pondered the enthusiastic cordiality of their welcome. The invitation that morning had seemed a little tentative, although the councilman had said he would consider his attendance a personal favor.

Taking his leave, Mahn-so-ni walked the length of the room. With a gesture here, and a nod there, he summoned the scattered little groups of men to the far end of the chamber where he seated himself behind a table.

As he waited for the conversation to quiet, he, too, was reflecting on the enthusiasm he had so spontaneously expressed toward Gart and his friends. Had he seen them as a good sign, a reassurance that he was justified in taking so much upon himself so soon after his appointment? His own sons had respectfully declined to come. He could hardly blame them. They were practical and hard working men. That was why he had turned the family business over to them. It must seem pretentious to think that he could change anything by working through the Council. He had watched its mumbling and bumbling for years, as an outsider. Still, his unexpected appointment to a seat just at the time that he became free from the family business? How could he ignore that?

He had waited too long. The hum of conversation was increasing again.

"May I have your attention, please?" He rapped on the table with his knuckles. "Yes, Cy?" He recognized a portly older man who had immediately jumped to his feet.

"Manz, before we get too deep here, could you tell me what is the nature of this meeting and by what authority you are calling it? I hadn't heard of anything coming out of the Council meeting which, I believe, was the first one you attended in your official capacity," Cy said, with a touch of sarcasm.

By what authority, indeed? Without a moment's mercy, Cy, the old fart, had put his finger right on what he had been struggling with himself.

"Very well, Cy, by my authority as a citizen who is gravely concerned with the decline in the quality of our life in this city. I have the right and obligation to call for your help in rebuilding our order and organization. Most of us can remember when it was much better. This is a glorious city, but our people seem to be moving into a shadow. Daily the gloom deepens. There is no clear public policy. Strangers, immigrants, keep coming in and our own people are cheating and killing each other while most of us ignore it. For some reason, we are not ruling ourselves. For lack of proper care, our civic body is showing signs of illness, weakness. If this becomes known by our sister cities, they will swarm all over us, like a flock of vultures."

Mahn-so-ni's color deepened, progressing upward from his dark gray eyebrows over the light skin of his forehead. He finally paused for breath.

"Yes, Cy, you seem restless. Speak up," he said,

"Well, Manz," Cy said, "I refuse to panic over a few street brawls. I recall my father telling about all the doom-sayers when Sargon of Akkad and his armies were taking every city in the land. Well, by the time they got here, they were too tired or too civilized to bother us much. Where is that disaster now? Oh, we still have plenty of Akkadians among us, but they are decent people."

With a benign and satisfied smile and a little nod to his audience, Cy turned and sat down.

"When Sargon died," Mahn-so-ni was quick to reply, "the Akkadians lost their vision, and their capital city is now covered by sand and mud. Couldn't this happen to us?"

Cy was back on his feet again. "We are different from the Akkadians. We have never relied on our warlords, or given them that much power. We have our councils and assemblies and, if things get bad enough, there is always a leader who pops up somewhere."

"How long since Demmuzi popped up?"

Gart could not identify the speaker, as the voice came from the gloom behind him. It was not spoken loudly and the speaker may have been surprised when Mahn-so-ni jumped up and began to pace the dais, obviously perturbed by the remark.

"We do have leadership. We have a great man at the head of this city. Indeed it has been a bad year," Mahn-so-ni continued. "Rumor has it that our king has been ill. I do not presume to tell you what to make of that, but if you count the years, it is very clear that he will not be with us much longer."

Mahn-so-ni stopped for breath, glancing self-consciously from side to side, then at the floor. Beads of sweat along his hairline reflected the flickering light of the rush and bitumen torches standing in the urns to his left. The tiny sparkles seemed to give him an aura of great sincerity. Suddenly, Gart noticed a silence had fallen over them, massive and warm. He sensed an invisible fermentation beginning in the room.

Mahn-so-ni sat down abruptly, staring directly at the table in front of him, as he recovered his breath and his composure. In a moment, his eye caught a signal from a younger man in the front row.

"Councilor, half of our neighborhood captains have fallen by the wayside. I feel that you, or we, should appoint new ones, preferably tonight."

"Thank you, Arp." Mahn-so-ni looked relieved. "How many neighborhood captains do we have here tonight?"

A knot of three or four advisers gathered around Mahn-so-ni's table, poring over a clay tablet. Gart presumed it was a list or sketch. He could hear dismayed remarks.

"I have no idea which streets."

"Make it up. No one will know the difference."

"What the hell? Redraw the boundaries."

"That's close enough."

Boredom was again beginning to settle in for the three visitors when Mahn-so-ni's voice pierced the background conversation.

"Gart, what quarter do you live in?"

"Southeast," Gart replied. His voice was strong and steady, but he couldn't resist the temptation to glance over his shoulder to read the eyes of those behind him. Orson was doubling over with silent laughter.

However, Orson was able to straighten up and answer, in a half-strangled voice, when Mahn-so-ni called out,

"Orson, what quarter?"

Kre-eg's small smile at Orson's plight began to relax and broaden when Mahn-so-ni arose to make his announcements.

"By overwhelming acclaim of this committee, the following are appointed neighborhood captains…."

The list of names included Gart, Orson and four other new-comers as well as the eight incumbents present.

"And as for you, Kre-eg," the councilman resumed, "can you write?"

Kre-eg sat stunned, taken completely off guard. Gart knew that Kre-eg could read and write credibly, if not with professional style.

Seeing Kre-eg nod, Mahn-so-ni said, "I, and this committee, need an aggressive and competent recorder and assistant. Do you accept this position?"

Kre-eg stood up suddenly and stiffly. His mouth opened and closed. Finally, a hoarse "Yes" came out.

They walked almost a full block in complete silence, except for their heavy breathing. The faintest of breezes had arisen, bringing cooler air from the waters to the east. The three greatly appreciated even this scant comfort, as all were damp with perspiration and a bit wrung out from the surprises at the end of the evening.

Gart and Orson both heard Kre-eg inhale deeply. Their heads swiveled in unison to observe the expected eruption.

"Have I ever been had! Recorder and right-hand man to Mahn-so-ni! As if I didn't have enough to do!"

"You could have said 'no,' Kre-eg," Gart noted.

Orson chuckled as Kre-eg stared at Gart.

Kre-eg's expression was perturbed and thoughtful but not angry.

"Well, I didn't hear any protests from you two, either," he sighed.

"All this stuff about feeling a personal calling to take care of the city.... You don't think Mahn-so-ni was just feeding us the usual stuff, do you?" Gart asked.

"I don't think so," Kre-eg said, with little hesitation.

Leah was asleep when Gart got home. Just as well, he thought as he slipped in beside her carefully to minimize the crackle of their bed of rushes.

Dawn was breaking when he awakened them both with his laughter. In his dream he was still at the meeting. Kre-eg was standing there open-mouthed and wordless.

"Serves him right, the smart ass." Gart knew he could never justify such language to Leah. Still, he savored the rare feeling of being one up on Kre-eg and without even planning it.

"For shame," protested Leah, "dragging the poor fellow down there and embarrassing him. Speaking of 'smart asses,' you seem to be taking a lot of satisfaction in this story."

"Well, I must admit, I feel a little proud that it was me, the country boy, who got the three of us fixed up with a situation where we can meet the insiders, some people with real influence."

"Oh — really?" Leah's question, if it was a question, seemed to just hang there. Gart squirmed a bit when she continued. "And just what are your duties, in return for this 'influence'?"

He was embarrassed. He had no answer.

About midmorning, he left the livestock market place to find Orson.

"Could you go with me to see Mahn-so-ni now, or will you be in trouble with your boss?"

"I can arrange it," Orson answered. "Just let me check with him."

They had found Mahn-so-ni in his construction yard where he was prowling, keen-eyed, through the maze of stacked bricks, timbers and bundles of thatch. For someone who had retired from his business he seemed to have a lot of suggestions for the workmen. His sons' expressions of forbearance gave way to smiles when their father left to greet Gart and Orson.

"Damned near anything you can do would be an improvement," Mahn-so-ni reassured them. "Talk to people, talk politics. Give them the sense that you are their connection with a government that is paying attention to them. Most of our people have neglected their tribal and clan ties. They don't feel connected to anything. Even the old families answer to no one in particular any more. Right now our main enemy is apathy." After an awkward moment he concluded, "Well, see what you can do. Come back and talk to me about it."

Gart walked back to his work feeling a little disappointed in Mahn-so-ni's answers. Certainly, the old Akkadian hadn't died of apathy. Had he expected too much from the new councilman? Was there really a craft to be learned here, or was he just one among many pushy and ambitious fools? He recalled Kre-eg's question. Why, indeed, should he get involved in this?

Within a month, Gart had overcome his dread of pushing himself upon others. He learned to present himself as everyone's link to the city council. He was enjoying recognizing more and more people on the streets and in the shops. From what he could gather, Orson was also meeting with some success.

Within a few weeks Mahn-so-ni was making remarks to Gart about how Kre-eg was making himself so available and helpful. Gart was amused, but he felt a bit jealous. After all, he thought, he had known Mahn-so-ni first.

CHAPTER TWO

Leah could hear Jeme screaming at his children. She peeked out the doorway in time to see several tangle-haired youngsters rushing out the door of the downstairs apartment into the courtyard. Such outbursts were frequent of late and not always quickly or happily resolved. Leah recognized in Jeme a dark and scary side, not unlike what was showing itself throughout the city. Jeme's stubbly chin and yellow-toothed grin was a regular feature of their building's courtyard. That grin could curdle into a thunderhead very quickly.

Jeme worked in the stockyards also. He would hold a job for several months, leave suddenly in a fit of boredom, sulk for a few days while he found temporary work, and then convince his old employer to take him back.

"I don't understand it," Gart had observed to Leah. "How have they managed to stay here in Banarum's building for all these years with Jeme's poor work habits?"

In spite of all this, Gart selected Jeme as the first testing ground for his political skills. To Gart's horror, Jeme embraced the program with great enthusiasm. He did not hesitate to hunt down and call on any person with whom he had contact at work, from the newest recruit among the wranglers to the superintendent of yards. Some of these people lived outside Gart's area, but it was not possible to halt the onrush of Jeme's enthusiasm.

"Hey, Mal-Shub, c'meer! You know Gart here?" Jeme had called halfway across the stockyard.

"Can't say's I do," answered the stolid, middle-aged man when he finally arrived within decent conversation range.

"Waal, you should," said Jeme. "He's a mighty good man to know. He's not only my friend and neighbor but he's a big time politician and a high officer in the Guard. If you ever need a favor from those city councilmen, he's your man. Don't be bashful."

"Jeme, here, is a good man," Gart said. "He does exaggerate a little, sometimes."

"Eggs-agger-ate?" said Mal-Shub. "If that means he runs off at the mouth, I know him pretty well. That don't take nothin' away from you, sir. Pleased ta meet ya," he nodded in parting.

Several months later, after another taxing evening of calling on people with Jeme, Gart sat at table staring over the remains of one more late supper into the tiny flame of their butter lamp. The occasional dull ring of dish on wooden shelf told him that Leah was tidying up the food stores, but the pace of her movements told him something was on her mind. She sat down next to the lamp and examined the contents of her sewing basket.

"I get the feeling you don't entirely approve of my being involved in this — uh — political thing," he said.

"Did I say that?" she asked, still rummaging through her basket.

"No, but you didn't say otherwise."

"I don't remember you asking me."

"Well?" he persisted.

"I'm interested in what you hope to accomplish. You've been at this for six months now."

"I just feel I should do this sort of thing. Everyone should. This city life is so complicated, someone needs to think about where it's all going or we'll be in really serious trouble, even worse than now. There are too many leaners and not enough pushers."

"You like to push?"

"Right. I'm no slacker. You know that." He stood up suddenly and turned to see her better.

"All right, sweetheart. You needn't get cranky just because you're a pusher."

"I think you're making fun of me."

"No, I'm not. I do wonder, though, about your sudden interest. I hadn't heard much about this until last summer."

"It isn't a sudden interest. It's just that this opportunity came along. Something leads me into these new situations."

"Something like ambition?" she asked.

"Hmmn, well, maybe something like that," he mumbled. Suddenly, he could see a vision of that doglike creature. It seemed to be laughing at him. How very strange. He couldn't share that, even with Leah.

"So, do you trust this *something* that leads you into things?" she asked.

"Umnn, no, not really," he mumbled as he sat down again.

"And yet, you very unselfishly give in?" she continued.

"Nothing unselfish about it. I like it. It's fun. It's exciting and interesting. I've always wanted to amount to something. Who knows? This might lead to something big."

"But sweetheart, you already do amount to something," she said. He was looking at her, doubtfully. Amount to some-thing. Amount to something. Her words were reverberating inside her head, then from somewhere came — *and is that all there is?*

"Oh yeah, yeah." Gart's tone was skeptical but his head nodded agreement with her affirmation of him.

For a few minutes the room was very quiet. The sounds of the neighborhood seemed strangely distant. Only the drone of a solitary fly disturbed the warm air as it looped and arced lazily through the mellow lamplight.

She looked up from her mending. The cloud had passed.

"Are you mad at me?"

"No, of course not, don't be silly."

"Prove it."
So he did. Convinced them both ... pretty much.

Directly behind Jeme's ground floor quarters was the apartment of Banarum, the landlord. Where Jeme was barely controlled chaos, Banarum was bare control.

"Preciate it," Banarum would say when rent was paid. "Be right there," when a ceiling leak was reported.

He did not seem cold. He simply rationed every response.

Gart's rap at the door was followed by an even and pleasant, "Come in." He entered to find Banarum seated and facing him from behind a table directly across the room from the doorway. The room was furnished rather sparsely, but the few pieces of furniture were of excellent workmanship with clean and simple lines. Banarum sat bare to the waist. In spite of this, only the faintest trace of perspiration was detectable and the scent of the room was fresh, seeming to say, "This place was aired and this man was bathed today." The skin of his torso and shaved head glistened. To Banarum's left was an attractive little butter lamp with black geometric designs on its red background. A thin line of smoke curled upward from the gleaming wick in its spout. In front of him was a stack of small clay tablets of the type often used for accounts.

"I was surprised when I was asked, a few months ago, to be a neighborhood captain by Councilman Mahn-so-ni," Gart began in what had become his standard opening.

"Ahh, very good. And just how much is supporting all you fine politicians going to cost me, today?"

"Oh, I'm not asking for a gift!" Gart answered, surprised. It did occur to him, though, that Banarum would have felt disappointed if this subject hadn't been mentioned. The man thought and dealt with concrete matters: houses, taxes, meat and barley. Banarum made his connections with a trowel or hammer, like most of the people who were holding the city together.

Gart met Banarum's steady gaze squarely for the first time. It seemed to him that he could see straight through to the back side of their conversation. They did not need to dance around with words to speak to their purposes. They were both ambitious, but both yearned to be known as orderly and honorable men.

The campaign to meet his neighbors had peaked for Gart after the first month and then slacked off. Once he met the challenge of organizing what he had to say, he began to lose interest. He began to worry that his income would suffer if he didn't get his mind back to the marketplace. Eight years ago he had been offered a job working with the livestock by the old Akkadian trader when he was in the city with the fall market flock. There had been lots of hard work and not much pay for two years, but Gart had learned a great deal from the old man about buying and selling. He already knew more than most about handling and rearing animals, thanks to Shelah, his father. He might have absorbed half of his father's knowledge but never equaled his enthusiasm for his animals.

Perhaps it was this lack that prompted him to move to the city and apply his ambitions to dealing with people as well as animals. Six years ago, Shelah had died suddenly, leaving Gart part of his flock. The old Akkadian, musing on his own mortality and lack of heirs, proposed that his employee buy him out with his new income, over several years. After four payments the old man said, "That's enough," to Gart's surprise and delight.

The hot weather had abated by now. Though it was still uncomfortable midday, people were less irritable. Nevertheless, at Guard meetings everyone talked about riots and street fighting. The three new lieutenants had not seen each other except at these drills. This particular evening, Gart resolved to visit with his friends. He offered to buy Orson a beer at the nearby eatery where, they suspected, Kre-eg was already at work. He had left immediately after drill.

"Oh yes, Gart," Orson said. "I'm still going around the neighborhood, telling the folks how lucky they are to know me. I meet a couple of new people every week. I enjoy it, but sometimes I wonder what it is we're doing. What does your friend Mahn-so-ni say?"

"I guess I've been afraid to ask him many questions," Gart said. "I want some answers from someone. What if no one has any?"

By the time they had finished their beer, Kre-eg was going off duty, so while they walked toward Gart's apartment he explained why he had paid so little attention to them that evening..

"I was doing my best to listen in on a couple of fellows who are part of a group that come in most days. Usually there are half a dozen of them, but sometimes more."

"You think they are up to no good?" asked Orson.

"I don't know that they are," said Kre-eg, "but they are so intense, very serious, no joking around. That doesn't seem normal for that age. It just doesn't smell right."

Kre-eg gave a little shudder, his expression unusually serious. "There have been a few remarks, like the other day I overheard, 'Do we have any yet?' and another fellow answered, 'No, just daggers.' Then, today I heard, 'Will she burn?' 'The storehouse you mean?' 'Yeah, she'll burn.'"

"I have to admit," said Gart, "that's a little disturbing."

The next day, Gart dropped into one of Kre-eg's family's canteens at lunch time. One glance told Gart that he had scored. He ordered his lunch and sat a bit apart from the cluster of young men who were lingering over their plates. They made reference to someone whose name sounded like "goose" or "the goose." These young men reminded him of his recent street fight experience. He could see Kre-eg, in the background, keeping a wary eye on the group. Could they really be dangerous? He could feel the fear coming back. Who did he really know here in the city except Leah? It was fortunate they could talk everything out, share their worlds, one-on-one, at a pace he could handle.

The group's talk stopped abruptly with the arrival of a sturdy, short young man of dark complexion and sharp features.

He got right down to business.

"Dungi. Dagan, Naram…." Each member was greeted by name and given a brief but intense scrutiny by the newcomer, who then dropped into an inaudible interchange with two of them.

Could this be "the goose?" He appeared quite young, perhaps twenty-two or twenty-three. He departed abruptly with two of the group and, within minutes, all of the rest were gone. Kre-eg accepted Gart's payment for the meal and made a face when Gart reminded him of the extra drill the following evening.

"Do you think that means anything, Gart?"

"Nah, the colonel is probably just trying to stir up some enthusiasm," Gart replied.

He was just leaving the canteen when he nearly bumped into the same intense young man, moving swiftly along the street carrying an elongated wicker basket covered with a cloth. His dark eyes swept by Gart without any sign of recognition or apology for the near collision. He was quickly gone, maneuvering himself and his basket skillfully through the crowd.

When Gart arrived home, Leah was gone. He had just begun to feel disappointed when she appeared with some fish for supper and a new dress from her father's tailor shop.

"Your cloth?" Gart asked, pointing to the new dress Leah had draped across the top of her loom.

"Yes, of course," she answered.

"Well, let's see it," Gart said. He *had* learned a few things in the months they had been married. She stepped out of her old gown and suddenly — startled — he beheld her as one perfected form. Her skin glowed softly in the twilight reflected from the wall. He could not speak. He did not move.

She paused, aware of his regard, accepting, waiting. She turned. The moment had fled but the image remained. His eyes followed with delight as the new garment slipped down over the lines of her back, buttocks, thighs.

"You are really — something," he finally said. "And the dress, the new one, that's beautiful, too. Your father put that together very well."

The garment was of a light wool material of natural color, perhaps slightly bleached to lighten its tone. A winter dress with a high neck line and short sleeves ending in decorative tabs bound with bright yellow embroidery, it was skillfully gathered at the waist, fitting her to full advantage before it swept out to a fullness at ankle length.

"He's very good at what he does," she said with a smile. "Oh, Colonel Alkohn was in the shop today."

"Your father knows him?" Gart asked, surprised. "What did you learn that I should know?"

"Well," said Leah, "he's from one of the real old line families and he was quite close to his majesty, Demmuzi-ki-ag years before he was made lugal. Then when Demmuzi accepted the throne eleven years ago, he made your colonel commander of the Royal Bodyguard.

"You probably know that he's been on the City Council for some time," Leah continued. "Dad says that some people think he will keep on advancing, maybe become commander of the army or maybe City Council president. Others say he isn't really politician enough."

Awaiting his supper, Gart stretched out on the bed to rest but he found he could not escape the colonel. All of Leah's story and some of his own memories were swirled about and came into focus in a mental picture of this sharp-nosed, square-jawed, middle aged man with the unwavering gaze and gray hair, close cropped, just like Gart's new haircut.

There was much that Gart admired about his commander. He seemed to stand tall, although he was actually only of average height. He moved swiftly and with precision. He spoke, always, with great certainty and conviction. He did not seem afraid of his responsibilities. Gart aspired to all of these qualities. Even so, he was not at ease with Colonel Alkohn.

That night he dreamed he was driving four beautiful white onagers hitched to a four-wheeled chariot. His hands were sweaty and clamped rigidly onto the reins. The team proceeded at a fast trot, following a trail westward into terrain like the sand-hills of his home district. Usually it seemed he was not alone in the wagon and he was driving for another someone. His features were vague, but the figure seemed taller, somewhat older, stronger, wiser and more confident in bearing. Gart glimpsed a black beard and some sort of shiny head-dress or ornament. These impressions were now beheld briefly from without, then felt radiantly within as the apparition fused with the dream driver. This fluctuation had occurred several times when the black beard became a black sky over the approaching pass. Now he saw showers of sparks. The sky loomed up, vast and black, transected by jagged lightning from top to bottom.

Thunder rumbled, but lower and milder than he expected. The rumble was coming from inside him. It filled and vibrated his chest and belly, rolling out pleasantly somehow to the surrounding shrubs and hillsides. The echoes seemed to converge on him, bathing him with a reassuring sense of harmony and connection. Brilliant, crooked arteries of light sought the earth and he sprang free of earth, reins and trap, spread-eagled in white, weightless space.

The full, sharp reverberations came charging out of some source in his chest, coursing along all his limbs and leaping from his fingertips and toes to fill all space. It was glorious, — transcending all form! He was not *actually* the storm god, at least not all of him. He did not feel very responsible or serious, but he was united with that deity. He and Enlil, god of storm and all the airy spaces, were one! He awaited the next coursing of the heavens but the newborn bolts blurred and the thunder muted and faded off.

The thunder was coming from his door, three series of thumps, moderate but demanding. Gart staggered to the door, struggling to get his eyes open and the world into focus. He had just succeeded by the time he got the latch undone. He pulled the door cautiously to him, the doorpost making a soft musical moan as it rotated in its pivot stone.

It was An-Nam, the colonel's runner. He was carrying a torch of reeds, still necessary on the dark landing, though the early light through their tiny windows dimly outlined the contents of the room.

An-Nam was right to the point. "Report to the armory immediately. Colonel's orders." He was already swinging around to go before Gart could question him.

"Is this a general drill?"

"Officers now, men later, sir." The "sir" faded as An-Nam was already halfway down the stairs at the end of the landing, his bare shoulders a dark shadow between the viewer and the glowing torch.

This was the first time Gart had been called at this time of day. Perhaps it was something serious. This was just an officer's call but, just to be sure, he donned his battle cloak, kilt, belt and bronze dagger before he ran downstairs and out into the deserted street.

Dawn was touching the east faces of the buildings with the promise of a sunrise. He met no one and saw no other sign of life in the streets before he came to the temple grounds. The gates to both the outer and inner courtyards were completely open, and he could see the full length of the esplanade and up the processional stairway that cleft the two massive, whitewashed buttresses on the northeast wall of the ziggurat. The first direct rays of sunlight struck the lustrous blue tile of the structure on the very top: the bedchamber of Nannar.

The simple little temple was located on a platform of masonry some three stories above the surrounding one- and two-story residential and commercial buildings. Well above the outer walls it dominated the city, its blue-glazed tiles connecting the heavens and earth.

At that time the main channel of the Euphrates flowed just west of the walls and the house of Nannar looked like the apex of the world to those who approached the city from the west.

Gart never forgot his first sight of it. At home he had seen hills just as high, but he was amazed such a mass could be created by human hands, even at the behest of the gods. He recalled the sacred grove on a small rise just before the road dropped down to the western edge of the river. There was a little amphitheater of palm logs. At certain full moons — precisely forecast by the priestly astrologers — one could sit in a certain section of the amphitheater and watch Nannar rise up directly from the roof of his bedchamber in his full and lustrous splendor to supervise the night-time activities of his special city, and to see his own face a thousand times in the reticulum of rivers, canals and lesser waterways crisscrossing the land of Sumer from the Arabian Desert southwest to the distant Lulu Mountains to the north.

Gart had never seen such a moonrise, but Leah had, several times. In fact, she had been there the very night Gart was arranging their marriage with her father. The bargaining had taken place on the roof of his prospective father-in-law, the very roof Gart had once rented as sleeping space for several months. He had to represent himself, as he had no family in the city. Old Elizamo's terms were surprisingly generous. Surely it must have been an accord of all the major gods that made their marriage possible. Of course, there might have been some influences within the household. Both Leah and her mother were acquainted with him and had not discouraged his interest.

Leah gave full credit to Nannar. She seemed attuned to the Lord of the Night Skies, perhaps through her visits to the holy grove and exposure to moonlight there. Whenever he and Leah were out under the full moon, she soon seemed to glow with a luster both soft and welcoming that seemed to say, "Let's let Nannar in on our secret." Or was Gart the one to be let in on *their* secret?

All of these memories flashed swiftly by in the time it took Gart to pace the breadth of a temple gateway, but the vivid image of the stairway to the sky persisted and Gart carried it with him nearly to the armory. The scene kept coming back to him. He felt a strong drawing sensation inside his stomach. He suddenly was convinced that the ziggurat was drawing together not only heaven and earth and the conflicting forces of this city but also was tugging at the threads of his personal life. The little temple at the top was a center point for whatever had drawn him to the city.

He knew he must hurry to the armory but further flashes of the view from the gateway pursued him. The lack of activity in the temple forecourt and on the ziggurat was reassuring. Several people went sleepily about their tasks in the courtyard; two sweepers moved in slow motion and several peasants crept along under large bundles of fodder for the temple dairy. Near the top of the stairway were three priests carrying baskets, probably the regular morning offering. He saw that the priests were naked. He imagined himself up there with them, shivering in the morning breeze, bearing offerings of parched grain and wine for the daily observance held just below the Bedchamber of Nannar.

"The celebrants take off their kilts to divest themselves inwardly of all self-willed aspirations and pretenses. This opens them, fully, to the breath of the gods, just as they were on that day when they were first given will and breath."

He could still remember *verbatim* this explanation, which had been gratuitously offered to him, probably in response to the puzzled and embarrassed look on his face, by an attending priest at the shrine of Enlil when he had first visited there. Well, he was still not ready for that stuff. It seemed silly. He was working hard to make it in the big city — and off to a good start, too — if he didn't daydream too much and arrive late for the colonel's emergency.

He was beginning to suspect he *was* dreaming this whole sequence when he saw two other Guard officers wheel around the far corner of the armory and hurry toward the control door. The long, low building was newly whitewashed and by now the sun's rays were coming in nearly perpendicular to the walls with dazzling effect. The door was recessed in a shallow portico and flanked by two fat brick columns. These were also whitewashed except for their impressive adornment, which was on each column a figure representing His Majesty, Demmuzi-ki-ag; the Servant of Nannar-Sin, bearing arms. This design was, in fact, a mosaic made up of the disclike heads of clay nails embedded in the mortar at the time the columns were laid up. The nails were of various colors, some baked of clay imported for the purpose and others of the light colored local stuff with added pigments. Whitewashing around these discs had been quite a problem. As a result, His Majesty was slightly grizzled at this time but still impressive. This struck Gart as quite appropriate. The king was rumored to be showing some signs of wear. Gart was reassured to see the Royal Arms-keepers still rubbing sleep from their eyes and trying to look busy. This must not be much of an emergency. Over in headquarters corner was a small group of men. He soon identified Colonel Alkohn, Mahn-so-ni and two others whom he presumed to be councilmen also. Slightly to one side was Captain Bruzi, the acting commander of the Royal Bodyguard.

Bruzi did not attend routine drills and was usually present only to prepare for ceremonies on state occasions. The group had now grown to about thirty officers, mostly junior or mid-grade. There were no enlisted men except for An-Nam, who was actually a slave but was entrusted to bear arms.

An-Nam now sounded for attention by clashing his bronze short-sword against a spear blade taken from the arms rack. The crowd hushed as Alkohn began to address the assembly in rapid, rhythmic speech.

"Gentlemen, this is not a drill. A state of emergency has arisen and we must act. We received word yesterday that a group of our merchants had been set upon on the road between Erech and Larsa. They were robbed and two were murdered. We do not know who did it, whether this brutal and criminal act was committed by organized troops or by outlaws. But considering all factors in our current situation...."

The colonel paused and paced a bit, looking first at the councilmen to his left, then at Bruzi to his right, then at the ceiling. To Gart this seemed an invitation for them to interpret what was being said. The murder of a few traders was not that rare.

"It is time for a reconnaissance in force to remind any forgetful neighbors that a mighty warrior holds this city and its lands in trust from the Lord of the Night Skies and that our lugal intends to fulfill that trust.

"Captain Bruzi will command this patrol. Second in command will be Lieutenant Gart-eber-Sin."

Gart flushed, suddenly very awake and self conscious. His naturalized name still sounded a bit awkward. It was rarely used by his friends and he didn't feel he quite owned it yet.

Alkohn continued at a rapid clip:

"The patrol will consist of sixty men at arms and twenty baggage slaves. It may return in two days but should be prepared to stay a day or two longer. The city walls will be doubly manned during this time. One half of the Guard will parade outside the walls each evening and the remainder will patrol the streets each afternoon and evening. The patrol should be ready to leave by midmorning and will parade through the main market place on its way out the North Gate — and I expect them to look and act like soldiers!"

Alkohn touched his forefinger to his temple, as if he had just remembered something else. He whispered to Mahn-so-ni briefly, then resumed speaking in a lower tone of voice.

"Lieutenant Kre-eg-el-Sheh will temporarily replace Captain Bruzi in command of the Royal Bodyguard. The household soldiers will explain your duties, Lieutenant."

Kre-eg started in surprise but quickly recovered his usual aloof expression.

Dismissed from the briefing, Gart set off for his apartment on the double. As his sandal-shod feet pounded the packed clay of the street, the military stride and the expression of manly determination he felt on his face seemed new and strange. He was flattered to have been picked and liked the idea of getting out of the city, but he was uneasy about leaving Leah and his business on such short notice.

By this time, a number of sleepy-eyed citizens were moving slowly through the streets. Some cocked a dull but questioning eye at him as he strode purposefully past.

He arrived at the apartment puffing and sweating. He swept through the door with his most military bearing to meet Leah's questioning glance.

"No big thing," he told her. "I will have to be out of town for two or three days — on patrol — partly training, partly politics. I don't expect any big trouble."

For the first time this morning Gart had a few moments to sit and organize his busy head. Suddenly, between one moment and the next, the night's dream came back to him. At first it was mixed with temple scenes, religious images and military imaginations. He felt compelled to tell Leah about it, even if she thought he was out of his head.

But she listened, and with growing interest although she looked perplexed at first.

"That was a good dream. It makes me feel better about this trip," she said.

Gart was satisfied with her brief comments. He felt clearer for having talked over the dream. Now he had to be practical.

"We'll need to get your kid brother to help you with the livestock while I'm gone. We only have four head at the yards. Mar-Ti was down there with me yesterday. He knows what to do, if you can just keep his attention on the job. If any one gives you a bad time get Jeme to help. Offer him a little something for his trouble but don't get carried away. The same for Mar-Ti. All right?"

"All right." Her response was so even that it gave no clue of how she felt.

"Oh, I think Mar-Ti should sleep over here while I'm gone. I'll tell Banarum to keep an eye out for you."

Her nod was barely perceptible.

In a flurry of motion Gart was out the door: Weapons, battle cloak, hastily eaten breakfast, water-skin and food pouch at belt, departure kiss on lips — stirred up, anxious, a little hurried. Enough thinking. Go now!

CHAPTER THREE

To his surprise, Gart found that most of his detail was already there when he arrived at the armory. This unit was new, put together for this occasion, and he had wondered if they could do it on such short notice. There were four senior under-officers who had each brought a dozen men from their units for this exercise. These sergeants, as well as Captain Bruzi, had some battlefield experience. This left Gart as the greenest officer. His fighting experience was minimal. His tribe's disputes over water and pasture were usually more noise and arm waving than serious combat. As though in a trance, Gart glided into his spot at the head of the column. To his far right, in the first rank, was Bruzi. Between them were the trumpeter and the standard bearer. They moved smartly out of the armory door. The unit saluted Colonel Alkohn, who observed them as they marched out without making himself unduly prominent. The colonel's gaze was appropriately severe, if a bit cloudy and preoccupied. Fortunately, Gart remembered to execute the column left into the marketplace and thus avoided launching his military field experience in disgrace. The unit slowed, often marking time in making their way through the busy marketplace with deliberate noise and display.

By the time they passed through the city gates the reinforced units were already on the walls and Bruzi and his men were accorded a departing blast from their trumpets. It was now midmorning and there was a cordon of people outside the gates: families, well-wishers, arriving tradesmen, and some farmers returning from the nearby fields to avoid the searing heat of mid-day. The general shouting and clamor was enjoyable but the ululations of the women sent chilly tingles down Gart's spine. As he attended to the formation and cadence he was aware of how he had been already melded into the strength and consciousness of this martial creature, moving inexorably onward. Its eighty synchronized legs carried it steadily into the marshy vitals and dry desert ribs of land to the north, toward the domain of Larsa.

He rejoiced in the feeling of prideful power. The feeling faded slightly when he imagined his herdsman family and ghostly ranks of forebearers looking on with skeptical smiles as this sweating procession passed by.

When the sun had reached its zenith, they were well out of sight of the city walls and had not passed a single traveler during the past half hour. Though only a week after equinox, no prudent person would travel at midday. But one would expect to see field workers taking a rest or eating lunch along the willow cloaked canal banks or in the planted groves of fruit trees. The spring barley was almost all harvested and Gart looked in vain for farmers tending the onion, cucumber and melon patches they passed. There were not even any children in the little birdwatch towers erected at the edges of the orchards and grain fields.

There was scarcely a bird on the wing or a song to be heard. Exception! Very high up, he spotted two tiny sets of wings seeming nearly stationary as they rode the updrafts. They were taking advantage of a shift of the weather, which had moderated, bringing some relief to the now fading part-time warriors of the Legions of Nannar.

"O.K. Break step!" Bruzi boomed out with more energy than he felt. "Over there, in the shade, fall out. Take a breather!"

All, except Gart, took to the shade of the nearby willows. He remained in the clearing. The men shed their heavy cloaks, weapons and packs and relieved themselves in all usual ways, including splashing themselves and drinking from the canal.

In spite of the heat, Bruzi was glad to be out here, away from the city and at least acting like a real soldier for a change. Only a few days ago he had been seriously questioning his decision to remain a full-time soldier. How long could he feed on memories of the glory days when they had chased fleeing Amorites? He had been young and impressionable then. He had been fortunate Alkohn had taken such an interest in him, had helped him get one of the few full time commissions and had later given him the job, if not the title, of Commander of the Royal Bodyguard. He knew his recent discontent was not his alone. He could see evidence of the same attitude in Alkohn, Demmuzi and some of the household troops. What should they be doing? Maybe this little foray, sham though it was, would help some.

He studied his second in command, who was still standing out in the sun, and liked what he saw — a little green and awkward, perhaps, but certainly not bored with his job.

Gart joined the others after a few minutes.

"What do you see up there, Lieutenant?"

Gart felt comfortable about having Bruzi in command, although he barely knew him. The captain presented himself with an air of quiet confidence. Gart wondered if that came from his social status as a member of an old-line family, not at this point particularly powerful, but still respected.

"Well, sir, I don't see much up there. It looks like a couple of falcons, but they are too high to tell. At least they aren't vultures. They are enjoying the sea breeze as much as we are, but it's unusual for the wind to come in off the sea in the middle of the day. Maybe there is a storm on its way."

Bruzi seemed mildly interested. Gart decided to push his observations a little further.

"In fact, I see damn little down here. I haven't been this way for a while, but doesn't it seem to you this whole area is unusually empty? Deserted?"

"Umn, can't say that I had particularly noticed," Bruzi admitted.

"I have seen hardly any sign of life in the last half hour except for us. That seems very strange to me," Gart persisted.

His commander glanced at him quizzically.

"No, wait! I take that back. I see something now!" Gart's peripheral vision had picked up a slight movement on the horizon. In this case the horizon was a finger of unwatered desert about two hundred yards to the left and slightly ahead in their line of march. "Looks like a head with two pointed ears bobbing along just over that ridge," he said. "It's only a jackal, I'm pretty sure. I think he has been with us for some time now. It just didn't register with me before. He's pretty cautious."

"You think he has been following us?" asked the captain.

"No, as a matter of fact, he has been ahead of us," Gart said.

"What do you make of that?" Bruzi seemed interested but Gart decided not to expand on the matter. He was not sure if the animal stories he had heard would be appreciated by such a city bred man.

"I don't know exactly. I'll keep my eye on him."

Because they had not departed the city until midmorning, it would be impractical to reach the recognized frontier of Ur by nightfall. Therefore, a search for a suitable camp spot was begun while the sun was still well up. It was agreed they should get off the main track to Larsa, even though there seemed little likelihood they would be disturbed during the night.

"Well, what do you think, Eber-Sin? Left or right?"

His new name still rang strangely in Gart's ears, the *-Sin* having been bestowed on him when he became an officer. Even as an officer the choice offered here seemed rather limited, but this was some progress from *"Lieutenant,"* and he was being consulted! He shaded his eyes with his hand as he swept the horizon ahead. Once again he caught sight of their jackal escort moving across what could be their path if they went to the right.

"Definitely to the right, sir. There is some high ground just above the marsh about a half mile over there. Maybe the breeze will help us with the mosquitoes."

"Fine," grunted Bruzi, who appeared a little faded.

The straggling column turned right and was soon preparing to bed down for the night. As secrecy seemed not an issue at this point; the men were allowed to cut rushes for bedding and start a fire from the embers successfully nursed along by one of the porters. They had no nets, but several of the men were able to capture a number of large carp amongst the nearby reeds to add a little flavor to their rations of grain and dried dates.

Nannar was late that night and when he finally arrived the slender crescent of his bull moon aspect interfered little with the glorious display of stars that lit the desert sky.

A rotating watch had been posted, more out of basic military discipline than any sense of immediate danger. With the four sergeants in charge, Gart was free to sleep. The soft soil of the old river bank, long abandoned by the wandering Euphrates, was comfortable and he fell into a deep slumber. He found himself quietly awake about midnight, judging from the position of the Great Bear in its rotation around the polestar. He was aware, at first, of the profound silence and experienced a feeling of peace and a contentment at being exactly where he was. This opportunity to be very still seemed just what he needed. This was a luxury known mostly to shepherds and astrologers. Now that he was more awake, he could hear an occasional jackal yip in the far distance. Once or twice, he thought he heard a sheep bleat much nearer, but he could have been dreaming.

As he gently drifted from one memory to another, it seemed he had been drawn to a special, coming-together place. He thought of Leah. He wondered if they would ever have children and grandchildren and if they would be looking at these same stars, just as his ancestors must have. He thought of his people, who would now be beginning their trek back to summer pastures. He thought of the city walls, so comforting but so confining, of the hustle, smells and squalor of city life, of the conniving commerce of the stockyards and the struggle for dominance and territory. He wondered why he had chosen this, and if, indeed, he had done the choosing. He thought again of Leah and of the gleaming white ziggurat, as he had seen them the previous morning. He pictured, hazily, the little shrine to Enlil inside the temple gate. Now he was staring into Enlil's true and vast domain, which included the moon and all the stars under the black vault of An: the remote and unknowable heaven god, progenitor of it all. The great sea-mother, Nammu, seemed even more remote. She must scarcely recognize these brackish sloughs as distant kin. Gart was getting sleepy. This earth, his bed.... supposed to be goddess, Ki....but seems inert, far off.... Herdsmen not stuck to Ki like ploughmen.... Herdsmen keep moving on. Got to keep moving.... Enlil keeps things moving. Not far off, Enlil all around.... The breeze bending the rushes caressed his cheek.

Gart rolled over onto his back and surrendered again to sleep.

The entire party was astir by the time dawn broke. Generally refreshed, if a little disgruntled and disoriented, they quickly broke camp. The border, when they reached it, proved to be a bleak and lonely place. There were some physical markings: a brownish stone stella and a badly deteriorated booth of tree limbs and reeds which served as a shrine of sorts. It was seriously in need of maintenance. The stella bore a brief inscription declaring its function as a border marker and promising peace and blessings on Ur and Larsa. This area had not been farmed for years. The stella, drab as it appeared, still commanded a certain respect. Such a piece of stone must have been hauled a great distance as there was no local stone in these river lands.

"Can you read it, Gart?" Bruzi asked.

"Yeah — some," he responded, claiming neither education nor ignorance. It pleased him he had progressed from "Lieutenant" to "Eber-Sin" to "Gart" after only one night in the field. "You pick up a little here and a little there. Besides, I get quite a bit of help with my business accounts from one of my fellow officers."

The stella inscription was largely in the old pictographic script that was not that hard to figure out.

"O.K., Gart."

Bruzi turned his attention to the little shack-shrine. Gart was still *Gart*. Perhaps he had made it with Bruzi.

On the deteriorating but still serviceable mud-brick altar of the shrine sat two small clay figures, local deities perhaps, or household gods left by refugees as a token of good faith when they crossed the border. They were in surprisingly good condition and free from dust and bird droppings. Their bland expressions would certainly not serve to scare anyone out of either land. It was unclear if their good condition was due to the care of unknown human hands or if the gods had made their own arrangements.

Stella and booth were both on the south bank of the boundary canal which was empty. Shutting the water out of a canal without consultation could be an excuse for a good fight, if one was needed. The water had evidently only been out a few days as the mud was still wet at the bottom of the shallow channel. The soldiers found this very convenient for their crossing. Perhaps there was a construction or repair project underway upstream from here. As they walked across on nearly dry land, Gart checked for footprints in the moist soil. There were no prints of humans or pack animals but, yes, there they were, firm and fresh! A single jackal had preceded them, probably that morning. Gart pointed this out without comment to Bruzi, who nodded without pausing as they took their places at the head of the column.

The party trudged resolutely down an old abandoned dike toward Larsa. Gart noticed an immediate increase in the number of blackbirds and even occasional rustles in the grass, probably rodents or snakes. The vegetation seemed greener and thicker. Why was this? Here came a large swarm of blackbirds directly toward them but now splitting and wheeling off in opposite directions. Something moved on the path ahead. As they approached, Gart got his best view yet of the jackal, at least *a* jackal. The gray, mottled, doglike creature was coming toward them at a slow lope, its head turned back over his shoulder. It seemed unaware of their presence. Then suddenly it stopped, dropping to a cowering position. It had seen them. In a matter of seconds the animal scooted off of the embankment and swiftly disappeared in the brush to their right.

"Hold it!" Gart threw up his hand reflexively with no thought of channels of command. "Captain, there is someone or something up ahead there, maybe coming toward us."

Bruzi, startled, quickly recovered his poise and his command.

"Right! Everyone take cover over there to the right. Get well off the path and lie low." His voice, though suppressed in volume was firm and definite. Even so, his follow up glance at his second in command seemed to seek confirmation.

"Yes, sir!" Gart responded in an emphatic whisper as he brought up the ragged rear. The moderate growth of waist-to-shoulder-high bushes became thicker and taller the farther they scurried to the east. These abandoned fields had not returned to desert. The bushes evidently benefited from spring and summer overflows from the canal they had just crossed. The bushes were now joined by willows and, within three hundred yards, they were at the edge of a large slough that extended off to their right, toward the border canal.

Bruzi's hand signals indicated he wanted the bulk of the party deeper into the willows and spread out for better concealment. Gart and one sergeant were to remain where they could observe the path they had just abandoned. Gart was concerned their tracks would be quite visible and would lead to a pursuit and a clash. How welcome this would be, of course, depended entirely on who and how many were out there.

After about a quarter hour passed; the troops and especially Bruzi began to grow restless. Gart wondered if he had muffed his first big chance as an up and coming officer, but he held his ground and signaled with more firmness than he felt the others should do likewise. He reasoned the birds should have resumed their chatter by now, as his party had been immobile for some time. The hush continued but still no heads or shoulders appeared above the brush bordering the path. Then he heard a faint murmur and an occasional clank to the north. These sounds gradually grew in volume and progressed and extended toward the east. If, indeed, someone had been headed toward them and the border canal, they must have taken a turn to his right. They could be following a levee built to control the canal during flood times.

Every soldier seemed to swivel in place, attracted by their prospective prey. Gart's neck prickled. A glance to his right caught several young soldiers hunkering down like he was, as if ready to spring immediately. Warrior blood suffused his face, crowded his heart, expanded his chest, moistened his palms. The sounds continued, extending to the east. If this was a Larsa border patrol it was fair game. No need to parlay. The mighty men of Ur would fall on them immediately and without mercy.

Gart could see himself two days hence, back in Ur, a seasoned officer, perhaps some captured armor, maybe a promotion. That wouldn't hurt him politically either! All this, if there weren't too many of them, of course. Maybe they would have to follow and attack that night. Umn... much trickier that way, more chances to foul up. Perhaps it was just an armed trading party, less glory but more booty. What if it was just a few unarmed traders? In that case they would probably have to cut a deal with them and let them go.

Gart's private strategy session was interrupted by a wave from his commander who beckoned him to come close enough to whisper some instructions.

"Lieutenant, I want you to send Ramlil and two men north toward the voices until they get a sighting."

"Yes, sir."

"I will take most of the men east as quietly as possible. We'll go parallel to the voices and try to head them off."

"Yes, sir."

"I want you to stay here with eight men and the baggage porters. Keep an eye on the old path but be prepared to go north and fall on their rear as soon as you hear a big ruckus."

"Yes, Captain."

The main body of the Ur patrol faded into the brush, and for fifteen or twenty minutes Gart was in command of all he could survey, which was damn little. He was not in control, however, of all he could hear. The mumbled voices continued, still moving off to the east only to be replaced by a fresh batch, and then another. Either they were taking their time or there were a lot more of them than would be expected for a routine patrol in these parts.

Who the hell were these people — or creatures? He was poised to scoot over to the next clump when he remembered he was under orders.

"Dirty, lazy, shit-eating jackass! Get going!"

There was no problem making out those words. At least they spoke some type of Sumerian.

"Get up, long ears. Not yet! Go a little farther."

These were other voices farther north. If the party had donkeys they must be on an extended trip, not likely to be a local patrol. Maybe just some traders. Gart quickly dropped that theory. Surbec, one of the baggage slaves tugged at his elbow and pointed to the west. An even line of upright spears was moving straight south along the old trace.

This was an alarming turn. The disembodied pikes stopped, waving in the air at random like the antennae of some huge insect pausing to deliberate.

If he were to stand up he could probably see the spear bearers — and be seen by them, of course. At this point, the sergeant, Ramlil, reached up and cut a brushy branch from the backside of a willow. Standing up behind the tree, he slowly moved himself and his cover around to the side. "They're coming this way. No, they've stopped now. They are just milling around," he whispered.

"Are they tracking us?" Gart whispered back.

"No, not at all. They seem to be taking a rest. Maybe they are going to fix their noon meal. Some of those helmets look like Lagashi."

"Lagashi! What would they be doing here, this far south?"

"I don't know, Lieutenant, but they are on their way somewhere. They have a lot of pack animals but they are heavily armed, too. Larsa wouldn't dare object, but if they were coming against Ur, why would they be turning east?"

They were indeed turning east. Traffic noises to the north continued and the lunch party to the west seemed to be growing. Gart felt they had little choice but to try to slip away to the east, although he feared the space between the marsh and the levee might soon narrow. This could expose them to detection. He whispered to Ramlil to move on out with the bearers and supplies, a few at a time.

"Talk to the bearers. Put a good scare in them, Sergeant. Tell them they eat slaves for breakfast in Lagash. I don't think we have any Lagashi slaves, so they don't have anything to gain by deserting us."

"Yes, sir, just as you say." The sergeant crawled away quickly.

The suspected space squeeze was soon evident and Gart's baggage and men were not entirely welcome as they moved in to share cover with Bruzi and the rest of the command. The scouts reported that the major portion of the eastbound contingent had left the levee and had spread out. Whatever reason these people had for making camp at midday, they had unknowingly pinned down Bruzi's patrol on the edge of the marsh.

Gart and Bruzi looked at each other, then looked away. They were stuck, at best, possibly done for. On their way out of this world in an inglorious whimper. Could the mighty warrior spirit, that they had so carefully rehearsed handle staying stuck? For about a halfhour everyone was very quiet, even the supposed Lagashi. Bruzi finally motioned to Gart to follow him and they moved about ten yards apart from the men. "Eber-Sin, we need to review all of our possible moves and make a plan."

"Have you considered breaking through to the north?" Gart asked. "We could be up and over that levee before they knew what hit them."

"I thought of that, but I don't know the lay of the land to the north. Do you?"

"No, sir, and they would be sure to pursue us. Bad idea."

"Looking at their numbers, we need to withdraw to the south," said Bruzi. "How much swamp do you think we would have to cross to get back to the border, and how deep do you think it gets?"

"It must be two or three miles and there is no way to know how deep it gets," Gart answered.

"Very few of our men can swim," noted the captain. "Add a few snakes, crocodiles and leeches and that doesn't sound any better than the first idea."

"How about attacking the small party to the west? Maybe they would think they were in big trouble and run?" Gart suggested hopefully.

"Naah, that would be a real long shot." Bruzi shook his head. "We had better withdraw most of our men and baggage as deep into the swamp as we dare, prepare to hide there. Go deeper into the reeds, if necessary. We should send sergeants and a couple men to check our limits north, east and west and to keep me informed if we have to move. I want you to cover the west again. Pick your sergeant."

"Ramlil will be fine," Gart replied.

"In that case, take Surbec the slave, too. He belongs to Ramlil's uncle who loans him to us for taxes. He spent several years in Lagash as a teenager. He probably understands their dialect."

"How did he get to us in Ur?" Gart wanted to know.

"Regular commercial channels, so far as I know. His owner probably picked him up in Larsa. He trades there sometimes."

"I'm wondering if we dare trust him. If we send him out to listen in he could have some choices to make," Gart said.

"You're right, Lieutenant. You will have to make that decision. I don't know him at all."

By the time the appointed lookouts were posted and Gart had somewhat reassured himself that Surbec was not unhappy to be in Ur, it was midafternoon and it seemed clear that the unidentified host was bivouacked for the night. As dusk approached, Gart and Surbec wriggled forward on parallel tracks in hopes of getting safely within earshot. Surbec was soon out of Gart's sight. He wondered if he would ever see the slave again. Now he could see campfires, the slow movement of several figures and hear an occasional burst of laughter.

Driven by impatience and voracious mosquitoes, Gart scurried on all fours across some ten yards of open space to the next thicket closer to the fires. He had scarcely regained his breath when he heard the crunch of approaching footsteps. He must have been seen! The tread continued, slow and deliberate, finally stopping about five feet away on the other side of the thick bush he had selected. Had he picked a guard post to visit? There was a rustling and shuffling; brush crackled. He dared not look up but he could envision fierce eyes peering down at him in his prostrate position and the firelight reflecting dully off of a copper helmet.

In the quiet he could hear the man breathing and the chilly trills of energy marched repeatedly up Gart's back. He heard a few grunts. Gart resumed his breathing. The strong odor of grain-fed human feces wafted across his nostrils and he realized the man's business was far less dangerous than he had feared. Still, he hugged the ground, his breathing carefully controlled until the footsteps receded. He could see the soldiers around the fire, eating, drinking beer and relaxing. There was an uncommonly large number of pack animals for a war party.

Not wishing to have further encounters, even with soldiers with such human needs, Gart retreated to his previous position. It was growing darker and all was very quiet except for the mosquitoes and frogs. After about a half hour he became aware of an intermittent rustling and slithering slowly approaching to his right. Certain that he was about to be a meal for a crocodile or similar swamp creature, he drew his legs up, ready to flee at all costs. "Plop." Just in front of his face — two bronze spearheads, shafts attached, horizontal to the ground. Gart's head jerked upward to face a copper helmet, its luster dulled by daubed mud. All else was lost in the gloom until the gleam of Surbec's broad smile brought his gleeful face into focus.

"Holy hell!" Gart whispered. "Where did you get all that stuff? Did you kill them?"

"Nah, drunk as skunks, both of them. Someone may kill them in the morning when they try to explain where their weapons went. Someone in their party will probably get the blame. Real jokers, these Lagashi."

"They are from Lagash then? Could you hear anything?"

Gart noticed that he had automatically shifted into a formal mode of address as he questioned this heavily armed young man now facing him on far more equal terms than when they had parted less than an hour ago.

"Yeah, I heard quite a bit."

There was no "sir" in this reply Gart noted, but it didn't seem important under the circumstances.

"Where are they headed? Could you tell?"

"Not to Ur. As best I could make out they will swing back northeast in the morning to the Zagros Mountains. I know they have a trading colony there. It sounded like they were going to relieve the garrison as well as pick up metals and stone. They may be taking this roundabout way for political reasons. They must have gone to Larsa first and now they'll pick up one of the paths through the swamps that become passable about this time of year."

"Do they seem to be on the alert?"

"Hell, no!" Surbec laughed. "They may not even be all that hostile, but I wouldn't trust them. They just finished their beer supply. They will be gone in the morning, hangovers and all."

Would Surbec be gone too? Gart wondered. How would a slave think under these circumstances?

"Let's get all this back to the captain. Uhh, good work, soldier. Maybe I should carry those weapons, the spears and what else do you have? Two short swords?"

"Oh, no, *sir*, I wouldn't think of it, *sir*. I'll lead the way."

"Very well, let's go." He was happy to have Surbec in view. He seemed awfully well informed for someone listening through the bushes. Would his nervous praise and calling him "soldier" be taken as a battlefield promotion? If so, could Bruzi be convinced? Who would pay off his owner? Who was entitled to the weapons — if they got out alive?

Their exhausted and sleepy commander was near the place where they had last seen him and he had little information to add to what they brought him. Bruzzi's best guess put the number of men in the surrounding encampments at two to three hundred. Relieved by Surbec's information, Bruzi seemed more preoccupied with the mosquitoes and getting to sleep than with Gart's concern about Surbec's allegiance.

A new watch was set with instructions not to make any unauthorized moves. The rest were to settle in and try to get some sleep. Dawn came soon and passed quickly as Utu, the sun god, soared suddenly out of the marshy plains to the east. His cheerful energy was little appreciated by the bedraggled sons of Nannar. The Lagashi must have slept better than they had, as they made a quiet and swift departure to the east. Whatever action they took regarding the two soldiers who had mislaid their valuable arms was carried out quietly. The weapons remained in Surbec's hands.

Before midmorning, satisfied the Lagashi were all gone, the mosquito- and leech-bitten legion swiftly retraced its route back toward Ur. They soon encountered local farmers on the way to Larsa, their donkeys loaded with melons. Some trades were arranged with the remains of their slightly soggy rations for the refreshing melons and the farmers were saved the long trip to town. From these farmers they learned that such large parties of Lagashi troops were becoming a frequent occurrence. Larsa seemed to be ignoring this, although the region was nominally under their control. When they reached the boundary canal, they found it was now full of water. By forming a human chain, they were able to ford it without incident and emerged bathed and feeling refreshed and more respectable. They were determined to reach Ur before the gates closed for the night.

The steady trudge home was interrupted only by a low mumble of conversation and several brief rests when a grove or orchard enticed them to seek relief from the sun. During these pauses, Bruzi seemed almost eager to talk to Gart. He expressed in both word and demeanor his great relief that they had gotten through the night with his command intact. "Gart, I don't know how our story will be received. What we found was not exactly what we went looking for. I do want you to know I will always appreciate your alertness. That may have been the only thing that saved us from total disaster."

"Well, thank you, sir." Gart was surprised at his commander's sincerity and open attitude. "I had a little help from my four-footed friend and a lot of help from Surbec."

After a brief silence, Gart continued, "You know, Captain, I have been thinking about Surbec. Aside from being damned grateful, I worry that it's going to look a little bad when the only man to really distinguish himself was a porter, and a borrowed slave at that."

Bruzi laughed. "You put that right well, Lieutenant. What did you have in mind?"

"Well, at least he should have the right to bear arms, if he wants to." Dare he push for more? Yes! "Maybe he should be made a freeman. Pay off his owner, somehow?"

Gart felt impelled by a sense of justice as much as gratitude, but having said this, he was surprised he still did not feel entirely clear about Surbec's trustworthiness.

Bruzi's smile faded slightly and he looked away.

"That would be quite a promotion for him. It would take some doing. In my present state of gratitude I might give him the whole royal treasury, if I had the keys. Let me think about it a little while."

When the march resumed, Bruzi motioned for Gart to march at his immediate left and for the next following rank to give them a little space so that they might converse more privately.

"I don't know, Gart, what the colonel and the higher ups will think of our performance. I can't say it was a success. I hate to make excuses in advance, but it does seem to me that this caper was just slapped together and the purpose was mostly political. I don't know how to call it, so there is no use to slant our story. We'll just tell them what happened. I will put in a word for you and Surbec, of course."

"Yes, Captain, I understand."

By the time the patrol had reached the causeway over the city's defense canal, the platoon had, without bidding, drawn itself into parade formation. They marched through the city gate in perfect cadence, spending their last reserves of energy in a burst of determination.

Because of the hour only a small knot of soldiers, beggars and traders were at the gate to greet them. Bruzi, hearing the puzzled buzzing of the people, threw them a quick smile and a wave. He was rewarded by an enthusiastic burst of cheers. Resolutely, they marched straight down the middle of the street to the armory, straddling the thin line between glory and ignominy.

Immediately upon falling out of formation at the armory, Gart sent a young boy to inform Leah of his return. He presumed he would be involved in a report and would be home late. The armory was full of men and noise. This was a regular drill night in addition to whatever state of emergency activities were underway. Colonel Alkohn inspected the unit with one sweeping glance. He asked everyone to remain until he had taken their report. Then he led the two officers quickly to a small private chamber at the rear of the building.

True to his word, Bruzi delivered a brief and factual account of the events of the last three days, including favorable mention of the contributions of Lieutenant Eber-Sin, Sergeant Ramlil and the slave Surbec, plus a general commendation of the discipline and cooperation of his men. Gart was impressed by his professional manner.

Colonel Alkohn chewed his upper lip and drummed the table with his fingers. He paced the tiny room several times. He would not meet their eyes, but directed his fierce gaze at their shoulders, shifting from one to the other.

"Both of you are officers," he snapped. "You should understand you're not paid to put on parades or save your own skins in games of hide and seek. You're paid to kill and destroy. That's what soldiering is all about. That's how we get respect. What have you accomplished so far? I hope I've made it clear that I expect more of you the next time!"

His face florid, he paced again with shortened steps, glowering at the walls but not meeting their eyes. “Come on, let’s go to address the men.”

As he followed his two commanders out, Gart could feel his neck growing stiff and hot with rage, his hands clenched and trembling. He was thankful for the protection of the gathering dusk. He and Bruzi stood apart as the colonel arranged for the assembly. Gart could contain himself no longer and he whispered to the captain in a hoarse voice.

“What the hell did the stupid ass expect from us? Were we supposed to eat two hundred Lagashi soldiers for breakfast? I’ll bet he would still be scraping his leg if he had been out in that swamp with us!”

Bruzi chuckled, as though relieved that his new protégé had spoken for them both.

“Sonny,” he continued to chortle, “you have just been initiated. Me, I’m no virgin. I’ve been had before. That was just a small sample. You should hear him when he really gets on someone’s back. Let’s see what happens now. This speech should be interesting.”

“Men of Ur, fellow citizens.” The colonel’s sharp, penetrating voice brought an instant and expectant hush. “This is a crucial and historic occasion. Captain Bruzi, his officers and men have just completed a brilliant reconnaissance that has confirmed our fears the treacherous rulers of Lagash are well on their way to a military program by which they hope to once again control the whole of Sumer. We have word they are supporting a traitorous conspiracy among the people of our neighbor, Larsa, which may well be their first victim. We will all face heavy responsibilities in the rearmament which we must accomplish for the defense of our beloved city. We are fortunate to have the examples of such brave men as those who have risked everything for our sakes during this patrol. I promise you their deeds will not go unrecognized. Captain Bruzi and Lieutenant Eber-Sin will be promoted and receive increased responsibilities. The loyal bondsman, Surbec, will become a free man within the week.

"Good night. You are dismissed."

A few steps toward the door and the colonel paused, signaling the two officers to wait.

"Oh, yes, you are to go to the temple, northwest audience hall, at sunrise to let them hear your report and to answer their questions. Please be extra respectful to them. We are in some trouble over there for sending you out without consulting them. When they are through, you are free to go. If I need you before the next regular drill, I will send for you. Uhh...Bruzi, you don't have to check in at the palace right now. We have other plans for you. Take a couple days off. Good night."

Gart directed his weary feet toward the apartment. His strength was fading fast and he was fighting the jumble of questions in his head. What should he make of Colonel Alkohn's double-talk?

By chance or by fate, he met, on the darkening street, nearly everyone he knew: Mahn-so-ni, Banarum, his kid brother-in-law, the garrulous Jeme and several councilmen. Politics be damned! Well, no, take that back, but the only one he wanted to see was Leah. He put on what he hoped was his most mysterious air and hurried past everyone with nods and waves of recognition.

Home at last! Leah and lamplight! He numbly drank in her steady gaze: a rich mixture of joy, relief and a dash of the resentment any woman rightfully feels when left for a lesser cause. A few fierce hugs, then she fed him and helped him with a quick sponge bath before he fell into their bed and a troubled sleep.

"Come on, soldier." Leah gently shook him awake. "It's getting light. We have to go to the temple." She would go with him to visit a shrine while he made his report.

Without further conversation, they dressed in their respectful best and proceeded directly to the main gate of the temple compound, arriving there before sunrise. They found Bruzi chatting quietly with two of the royal guards who were posted at the outer gate. Gart introduced his wife to the captain, even though everyone seemed too sleepy to respond.

As the royal palace was inside the temple compound, Gart presumed he could rely on Bruzi to guide him to their appointment in this little city within a city. Located here were not only the shrines and libraries, but also the administrative offices and services which processed the tithes and taxes that clothed and fed the large number of priests, astrologers, priestesses, bureaucrats and temple prostitutes who lived here. Bruzi had a knowledge of the system that was based on many generations of belonging.

"O.K., Lieutenant," said Bruzi. He gave a polite nod to Leah, who was taking her leave, and a soft little salute to the guards who had, until recently, been under his command. "We might as well move on up to the next level. Someone will be expecting us shortly." The two officers strolled to the east corner of the ziggurat and slowly ascended the wide stairway of burned and burnished brick at the northeast face of the massive, manmade mountain.

"Sir," Gart continued formally, "who are we likely to be meeting here?"

"Well, the hall up there is usually referred to as the high priestess' reception room. It's likely we will see the *Nin-An*, herself, and I know not whom else. We can count the number of interviewers and figure just how interested they are in our expedition. You do know that for every major official in the royal household, there is a counterpart on this side of the compound?"

"I didn't know that. Is this temple a restricted area here?"

"No, Gart, everyone is welcome here. If you look down there, to the north, all you see are dairy yards, granaries and dormitories. If we were to go around the corner to the west face, the structures and functions of the temple get more strange and more exclusive. Here is the room we are looking for."

They paused a moment to look back at the courtyard. Near the east entry-way to the court, Gart spotted a familiar figure. Kre-eg was coasting along with his usual easy stride, evidently on his way from his favorite haunt, the temple prostitutes' quarters, to his new post with the Royal Bodyguard.

Their timing had been good, for they had just arrived at the solid wooden door under the extended eaves of the lean-to structure, when they heard the morning party of officiants descending the central stairway from the upper levels of the ziggurat. Nannar was officially bedded for the day and Utu's gleaming helmet peeked up from the great, marshy lake to the east. The rustle of skirts stopped at the other side of the anteroom. Very shortly the door opened and a young woman, a novice priestess, motioned them to enter.

Nin-ana-Me waited as the two officers stood in the dim chamber, their eyes not yet adjusted enough to see her and her co-interrogator. She was thankful for even this brief pause to settle herself before they began. She had just left Ni-Zum-Ka, the high priest, who at the last possible minute gave his blessing to this inquiry. She had realized any idea originating with her could be a problem for him. She was beginning to understand the old man was afraid of her or of something he felt she stood for.

There was no hurry to begin her questions. They were not fully formed, as yet. News of this strange little foray had come as an unexpected gift, rescuing her from the despair she was beginning to feel for herself and for Ur. Here were two officers who, for whatever reason, had broken out of their usual confines to encounter a wider world. How she would have liked to go with them! Perhaps there was some meaning to be gleaned from their experience.

She had immediately started a tactful series of requests to set up an interview with them on their return. Mer-luke seemed the most likely ally. He might even be sympathetic with her need for contact with real people with day-to-day concerns. Considering his office and nightly schedule, he must feel nearly as isolated as she did, although he never complained. If she judged him correctly, Mer-luke would also be the most likely one to see the patrol as part of something bigger and not just a temporary distraction for political purposes. His reaction to her proposal had been puzzling. At first he seemed quite startled, but on further explanation he moved quickly from suspicion to an uncharacteristic enthusiasm.

Now she must try once more to reach out and make contact with a real world and real people. She had come to Ur somehow convinced she was there for a purpose, to be part of something very important. The years were passing. The flower that was the city seemed to be wilting from some mysterious malady and she felt herself floundering. Oh, how grievous if this city lost its way! How bitter it would be if she were asleep and missed her call!

Mer-luke was also using the quiet to review why he was here. He had been startled by the priestess' suggestion they look at the predicament of the common folks he was inclined to forget. He now realized he needed to be brought back to earth by any means available. The excitement and frustrations of his work in the observatory the past few months had left him exhausted.

He did not understand how he had become so obsessed by the relationship between Nannar and the star of Inanna. He felt he could see the great light of the nighttime nudged off course every time he passed that lady of mixed deportment. If that were so, he might be on to an explanation of the troubled times in the city. If Nannar was straying it would certainly be observed and not appreciated by Nin-Gal, his virtuous wife. How odd that just at that point in his musings he is summoned by the priestess of Nin-Gal to this unusual inquiry.

It is true that he had failed to demonstrate his theory and his young assistants had begun to look at him strangely when he tried. The thing that fascinated his assistants was the persistent and increasing meteorite showers in the northern sky. Some seemed headed toward Larsa or Lagash, but most seemed to come strait toward Ur.

News about these celestial events was seeping down into the general population. More people were showing up at midnight to watch the display and to pester him with questions about what it meant in their lives. How could he answer? He couldn't turn them away, but how could he admit the depth of his ignorance or how could he explain the awe he felt or the utter conviction that there was something out there, living and growing and about to break through for them all?

When their eyes had accommodated to the relative gloom of the room Gart became aware of two figures seated on simple stools on a low platform against the burnished brick wall. That wall would be a part of the outer sheath of the ziggurat.

On the left, they could now see an older man of slight stature with white hair and beard, both meticulously trimmed and nicely set off by the contrast of his dark skirt and shoulder shawl and his dark, sparrow-bright eyes. On their right was a woman who appeared to be in her third or fourth decade. Her sturdy, yet supple, figure was artfully draped in a garment of deep blue material which was an insignia of her high rank. Her fine features seemed poised in an expression of patient expectancy. The eyes were neither bold nor timid.

The woman spoke first.

"Good morning, Captain Bruzi and, I take it, Lieutenant Eber-Sin."

"Yes, my lady," replied Bruzi, pulling himself up to a more soldierly posture.

"Lieutenant, my name is Nin-ana-Me," she said, looking directly at Gart, "and the gentleman to my right is Mer-luke, our most senior astrologer and counselor to His Royal Highness, Demmuzi-ki-ag."

The stiff little bows of the officers were acknowledged by Mer-luke with a minimal smile and nod of his head. His expectations for this interview were limited.

"Gentlemen," the priestess resumed, "we do not get out to the countryside very often any more, as much as I regret that. We feel the need of additional observations so that we might more wisely direct the affairs of the temple and, in turn, be of benefit to the state. We have noted a decrease of over one-fourth in the harvest from the temple lands this year as well as a similar decline in votive offerings. There seems to be no drought or indication of plague to explain this. Even the heavenly signs seem increasingly obscure. Perhaps mother Ki can give us hint. What did you see of her?"

The woman seemed very much at ease in her role as spokesperson. Her voice was low and unhurried and possessed a momentum that carried her listeners along willingly.

"My Lady," Bruzi cleared his throat, "I would like to defer to Lieutenant Eber-Sin in this matter. He has very ably demonstrated his powers of observation at times when I might be preoccupied with administrative matters."

"My Lady — and, sir," Gart felt he must proceed without further preparation. He was careful to include the astrologer in his salutation. "My first impression, once we got into the countryside, was that of the quietness. Except for the sound of our footsteps and the rattle of our gear, there was almost nothing to be heard. When we stopped, there were no insect noises, no birds, only the faintest breeze. The only animal I saw during the first day was a wild dog or jackal who kept us company at a distance most of the day and even into the next morning, when it evidently found the Lagashi more interesting."

"It followed you?" Mer-luke asked, mildly interested.

"No, as a matter of fact, it always preceded us. It seemed to be waiting for us to come along."

"Now that *is* interesting! Most unusual, wouldn't you say?" the astrologer asked.

Both officers nodded assent as Mer-luke leaned forward, stroking his white-bearded chin.

"And you say it deserted you for the Lagashi?".

"I don't know that for a fact, but I feel it did. It came back toward us and then turned to the east at just the place they turned later."

Gart's interlocutors shared a bemused glance.

"Yes, yes, continue!" The old man was becoming more involved in the story.

Gart described the marked increase in signs of bird and insect life once they crossed the drained canal with its border stella and ramshackle shrine. He also noted that on their return on the next day the contrast was less remarkable. The countryside seemed subdued but not dead.

"And the night sky — did you notice anything special about it?" Mer-luke persisted.

Gart paused for some time. He presumed that the astrologer had been watching closely that night and was looking for some specific confirmation. He searched his memory for some forgotten starry message but came up with nothing. He looked questioningly at his commander but Bruzi's slight, empty-handed shrug promised no help.

"No, sir, nothing really different, except that, due to the lack of moon and the fact that it had been some time since I had slept in the open I was very impressed by the Milky Way. It seemed closer, stronger and I hadn't remembered it spanned the entire sky. I must have awakened every hour. It seemed each time I opened my eyes I was looking at the Star of the Northern Quarter. All of the other stars had moved, but it and I were in the same place."

"Tell me, Lieutenant," Nin-ana-Me resumed, "is there anything else you can describe? Did something in particular attract your attention? Have you any general impressions or strange ideas?"

"Umnn...well, odd you should ask, but yes. Both nights. The first camp seemed a special place, though it looked like a common old silt bank. That night I had a sense of a coming together of everything; earth, stars, men. I guess I'd say...awe?" Gart looked quickly about in embarrassment, but he was met by encouraging, interested looks from both interlocutors and even an affirmative nod from Bruzi.

"The first night the feeling didn't seem to have any connection with what we were doing," Gart resumed. The second night, I was really excited and exhausted at the same time, yet underneath, it seemed safe enough. This assured me that what we were doing was all right, at least after it was clear what we needed to do and not do. I am sorry if I have rambled on. All of this is probably off the subject."

"No, no, not at all." The priestess looked around, then beckoned to the attendant who quickly provided stools for the two officers.

"Now, Captain," she continued, "I realize you are personally responsible to His Highness as well as to Colonel Alkohn. I do not wish to put you in a bind by asking for sensitive information, but as you realize, the temple and the palace are, in our understanding, the two arms of the will of the God. There is always quite an interchange of information and people across the courtyard here. I will try very hard to keep my questions above the gossip level. However, we do need your observations to confirm what we think we see in the condition of our king. May I proceed?"

"As you wish, My Lady," Bruzi answered cautiously.

"Have you not noticed, as we have, quite a marked change in His Majesty's behavior? And for how long?"

"Yes, My Lady. It has been noticeable and increasing for about six months. He seems more remote, withdrawn, forgetful."

"And would you say this is progressive?" Nin-ana-Me sensed it would be difficult to get Bruzi to say much.

"Well, yes and no. In general it has gotten worse, but it is rather variable from day to day and at different times of the day. In fact, his personal staff have had to change their schedules. He is often up two or three hours before sunrise, pacing about, quite agitated and distraught, yet by the time of his evening meal, he can chat and joke a little, almost like his old self. The evening meal is the only time he eats or drinks much of anything and he appears to have lost considerable flesh."

"Anything else, Captain?"

"Umnn — well, as you have undoubtedly been informed, he has not visited his harem, or attended religious services, or asked to review his guard for several months. In summary, I would say he has been very quiet and not very productive."

"That sounds somewhat like the lieutenant's description of the countryside, wouldn't you say?"

"Yes, My Lady," Bruzi answered with a puzzled look.

The woman glanced down as though studying her hands, which were spread palms up in her lap. Having evidently reached some conclusions, she looked up.

"Thank you for your time, gentlemen. Your observations are very helpful, though disturbing. These days seem filled with puzzles and challenges. I am wondering if there is anything we can do about it." While speaking she had gradually turned toward Mer-luke.

He sighed, still frustrated and bemused. "It's in the hands of the gods," he answered in an flat, fatigued tenor.

"In the hands of the gods, indeed — among others," she answered impatiently. "I just hope the city of Ur doesn't perish in committee meetings while the gods are off settling their differences about something else. Our City Council seems just as contentious and no more attentive than the gods described in our legends. Thank you again, sirs. You may go now."

They descended the stairway to the main plaza in silence.

"Now, what was that all about?" Gart looked to his commander in earnest supplication.

Bruzi appeared equally mystified. After a moment he silently dismissed the matter with a little shrug and an opening flip of his hands.

Taking leave of Bruzi, Gart headed toward the east gate where he could see Leah waiting in the shadow, protecting herself from the bright rays of the sun, which was now well above the walls and rooftops.

"Gart! Lieutenant! How fortunate! You are just the one I want to see."

Squinting into the glare of the morning sun, Gart made out the rumpled kilt, the burly bare chest and now the resplendent bald dome of Shem-ki. This hearty lay brother of apparent middle age had taken his vows only a few years ago and now served as chief administrator of the vast temple enterprise. Gart was familiar with his affable but shrewd business ways through several negotiations at the stockyards. He was no pushover, but he would sometimes give you a break.

"So, which hat are you wearing today? Are you the valiant young soldier or the sharpest trader in the yards? Hey, I may have a real interesting job for you." With the last phrase Shem-ki's voice switched abruptly from hearty, affable to hushed, conspiratorial. "Have you got a few minutes?"

"Well," Gart scrambled to reorganize his thoughts and to match the joking manner, "the gleam off of my head is from the copper helmet of His Majesty's service, but once out that gate, I am interested in your proposition. How long will this take?"

"Oh, no more than a half hour. Come on around this way to the receiving pens." Shem-ki had Gart by the elbow as if to carry him off with enthusiasm.

"No. Hold on." Gart resisted. He had caught sight of Leah, eyes downcast, pensively drawing patterns in the dust with her sandal toe. "I'm sorry, I must first speak to my wife at the gate. She has waited for some time. I'll either be right back, or I'll return this afternoon."

"Oh, I'm sorry, I didn't even know you were married. Got kids?"

"Good question," Gart threw back over his shoulder.

As he approached the gate he gave his wife a careful look. Something was here that he had not experienced before.

"Sorry for the delay, business matter," Gart began.

In reply, Leah flashed him a momentary pout, quickly supplanted by a radiant smile. "I'm even a little nauseated," she whispered, in obvious triumph.

"What's this?" he asked, a bit confused, "You mean...You're.... Are you sure, Leah?"

"Well, mostly." She nodded and patted her belly. "The priestess says I am, or will be soon. She predicts I will have a baby at the winter solstice."

"Oh, how wonderful!" Gart beamed. "I shall be very proud. Now, best you scoot home and rest — and I had better get myself over to the stockyards and try to make us all a living. Here, take this with you." He handed her his helmet. "Are you feeling all right?"

She nodded vigorously. He watched as she departed and saw the little skip in her step.

He had given her the helmet to continue his joke with Shem-ki, but he also felt some relief to cast it aside and get back to his work.

"Yes, Gart." Shem-ki was ready to deal. "We have this medium-sized awkward situation. Someone with your tact and cow savvy could render a real service to the temple and your fellow citizens. Yes, the gods will thank you, I'm sure."

"So far, so good," said Gart noncommittally.

"We will even make it worth your while," the older man added.

"Better and better. Go on."

By this time they had reached the livestock receiving pens where both offerings and the landlord's share from temple tenant farmers were received. This was adjacent to the temple dairy which produced milk, not only for votive libations, but also for drink, butter and cheese for the temple community.

"See that fellow over there?" Shem-ki pointed to a handsome brown bullock standing in the pen with several sheep and goats. "Looks great, doesn't he? He must have cost our benefactor quite a sum. The problem is, he's lame. That's a *no-no* for the god's table. Let's presume our banker friend didn't know about that. If we return the bullock, he's going to be embarrassed and out of sorts at the very least. He likes lots of credit and I suspect his charity to be very self-serving. It would be best if we didn't have to deal with this. Would you look at that leg and tell me what you think?"

Examination of the leg indicated to Gart this was a recent injury that had some slight festering. With proper care, the animal would recover and could pull a plow again. He would be suitable for slaughter now outside of temple auspices, but recovery could take several weeks. This animal wouldn't be ready in time for the upcoming feast days.

Shem-ki pondered these comments while Gart waited.

"I have an idea, Gart! I'm pretty sure we have another one on a nearby farm that looks a lot like this one. Assuming that our banker and this bullock are not personally acquainted, we should be able to pull a switch in time for the sacrifice of the fifth new moon after New Year."

"Your farmers will take the lame one then?"

"I see some problems with that. I would like this one out of sight as soon as possible. I am not very happy with these tenants. They would raise a fuss if they couldn't work him right away. I would prefer to send him way out of town. We have a farm on the outskirts. Could you take him out there and instruct the tenant how to take care of that leg?"

"I can do it, or have it done. How soon?"

"As soon as possible. If you will also go out and check his recovery in a month or so. I'll see that you are paid."

"All right, sir, I will send my man Jeme around early in the morning to get him out of town before the rich folks are awake. I will go out later."

"Jeme? *do* you mean *Jeme*, that wild-talking fellow from the stockyards?" Shem-ki seemed alarmed. "Do you think that man can keep a secret?"

"I'm sure he can, especially if he is let in on the conspiracy. He would delight in putting one over on a banker. By the way, it would be good if you could give him a written bill of lading and some instructions for your tenants to receive the animal. I know your tenant can't read, but he would recognize your seal and be impressed by the tablet."

Gart savored a little pride in his growing sophistication in business matters.

"I'm willing to do that," answered Shem-ki. "I just hope I can find a scribe to do it for me. They don't want much to do with the business end of it here. They all think they should be up there learning to write all that high-falutin' stuff." The glistening, now perspiring, bald head jerked toward the cloisters on the northwest face of the ziggurat. "It's quite a problem sometimes. Do you know a good accounting scribe I could hire part-time?"

Gart's gaze had followed the trajectory of Shem-ki's nod and his eye was caught by the distant but unmistakable blue-robed figure of Nin-ana-Me leaning forward with her elbows on the balcony adjoining the cloister side of the audience room. He felt an impulse to wave to her but suppressed this immediately when he realized where he was.

"Umm — umnn, well, yes, as a matter of fact, I have a friend. It may be just the thing. I'll send him around." Gart hurried off toward the east gate, his thoughts turning quickly to his business and the livestock at the yards.

CHAPTER FOUR

On his arrival at the yards, Gart found Mar-Ti, Jeme and two of his sons watching as the cow he had recently bought cleaned up her newborn calf. After the livestock were watered and fed, he beckoned Jeme aside and offered him the job of escorting the bullock to his assigned hideaway.

"Yes, sir, and I will keep it real secret," Jeme promised. "How about if I take this young feller with me?" He threw an arm across the shoulders of his delighted eleven-year-old as Gart nodded in agreement.

"By the way, Gart, while you were away your cousin came by the yards. He said that the family would be leaving their winter quarters in about a month and they will be expecting you to come out, like usual, to help them mouth out the sheep and goats and to decide when to bring the ones with poor teeth in to market."

This was something to which Gart usually looked forward. Prices should be good this spring and he still had an inherited interest in the flock.

About midafternoon, An-Nam, the colonel's runner, came to the yards looking for him.

"Oh, Lieutenant, the colonel would like you to come to the armory to talk to him sometime before the drill this evening."

As usual, the little man turned quickly and left before further questions could be asked.

Within minutes Gart was on his way.

"Thank you for being so prompt, Lieutenant." The colonel seemed relaxed and friendly. Gart could detect no trace of animosity left over from the lecture of the previous evening.

"You may already know," the colonel continued, "that the City Council will soon authorize an increase in both the full-time army and the Civil Guard. What you do not know is that these plans include promoting you, Lieutenant Eber-Sin, to Senior Lieutenant on a full-time basis and giving you the responsibility to form and train a platoon, which you will command."

The colonel's words were coming too fast for Gart. He was having difficulty with the implications of "full-time" and "command." Did he have a choice? What could he do about his trip back home?

"I do understand, Lieutenant," Alkohn resumed, after a brief pause, "that you have other business and political interests. We will allow you to adjust your time as you can, at least for now, barring a real emergency. You may draw full pay and rations starting next week."

Even as he struggled with all this news, it struck Gart the terms offered were surprisingly considerate.

"You may also be interested to know, Lieutenant, that your fellow officer, Captain Bruzi, will be given a double promotion and will be placed in charge of the entire rearmament and training program. We will need you and all of the officers most of tomorrow afternoon and evening," Alkohn continued. "We will be working out the expansion plans, so come prepared to assume your new responsibilities."

If Bruzi was being double promoted they must not have disgraced themselves on that patrol, Gart thought to himself as he practically floated out of the commander's presence and down the street toward home. On the way, his first doubts caught up with him. Was a real war in the making? What did the higher-ups know that they weren't telling? Had he let his ambitions lead him into serious trouble?

"You need to know, Leah, that I will be spending more time at the armory. I have been asked — maybe told is the word — to go full-time and to train and command a platoon of my own."

He was not sure she fully heard him.

"And who will take care — of — your livestock?" she finally asked.

There is more here than livestock, Gart was thinking. The tone of the question was so serious, a bit distant.

"Are you really pregnant, Leah?" he asked when he was finally able to catch her eye.

Her slow and solemn nod did nothing to dispel the serious tone of that moment. Without further comment she proceeded to serve their supper, which had been prepared with great care and generosity. He did not pursue her eyes further as he silently weighed and discarded a response.

This was the first full meal he had been able to sit down to in four days. After his fill of grilled fish and onions, pan bread and beer, he began to relax. His beautiful wife, the richness of their relationship and the joy of her pregnancy filled the fore-ground as he allowed his self-doubts and feelings of estrangement from Leah to fade away.

Downstairs, Jeme's family was unusually quiet. Possibly they were preparing for the early departure to the countryside.

Gart awakened slowly on the first day of his "full-time" military career. He became gradually aware of two sets of rosy rectangles on the smooth white plaster of the wall he was facing. The coming dawn was projecting itself through the two tiny windows of their apartment. The shadow of the vertical wooden rod bisected each frame of faint light. As it became lighter, he could make out the details of the room, now familiar, but so strangely different from the waking sights of his earlier years. All of the lines of the room and its furnishings were so clear and symmetrical, thanks to Banarum, the constructor, and to Leah, who so ardently chose, arranged, cleaned and cared for their furnishings and possessions.

The simple, rectangular room could be divided by a curtain of rough linen, artfully designed from scraps from his father-in-law's tailor shop, but it was seldom used. The end wall of the food preparation area was completely lined with the carefully matched large earthenware jars used for water and food storage. Under the windows, arranged in tiers, were the baskets that contained all of their clothing, tools and mementos. Their bed was on the floor itself. A shallow ridge of packed clay had been laid over log rafters, woven reed mats, and the clay seal of the floor. The ridge dammed off a rectangle in the corner to retain the loose rushes of their bedding. The low table, on an earthen pot pedestal, bore a single small bowl of semitranslucent stone, Leah's prized possession. Her loom, four low stools with wicker seats and one bench completed their simple furnishings.

In the stillness of the dawn, the harmony of these carefully fashioned objects spoke to the awakening ex-herdsman:

"This is something new. No riot here of the infinite variations of nature you found in the brush shelters and mud huts of your youth. Here is something that springs from the mind and heart of humankind."

Before his eyes, now wide and rested, unfolded a picture of the purity and strangeness of thought itself. Freed from the tapering cylinders and endlessly duplicated spirals and scallops inherent in the flow of plant and animal life, here were pure planes and parallels, rectangles and cubes of space rendered in the wood and plaster of this room, his home, but not confined to it alone.

These shapes seemed to address him, not in each artifact, but collectively as one truth. Without formal words, it came clearly to Gart: The ziggurat is no imitation mountain. It is this room on another scale.

The flavor of this experience faded along with the rose tinge of the dawn light. Brzzt.... Brzzt.... The first fly of the day sailed through one window, looped upward and left through the other. The day had begun, though silence still prevailed throughout the city. Gart listened without stirring.

Was he hearing something else besides the occasional drone of the fly? Yes, there it was. It seemed familiar. Could it be the masonry talking, settling, warming? No, that *Hummnn.... Hummnn.* It came — and faded. Much too regular. Yes, he had heard it before, every time he came back to the city after visiting his home village. Several times he had noticed it when he first crossed the canal onto the irrigated land. It always seemed to get louder as he approached the city. He had never noticed it before inside these walls, but maybe he had just never listened.

Could this steady *Hummnn.... ummnn...mmnn* be some *presence* hovering over this land between the rivers; this land of marshy plains and fertile fields? Was this the power that was drawing people like him into the cities from their farmsteads and drovers' tents? Was there some connection between that Hummn and the powers that must be collecting here?

Abruptly, Gart arose and scrambled through his preparations for the day. Fending off any memory of Leah's discontent, he crossed their courtyard. In the first full light, he saw Jeme and his son in the street toward the temple compound. They had started on time.

Today's session at the armory would be the first general meeting of all the officers of Ur during the eight years he had lived in the city, and he was eager to see who they were. Soon they began to trickle in. He estimated there were between two and three hundred men. Their dress and equipment varied widely, from fancy and combat ready to casual kilts and sandals. Except for the Royal Bodyguard and a few high-ranking officers, these were part-time citizen soldiers.

The meeting was slow in starting and boring in content. There were talks by Alkohn and three other colonels as well as Bruzi, who must also be a colonel now, and General Mem-el; the senior and overall commander.

"Gentlemen, our city is once again in grave danger." General Mem-el was concluding the series of speeches. "Those of us responsible for her defense have called you to prepare for a heroic struggle. We have word that the armies of Larsa and Lagash are mobilized and in the field. So far, they have been too occupied in the northeast to meddle directly in our affairs. We do have time to prepare before they turn on us."

History might well bear out the general's conclusions, but Gart wondered how their commander had arrived at them. The officers meeting was dismissed an hour before evening drill. Gart took the opportunity to find Orson, Kre-eg and Bruzi. He proposed they meet for food and beer at the adjacent canteen. This was, of course, one of the several where Kre-eg worked. So far as Gart knew, Bruzi and Kre-eg had hardly met.

"Well, Lieutenant Til-Chah, how did you hit it off with Ni-Pada-Dan?" asked Bruzi with a smile of anticipation.

"The Lord High Chamberlain? Oh, fine, fine." Kre-eg paused to make sure he was getting the message. "Fusty old fart isn't he? He has given me daily grades on my uniform, my posture, military bearing and general attitude. I know, appearance is important in that position. It's much more show than security, but yee gods, who's looking?"

"Ni-Pada-Dan, that's who." The ex-commander of the Royal Bodyguard was enjoying this more and more. "I'll tell him to slack off a little. He's my second cousin, you know."

"Ehhe — I guess I blew that one. You're probably related to his gloomy highness himself, if my luck holds."

"Well, as a matter of fact," Bruzi averted his face in feigned modesty, "third cousin, twice removed. But don't worry. He was just plain folks before he got this job. They say he was a damned good soldier, though. I've heard he wasn't overjoyed with the nomination. There are some drawbacks to the job, if you know what I mean."

Kre-eg's expression betrayed that he did not, indeed, know to what Bruzi was referring.

"You don't know about that?" Bruzi asked. "How long have your people lived here?"

"Oh, my grandfathers were born here, or at least they grew up here," Kre-eg replied rather quickly.

"And before that?" Bruzi continued, not unkindly, but showing no evidence he recognized this as a sensitive issue.

"Umn — out east, Elam or thereabouts, I understand." Kre-eg got up from the benches where they were seated and went to the kitchen area where he could be heard rebuking their waiter sharply for his tardiness.

"Hey, you are still working here? Aren't you full-time military now?" Orson asked as Kre-eg returned. He had been listening to the outburst in the kitchen also.

"Full-time both places, at least for now. I'm doing double shifts."

"What's the matter?" Orson pursued. "Won't your uncle let you off the hook?"

"My uncle is no problem. It's my father. He wants me to learn the business from the ground up."

"So, what did your father say when he heard you were to be commander of the Royal Bodyguard?" Orson asked.

"I suspect he must have known about it before I did." Kre-eg looked a little surprised at his own remarks. Then, as if he had said more than he intended to, he pressed his lips together and hurried back to the kitchen. Shut up Kre-eg, he scolded himself silently. This is a family matter. You don't really know Dad was behind this.

The canteen became increasingly crowded and noisy. Actually, *canteen* was a rather generous name for the establishment. The cooking and storage area was somewhat screened from view by a low brick wall. A small dining area with low tables and stools was covered by a pole framework and a thatched roof. Once the sun went down behind the armory, more tables appeared, spilling out into what was supposed to be a small public square facing the armory. Bruzi had been scanning the clients and passersby, but now he gave full attention to Gart.

"Eber-Sin, what about you and your grandpas?"

"I guess I am one more variety here, Bruzi. I am the first of my family to actually live in the city. However, my people are one of the tribes loyal to Ur since the time of the great flood. We have always been in and out of the area, seasonally, and we market all our livestock and cloth here in the city."

No one commented. Gart felt some anxiety coming back. He turned to Kre-eg who had rejoined them.

"It must have been a lot of hard work for your family to get so well established, coming here when they did."

Kre-eg straightened up and stretched a bit, one hand behind his neck. He chuckled, then picked up the cue.

"My father's father raised a big family and even served a couple terms on the City Council. They were all hard drivers. I'm not so sure I need all that, myself."

"Oh, really?" said Bruzi. "I knew your father was an important business man. Is he involved in politics, too?"

"Involved? Yes, you might say he politics the politicians. He doesn't miss much."

At this point Kre-eg heard another call from the kitchen and went to take care of it.

"Doesn't miss much?" Orson mumbled. "That's right, for sure. I have heard about that old boy from my boss, who does lots of business with him. He is one rough trader."

Kre-eg returned, accompanied by a waiter carrying baskets filled with wheat cakes and small cheeses. Another waiter followed with a jar of beer and drinking reeds. During this commotion, Gart noted the arrival of three youths. He recognized the intense young man whom he had previously seen in this canteen and presumed to be the leader of the group that gathered here. With him were Surbec and a stranger.

The fiery-eyed young man approached their group and with an impudent grin threw Bruzi a mock salute.

"Evenin', General! Oh, I hope I am not interrupting a staff meeting."

"Oh, hi Junior. Gents, meet Bar-shin, my kid brother," Bruzi answered, a bit startled.

"Oh, this is a good day, today." Bar-shin nodded confidentially to Orson and Gart. "On bad days, I'm his half-brother."

"So I take it you're here to join the new army?" Orson hastened to break the short but awkward silence.

"Hah! They would be unhappy with me, I assure you," Bar-shin said. The young man's voice and departing wave faded as he went out of the dining area, followed by his two companions. As they had turned to go, Gart's eyes briefly locked with Sur-bec's. The tall young man quickly averted his gaze.

"Spoiled," Bruzi said, "but not really a bad kid. I hope he stays out of real trouble. By the time he came along, our father was too old to really discipline him. His mother is half Lagashi and a bit of a malcontent."

Why am I telling these fellows all this? Bruzi was asking himself.

Kre-eg returned as soon as the three young men left. He began to eat rapidly. Drill would begin shortly. However, Orson was not content to let the subject of fathers drop.

"Well, my father is ambitious too. Unfortunately, most of it involves me. I would have given up this scribe training thing long ago if he hadn't kept the pressure on. He was always determined that I was to be *Mister Superscribe*. He hasn't given up yet."

Kre-eg flashed Orson a wide smile of understanding and retreated to the kitchen again.

From where they were sitting, they could see the open doors of the armory and watch the enlisted men arriving, but they chose to wait for Kre-eg, while he finished his duties.

The three of them sipped the remaining beer in silence, avoiding eye contact. Gart was surprised at the turn the conversation had taken. He had been wanting to hear about life in the Royal Residence. For him, the lugal, Demmuzi, was still a mysterious figure. How had they gotten on the subject of fathers?

"What about you, Gart?" Bruzi asked, re-opening the conversation. "Are you a self-made man?"

"Hardly! My father has been dead for several years. He taught me whatever I know about livestock. It was my uncle who was the hard one to please. He taught me how to shoot the bow and to fly falcons, but he was never quite satisfied with what I did." Gart made a little face of forbearance.

They all saw Colonel Alkohn enter the armory door and sprang to their feet in unison. Drill had begun.

Climbing the stairs to his apartment that evening, Gart remembered Jeme and his son were not expected back that night. Although the distance was not great, the bullock's injury would slow them considerably on the way out. It had therefore been planned the pair would spend the night with the temple tenants. They were to wait there for Gart's midmorning arrival.

In spite of his great fatigue, Gart's sleep that night was frequently disturbed by dreams of a limping bullock. He became fully awake shortly before dawn and decided to get an early start. Taking leave of his sleepy wife, he put on only a light kilt and at his belt a skin of beer and a little bag of parched grain.

He had exhausted his early enthusiasm as well as his beer and breakfast by the time the sun was well up. He had reached the cross path that led off from the northbound main track to reach the tenants' village. The footprints of his trio were easy to see.

He was glad to do a favor for Shem-ki and this little subterfuge was no big thing. Still, as he loped along, he became aware of a certain distaste. Why should a high temple official like Shem-ki have to go to such lengths to protect a money lender's feelings?

After sighting several thin columns of smoke from the village cooking fires, he suddenly came upon his party, still bedded down on the bank of a canal some one hundred yards short of the village proper. As Gart approached, Jeme was just returning from washing up in the canal. His smile and wave seemed to indicate all was well.

As Gart sat down to rest a bit and chat with Jeme, the boy and the bullock began to stir. Suddenly the boy's eyes popped wide open and he screamed.

"Look out!"

The bullock was up, had broken its tether and was charging straight at them. As they scurried out of its way, the beast stopped short at a brush pile about three yards beyond where Gart had seated himself. It lowered its head with a sharp snort, then suddenly threw it high, bellowing loudly. Attached to its muzzle was a long black snake, perhaps five feet long. The stricken animal swung his head violently from side to side, at the same time trying to trample his assailant or to rub it off on the brush pile. After about five such flings, the snake went flying onto the canal bank and swiftly began to climb it. To the men's horror, the boy went in hot pursuit. Fortunately, the snake entered the water and they watched as it quickly ascend the opposite bank and disappeared.

Men, boy and beast stood immobile and silent for a moment, all very much awake now. Suddenly, Jeme reached into his bag and handed the clay tablet bill of lading to his son.

"Quick, run down the road. Give this to the head tenant and tell him to come right now!"

Gart thought to himself, I have underestimated this fellow. He is going to be sure he delivers the goods alive, even if just barely.

The two men and the animal continued to look at each other silently. All were perspiring, but now the bullock began to tremble violently. They did not have to wait long until voices and footsteps came running rapidly from the village. Jeme's son returned with a boy his own size and his father who declared himself to be the chief tenant. A few words of explanation and a quick look at the bullock were enough for him to send the two boys back for more help.

"Quick, son, get the shaman. Do whatever he says, bring anybody else that is around."

The village, already alerted, was soon to be heard approaching *en mass*. Among the first arrivals was a tall thin man with matted gray locks and a scraggly beard. His gait was a jerky hobble but no less swift than the others.

By this time the bullock lay on its side trembling and sweating profusely, jerking its limbs and rolling its eyes. It began to gasp noisily. The old man turned to a knot of the excited young boys and instructed each with his clear, decisive voice and a long bony forefinger.

"You, bring four bricks. You, the same. You, live coals in a fire-pot. You, six drinking gourds. You, tinder. You, six sticks of dry firewood." The shaman turned from the flying, young feet and pulled from his belt the longest flint knife Gart had ever seen. The old man faced the bull, then bowed very briefly to each of the four quarters of the earth. He firmly grasped the bullock by the ear and slit his throat swiftly, cleanly and deeply, on both sides. The jet of pumped arterial blood spattered the bystanders. The cups and materials arrived and the blood was collected. Each spectator was pressed with a cup of the warm, living liquid.

"Drink and live. He was kissed by the God. Drink and live," the old man insisted. "The God has chosen his own sacrifice. Only He can judge who is worthy to serve Him."

Shortly thereafter, a small fire was established on the eight assembled bricks. The butchering of the quiet but still-steaming carcass proceeded at the hands of several of the adult villagers. Pieces of fat, kidney and liver were cautiously introduced to the young fire and a thin line of black acrid smoke ascended into the calm air. Thin slices of warm raw liver were distributed to each person in attendance. This was a rare treat, accepted eagerly by some and with questioning looks by others.

"Eat and live. It is a boon to you from the God." The old man repeated this over and over, rhythmically, insistently.

With unbelievable rapidity, the carcass disintegrated and disappeared under the firm direction of the chief tenant.

The old man washed himself thoroughly in the canal and also disappeared. Gart found himself facing the chief tenant with no idea what to say about this development. His problem was solved when that man spoke.

"Please tell Brother Shem-ki we will keep half of the meat in the smoke shed for a few days but then, unless we hear other-wise from him, we will distribute it to the people before the flies get to it. Be sure to remind him this was not our idea and the animal was used for its intended purpose. It was sacrificed, and from what I could see of the smoke, the God is happy with it. If we are happy, too, that doesn't mean Shem-ki can charge us for the meat."

"Yes, Sir, I certainly will." Gart was impressed by the swift recovery to business as usual by both the tenant and Jeme. Why didn't he feel the same? He was supposed to be the business man, but all the way back to the city he kept asking himself, Why do I feel so awed by all this? Why would such a thing move me so?

The following morning dawned all too soon for both Gart and Jeme. They were both still shaking off tatters of sleepiness and fatigue when they arrived at the east gate of the temple compound. It must have been near the appointed time, one hour after sunrise. Awaiting them was Orson, who was there to be introduced to Shem-ki.

"Oh, what a fix that puts us in!" Shem-ki groaned when he heard their full report about the last day of the lame bullock. "No, come to think of it, the embarrassing evidence is gone. We can handle it with a little creative accounting. I presume you have brought me a rescuer." Shem-ki nodded toward Orson, who was still standing apart.

"It looks like we won't be needing you for that follow up in a month, Eber-Sin. Sorry for the bother."

"That's no problem," Gart said. "However, you *are* going to pay Jeme and his young helper for their two difficult days are you not?" His tone was something short of coercive but Shem-ki quickly got the message. He did not want a disgruntled Jeme at large.

Gart introduced Orson and, feeling his duties discharged, turned to go. In so doing, he once again caught sight of a blue-gowned figure leaning on her balcony halfway up the ziggurat.

He was surprised, however, to find Nin-ana-Me's attendant awaiting him at the gate.

"Excuse me, Lieutenant. Her Ladyship would like a few minutes of your time if at all possible. Follow me, please."

"I hope you will forgive me for imposing on your time again Lieutenant," the priestess said. Her manner was much less formal than before and her tone almost confidential. "I happened to notice you introducing someone to Shem-ki this morning. He seemed to be carrying a scribe's supply basket. Would this be someone from outside the temple?"

Gart nodded in assent.

"I am in need of some part-time services that, for various reasons, I do not feel our regular scribes can provide. I need someone I can work with. He can be taught the vocabulary.

"Do you know him very well? Do you think he would have a problem working for a woman? Is he married? Does he respect women?"

What's all this? What strange questions! he was thinking.

"I know him fairly well, but I don't know if I can answer all your questions. If you wish, I can ask him to call on Your Ladyship in a few days," Gart said.

On his way to the armory Gart passed directly by the headquarters of Mahn-so-ni's construction business. This was now supposed to be under the direction of his sons. However, Gart was not surprised to see his gray-haired mentor in the midst of the knot of workmen assembled for morning instructions. Mahn-so-ni recognized Gart and signaled, with various head jerks and finger stabs, that Gart was to wait for him at the gate.

"Gart, my friend, I wondered if you might be interested in getting in on a deal that some of us are putting together? We need some good men, plus more trade goods. With this rearmament activity, the demand for metals is brisk. We are hoping to finish a large ship now under construction and send it to Dilmun. We should be able to bring in a big cargo of copper or copper ore at a very nice profit. Interested?"

Interested*?* Who wouldn't be? And *Dilmun*? Some stories claimed it was the island from which the founders of Ur set sail on their voyage west. Now it was the established source of metals, precious stones, spices and many fantastic stories. Here again, Gart found himself flooded with so many new ideas that he simple could not sort them fast enough.

"Pos — possibly some trade goods. I'll — I'll see if I can get something together. I'll let you know in a few days," was the best he could stammer out.

At the armory, he was surprised to find Kre-eg waiting.

"Gart, I need you to go with me for a few days, out of town. This is important, official but very, very secret. I know you were going to visit your family soon and it's in the same direction. Don't tell it any different to anyone."

"Really, Kre-eg, I am juggling all the things I can handle. We have gotten all our recruits for my new unit."

"No, Gart, I need your help. This is too touchy to go through regular channels. You're the only one I can trust. Also, I will need you to find two more men just as trustworthy. We will leave in three days, very early in the morning. I will not take *no*. And — uh, besides, I outrank you, as of this morning."

Now it was *Captain* Kre-eg! Gart was taken aback by this news and the way it was used. This was a very rapid raise in rank for a junior officer.

"Well, where exactly would we be going?" Gart felt himself losing ground.

"I can't tell you. I don't know exactly myself yet, but —" Kre-eg jabbed a bony forefinger repeatedly up over his shoulder in a northerly direction.

That would likely be Larsa, thought Gart. Kre-eg turned and, with only the slightest salutary jerk of his head, walked out of the armory door.

As Colonel Alkohn was present at the close of drill, Gart forced himself to use that opportunity to ask for a week's leave for himself and Surbec who was now a guardsman and who had agreed to come. Gart dreaded making this request and was expecting a thorough grilling, but to his great surprise, Alkohn paused only briefly and replied:

"Yes, of course Lieutenant. We will manage. I understand that you have other obligations. Travel safely."

Gart left the armory, fatigued from the long day but, at the same time, feeling rather wound up. He would have to put aside his concerns about Surbec and Jeme. They were still his best bets.

Gart's homeward trudge took him by Orson's door and he remembered his promise to the priestess. He needed to take care of that detail.

"So, Orson, how did the day go with brother Shem-ki and the great big store house? Did I do you a favor?"

Orson chuckled briefly and rubbed his head before replying.

"It wasn't too bad. I spent all day recording a big transfer to the palace account. This evidently happens only once a year and Shem-ki was very particular as to how this was done. He seems to want it on the record, but not too obvious."

Secrets, secrets, always secrets, Gart thought.

"Well, I may have something further for you, if things are still slow at the warehouse," Gart said. "This is at the temple also, but an entirely different part. You will need to keep this work secret from Shem-ki. I have no idea why, or how much time is involved. Are you free in the morning?"

Orson moaned and looked at his wife, throwing up imploring hands in Gart's direction as if to give him the blame. He was still protesting early hours, but there was more to it than that. This fellow Gart, he thought to himself. What makes him think I am always available? Secret temple work! What will it be next?

Gart was getting up to leave and took no notice of the pained and quizzical look Orson was giving him. He continued, "Take your working gear and as soon as the morning observants come down from the Bedchamber go to the second level of the ziggurat. At the northeast corner you will find the reception room of the high priestess. Ask for Her Ladyship, Nin-ana-Me. I would introduce you, but I am pushed for time. I have rescheduled my trip home. I will be leaving in three days. Oh, by the way, Kre-eg is going with me."

"Kre-eg, the city cynic? The grand pooh-bah of the royal palace is going to the ranch with you? What is that all about? Is some outraged father after him?" Orson asked.

"I was a bit surprised myself," Gart said.

"I would advise you to keep close track of your girl cousins," said Sari, sounding somewhat testy. She had been following the entire conversation with a great deal of interest.

"Really, it's that bad?"

"That bad." Sari spoke with authority, and Orson, standing behind her, nodded concurrence.

Gart did not need another worry in regard to this damned trip. He still had to get home, check out Jeme, smooth things over with Leah, make arrangements with his brother-in-law and get some sleep.

"Lieutenant, Lieutenant, time to go."

Once more he was being wakened by the rapping of knuckles on his door-post. The voice was hushed and Gart couldn't quite identify it. He stumbled to the door. The faint star light from the courtyard was enough for him to identify An-Nam.

"If you don't need me, Lieutenant, I'll go back down and help the Captain with the pack animals." Gart could hear some slight scuffling and mutterings in the street below.

In spite of the hour, Gart was reasonably awake and well prepared. The anticipated problems had never appeared. Leah was not upset. She now felt excused from any obligation to accompany him and meet her in-laws, a project she had mixed feelings about. Jeme had agreed to go with great enthusiasm, in spite of his recent experience.

At the foot of the stairs he could make out Jeme and Surbec. The latter had slept on a mat in their courtyard to be available early. They filed into the street where they found Kre-eg and An-Nam trying to quiet the pack animals. It was getting lighter and Gart could make out the four loaded animals. Their light gray coats reflecting the faint dawn. He could see that the packs contained local pottery, a legitimate trade item, and bundles of dates, an item that grew in both cities that might be traded or eaten if the market was off. He presumed the payload, of whatever nature, was under this top layer. As the light increased, it became clear to him that their pack animals were none other than the lugal's war chariot onagers.

Immediately, Gart began to worry. These strikingly handsome animals would be recognized as very valuable. That could attract attention and bandits. At the same time, he was aware of chilly prickles on the back of his neck and a feeling of strange familiarity. Suddenly he remembered. The last time An-Nam had called him — the dream — these were the onagers in the dream! Here he was, headed northwest with them! But there was no chariot, no apparition, no storm clouds – yet.

"Kre-eg, I doubt we are going to fool anybody much with this fancy outfit. Could we at least change their halters?"

"Lieutenant, what *is* is the way it will be. Stop nattering and let's get on our way," was Kre-eg's testy reply. He quickly handed a lead rope to each of the four men and stomped off toward the north gate, the column following as best it could.

The day was mild and proved to be much less exciting and mysterious than its beginning. The journey to Larsa was too far for a single day, at least with pack animals, but it was an easy two day march. The plan was to arrive toward evening of the second day. In between would be a steady trudge with plenty of rest breaks. These breaks were a mixed blessing, as the donkeys were not used to baggage, and either had to be unloaded or watched constantly to keep them from rolling on their packs. Even so, there was time for some visiting and for private thoughts.

Gart noted that Kre-eg's mood seemed to shift by the hour. One rest break he would visit and joke with the rest; the next, he would anxiously search the horizon, or become morose and withdrawn. Gart was surprised that An-Nam was coming all the way with them. This must indicate that Colonel Alkohn was involved in some way. With five men, they were not likely to be set upon by casual robbers.

Gart and Jeme spent considerable time covering or removing the fancy brass ornaments from the donkey's halters. They made camp that night without a fire, but fortunately they found a well whose waters were sweet and inspired more confidence than those of the canals they crossed. They withdrew from the main path some two hundred yards and made their beds on a canal bank. Without a word to each other, Gart and Jeme thoroughly searched the area for snakes or snake holes and cleared rather more brush than they needed for bedding. Four of them split the night into watches, leaving their commander free to sleep, if he chose.

But Kre-eg slept little and was up with the watch frequently during the night. He investigated every sound and fidgeted a great deal. As he stepped carefully around the pack animals, pretending he was checking them, Kre-eg thought to himself, Father must be mixed up in this deal, too. I'm sure the man I saw leaving the house last night was Ni-Pada-Dan. It was Alkohn who gave the orders. It seemed very strange that he asked to meet me at the royal treasury. At least I thought so until I saw what was in the packs. Now, that warehouse in Larsa that we are going to, I'm sure the name is the same as father's agent there.

Gart had awakened and was lying propped up on one elbow as he watched Kre-eg pace back and forth.

"I'm used to better company at night than sweaty old men and donkeys," Kre-eg explained, aware his restlessness was noticeable.

"You know, it's been three days since I've had any. That's bad for your health."

"Oh, really?" Gart's voice was skeptical, but he was counting days on his fingers, behind his back.

"Yeah, my old man told me a young buck should get laid as often as he can."

"He told you that?"

"Sure did."

"Hah!" Gart chuckled. "Mine told me, 'The more you pound it the flatter it gets.'"

"And there, Lieutenant, you have the difference in our whole approach to life. Damn" His voice dropped to a whisper, Kre-eg thought to himself, Even in my sex life I wind up quoting my old man.

Gart said nothing. He couldn't disagree with what Kre-eg had said.

Day broke without fanfare. The sun simply rose up. No robbers, no big black snakes. There were only aching bones from sleeping on the ground. They broke camp quickly out of boredom with the place.

Soon they could see the city walls of Larsa. Gart suddenly realized he had never been in a walled city other than Ur. The little column entered the city gates along with a sudden rush of incoming people and animals. A small gift got them by the guards, who were in a good mood. The gate watch did question their destination, which Kre-eg gave them. They soon found the warehouse in the southern part of the west quarter.

At the entryway, Kre-eg approached a man who was dressed as an officer, evidently a Lagashi officer judging from the helmet. He waved them into the courtyard, men and donkeys, without a word being spoken.

The officer indicated they were to unload the animals at the far side of the warehouse. He was the only person visible inside, except for their party. Kre-eg gathered his men and instructed Jeme and An-Nam to unload the donkeys, except for the pack harness and the rest of their rations. Surbec was asked to keep his sizable body between the Lagashi officer and the door, and to discourage his exit until Kre-eg had received a proper receipt.

"Gart, I need someone to check off the bill of lading and receipt. You read some don't you?"

"I recognize *cow, barley* and *beer*."

"How about *gold, silver* and *lapis lazuli?*"

"I could learn real fast."

Kre-eg and the Lagashi each produced sets of scales and weights which they compared to their satisfaction. Kre-eg began weighing out the irregular castings of yellow metal. There were twelve such, each about the size of a small quail egg. These were followed by an equal number of silver and then about twice that mass of fine blue stones. Finally, there were two small carved figures of ivory, evidently household gods. Gart scratched off the items on their clay tablet while the foreign officer did the same on his copy. He did not dispute their count or quality. However, when they had finished he said:

"That's not good enough. I know you can do better than that, but I will sign off if you throw in the pack animals, too."

"There is no way we could agree to that, Colonel, sir!" Kre-eg immediately drew himself up to full height. The extra two inches allowed him to look slightly down and directly into the officer's eyes.

"It seems to me, Captain, you are in a rather awkward position to be bartering."

"This has nothing to do with barter, sir. What we have delivered more than adequately fulfills the agreed and customary amount. Our position may not be as precarious as you believe. We have adequate contacts at your court to ensure a careful review of the accounts and income of the commander of the royal guard."

If this was moving the Lagashi colonel to reconsider, he gave no sign. His face remained stolid and his posture rigid.

"However, as a token of good will...." Kre-eg stepped back to the remaining packs. "I could return this to its previous owners." Kre-eg pulled apart the reed packing to reveal a translucent alabaster vase about sixteen inches tall. Gart involuntarily stepped forward to inspect the detailed engraving just below the neck of the vase. At the same time the colonel moved to do the same. They were nearly forehead to forehead. The engraving was extremely well done. It evidently depicted the patron god of Lagash dispensing judgment or boons to his subjects.

"How did you get this?" the colonel said sharply.

"I have no idea," Kre-eg said. "It probably left Lagash two or three wars ago and has been in commercial channels since."

The colonel took the vase carefully in both hands. He held it toward the fading light, inspecting it with obvious satisfaction. Suddenly, he tucked the vase under his arm, stooped to gather up the protective wrapping and started toward the door.

"Very well, Captain, consider the matter resolved. Have a safe journey home."

"Sir! your seal!" chorused Kre-eg and Surbec. The latter was planted squarely in the officer's path.

"Oh, yes, of course." He fumbled in his pouch for his cylinder seal, which he rolled firmly across the soft clay additions to both copies of the bill of lading held out to him by Gart. He departed with a smile. No vase was on the list.

Gart, Kre-eg and Surbec all turned their backs as three Lagashi soldiers came in to wrap and remove the booty. They did not wish their relief to be too obvious.

Kre-eg was able to arrange with the owner of the warehouse for them to spend the night there, but he joined in the grumbling about the restrictions he had to impose on everyone to keep out of sight in this new and strange city. He and Surbec went to a nearby market where they traded dates and pottery for beer and bread. They paid dearly, but returned with enough for the night, plus some to take as a gift to Gart's family the next day.

CHAPTER FIVE

Sunrise found them all awake and eager to be on their way. Even the onagers were quiet and cooperative. There was a new shift of guards at the gate, but they, too, were in a good mood and waved them on their way.

Gart was a little uncertain of the route to his peoples' winter quarters. Although he had never been in the city of Larsa before, he had several times helped tend flocks within sight of the city to the west and north. Their spring and fall migrations skirted the edge of the cultivated lands and their associated waterways. Unfortunately, the Euphrates was notoriously fickle and landmarks could be swept away in a year as the river changed channels. Without voicing his reservations, he struck out boldly on the first well-traveled trail heading west.

Gart and Kre-eg walked abreast at the head of the little column. Although everyone was content at the completion of their assignment, Gart was troubled as to its meaning.

"This was tribute, right? Taxes for the King of Lagash?"

"Looks and smells like it." Kre-eg did not elaborate.

"Our proud city is paying for protection?" Gart's disappointment was evident.

"I don't like it either," said Kre-eg. "Most people don't know. I didn't know it myself until last week."

"How long has this been going on?"

"Evidently for quite a few years. Someone cut a deal and has kept it mighty quiet." Kre-eg said no more on the subject but as they walked along he continued to wonder about the extent of his father's involvement in this murky arrangement.

By midmorning, Gart began to recognize the terrain and could see they were on the main drovers' route skirting cultivated land, but by midafternoon, the party was feeling thirsty, tired and bored. His companions were beginning to ask rather pointed questions and Gart was greatly relieved when the trail entered and began to follow a gentle depression that soon deepened to form a draw familiar to him. He was now able to assure the others that a brisk hour's march would bring them to the mouth of the draw and the settlement that was home to him and shelter and a welcome rest for them. He inspected the cropped dry vegetation and the fresh sheep droppings along the slopes and surmised that his family's flock was still in the immediate area. Although he was several days earlier than expected, he should be able to fulfill all of his obligations.

Home was very humble, indeed, and Gart had been careful not to arouse any great expectations in his companions. The little huddle of about thirty one-story mud brick buildings was sometimes referred to as Nafti or Junction. More precisely, it was *Nafti Junction.* Here two trails crossed near the banks of what was sometimes a river channel and sometimes a dry wash, depending on the meandering of the Euphrates farther upstream. The population varied from about three hundred in winter to forty or fifty in summer. The elderly and infirm, plus a few caretakers, were left to cope with the summer heat as best they could while the rest sought pasture on higher ground. The bleakness and isolation was compensated for by the relative peace that had reigned here for hundreds of years. They were on the fringe of what was considered civilization and well out of the path of invading armies from the quarrelsome cities to the north and north-west.

A few scattered bleats and the tinkle of a bell had been audible off to their right for the previous quarter-hour but it was not until the first buildings of Nafti Junction came into view that Gart's companions became true believers. A sizeable herd of goats and sheep was approaching the settlement on a parallel course. The drovers of this herd were the first to spot them. They were too far away to be recognized. Gart waved his spear in greeting, then had some second thoughts. He reversed the shaft and waved the butt end. This brought better results. He was soon embracing the gangly youth who came bounding through the brush. It was one of his many cousins and he had grown almost a foot since Gart had seen him.

To Gart's considerable satisfaction, his early arrival from the wrong direction, armed companions and especially the four matched onagers caused quite a hubbub,. His mother, sister and brother-in-law soon came running. Within a half hour, Uncle Eb arrived with more livestock. He seemed as straight and wiry as ever. He inspected Gart's troop with his usual skeptical eye, but quickly arranged for a large tent to be cleared for their use.

"You all right son?" Uncle Eb inquired in a very low voice, scarcely moving his lips.

"Why, sure. Why do you ask?"

"I mean you're not in trouble or nothin'? All these guys waving their weapons around, are they with you?"

"Oh, sure, they're with me. Well, actually, the tall fellow, Captain Kre-eg, is our commander. We are all in the Civil Guard, except for my friend, Jeme. He works for me. We're on a training exercise, sort of, checking out the area. I thought I could roll it all into one trip."

"Commander, huh. You mean he's your boss?"

"Well, yeah, this trip, anyhow."

"Humph, well, you are a few days early, but there is no reason we can't sort sheep tomorrow if you think you can find a market for them. It will be good to have some extra help."

"Uh, Uncle Eb, I uh, I'm not sure I can ask them to help, but I will be there, bright and early."

"Umn." Uncle Eb turned on his heel without further comment. Gart was reassured, however, when he saw his uncle go directly to two young men who soon departed, knives and ropes in hand, for the corral. One or two goats would not make the sort. There would be fresh meat for supper.

Gart declined an invitation to stay at his sister's house. He felt he should stay with his companions to help bridge the gap between strangers, but Jeme had never met a stranger and was soon talking livestock with some of the older men. An-Nam, who was rather shy, dutifully arranged their packs in the tent and then took the onagers to water at the nearby river channel. In so doing, he formed a quick and easy alliance with half of the children of the village. In the meantime, Kre-eg and Surbec strolled the village, checking out the general population. They were easily persuaded to inspect the loom houses where the women and girls were still busily engaged in the spring weaving program. Kre-eg seemed much more relaxed today. Gart had seldom seen him more charming and cheerful.

By the time the evening meal of roast kid, onions, bread, dates and beer was ready to be served around the central cooking pit they were all friends and the air quite festive. Gart felt this was the time to draw his sister aside and relay to her the essence of Sari's warning about girl cousins in very polite and general terms. From her look, he was certain she understood his message.

All of his companions were asleep in the tent by midnight. He lay awake for some time as he tried to gather together his two disparate worlds.

It was Gart's faithful awakener, An-Nam, who sensed the early stirrings of the village and shook Gart gently out of his troubled sleep. To Gart's relief, Jeme and Surbec were awake and volunteered to help with the sheep. He was very appreciative. He was gaining confidence in both of these men.

An-Nam was happy to remain at the tent to mind the property and Kre-eg was left asleep.

After a quick breakfast of warm barley gruel, they were off to the nearby corrals with a dozen or so of Gart's kinsmen. Their job was to sort the flock of both sheep and goats. The breeding ewes and nannies who were in poor flesh or whose teeth were badly worn down were to go to slaughter. The bulk of the male lambs, whether castrated or not, would also be separated and marked for local use or sent to the city. This was hot, dirty work often involving a tackle, a forced mouth inspection and a drag to the holding pen. All of the men were soon wearing a mask and cloak of dust and powdered sheep manure. Fortunately, they were through by mid-morning and could go to the river to bathe. The breeding flock was released and driven off to graze, in spite of the bleating protests of their forsaken companions.

Kre-eg joined the bathers. He was still in good spirits and showed no resentment at having been left out of their morning labors.

"Oh, Captain, *my commander*, are you eager to start the trip back?" Gart was uncertain how much he should detain the party for his own personal purposes.

"No hurry, fellow. I have the week for it and this is only the fourth day. This country living is not so bad, as long as *you* take care of the dirty work."

Gart was pleased with the chance to spend a little more time with his family and to work out some business arrangements. He still had an interest in the community flock, some twelve ewes inherited from his father and managed on shares by his sister and brother-in-law. He had been mulling over the possibility of trading his entire interest for finished cloth, which he could then invest in Mahn-so-ni's overseas venture to Dilmun. One good storm or pirate raid would wipe out his savings, but the mystique of the whole proposal prevailed. He was able to make a mutually agreeable offer to the woman who headed the weavers. He was to take three-fourths of the stock on hand at this time. His account of the venture attracted such interest that the village headman and the chief of the weavers insisted he take the rest of the stock on consignment and invest it for them. This raised the stakes considerably, but Gart agreed to arrange it.

His visit had gone so well that he decided to push his luck a bit farther. Since none of his companions knew exactly where they were, he would select a route that would allow them to spend the night of the following day at the settlement on temple property where he and Jeme had witnessed the memorable sacrifice of the snake-bitten bullock. Although he had many vivid memories of the incident, it was the shaman who kept coming back to him in his dreams, both day and night.

Gart had not heard anyone use the shaman's personal name, but he was inclined to believe this was Man-to-Shi, whose reputation as a wise man, conjurer and herbalist was widespread among all the border tribes. Gart was considering how he might represent himself to the old man when he heard the shouts of children.

"Someone is coming down the draw!"

"Who is it?"

"I don't know them, five or six men and several animals."

"Let's go see! Better tell the headman first!"

"They have big packs, probably just traders."

"Wait! Be careful!"

"Hey, look at that last donkey!"

"Is that a donkey? I've never seen one like that!"

Gart joined the crowd of the curious of all ages. It was quickly recognized that two of the men were of their own; born and raised here, but now turned to commerce. They were returning, as was their custom, to their home to trade, visit and reorganize their wares. With them were three others, who soon proved to be an Akkadian and two Elamite traders.

The animal that had excited the children's interest was no donkey. Gart had never seen anything like it either. This creature was firmly secured by a halter and lead rope to the last pack animal but carried only a very small pack on its back. Its coat was a reddish golden hue and it stood a good four hands taller than the donkeys. Its ears were short and its eyes wide and lustrous. As the children approached, it tossed its head nervously, prancing about, flaring its nostrils and snorting. Gart now recalled having heard of such a creature, but he had not known if they were supposed to be real or imaginary. There was no name for it in Sumerian, but these Elamites used a name from a northern language that was to come to identify the horse.

Gart noticed Kre-eg as he sauntered out from the tent where he had been resting. In the meantime, the Elamites had calmed their fractious animal, who was now nibbling at their ears and sniffing tentatively at the children's hands as they held up bunches of dry grass for him. Kre-eg walked around the group several times, looking the animal up and down. He seemed to be listening intently to the conversation. Gart had never seen him express the faintest interest in an animal before. Suddenly Gart had to stifle a snicker.

Perhaps Kre-eg and this animal were spirit brothers! They even looked alike: tall, thin, excitable and moody. Yes, even their long bony noses had something in common.

"Do you speak Sumer?" Gart addressed the Elamite who was soothing his charge.

"Speak everythings. You want buy good horse?"

"Is that what you call him? Where did you get him? Where does he come from?"

"We buy this spring north of Zagros Mountains."

"Do they grow there? Are they wild animals?"

"No, grow far, far north. Mostly wild, some tame. This one catch when little. Came south with trader."

"Why is he carrying such a small pack? This is a big animal."

"This one still baby yet, still growing. Very silly sometimes. This one not like pack on back much. When big, northern tribesmen can ride, go fast, like the wind. Very fierce warriors."

By this time, the colt had become almost as interested in Kre-eg as Kre-eg was in him. He was nibbling at Kre-eg's skirt.

"He does lead doesn't he? May I see?" Kre-eg asked.

"Leads mostly but very silly sometimes. Be careful please." With definite hesitation and anxious glance the Elamite handed the lead rope to a potential customer. In the meantime, his partner had removed the small pack.

"He likes you mister, but be careful."

The animal followed Kre-eg nonchalantly, not even waiting for tension on the lead rope. The delighted Kre-eg made several passes in front of his audience, then led the colt to the small incline in front of the tent. Stepping quickly to the colt's side, to everyone's amazement, he vaulted astride the animal's back.

A sudden hush settled over the entire assembly. The colt turned his head to the left, rolling his wide eyes in disbelief. He turned his head to the right in the same manner. He pranced to one side, then to the other.

Trembling, he squatted on all four. Then he exploded, his back formed a perfect arc. Daylight appeared beneath all four feet, now closely bunched and daylight also appeared beneath Kre-eg's posterior. Miraculously, he landed back aboard, halter rope still in hand. The colt twisted right. Kre-eg persisted. The colt twisted back. Kre-eg shortened the rope, sending his mount into a left-spinning whirl that mowed down the guy ropes to two tents, crashed sideways against a brick building and with a final posterior-over-anterior snap catapulted his hapless rider into the bramble-reinforced fence used to protect the flocks at night.

The crowd was still speechless. The horse gave three more hops, until he realized his success, then turned to sniff curiously at his bloodied and bedraggled deposit for a moment before he trotted off with his owners in hot pursuit. The onlookers now erupted into a melange of sound and motion, each one going a different direction, making a different exclamation.

"Did you see that?"

"What a ride!"

"That critter is plum crazy!"

"That soldier is crazier. Has he come down yet?"

"There, in the brush fence. His face is bleeding!"

"Did you see him jump on that thing?"

"He's not jumping much now."

Gart was the first to reach the dazed and scraped Commander of the Royal Guard. Fortunately, the bramble fence had cushioned his fall, although it had inflicted cruel scratches on his face and arms. Gart and others were still in the process of separating Kre-eg from his brush and thorns when Gart's mother and sister arrived.

"Bring him to our house," his sister said. His mother quickly sent some older children to the river bank to collect green willow and alder leaves for dressings. There were visible abrasions on Kre-eg's right arm and leg. His left knee was already beginning to swell but did not seem broken. Gart and Jeme carried him to the house between them as Kre-eg greeted his audience with a twisted smile and an occasional grimace. An-Nam and Surbec reconstructed their tent as the breathless and perspiring traders returned with their triumphant, though recaptured, colt.

That evening Gart watched carefully as his mother changed Kre-eg's dressings. She was very good at this, as he remembered well. She was a woman of few words who expressed her caring best with her gentle and reassuring hands.

"Are you the village herb woman now? I know you used to study that."

"No, not really. There are three or four of us who collect the desert plants. I know the names and locations of most of the plants and some of the uses, but I can't always tell what the people or animals need. I should have paid more attention. You remember the old herb woman, An-Ras, don't you? She died when you were about five. She was a good teacher. No one since has her gift."

"Mother, are you the one who told me about Man-to-Shi, the shaman from the marshes? Is he still alive?"

"I could well have. I did meet him, you know. I used to go with An-Ras to see him. She would take him desert plants and he would trade her some from the marshes and even from the sea. He may still be alive, although he is older than I am. I was a young woman and he was a mature man, even then."

"He lives in the marshes then?"

"No, not really, that is just the way the story goes. He actually lived on temple property. The one nearest to here. It may have been marsh at one time but it had been drained and was being farmed when I was there. It still is, unless the river has changed again. One story has it that Man-to-Shi was always there from the beginning of time, or at least since the flood. I don't believe that, though. He told us he learned everything important from his mother who was a famous healer in her time."

"That must be the same shaman I saw there a few months ago."

"Probably so. He hasn't always been there, though. I have heard that as a young man he was called to the city to study for the priesthood during the time the previous ziggurat was being built. He came back after three or four years. He said it wasn't right for him. They say people he knew there still visit him, sometimes."

The following morning it became obvious to Gart that if they were to travel that day, some special arrangements would be necessary. Although Kre-eg could hobble around, he was in no condition to walk very far. It was therefore arranged to borrow two additional donkeys; one that was well broken to ride and another to carry the cloth in excess of what they felt their four animals should carry. In a week, when the herdsmen brought the for-sale herd in, they would return the donkeys. As they prepared to depart, Gart's mother approached him with two small bundles.

"Here, take these for Man-to-Shi. Tell him they are from a student of An-Ras. He liked her and that might help. He only sees people when the mood strikes him. These are bitterbrush and quat. One makes people sleep without dreaming and the other causes people to dream while they are awake."

The route to the temple farm was familiar to Gart and presented no special perils. It was less than a full day's journey, even though they had to slow down because of Kre-eg, who alternated hobbling along to keep from getting stiff from riding Old Deadhead, the donkey. Once they had devised slings to keep his long legs from dragging, Kre-eg was free to reflect.

If I'd had a rope around him I could have ridden him, he told himself. If I had remembered to squeeze my knees..., he thought.

"Ouch," he gasped aloud as he had, by reflex, clamped his legs onto the donkey. 'Runs like the wind,' they say, he continued to himself. 'Mighty warriors' they say — who knows? Just to be up there! Something entirely new. He could recall the sensation, as if he had been suddenly been jerked upward and on board by some daemon. But it was his own legs, his decision. He had done it. Well, almost.

"Maybe next time," he muttered. Then, directed at Gart, "Do you think they will keep him there?"

"You haven't given up on that critter, yet have you?" Gart commented.

Suddenly Kre-eg's donkey stopped, head high, ears pointing ahead and to the left.

"Hey, what's this? Old Deadhead here is onto something out there," said Kre-eg. He and Gart both shaded their eyes against the midmorning light. The donkey's ears were tilted toward a gap in the line of bushes off to the left of their path. An odd shaped shadow stretched most of the way across a gap in the line of bushes. The base of the shadow was the blob you would expect from a bush, but there was also a smaller blob on top, then two short streaks not unlike donkey's ears, but parallel, pointing straight up. As they watched, the farthest part of the shadow diminished almost into the bush, then reappeared. This repeated three or four times. There was no wind. The donkey stood still. The bush stood still. It seemed that the sun stood still, but the shadow moved. The donkey sighed, seemed to lose interest, and voluntarily resumed his plodding course.

"What was that, Gart? An animal of some kind?"

"Must have been. Something was moving."

"If it was that big, why couldn't we see it above that little bush?"

Gart was silent for a while. "I can't figure that one out, but Old Deadhead doesn't seem worried, so maybe we shouldn't be, either." His dismissive comments did not block the prickling sensation at the back of his neck. He scanned the trail ahead: old sheep tracks, dry droppings, a large black beetle. No! There they were, jackal or dog tracks ahead and going in the same direction! It must have doubled back and stopped to rest. Within a few minutes though, Gart was convinced their observer was back on duty and ahead of them. Several times he noted the motion of something gray-blue through the brush.

Suddenly, they were there. The pack string rounded the end of a line of trees, easily crossed the nearly dry canal and found itself in a farmyard surrounded by a few combination brick and wattle buildings, brush lean-tos and livestock pens. Gart's plan was to find the head tenant, whom he expected to be friendly, considering their last encounter, and make arrangements to stay the night. However, directly in front of him walking stiffly across the courtyard, was the man of gaunt figure and long gray locks who had been on his mind for several weeks.

"Excuse me, sir, but are you Man-to-Shi? The healer?" Gart added, after a short hesitation.

"I have been called that." The reply was deliberate, unhurried. "And who are you?"

Such a simple question. Such a civil manner, but Gart suddenly felt himself flustered, unprepared. He had not decided yet how to explain his reason for being there or how to present himself. He was comforted to hear his smoothest and most cultivated voice begin, just like in his recent door-to-door political endeavors.

"I am Gart, a member of the Nafti Junction community, though now living in Ur. I bring you some small tokens from my mother, who was a student of An-Ras, and who has often mentioned your special healing skills to me. You may recall, also, I was here a few months ago on the occasion of the sacrifice of the snake-bitten bullock."

"And these…?" The old man's extended hand traced a slow zigzag indicating the tips of the spears, the waiting men, including the battered Kre-eg, and the laden animals.

"Oh, yes, this is Captain Kre-eg-el-Sheh, Commander of the Royal Bodyguard for the lugal of Ur, and the rest of us are citizen soldiers under his command. We are returning from an assignment of official — training." Here his melodious explanation had been interrupted by Kre-eg's sharp scowl. "It is as a favor to me the captain agreed to stop here. If we should be welcome, I had hoped we might spend the night here. If I would not be imposing, I would like to make your formal acquaintance and to ask you some questions about medicinal plants."

"I do not believe you, young man. You sound too much like a politician." Man-to-Shi turned to Kre-eg.

"And you, Mister Captain, sitting there so quietly on your poor tired donkey. What do you say to all this? Is there a war on? Is this your booty, or are you just collecting more taxes?" Man-to-shi's hand again indicated the laden donkeys. "You are wounded and appear to be in pain. Did you hope I could help you with that? If so, why not just say so?"

Kre-eg, startled out of his spectator role by the old man's brusque questions, was no better prepared than Gart to deal with him.

"Why — uh, no sir. I mean, the Lieutenant is quite truthful. I have no right to expect you to help me with these wounds—I mean, injuries. Yes, I am in pain and, of course, if you could help, I do need to rest a while."

"As to these," Kre-eg pointed to the men and laden donkeys with the same sweeping gesture Man-to-Shi had used, "it is rather complicated."

"Yes, rather complicated," echoed Gart.

"And so is your story, Lieutenant. Gart of Nafti; Did you expect me to believe it?"

"Believe me or not," Gart said angrily, "every bit of what I said is true. Maybe it doesn't explain all the reasons I am here. In fact, I don't know myself why I had to stop here. I have had it on my mind for some time. It just seemed like something I was to do."

"Now, I can believe you, young man. Sometimes I feel the same way. If the tenant will have you here, I will see you both after sundown." The old man turned and continued across the courtyard.

Kre-eg, observing his slow, stiff gait, remarked. "He sure doesn't talk like he walks. Feisty old bird, isn't he?"

Gart was soon able to locate the chief tenant who remembered favorably the incident of the bullock and the free meat that resulted. They were invited to use two brush shelters on the east side of the compound, and several boys were dispatched to help them cut willow boughs to bring these booths into usable condition for the night. They were invited to share the communal cooking fire in the center of the compound to prepare their evening meal. It was from this hearth that Gart and Kre-eg departed, in response to Man-to-Shi's hand signal, after all had eaten.

The old man led them to a rude shelter to the north of the compound. Many bundles of drying plants hung from the roof poles. Gart guessed he must live there, although it was sparsely furnished.

"Did I understand you wanted help with your injuries?" Man-to-Shi asked Kre-eg.

"Yes, yes, of course," he answered.

"Then lie down on that pile of mats. Do you wish your companion to remain?"

"Well, sure, I don't know why not." Kre-eg's tone betrayed his insecurity in this strange situation, but he moved stiffly to do as the old man asked.

Man-to-Shi sank to his knees beside Kre-eg, and Gart sat on the earth floor about three feet behind him. The old man removed Kre-eg's overskirt but not his loincloth or the bandages on his thigh and arm. He now rubbed his gnarled hands together, then shook each hand in a circular motion with the fingers hanging down loosely.

Kneeling beside him and leaning forward, he began passing his left hand over the surface of the young man's body but not actually touching the surface. Systematically, swiftly, the hand scanned the entire surface, saving the battered knee until last. From his angle, Gart could clearly see the knee was not touched. He saw the quick flinch and surprised look on Kre-eg's face as the hand passed the knee. The healer supported the knee with a roll of cloth and moved closer. The extended hands, fingers widely separated now, formed an arc with the wounded knee interposed in the gap, still not touching it.

Man-to-Shi sat motionless, breathing deeply and with a relaxed rhythm. From time to time, he would remove his hands to stretch and rest them. Then he would resume. This continued for what must have been nearly a halfhour.

Kre-eg became increasingly aware of warmth in his knee, little bursts of prickles, a warm glow and then another burst. He could feel the spasm in his leg turn loose each time. The healer seemed to hover over him. It occurred to him that holding this position must be costing the old man in discomfort. More prickles and then tension relaxed deep within Kre-eg's chest. He had never paid attention to that tight spot but it must have been there for a very long time. Whoa! he thought. This *is* different, really weird.

The knee was put back to rest and the healer leaned forward, stroking the air with both hands over the feet, legs, pelvis, abdomen and chest, where the hands made a circular motion, then left the surface, to be shaken sharply off to the side. This peculiar maneuver was repeated several times.

Man-to-Shi then removed the bandages and their leaf dressings from Kre-eg's arm and thigh. The surfaces were smooth and dry with fresh, thin scab formation.

"That is all I can do for you, young man. The rest is up to you. With reasonable care, your injuries should heal in a few days."

"I thank you very much, sir," said Kre-eg, sitting up and gingerly rubbing his knee. "I could feel the spasm letting go gradually, a tingly feeling and warmth."

The old man nodded, then squinted, as though weighing his next words.

"How did you get these bruises?"

"I was trying to tame a wild horse," Kre-eg replied.

"Horse? I do not recognize the word."

"It's like a tall donkey with short ears," explained Gart.

"It is nothing like a donkey at all," Kre-eg protested.

"Ah, yes, the swift animal from north of the mountains," Man-to-Shi recalled. "If I understand what my hands were telling me about you and your body, you have plenty of wild horses inside you in need of training. Take great care or they will rule you.

The old man's words, measured and carefully enunciated, carried such conviction that Kre-eg, in distress, turned to catch Gart's eye.

Gart had never seen those eyes so wide.

"And as for you, young man," Man-to-Shi turned to Gart. "What did you mean that you wanted to make my 'formal acquaintance.' Or did you just want to get your hands on my medicinal plants? I see you eyeing all my little bundles, my friends and helpers." The old man pointed to the many sheaves of drying plants hanging from the rafters of his shelter. "Were you about to make me an offer for the lot of them? You are a business man I believe."

Gart flushed. The thought of dealing in such plants had occurred to him, even though he knew little about them. This encounter with Man-to-Shi was turning out badly. He sidestepped the questions. "About the dressings — I notice the scrapes are nicely covered over. Did my mother choose well? Was that the best choice for such a wound? Is that what you use?"

Man-to-Shi replied, "She chose well, as you can see. Many other leaves would do well also. Our plant cousins are happy to soothe our wounds if we respectfully ask. Your mother's faith in them and her care in binding up the wounds account for the good results as much as which plant the leaves are from.

"You said you had questions about medicinal plants," Man-to-Shi repeated. "Surely you didn't come all this way to ask about dressing a few scrapes. Are you saying that you want to forsake the big city and come study with me a few years, or did you expect me to cook up a decoction and pour all my secrets down your throat during your overnight stop?"

The pervasive calm that had covered the wiry old man during the healing exercise was gone. Man-to-Shi got to his feet and strode back and forth in front of the lean-to with increasing agitation. His voice crackled with annoyance. Stiffness was no longer evident in his gait. Gart felt embarrassed and frustrated, once again. He could not find any direction in the old man's moods and remarks. Every time he started to open his mouth and organize a reply he was blocked by the fresh memory of "I don't believe you. You sound too much like a politician."

"I'm sorry to waste your time with my half-baked questions," he said at last. The old man's rising tones were beginning to attract the attention of several children across the courtyard.

"You are *not* wasting my time. I will not permit that, but you are annoying me because you are not being straightforward. You are not speaking from the heart." Here, Man-to-Shi paused briefly to catch his breath. "So, proceed, *proceed,* finish baking your ideas, talk them out."

Seeing no way out, Gart began. "There are so many questions.... Even if you know the names of plants and can recognize them, what are you to believe about their use? There are so many old tales. This plant or that tree was supposed to have sprouted from the body of that god, or that ancestor — but what does that mean to us? Why should the plant want to help us? We kill them and eat them or boil them alive.

"How can some plants be used to treat illness when they make you dizzy or nauseous or give you diarrhea? How can we know how much is good and what can kill you?" Gart noted the glazed look coming into the eyes of both Man-to-Shi and Kre-eg. Maybe he was overdoing the questions.

"Yes, yes, I see I am asking too much. Answering all of this would take a long time. Indeed, I would like very much to study with you, sir!" Gart was astonished to hear himself say this.

"You lie once again, young man," said Man-to-Shi, disdainfully. "You say this either out of ignorance or out of greed for knowledge and power. I assure you that you would not like studying with me at all. You would be consumed by the mosquitoes, bored by the silence and embarrassed to have the children hear you talking to plants."

"This conversation was obviously a very bad idea on my part," Gart interrupted. "We shouldn't have stopped here. I thank you very much for what you have done for Kre-eg, but I feel we should leave your presence and not bother you further tonight." His anger gave him the energy to try to stop this rout.

"No, wait." Suddenly the old man was surprisingly calm. "It is only fair, since I demand that you be straightforward, that I tell you the real source of my annoyance with you. I asked you to finish cooking your ideas. I should do the same.

"Talking to myself and the family here," he waved his uplifted hand in a circular motion around the farm compound, where a small group of spectators had began to gather, "is not always enough to keep me totally sane.

"Ever since you descended upon us so unexpectedly with your bullock offering, I have been thinking about my reaction at that time and what it might mean. Now I must put it into words."

However, the old healer stopped talking and fingered his gray beard, looking across the courtyard at the faint embers of the cooking fire. Gart slumped to the floor of the booth, and resumed his sitting position. His sense of relief at the return of Man-to-Shi's composure was just beginning to relax him when he had a very interesting thought.

That was it! The tenant had said "Get the shaman," but what followed had not fit anything he had ever heard about the behavior of a shaman. Was that what had kept on bothering him and leading him to return here? He was just on the verge of saying this to Man-to-Shi when Kre-eg spoke up.

"Gart, why don't you ask him about the jackal, or whatever it was? A shaman is supposed to know about those things."

"Shaman! Who called me that? Is that what you were expecting?" His voice was halfway back to its previous high, irritated register. "You were probably hoping to see a good show here! Song and dance, some weird old man frothing at the mouth and flopping around in a trance. Well, you may be disappointed. I resent being dismissed as a shaman." He inhaled sharply. Gart and Kre-eg looked at each other in alarm. Now the old man let his breath out slowly, looked briefly at the fire once more, and said, in a perfectly calm voice:

"I am sorry. You touched on a sore point there. Yes, indeed, they do call me *shaman*, as they did my mother and grandfather before me. But as you can see and will hear, I am not entirely content with that. I'm not yet quite composed enough to talk about the bullock. Why don't you tell me about the jackal?"

Gart hastened to comply. He told briefly of their impression they were being both watched and preceded by a creature as they had approached the farmstead that afternoon. He mentioned, in detail, the puzzling shadow and the tracks going in the same direction they were. Man-to-Shi's quizzical expression made Gart realize his story did not do justice to their experience.

"And what makes you think the jackal was not just a jackal?" asked the old man patiently.

"I know," said Gart. "I haven't made my case. It was mostly a feeling, but a very strong feeling, perhaps of danger, or excitement, maybe anticipation. Maybe it has something to do with a more direct encounter I had with a jackal a few months ago. Few jackals have been seen around here in recent years. I did hear one, or perhaps more, on the first night out of Ur on my previous trip and saw one the next day, but none since. This may sound more like just a feeling than a logical observation, but still…."

"Such a feeling can be very convincing," Man-to-Shi replied. "Such an animal, or such a presence if you prefer, appears in the legends of our people. Do you know your guardian spirit? Does it have an animal form?"

"I'm not sure I know what you're talking about," said Gart.

"Does your tribe have initiation practices?"

"Oh, well yes, sort of. Now I know what you mean. There is a coming-of-age party when you are welcomed to sit with the men at meetings and so forth. It's nothing like they tell about in the olden times. I think there is still a secret society among those who are drawn to hunting. I'm sure my Uncle Eb has something to do with that. For that initiation, you still have to go out into the desert and fast. I don't know much about it. My father was more interested in taking care of the livestock. He tried to teach me about that. Uncle Eb taught me to shoot the bow and how to fly his falcons, but I don't think I quite made the grade as a hunter. I didn't hear anything about joining the secret society."

"So you never went to seek your guardian spirit?"

"No, I did not."

"Well, you have one and it might even come looking for you," the shaman continued. "If you are not too interested, it will probably get bored and wander off. I don't know if this is what's happening here, or not. Do you really want to pursue this? Here? Tonight?"

"Oh, yes, yes," Kre-eg replied swiftly.

Gart noted Kre-eg seemed to have more enthusiasm for this project than either he or the weary old man. However, he nodded a wary assent.

"Very well, we can do some things tonight." The old man gave a deep sigh, then spoke to Gart in a confidential tone. "For some reason, I am also interested in your story. I do not believe this jackal is just a jackal. I must go to the underworld and retrieve your guardian spirit — jackal or whatever it may appear to be.

"I am sure," Man-to-Shi raised both his voice and his eyes in oblique, yet tactful recognition of the rapt attention being paid by the nearby group of boys, "my nephew, the apprentice shaman, and his assistants will quickly bring us some torches, a drum and rattle, and my medicine bundle so that we may go to my other booth across the canal. We must not further disturb the sensible people of this village."

The boys scurried to do as bidden and the little procession was soon on its way. The path was evidently not in heavy use, as they frequently had to push aside small branches. In about fifteen minutes they crossed the small canal by a rude and flimsy bridge woven of poles and tree limbs. Its springiness and uneven surface might have been fun during the day, but Gart found it unnerving in the torch light. Shortly, they reached another brush covered lean-to similar to the one that they had just left. This one was situated on higher ground and faced east across the canal and overlooked a clearing that would allow a good view of the sunrise.

A small fire was soon lighted to supplement the flickering torches. At Man-to-Shi's direction, a space in front of the lean-to was cleared of debris. The nephew with the drum was seated to the south with his three young friends in a row behind him. Kre-eg was seated to the north. One of the boys tied the medicine bundle to the middle rafter of the lean-to. Gart was directed to lie down with his head toward the bundle and his feet to the east. At this moment, the moon, now in its first quarter, began to show itself in the east. Its arrival was acknowledged by a smile and a nod from the old man.

"Now I must go to the underworld, just as they say Inanna did. Since my motives are purer, and my task simple, I promise not to stay as long as she did."

The drum began its low, monotonous throb. The shaman began to shuffle with tiny steps in a circle around the reclining Gart. At each cardinal point, he would stop, face outward and bow, then raise both hands above his head and shake the gourd rattles he held in each hand. This went on and on. Gart could see Kre-eg, glassy-eyed and immobile, sitting as though fixed in a trance. Gart's eyes were getting heavy, but when he closed them he was so overpowered by the sound of the drum, which seemed to move inside his chest, he felt compelled to peek out from under his eyelids to stay oriented. In time, he felt calmer and seemed to float.

Now he noted the shaman was beginning to stagger and he feared he was about to fall on him. Instead, Man-to-Shi dropped to his knees at Gart's right side and quickly bent over. He placed his cupped hands over Gart's breast bone and blew forcefully into the cone he had formed. Immediately, Gart's eyes came open, his vision became very acute and he felt powerful contractions in his shoulder muscles. The old man's left arm swept under his shoulders, urging him up into a sitting position. Gart could hear the word "falcon" as Man-to-Shi scooted around behind him. He could feel another hand-cone on the top of his head and then a forceful blast of breath.

"Receive him!"

The harsh whisper had scarcely entered his ears when, with a buzzing roar, Gart's perception was filled with the vision of a huge falcon. It was a brilliant, deep blue with gray and tan underparts. The eye was much larger than those of his uncle's falcons, more knowing, yet fierce enough. He could not see the legs but was convinced there was no tether there.

Suddenly, he saw again, very briefly, his dream of the soaring chariot and his ghostly fellow driver. The correspondence to the present vision was vague, but Gart was immediately convinced the assistant driver and this falcon were two forms of one being.

"Up! Dance! Sing!"

The old man pressed the rattles into Gart's hands and traded places with him. The drum, which had fallen silent, resumed and Gart's feet began to shuffle.

"Dance your totem. Raise your spirit. Sing!" the hoarse whisper from the mat below him urged

Gart could hear:

"Falcon soar,
falcon soar...,
See far,
see far…,

Falcon soar,
falcon soar...,
See before,
See before…"

Could that be him? The words appeared from nowhere and the sound was much sweeter than he remembered his voice.

"Falcon soar,
falcon soar…"

The drummer and his friends had picked it up. Even Kre-eg seemed to be mouthing the words. All of Gart's usual feelings of self-consciousness, awkwardness and skepticism were right there, but they seemed to lack power or pain.

His shoulders dipped and bobbed as he soared and coasted, catching the updrafts, then diving, dipping and gliding across the surface of waterways, fields and plains. Rivers changed their courses, seas receded, strange and magnificent cities rose and fell. Mountains erupted and dissolved.

Strange silver birds with fiery tails flashed by and dipped! Suddenly, all was calm. Gart shook his rattles, the drums stopped. He slumped to the ground and fell into a deep sleep.

When he awoke, the sun was peeking over the fields and marshes, striking him directly in the eyes. He was aware of a faint stir about him. Man-to-Shi returned, face and torso still wet from his morning ablutions at the canal. Kre-eg moaned, stretched, yawned and rubbed his eyes. A couple of the boys were still asleep. The missing drummer appeared, followed by an anxious- looking

Jeme crossing the springy little bridge. They carried a pot of steaming gruel and a number of drinking gourds. One of the boys was reviving the smoldering embers of the fire with tinder and blowing. The fire's function at this point was not clear to Gart. Perhaps the rekindling was necessary to reconvene the little group. All members and Jeme sipped their breakfast gruel. Kre-eg was the first to break the silence.

"So what happened to the jackal?" he asked, looking in turn to Gart and Man-to-Shi.

"Did you see him at all?" the shaman asked Gart, who shook his head.

"No, only the falcon."

"I am not surprised," said the old man. "I did see him, though, at the entrance to the underworld. He seemed to be guarding the gate or, perhaps, simply marking the place. He made no objection to my passage. It is the falcon who represents your guardian spirit. The jackal can be a helper though, not just to you, Gart, but to anyone. On your previous trip, did your companions see it?"

"I think so," said Gart, struggling to remember the exact details. "Yes, I know Bruzi, my commander, did."

"And you, Kre-eg, you saw something?" the old man asked.

"Well, yes, tracks, a shadow. Yes, something was there."

"Either of you may see this fellow again, maybe not in quite the same form. It will probably be there to tell you are about to cross a limit or boundary of some kind. Be careful though, or you may be tricked into missing the line. As you know, boundaries are not always well marked. Some seem arbitrary, but without boundaries, confusion reigns. The jackal may alert you, but he will not tell you what kind of frontier you are crossing."

The entire group was silent. Gart struggled to remember, review, make sense out of what he was hearing about crossing borders. It seemed important, but it was all very vague to him at the moment.

After several minutes, Man-to-Shi spoke again.

"Now it's my turn. You can help me by listening while I explain my afterthoughts about the sacrifice of the lame bullock. You —

Jeme, Gart and most of these boys — were there. You saw I acted without hesitation or deliberation, and you may remember I acted, not as a shaman but as a priest in a formal ceremony of sacrifice. I was once trained to do this, so my actions may not seem as surprising to others as they were to me.

"You should know many years ago I strongly rejected what I had seen at the temples and returned home to study the old ways of the shaman. For some reason, the temple administrators have allowed me a subsistence on their property for all these years, even though my activities and interests were quite different from their ways. Suddenly, a lame bullock and a large, black snake appear and I am a priest again."

"This was why you were so upset to see me again?" Gart asked.

"Yes, your reappearance brought it back into my mind. I had been mulling it for some time. It was not what I did, but the swiftness and surety of my reaction and the feeling of utter rightness that surprised me. Is it possible some of what I rejected has some merit?"

"Well, what choice did you have?" Kre-eg asked.

"Thank you. Precisely the point," Man-to-Shi continued. He was becoming more animated and seemed appreciative that, at least someone, was following him.

"Now that I have examined it in detail, only three possible courses of action occur to me: First, I could have said, 'This is taboo, an evil omen,' or simply, 'poisoned meat.' What a mess that would have been. Of course, Jeme and Gart would have had to bury the old fellow, bill of lading and all, as none of us would have dared to touch it.

"The second possibility would be just the opposite. If I had simply said, 'This meat is safe. Dilution and cooking will make the poison harmless,' most of the people would have believed me. If I, or the chief tenant, had said, 'Free meat! Eat! Enjoy!' we would have had a three-day party."

The apprentice and his friends all nodded their heads in agreement. The old man took a deep breath and resumed.

"Greed could well have stepped in and our unexpected boon could have led to a degrading squabble over the spoils."

Silence again. Regarding this prospect, no one wanted to speak.

"But what happened was the third, and least probable thing," Man-to-Shi resumed. "Through no insight that I was aware of, a lame bullock, a cranky snake and an ex-priest meet, an improvised ritual is performed, a little fire produces a column of smoke that reaches upward and what was chaos takes on form. Its name: sacrifice.

"That occasion has already become memorable for some of us," he said in a husky voice. "I'm not sure its effects are over with yet." He turned to go, but in the middle of the first step he looked back, a faint, moist gleam in his eyes. "Thank you for your kind attention. Maybe I can let this matter rest now." He hobbled off toward the little bridge leading to the village, his gaunt frame flecked by the dancing spots of light as the morning sun poured through the overarching willow trees.

CHAPTER SIX

Gart had been back in the city for an entire week before he had a sense of being totally there. He had trouble paying attention and his sleep was full of dreams, some fretful and some rather satisfying. After several contained glimpses of soaring falcons, he awoke feeling invigorated and powerful.

He finally remembered a few minutes after they had left the temple farm they had been overtaken by a young runner, the shaman's assistant. He was bearing a bundle for Gart. The runner had explained that the bundle contained leaves of cassia, myrtle and thyme, plus some lumps of the gum of a tree who's name was unfamiliar to Gart.

"Could you please deliver these to Lah-ma-Nah, the Royal Physician?" the runner asked. "Be sure to warn him this year's leaves are very potent."

Of course Gart could deliver the bundle, and of course he promptly forgot. Once remembered, the simple task was put off for another two weeks until he finally presented himself and his bundle at the gate to the Royal Residence. This was a substantial, rambling, two-story building of burnt and burnished brick located in the southeast corner of the temple-palace compound. It would have been impressive if it were not dwarfed by the ziggurat and the surrounding temples. He was admitted without difficulty, but was then sent with an armed escort who informed him the physician would likely be on the second floor, near the lugal's private quarters.

This was Gart's first look at the inside of the palace and, although it was spacious and furnished in good taste, he judged that it was really rather modest if one compared it to the size and workmanship of some of the homes of the wealthy.

Ushered into a small room with one small window and three doors, Gart was offered one of the several stools there. The room also contained a couch and many little storage baskets. The guard soon returned with a bland faced, smiling man who introduced himself as Lah-ma-Nah, the Royal Physician.

The doctor seemed quite pleased with the bundle. He paid sharp attention to Gart's relayed caution that this year's leaves were unusually potent in spite of poor growing conditions for crops.

"And how is my old friend Man-to-Shi?" he asked, as he drew up another stool and looked expectantly at Gart.

"Well, I don't know exactly," Gart hesitated. "He looks like a skinny old wreck, but he didn't seem to have any problem staying up all night and totally wearing us out."

The physician laughed, but muffled the sound with his hand. "Not so different than when I last saw him," he chuckled. "I try to get out there every year, but this year is difficult." He indicated with a motion of his head that the difficulty was in the adjacent room. "Yes, we have had poor growing conditions here, too. Perhaps the two are related." He opened Gart's bundle and nibbled cautiously on a dried and brittle leaf. "The leaf is bitter, the king is bitter. Maybe a little of this will help. I certainly hope so." He thanked Gart warmly and was escorting him to the door, when he paused.

"You must come again, so that we can talk some more," he said. "That old swamp doctor has often given me some things to think about."

"I would like that. I'll look for an opportunity," Gart promised.

He set out briskly from the palace, north along the main wall of the temple compound and out the main temple gate, then back south, toward the stockyards.

Within a few minutes, however, he thought better of it. He simply must go home and get things in order. There were all those goods he had brought from Nafti to store and he had planned to talk to Banarum in hopes of interesting him in the Dilmun venture.

As he entered the courtyard of the apartment building, he could hear Leah and Sari talking on the upstairs landing. He stood to one side and greeted Sari briefly as she came down the stairs with two shoulder baskets of clay tablets.

"What's with Sari and all the clay tablets?" he asked Leah.

Leah's silent, steady gaze indicated to him he must have forgotten something major.

"Oh, yes, now I do remember. You told me all about it the first night I was back. You have a job, right? You and Sari are working as copyists for Orson and his project with Nin-ana-Me."

"Well, thank you for remembering," she said in a very cool tone. "You must have been listening to at least some of what I said."

"Now, Leah," he assumed his most serious tone, "It is just that it's a bit unusual for a woman to learn much about reading and writing."

Leah seemed to be weighing his statement. Unusual, indeed, she thought as she silently surveyed what had already become very usual for her. Her world; crocks and bowls, broom and loom. And you, Gart, are you ready for me to do anything other than the usual? she asked, but only in her thoughts.

Gart chose not to deal with the silence but excused himself to go find Banarum. As he descended the stairway there flashed into his mind a fantasy of Nin-ana-Me seated at a table on a huge dais. Flanking her and also wearing sky blue robes were Sari and Leah. As the priestess pondered and nodded gravely, her two new assistants were hurling little silver lightning bolts at an unseen audience. Seated below them, a cross-legged Orson industriously recorded the proceedings.

"Yes, Gart? Problems?" Banarum was just coming home as Gart arrived at his door.

"Oh no, sir, no problems. In fact, opportunities!"

Gart mentioned in what he hoped would pass as a casual manner that he was preparing a shipment of goods, cloth, hides and rope to go to Dilmun. Just as casually, he dropped the name of Mahn-so-ni as one of the organizers.

"Would you, by any chance, be interested in joining us in this project?" Gart asked.

"The goods are to go directly from here by boat?" Banarum asked.

"Yes, sir."

"And do you have a boat?"

"Well, almost," Gart said. "Someone started a large reed craft but ran out of funds. We could finish it in about six weeks."

"A reed boat?" Banarum arched his brows, wrinkling his forehead well up onto his bald cranium. "You mean one of those pointy-prowed little things the marsh people skiff around in? On the open seas?"

"The same style and materials, just twenty times larger."

"I don't know about this. Wouldn't a good puff of wind tip the damn thing over?"

"I hope not," said Gart. "It wouldn't sink, that's sure."

"Well, it wouldn't hurt to look at the fool thing," Banarum admitted. "Could we do that and maybe talk to Mahn-so-ni, in the morning?"

"Agreed. I will be at your door an hour after sunrise." Gart felt his lungs finally filling with fresh air. It was as though a tide of good fortune was lifting his affairs.

"All done! How was that for timing?" he announced to Leah as he returned from having removed the last of his trade goods from their apartment.

"Far better than you realize. Nin-ana-Me is due here any minute."

"Nin-ana-Me? The High Priestess? Here in our home? Why — why, it seems hardly proper she be asked to honor our humble home!" Gart was flustered.

"She's been here twice already and liked it fine. In fact she said she enjoyed being here very much." Leah sounded impatient, perhaps even a little scornful of his protests.

"Why is she coming here?" he asked. "Why haven't I heard about this? Is there some big secret? This is her third visit already? Does she just come here to see you? Aren't you going to answer my questions?" He looked at his wife in alarm.

Leah, who had been stooped over and scurrying about with her cleaning, now stood up in front of him to catch her breath. She put her open left hand in front of his face and began counting off his questions, plucking one finger at a time with the other hand.

"First, I do not know entirely why she wants secrecy. It may have to do with temple politics. She wants to remain the unknown author of certain writings which she hopes to plant or circulate in certain places. Second, yes, this is her third visit. Third, the big rush seems connected with the growing public interest and discussion about the appearance of the snake. Fourth, she doesn't come just to see me. Sari and Orson come later to write the new work down and check copies for errors, but first she likes to practice on me what she is going to write. She says she wants to know if she is understandable."

"See, I do listen to you," Gart said as he began to relax the rigid posture of attention he had assumed.

Leah dropped her hands from in front of his face and looked away as though remembering something. She continued in a lower tone. "I think there is more to it than the writing. I think she is lonely and misses having a normal family life."

Gart was silent for a moment while he reviewed Leah's lecture.

"The appearance of the snake?" What was this about? Immediately, his own snake experience came to mind. Had the matter of the lame bullock become general knowledge? That snake had disappeared far from here. What was this?

"Oh, I suppose it came out while you were away. I think Nin-ana-Me had known for several months. It seems a large black snake, probably a cobra, has taken up residence in the great urn before the image of Nin-Gal in her temple. It lives mostly on the milk offerings and may or may not be in the Vessel of Containment when anyone has the courage to look. A couple of shrine attendants claim to have been chased by it, but not everyone believes them. On two occasions it has shown itself during services, which created quite a stir. Many more people are going to the ceremonies in hopes of seeing it. Nin-ana-Me says this is a great opportunity to wake people up and give them some new ideas."

"I can understand the excitement," said Gart, "but what is all the discussion about?"

"Well, Nin-ana-Me says.... Well, why don't you ask her?"

Gart followed Leah's gaze. There, in the middle of their doorway, her nose one inch from his languidly waving fan, was Her Ladyship.

"Oh, Your Ladyship! Do come in. Welcome to our humble home!" Gart was flustered again. He always hated not being in control. He just hoped he sounded sincere to their guest.

"Thank you, Lieutenant." She swept into the room with a swish of her linen garments, not the temple blue Gart associated with her, but the light tan of unbleached commoner's clothing. She moved toward the bench at her right with the surety of one familiar with the room. Oddly enough, she did not address them immediately but seemed to be studying a shadow cast on the wall by the bar in the tiny window.

"And what is it that you are to ask for yourself?" The question was for Gart, but she was looking at Leah.

"Oh, about the snake, all those arguments," Leah answered.

"Ahh, yes, that is quite a controversy. People have been talking of little else. Some say the snake is just a snake and they speculate as to whether it is male or female, cobra or blacksnake, mean or playful. So far as I know, no one has consulted the snake."

Here the explanation stopped. Nin-ana-Me's ending inflection was ambiguous. Their guest had seated herself on their one proper seat, the little bench against the wall just to the right of the door. As Gart helped Leah pull their table out from the opposite wall and place it in the middle of the small room in preparation for the work that was to follow, he was asking himself, What does this all mean? She hasn't really said anything so far.

Finally he asked, "And do you think this snake is just a plain old snake?"

Again she did not answer directly, her gaze roaming the upper reaches of the little room. "Some are saying the snake was planted there by someone. Was the temple staff just trying to boost attendance or were foreign agents sent here to disrupt our worship and undermine our citizen's confidence?"

Once more Gart noted that she had taken no position. "So you see this as a hoax?" He was partially teasing, as he sensed she was concealing some strong feelings on the subject.

"No, I do not."

"You see some special meaning in the snake appearing in this way then?"

Once more she evaded him.

"Our most senior military man, General Mem-el, is convinced the snake is a message from the gods and is not only an omen in favor of our present rearmament program but even calls for us to strike out against our oppressors. He won't say who our oppressors are, though some of us may have an idea." Here her left eyebrow made a little arch in Gart's direction. "What do you think about that, Lieutenant?"

Did that quirk of the eyebrow mean this lady knew a lot more about his recent trip than he realized?

She awaited his reply.

"That's a little too convenient for the general. There must be more to it than that." He chose to be a little vague himself.

"Mer-luke and his astrologers," she resumed, "will tell you when the snake rises up out of the vessel, it points to the heavens. This is supposed to mean we must redouble our observations and calculations as something important is happening there. Who can say they are wrong?

"On the other hand," she said, "one of my very old priestesses has whispered to me that power has returned to the house of the Goddess and that she will again reign supreme, as she did when we were all tillers of the soil. She is careful not to let the chief priest hear her. He would have a stroke and probably use it as an excuse to shut down our side of the temple compound."

"And what do you think of it all, Your Ladyship?" Gart was increasingly determined to get an opinion from her.

At this point Nin-ana-Me arose from the bench and struck a pensive pose, hand under chin. This Gart fellow is surely persistent, she thought. Is he really interested? Can he understand the issues involved here, or has he just noticed my evasions and decided to have his way with me in this conversation? Leah, I can instinctively trust, but what about him? She took in a long slow breath and looked directly, searchingly at Gart.

Gart did get the impression she was weighing not only her words, but also her listener.

"I was present both times when the serpent rose up during the worship service," she began in a lower, softer tone. "I have dreamed about it every night since, but they have not been unpleasant dreams. I cannot dismiss this. It was a special happening with a message for those who are prepared to receive it. Perhaps any time can be special if we are awake and receptive to what is trying to happen. Maybe this is special right here now; my trying to share this with you."

The intensity of the woman's words and her gaze held Gart transfixed, scarcely breathing. The silence seemed to ask nothing of him, but soon the need to breathe, to move, sent him fumbling back to the obvious question.

"And what do you feel is trying to happen?"

He noted Nin-ana-Me's silence this time was more of a hesitation. She seemed less certain.

He just keeps after me, she thought. Are these convictions of mine based on anything but self-delusion? I have asked myself this many times. I can't give them up, so I shouldn't be afraid to answer his question.

"I must warn you," she began, "what I say will sound a little strange, vague perhaps, but it is very real to me. In fact, if I had not been the favored daughter of the King of Erech, people would probably still call me strange."

"Oh, that is not so at all," Leah protested.

"Yes, something very important *is* trying to happen right here, and now!" Nin-ana-Me's hand dropped from her chin. The chin thrust forward and her voice rang with conviction. "And," she continued more softly, "if we are alert and try to keep a pure heart, perhaps we can help it happen."

This was still not specific but it was *an* answer and it was sincere. Gart was content when he heard Sari's laugh from the courtyard. As Orson and Sari's footsteps could be heard on the stairs, Nin-ana-Me turned to Gart and said:

"I feel bad about disturbing your home, but we will be through in about an hour."

"I told her you wouldn't mind, Sweetheart, and you'd probably be at some meeting or other, anyway." Leah's rapid explanation sounded slightly apologetic, but he thought there was a resentful edge to her voice also.

"That would be a good guess," he said in Leah's general direction as he went out the door without further leave taking. Deny a man access to his own home? Now that was a hell of a note! Not that he wanted to stay anyway, not that he needed to hear any more of that stuff, not that he wasn't going out anyway. Sari and Orson got the faintest of nods as he passed them on his way down the stairs.

The streets were very dark now. There was no moon yet and the stars hadn't made their appearance either. Maybe he should drop by Mahn-so-ni's house. He was supposed to have a standing invitation there and it wasn't far.

Something was going on when Gart arrived there. Torches were flickering outside the house and people were coming and going, laughing and having a good time. Maybe it was a family affair. This did not seem the time to drop by.

Well, he would just go over to the stockyards and check on things. The cows would be glad to see him. Run off by a bunch of women — and Orson, of course. Orson, himself, was a bit of an old lady at times. Now that wasn't fair!

Was he there already? Still talking to himself, Gart rounded the corner of the building just outside the entrance to the yards. He saw a glow and heard a commotion at the far corner of the yard: bleats, thumps and crashes. A lion in the herd or jackals? Then Gart remembered, he was in the city. The gates would be shut — guards on duty.

He had just broken into a trot when he stumbled over something. Feet — and legs! It was the watchman of the yards! Was he dead? Gart stooped and shook the man who stirred and mumbled. He reeked of beer. Be it from charity or bribery, the watchman was very drunk.

Glancing up, Gart could see that the glow had spread into leaping flames. A strange figure moved across the path of light between the fire and Gart. Was it a dog? Size and distance were hard to judge but in his quick glimpse its gait was lumbering and awkward. Could it be a human on all fours?

Gart began to run through the alleyways between pens. The animal cries, bleats and crashes were welling up around him. Now came an intense, full-bodied shriek, like none he had ever heard, prolonged and expressive, a most terrifying sound. He could see three young men, bare torsos glistening in the firelight. They were throwing themselves against the pole partitions of the pens, crashing through them, stomping jumping, twirling. One young man was directly before him, wild-eyed but rigid-faced.

"What the HELL do you think you're doing?" screamed Gart, lunging forward at the demonic mask.

The next thing he was aware of was Mar-Ti pleading with him to awaken.

"Gart! Gart! Wake up! Are you all right?" The boy was in tears. His hand on Gart's shoulder was shaking him, perhaps gently, but every repetition brought a cascade of pain throughout his head, neck and chest.

He tried to lick his dry lips to speak but found his tongue was not long enough to reach to the outside of his swollen lip. He tried to turn his head to look at Mar-Ti, but found movement impeded by an egg-sized bump on the crown of his head.

"Sure, kid, I'm fine now. That must have been a hell of a bad dream I had."

"Sit up, Gart. That was no dream. Let's get you out of here. Can you walk?"

"Sure, why not?" He soon found out why not. As he attempted to rise he experienced intense pain in the side of his right ribcage. He seemed to remember a voice and a thudding heel to the ribs.

"You greedy son-of-a-bitch, take that!"

"Yeah, you friggin sheep herder." This was a second voice. "How do you like it?"

His eyes began to come into focus, but the sources of those voices were nowhere to be seen. The pale moon, now in its last quarter, had risen and was dimly illuminating a scene of desolation. The fire was out, but the smell of smoke and burned wool was heavy in the air. Gart could see Jeme and several members of the night watch trying to put back partitions and round up loose animals. The bleating was now much less, but Gart could see several dead or dying animals and a few others, mostly goats, wounded and bleeding, slashed in strange, random fashion.

"Can you make it, Lieutenant?" Jeme had joined them now.

"Yeah, I'm O.K. now." Gart did not sound too convinced.

"You help him on home, Mar-Ti. I'll check on the stock and let him know a little later," Jeme said.

As the pair moved out into the street more guards arrived. Here came reinforcements, even a squad of the Royal Bodyguard, on the double. Not leading them, but following closely in their rear, was Captain Kre-eg-el-Sheh.

"My God, Gart!" he exclaimed as he caught sight of the hobbling figure. "What have you been doing?"

"Ridin' a damn horse, of course," Gart answered thickly.

Kre-eg had to laugh at this quick association. "Can you make it O.K.?" He looked at Mar-Ti, who nodded. "I'll tell the colonel not to expect you tomorrow, that you were wounded in the line of duty, no matter how it happened."

Leah had lit every lamp in the house before he arrived. Even through his pain, Gart thoroughly enjoyed her wide-eyed concern and expressions of relief and compassion. She cleaned his wounds and put him to bed. If he didn't move he felt pleasantly numb, but he could not sleep.

"Leah."

"Yes, Gart."

"What were Mar-Ti and Jeme doing there that time of night?"

"I sent them. I asked Jeme to get Mar-Ti and go look for you."

"Jeme, good old Uncle Jeme. He hasn't failed us yet. You sent them to the yards?"

"Yes."

"How did you know I was there?"

"I just knew," she said.

"Of course," he said. "That's where I attend all my meetings."

He was still deeply asleep when Leah's gentle stroking of his bare arm gradually brought him into awareness of daylight and his surroundings.

"Gart, Jeme is here, about the livestock."

Gart struggled painfully to his feet and limped to the door. As grateful as he felt toward Jeme, Gart was not ready to drop all formality.

"Are the cow and calf O.K.?"

"Not a scratch that I can see," replied Jeme. "She's a little spooked though. She may have had to defend herself. Even Mar-Ti had to be a little careful when he went to milk her."

"How about the sheep?"

"One has an ear partly cut off. The other three are O.K. It's hard to stab a sheep on the run. All three goats are in a bad way though. I'd butcher them out if I were you," Jeme said.

"Who would do a thing like this?" Leah looked searchingly at them both. "They didn't even steal anything!"

Gart could only shake his head, and that very gingerly.

"Well, ma'am," Jeme finally answered. "Some folks are just full of hatred. I never understood it myself, but it's a fact."

"Get a little breakfast, Jeme, and I will come with you. Do you have time to help?" Gart asked.

"I'll make time. Are you up to it?"

Gart nodded with forced conviction and Jeme went downstairs.

"Gart, you can hardly walk. You have no business going," Leah scolded. "Can't Mar-Ti do it?"

"No! I'm the one that got him to make friends with those animals. I can't ask him to slit their throats. My father wouldn't send me to do it until I was a man grown. I know he could hardly bear to do it himself."

By midmorning their arduous and bloody work was done and the meat in the hands of hawkers or consumers. Cleaning himself as best he could, Gart made his painful way to the armory to make sure Kre-eg had not forgotten to excuse him. He had not forgotten. Colonel Alkohn rolled his eyes at the sight of Gart, but his questions seemed to indicate sincere concern.

Gart spent the remainder of the day at home, grateful for the opportunity to rest his tender ribs and dizzy head. Leah remained solicitous, but Gart detected a certain underlying reserve that made him uneasy. He might as well try to get to the bottom of it.

"Leah, I had the feeling you were not too happy with me when I left the house last night."

"Now why in the world should I have been unhappy with you?"

"Well, could it be that I seemed impatient…a little pushy with my questions, a little irritable. Maybe you saw it as a bit rude?"

Rude? Leah thought. He just doesn't see! I had so looked forward to hearing Nin-ana-Me talk and work out her ideas. Finally, she answered him.

"Who am I to contradict my Lord and Master?"

"Sarcasm won't help. What, just exactly, made you mad?"

"Specifically, I was looking forward to having Nin-ana-Me here again, not just her honoring our home, whatever that means. I was shocked and embarrassed when you whom I didn't even expect to be here, seemed to have to take charge and question her every opinion."

A long silence ensued. Gart was certainly in no condition to stomp out in a huff. He even wondered if it had been his petty preoccupation that had made him such an easy victim the night before. It would be best he not confess to that. Lame excuses wouldn't help him. He was still searching for a suitable peace offering when Leah spoke.

"She is really quite impressive, don't you think?"

"Now that you point it out, yes," he answered. "She made quite an impression on me when I first met her, but I thought it was mostly the situation. All her titles, the setting, the fact that she paid a lot of attention to my opinions."

Gart slowly and carefully arose from the bed. His ribs had gotten stiff and he had to breath shallowly to avoid sharp pain. Other bruises were trying to compete for attention also. He needed to go out back to the drain to relieve himself. He was a little shaky on the stairs but too proud to allow Leah to help. After his slow, painful return, he resumed his observations about Nin-ana-Me.

"I was quite self-conscious during that first interview. The second time I saw her I was flattered she remembered my name and asked me for help. I guess I was looking at me rather than her."

He remained silent for a while.

"What is it about her that impresses you?" he asked, looking at his wife with a quizzical expression.

"There's just something about her," Leah said. " It's her bearing, I guess, and you can see it in her eyes. They are gray...maybe blue-gray...with little flecks of gold. Did you notice?"

"I can't say that I did, but I believe you are right. 'Blue-gray with flecks of gold.' That's very unusual here in Ur. I don't know about Erech. Yes, you are right. Those eyes sort of see right through you."

"No, that's not quite right, either," replied Leah. "She sees beyond you, but she always sees you, too. Even when she's talking in a very general way, even in verse, she seems to take you along with her, like you were going that way, too. She seems to precede you, but she doesn't lose you. That is even more unusual than the color of her eyes. That's why I have so enjoyed her."

Gart was silent again for some time. Peace seemed to have settled on the household but it was a simmering peace. Blue-gray with flecks of gold...they precede you..., he was musing. Is there really something to this, something about to happen here?

Late that evening, Gart, fed and rested, decided he would risk reopening the subject of Nin-ana-Me's project with Leah.

"'Verse,' you say. You said 'she takes you along, even when she talks in verse.' Is our priestess a poet? I was afraid she was into politics."

"What we are working on now is in verse form, sort of. It's different. You have to stop and think about it."

So far, so good. He pressed on.

"Who is she trying to reach with these secret messages? What is she trying to do? What does she call it?"

"Really, Gart, I don't know that I have any right to discuss this with you," Leah answered with a slight chill in her voice. This sounded to her like another take-charge session.

"Oh, you're afraid I will be reciting verses to the cows down at the yards?"

"You have done stranger things," she said, her voice still decidedly cool. He keeps asking all these questions, she was saying to herself, then if I can't explain it all, and I can't, he makes bad jokes about it.

"I suppose I could ask her if she will explain it to you, if you are really interested in what we are doing."

"I would be obliged if you would do that, *ma'am*."

The next two days were difficult, strenuous and painful for Gart. He had to finish preparing for the arrival of his kinsmen and their market flock at the badly damaged stockyards. At the armory, the ranks of his new unit had finally been filled and now the job of equipping them and turning the recruits into soldiers must begin in earnest. Although the new recruits were enthusiastic, Gart and his fellow officers had noted with concern the growing moodiness of their commander.

Alkohn reported to them that on the night of Gart's injuries there had been three other major acts of vandalism and, the following night, a murder and several serious personal assaults. The Lord Chamberlain, General Mem-el and the City Council President were all looking to him to deal with these problems. His scowling countenance and air of fatigue made it quite clear he had no taste for this task.

A week after the stockyard fire, Gart's wounds had largely healed and he had completed preparations for the arrival of his kinsmen and the market flock. Tonight he was specifically invited to attend the transcribing session in his home. Nin-ana-Me would not come as early, out of respect for his supper hour. In preparation, Leah busily stored things away to clear a work space.

Their three guests arrived together and, after a brief hug for Leah and a pleasant nod to Gart, the Priestess gestured they should take their accustomed seats. Gart had placed his stool in the north corner, outside their circle.

"If I remember correctly," she began, "when we last met I was attempting to explain what had led me to this project. I fear I did not do that very well. Let me try again. I may not have gotten across what a strange and powerful effect the appearance of the snake had on me.

"The sight of the serpent rising up caused me to wake up and to realized how numb and self-satisfied I had become. I also noticed how widespread and deep that attitude appeared to be among those around me. The King, may the God save him, seems so numb that he must be ill. The Lord Chamberlain seems scarcely better. At least the King suffers. Most of his retainers are so occupied with keeping things the same, pretending everything is all right, they could be sleep walking. This is a great tragedy, and I hadn't even noticed it."

"So this is about politics? You want to wake up the government?" Sari asked. It was unusual for Sari to speak out so quickly.

"That too, but that doesn't really cover it," said Nin-ana-Me. "It isn't just the royal household, at the temple also. Forgive me," she said. "I need a few moments to collect my thoughts."

She cast her eyes down to the table, half closing them. Immediately, out of many memories, resounded the morning chant.

"Oh Lady Nin-Gal, shadow bride of he who illuminates the skies by night, be present here with us. Summon to this place all gods and daemons who reach down to mankind as they stretch upward to touch hands and span the void created when Enlil split ancient Tiamat, separating Heaven from the earth."

The sound of the chorus echoed back from many mornings before the altar. She could feel her tension ease, her hands relaxing their grip on the edge of the bench as she leaned forward. The familiar words were soothing her and diluting her unexpected sense of excitement.

"We thank Thee, Oh Nin-Gal, and all of the heavenly creator gods that we have been placed here where the mighty rivers meet the sea, where the earth is fruitful and the waters yield many fish. We know that, among you, you have established this city for a purpose. You have aligned it with the stars, divided it into quarters and assigned the families to worthy crafts, each with its unique task."

At this point the chorus faded and she could hear her own whispered private devotions. "And I thank Thee, Nin-Gal and all the friendly Creative Ones, that I have been chosen into the guild of priestcraft and have been privileged to dwell on such a high place, the very ziggurat itself, where you descend to meet us. Grant, Lady Nin-Gal, that though I, like you, persist in secret at labor that reveals mere glints rather than dazzling light, that my works, like yours, may lead others to perceive the fullness of creation, to know that the harmony that rules the motion of the planets is destined to prevail in the affairs of men."

This prayer, too, was very familiar and flowed smoothly out of her memory, but seemed more demanding than the chorus. Why then did she feel so refreshed? She looked about the room to try to explain this feeling of newness, a richness she had not previously noted. Her task was the same. The text, there on the table, still seemed valid, but the moment she ceased her prayers and looked up at the group something changed.

To her left, in front of the door, Orson was already engrossed with the tablets on the table. To his left were shelves of bags and bowls and jars for grain and water. Next was Gart, sitting rigidly alert on his stool. To his left was the far wall with its high little windows and rows of baskets so carefully arranged by color and size. Toward the south corner was Leah, wide-eyed and at ease, leaning on her loom. Just to Nin-ana-Me's right was Sari, looking openly at her in a way that was entirely new, intense.

Finally Nin-ana-Me spoke. "It is true that the numbness I speak of can lead to our fair city being sacked and burned, and our being murdered or enslaved by our neighbors, as so often happens in this land, but even that would not explain the full tragedy that could be in the making here!"

"What could be worse than that?" Orson spoke just as Gart was about to ask.

Instinctively, Orson searched for a joke to relieve the intensity he felt building in the room, but he could find no joke here. He could only hear a ringing in his ears. It had been so very quiet. He glanced down and it seemed that the little wedge marks on the tablets were swarming upward in a spiral, surrounding his head. "Whew," was all he could say.

As they all waited in vain for an expected further comment from Orson, Nin-ana-Me looked up at the little windows, then back and forth to the far corners of the ceiling. This was a small deception. She did not want them to know she was praying again, a special plea for this time together.

Oh powers that be present in this place, she heard within. This was a strange salutation, new to her. *Protect me from foolishness, from wishful thinking. Help me to not expect too much from these people out of my loneliness.*

Though I am a foreigner and a priestess at a shrine where we are in danger of complacency and of falling away from the truth, let me not flee my solitude, nor shrink from serving what may be possible in this moment.

Her prayer ended and she looked slowly around the room. They were all watching her. She felt very vulnerable. She could only gesture mutely at first at the tablets on the table. Finally she said, her voice low and rather hoarse, "You may see something here, and you may not. Don't feel you have to be impressed unless it makes sense to you."

Her words hung there for a moment, then Sari leaned forward, her body turning to face Nin-ana-Me. Sari's features were twisted with effort, her voice husky as she stammered out, "If it please Your Ladyship…it…feels like…feels like…it needs to be done!"

They all straightened up in their seats, jolted by the transformation they had heard. Sari had never spoken with such authority. Savoring the moment, Orson and Leah quietly resumed their work.

Silenced for the moment, Gart looked to Leah. Then, for some reason, his eyes dropped to where her hand lay on her abdomen. Was that a kick from within he saw? This was confirmed by Leah's smile as she caressed the spot. She did not look up, however.

Distracted, Gart simply waited but eventually he resumed his search for answers in terms that were more familiar to him.

"So if it isn't just the government, whoever that is, that you want to wake up, whose attention are you trying to get with your verses?" Gart was tempted once more to try to gain some control of the conversation. He was also trying to understand how poetry and politics could fit into one world.

"Gart, I cannot honestly tell you who's attention I need right now. It can't be just the lugal or his retainers, or even the temple people. And don't think for a moment that I am just being critical of Ni-Zum-Ka and his priests. We owe an enormous debt to the whole priestly guild. It was out of their inspiration, their labor, that our cities were conceived and could begin to function at all. They were the first to see order, yet dormant, in men's affairs and recognized there a reflection of the movement of the heavenly bodies.

"But they must not, we must not, settle for old truths alone. Just applying them, just beating people over the head with them will.... Well, maybe that's what is happening to our city now. Someone must keep reaching, deeper, higher, wider, to understand what is yet to come forth."

She looked directly at Gart with such wide-eyed intensity that he had to avert his gaze. "Not just one person must wake up," she resumed, "but a community, maybe many, maybe only a few."

She caught her breath as if to say more, then thought better of it. She gave her head a sharp little shake, as if to clear it of the complexities of the question. "Shall we get back to the details?" she asked.

Gart didn't feel settled, but he didn't want to prolong this discussion. What was it that she was expecting to "burst forth"? What was going to come out of Ur, other than his child, of course?

While the work party went over what Orson called "the tenth revision" of a tablet closely packed with wedge marks, Gart found an excuse to withdraw completely from the field.

"I need to go down to the courtyard and check the fire," he fibbed without addressing or looking at anyone in particular.

The following afternoon, Gart had just arrived at the yards when he heard a familiar bell coming through the sheep gate. There were three men with the flock. The two younger men were Gart's cousins and the older man was the owner of the donkeys Gart had borrowed.

"The horse colt, are you going to keep him?" Gart was surprised to hear himself ask this as his first question.

"Yes, yes," the cousins were quick to reply.

"We will have to see about that," said the older man rather firmly.

"What about the cloth, Gart?" his older cousin asked.

"The cloth?"

"Yeah, you know, that we all put in to go to Dil...something? Dilmun?"

"Oh, yes, I have it here. It's in storage."

"It hasn't even left yet?"

"Well, no, the ship isn't quite ready but we are making good progress." Gart knew he needed to check on the Dilmun deal. The hopes of the home folks were riding on his shoulders and he wasn't even sure that there really was a Dilmun.

"I can show you the cloth. It's not far."

"No, no, we trust you."

They still looked disappointed.

"I'll tell you what I'll do, fellows," Gart proposed. "We will celebrate your safe arrival tonight and in the morning we'll go talk to Mahn-so-ni, one of the big investors, and then we can go inspect the ship!"

This seemed to mollify everyone. He must move quickly. Leah was expecting company, but he had implied a small feast. He would slaughter one of the three lambs which were his share of the crop. He would send Mar-Ti ahead with the news, some firewood and some tokens to buy beer. He could save a choice cut to give to Mahn-so-ni in the morning.

After sending his kin off to reconnoiter the bazaar, Gart sharpened his bronze knife on a stone and led the balky young ram outside the walls to the regular slaughter racks. It seemed hardly fair that he had to walk all the way to the city, just to meet his death.

Once in position, Gart jumped astride the woolly beast, pulled its head up and back to slit its throat. The ram's vigorous struggles made Gart's task easier by forcing him to focus on getting the job done.

He waited now, still astride the fallen animal. He would wait for the blood to stop gushing and the kicking to cease before he hoisted the carcass onto the pole racks to skin and gut it. Death in the city was no prettier than death out in the brush. Already, the scavenger dogs were gathering, awaiting their chance at the offal. In his mind's eye, Gart saw Man-to-Shi bowing solemnly to the four corners of creation before the death of the bullock. Somehow, he wished this could be a proper sacrifice rather than just a smart move to promote his business.

The party that evening was at least a moderate success, thanks in part to his mother-in-law and Mar-Ti who pitched in to help the pregnant Leah. Jeme, by now feeling well acquainted with Gart's cousins, drank and talked more than the others appreciated, but Gart considered that mild annoyance a fair price for Jeme's continuing loyalty.

The following morning, at the earliest decent hour, Gart and kinsmen went in search of Mahn-so-ni.

"Come on, let's go see our baby," Mahn-so-ni beckoned.

He was referring, of course, to the reed craft now nearing completion. It was moored in the lagoon inside the city walls and would have to pass the narrow canal gate to find its way to the Euphrates and the sea.

"There she is!" Mahn-so-ni flung his arm in an enthusiastic, if unnecessary, gesture. The fat bundle of reeds with upswept prow and stern was easy to see and familiar in form, if not in scale. This skiff was thirty paces long.

While the herdsmen were examining the craft in detail Mahn-so-ni drew Gart aside.

"You probably should know, Gart, that Kre-eg, Nam-Ku and Ni-Pada-Dan called on me last evening.

Gart's eyebrows went up in question.

"It seems," Mahn-so-ni continued, "that the night of your fracas, a number of other bad things happened, including break-ins and theft and destruction at Nam-Ku's brewery and warehouse. He was very upset and feels our present government is putting us all in danger through its inability to act. Ni-Pada-Dan is in complete sympathy and says the condition of our lugal is not likely to improve.

"In spite of our recent efforts, Gart, I don't see anything helpful coming out of the City Council. I agreed with their suggestion last night that something else must be done; perhaps an emergency council, small enough to act, but big enough to represent most factions. What do you think?"

"Oh, I agree," said Gart, rubbing the remaining tender spot on his head, surprised he was being consulted regarding such a serious matter.

"I thought you might," said the councilman. "We may need you to talk to Bruzi for us. We should have no problem with the army, if we go about it right."

The cousins had now completed their inspection and now came right to the point.

"When will it be ready to go, sir?"

"Umm, yes...well…" Mahn-so-ni hedged. "The craft is almost complete, but a few things have held us up."

"So, when?"

"Very soon, we hope," Gart said, trying to get Mahn-so-ni off the hook. His kinsmen looked a little skeptical but soon departed to complete their trading and to return home. They received a promise that Gart would visit them next spring before the herds went out. If possible, he would bring his wife and firstborn. Next spring was far off, but he felt a sense of foreboding as he made his promises.

It was nearing midday and Gart had just interrupted his work to speak to Bruzi when Kre-eg came striding out of the noontime sunlight into the shadows of the armory. Once he spotted them, Kre-eg gestured with forefinger and arm that he wanted them both to join him across the street for lunch.

They were early and the eatery was deserted. Kre-eg ordered the waiter to bring them barley cakes and a jar of beer. Then he turned his attention to Bruzi.

"Bruzi, we are forming a committee to act for the lugal. As you probably know, he just isn't able to take the lead now and we have some serious problems. We would like you to be a full member of a small, carefully selected council, to act as regent."

Bruzi decided to forego the beer. He sat back. He could feel a cold wave rolling upward from his feet. This sounded like treason! Had he misjudged these young men? He would never have taken them for conspirators. On the face of it, what they were talking about in such careful terms was against everything he had ever stood for. He looked around to be sure no one overheard.

"Overthrowing the lugal, especially now, when he has so little time? Is that wise? This could be very dangerous. After all, there are steps to be taken, customs to consider."

"No, no! you misunderstand," Kre-eg protested. "There is no exact precedent for this situation, but we are being as proper as we can be, contacting all the right people, including you.

"Ni-Pada-Dan assures us that the Royal Physician, who is sympathetic, can get Demmuzi to agree to step down. We could say it was temporary, in case he should recover soon."

"Soon?" asked Gart, not realizing why and immediately regretting his intrusion.

"Yes, Gart, he doesn't have that much time," Kre-eg replied, keeping his eyes on Bruzi.

"But why me?" Bruzi resumed, somewhat reassured, but still feeling a little tremulous over the magnitude of the matter.

"We want the army well represented," Kre-eg said. "And you are young enough to have some new ideas and...."

"And...?" Bruzi questioned.

"And ...well," Kre-eg flashed his famous charming smile, "Of course...if your family and their friends understand our purposes here..."

"Of course," Bruzi answered dryly. Am I being played for a sucker here? he asked himself. I smell Nam-Ku behind this. "And just who would make up this council?"

"Nothing is final yet, but the way it looks now, there would be six full members: two for the army, including you, one seat for the temple, one seat for the city council, and two seats for the royal household."

"Representing the royal household would be...?"

"Ni-Pada-Dan and — myself."

"Representing the royal household?"

"Yes, as acting commander of the Royal Bodyguard and...."

And, perhaps, representing certain financial interests, Bruzi was thinking.

"Of course," he answered as dryly as before. "And the other seats?"

"For the temple — it would be awkward if we didn't ask the high priest, Ni-Zum-Ka. For the city council, the official leader is Shi-ten-Ku. For the other army seat, I don't think we dare bypass General Mem-el," Kre-eg said.

"Well, Kre-eg, that's not exactly a bunch of firebrands you are asking me to join. Can this group change anything? What about Alkohn? He won't take this lightly. You say you were just with Mahn-so-ni. Where does he fit into this?"

"Oh, I forgot to mention something," Kre-eg resumed. "Each full member would select an alternate, who would attend but not vote unless the member was absent. It's likely that the names you just mentioned will be chosen. What do you say, Bruzi?"

"I have no taste for this whole matter, but I couldn't agree more that something needs to be done, and if we don't do it, who will? Bruzi heard himself saying, as though his voice was far off. "My inclination would be to say *yes*. I will have to discuss it with my family first, of course."

"Of course," answered Kre-eg with a faint but understanding smile.

"Time to go," announced Kre-eg as he arose. "By the way, Gart, you are to be my alternate on this council," he dropped this in his most matter-of-fact tone of voice.

Now it was Gart's turn to draw back with concern.

"Me? Why me? I have no influence. I don't represent anyone but myself!"

"Precisely! You are probably the only person I really trust," Kre-eg answered crisply.

"Why would you trust me?" Gart wanted to know.

"Because you don't buy any shit from anyone, especially me, without a lot of questions. I'll see you later."

Gart said neither *yes* nor *no*. This, of course, meant *yes*, but without his formal consent. He had just bought into something, but…what? As he picked his way through the crowed street Gart was as wide awake as he had ever been, yet he could feel a sense of oppression, a heaviness sifting down through his body.

"Gart! Oh, Gart! What a stroke of luck!" It was Mahn-so-ni and one of his grown sons. Gart looked up, surprised. Then he realized his feet had mysteriously brought him to the front of his mentor's house.

Mahn-so-ni's son threw Gart a brief wave and sauntered on into the family home. At first Gart could say nothing in response. Then, grasping a few mental shreds from this other world of his, he said, "By the way, about the lugal, someone said that he didn't have much more time. Is his health worse?"

"Not that I know, Gart. However, it is now eleven — maybe eleven and a half years since his coronation."

Gart looked at Mahn-so-ni without comprehension.

"You do know about the twelve year term, don't you?"

"I can't say that I do."

"I'm surprised at that... but I shouldn't be. I suppose it has been a hundred, maybe a hundred and twenty years since a lugal actually completed a twelve-year term. You need to have the background on that." The councilman squinted as though lost in his calculations, then nodded as if agreeing with his result. At this point, the son reappeared at the entry gate to summoned him to the evening meal.

Still stuck with his mystery, Gart turned homeward. On his way he remembered there was probably another work session at his house that night. With all that had been dropped on him today he should keep quiet this evening.

His foot was on the first tread of the stairs to the apartment when he heard:

"NO," (The word was obviously inside his head.) (step)
"SOMETHING"...(It was his voice but so very certain.)(step)
"IS"... (step)
"IS"... (step)
"TRYING"....(step)
"TO HAPPEN.....(step)..
"HERE"........... (step)

These were *her* words but *his* voice.

"NOT BETWEEN YOU"....(Step)...
"BUT...AMONG..YOU"....(Step)... (Step)...
"AMONG...YOU .."
Whew! The landing. He was drenched with sweat.

Everything was very quiet. He peeked through the door. Leah, Nin-ana-Me and Sari were leaning over the table, poring over a series of tablets by lamplight. All glanced up, smiling, except Orson who waved a greeting with his stylus as he kept his eyes fixed on his text.

"May I?" Gart approached the table, indicating the tablets with his hand, forgetting his resolve to be a listener only.

"Surely," answered the Priestess.

The light was very poor and the characters quite small. Many of the characters were unfamiliar to Gart, in spite of some recent coaching from Leah. He did notice that empty spaces had been left between groups of lines. This was not usual. He had stooped to inspect the tablets but now straightened up, fearing his question was a dumb one.

"I hesitate to say this," Nin-ana-Me said, "because the gods have not allowed me to have the usual experience of pregnancy, but I am convinced what we are doing here is something like a pregnancy. It is like a pregnancy *among* us."

"AMONG US?" Gart said, louder than he intended.

"Yes, that's it," she continued. "I admit that is an awkward way of putting it."

"You're expecting something really important to happen here, in Ur, soon?" Sari's face revealed a luminosity not seen before.

"Yes! Yes, right here in Ur. Soon? Well, that may not be quite the word and maybe someday it will move on to another place, but right now it is going on here, among us."

"What's going on? Did I miss something?" Orson with his heavy bundle of tablets had just come through the door.

"No, I don't think you missed anything, Orson. It's you who had the imagination to invent new symbols for those little connecting words that are so important to our work."

"It's not just the words," said Sari. "It's the way they are arranged and the pauses, blank spaces, in between. It gives it rhythm, like a singer would do." Here she looked at Orson with a triumphant smile.

Orson beamed at her with a crooked, self-conscious grin.

"I hope it is like a song," said Nin-ana-Me, calmer now.

"So..., How many final copies do you need?" Orson asked.

"Twelve will do very nicely," his employer answered. "How much time will it take?"

Orson looked questioningly at his assistants. "Oh, say...three, four...maybe five days, including the firing."

"Shall we start tonight?" asked Leah. "The cooking fire in the courtyard probably isn't out."

"So where will all these copies be going? "Gart asked.

"In the dead of night and surrounded by a great cloud of mystery," the Priestess answered, "one copy shall be installed in the masonry of each of the four principal gates of the city. How is that for impudence?"

"But you are the Chief Priestess!" protested Gart. "Surely you would have the right to do that, in broad daylight, if you wished, although I'm afraid most of the people who use those gates can't read."

"Chief Priestess! Hah!" that lady answered. "If anything could kill the desire to read, it would be a title like that. "Four copies will go to the palace and temple compounds. I can put them in not too obvious, but visible, places in the palace and temple record rooms. A copy will be placed on altars in the House of Nannar and the House of Nin-Gal, the snake permitting, of course.

"Gart, would you arrange for the gateway installations?"

Gart nodded in assent. "When is this to be done? And what about the other four copies?" he asked.

"It should be carried out very soon. I'll keep one copy. One is for Orson and the other two must await the arrival of my brother from Erech. He is a man very wise in the ways of both men and the stars and I would like his opinion before we distribute these. I received word yesterday he will be here within a week."

Sari had returned and was standing silently, still holding the fresh clay tablets. "There's a man down by the fire. I don't know who he is," she said.

Gart stepped out quickly to the landing and down three or four treads before he turned and came back.

"It's Surbec," he said. "I suppose he's expecting to spend the night there again." He turned to Leah. "Do we have any left-over food, some bread or something? He can just as well tend the fire for us and turn the tablets tonight."

"I'll find something," she said. "What about these?" She pointed to the rejected copies in the corner.

"Those should go to the dump outside the city walls, but be sure to smash them thoroughly to protect them from the wrong kinds of curiosity," Nin-ana-Me explained.

"I'm sure that Surbec can do that in return for breakfast," said Gart. I'll tell him what you said."

Nin-ana-Me, Sari, Orson and Gart all filed down the stairs, laden with various bundles and baskets of supplies. It was near midnight and their excitement had given way to a deep weariness.

CHAPTER SEVEN

The following day, Gart left the armory early to meet with Mahn-so-ni before the big meeting. When he arrived in front of the Royal Residence the entire plaza was deserted, except for a small knot of workmen who were doing something to the north wall of the building. As he approached them he recognized Mahn-so-ni's voice giving meticulous, slightly impatient, instructions to someone who was on his knees repointing the mortar between the bricks. After a few minutes, Mahn-so-ni noticed Gart and his intense scrutiny of the proceedings.

"Oh, there you are, Gart, and right on time, as usual! Ah yes, this is an opportunity for me to fill you in about that twelve-year term."

Nearby Gart saw Kre-eg, Ni-Pada-Dan and a third man. As he turned, he could see his florid face. It was Nam-Ku, Kre-eg's father, and he was doing most of the talking.

"I'll start with the most stickery part," said Mahn-so-ni. He paused and thought to himself, I should take care to present this story in a fair way. Gart is from out in the sticks. I'm not sure how this will sound to someone who isn't city-bred. Why is it that I feel I need to be protective? Why have I taken such an interest in him? Maybe he reminds me of myself at his age. He has more hustle than most, even my boys. Good men though, good solid men. His frown was directed at mid-courtyard as he resumed his explanation.

"It seems that in olden times our wise forefathers decided if a king was able to reign for twelve years, he was worthy to be sacrificed."

"Sacrifice him? Sacrifice the king?" said Gart, dumbfounded. "I don't understand that at all!"

"Neither did I — when I was reminded of the story," the older man responded. "After I had agreed to take an active role in the city council, both Ni-Pada-Dan and Ni-Zum-Ka, the High Priest, sought me out to remind me that this issue was coming up."

"They actually sacrificed the king — to Nannar?" Gart was visibly struggling with the idea.

"To Nannar — well now, even that question is more complicated than it sounds. I'm hardly the one to be explaining these things to you. I'm just a businessman, an old construction worker."

The councilman paused, staring off toward the wall under repair some fifty yards to the east, then he turned to Gart.

"You really didn't know about this?" Mahn-so-ni's voice had a slight pleading quality, as if he hoped to be excused from defending the matter.

"Not at all. You say it hasn't actually been done for well over a hundred years? How did that happen?"

"That's what I asked Ni-Zum-Ka," Mahn-so-ni answered. "Ni-Zum-Ka can be a bit of a bore, as you may see shortly, but he knows a lot of history. He claims there have been nineteen lugals since the last proper ritual sacrifice."

"So what happened to them?" Gart asked.

"According to Ni-Zum-Ka's count, seven died in battle, several died in fires or epidemics and three died of mysterious causes in the eleventh year. Six others managed to stretch out their time a few years. Some appointed slaves as substitute kings for a few days, strangled them and then pretended to start over, or just ignored the rule. But none lived for long after such maneuvers."

"They could do…that?" Gart was incredulous.

"Well, they did evidently. In one case it got rather out of hand. The slave was smarter than the king. In most cases where substitutes were used the lugals were deposed in a few years and that method hasn't been tried recently." He fell silent but continued to think, surely Demmuzi — poor old guy — he must have understood all about that when he agreed to be lugal. What could he be thinking these days?

Gart was still trying to make sense of what he had heard when he noted several of the small groups nearby were going into the lugal's residence.

"That's Kre-eg's father with him, there," he said to Mahn-so-ni. "Will he be on the council?"

"Yes, that's Nam-Ku, all right. No, he won't be going inside tonight. But as long a Kre-eg and Ni-Pada-Dan are there, he'll be a factor."

Gart and Mahn-so-ni entered a wide foyer on the ground floor. A handsome wooden staircase hugged the right wall of the entry hall. Just beyond this was the large Royal Audience Room, which extended the width of the back of the building. Gart admired the wooden pillars and beams of the ceiling. These were the largest timbers he had ever seen used in construction. The room was rather dark, as the only windows were a series of peepholes placed very high on both side walls. Soon servants appeared with lighted torches, which they placed in large pottery urns on a low dais against the back wall. Gart could verify this was their usual place from the large deposits of soot on the ceiling above each holder. Evidently the staff was expecting a long meeting, as they quickly returned with large baskets of pitch-soaked replacements. Low stools had been arranged in two concentric arcs at the back of the chamber. Two of the stools were on the front edge of the dais. The semicircles faced them.

As the members continued to file in, and the room came into focus, Gart began to feel slightly awkward. Except for Kre-eg, he was by far the youngest man in attendance.

At this point Lah-ma-Nah, the physician, came down the stairs and walked directly to Kre-eg. After they had spoken a few words, which evidently included some humor, Kre-eg drew himself up to his full height and announced:

"Sirs, please continue to take your ease for a few minutes. We are still expecting two members, and we are hoping for a message of welcome from His Highness — soon!" Lah-ma-Nah was still chuckling when he spotted Gart and Mahn-so-ni. He walked over to them, greeting each in turn.

"Is Ni-Pada-Dan up there with Demmuzi?" Mahn-so-ni jerked his head toward the top of the stairs.

"Yes," laughed the physician. "The old fellow ran me off. He said he had had enough of my clucking over him and that he could handle that uppity Lord Chamberlain just fine without me. Ni-Pada-Dan will earn anything he gets from him tonight. His Highness is feistier than I have seen him in a long time. That's a good sign, I think!

"Let's grab some stools and go over to the corner where we can talk," Lah-ma-Nah said. But, once seated, he stared silently at the floor for some time before he looked up and began. "Actually, it is not thoughts of impending death that bother Demmuzi, it is his overwhelming, if off and on, experience of utter gloom. He says he wants to die but is sure he must live on in misery and disgrace. He feels he is not fit to die in any way, and that he certainly is not healthy enough to be a proper sacrifice. I think that is the opinion of the High Priest, also."

There was an extended pause. Lah-ma-Nah again studied the hard-packed clay floor in front of him.

"What I don't understand," said Gart, squirming a bit, "is where the idea came from in the first place. I know it hasn't actually happened lately, but evidently our present lugal agreed to it. How was such a thing supposed to help the city? How could they expect anybody who had any ability to lead, who had any ambition, to agree to such a thing?"

"Ahh, you have it, right there," said Lah-ma-Nah.

"Protecting the people from the ambition of their leaders — personal ambition anyway — and unrealistic dreams of empire has been a special tradition in Ur," said Mahn-so-ni. "That's why the official title is *Lugal, Tenant of the God.* We get sloppy and talk about the 'king' and 'His Highness,' but that is incorrect, if you understand the tradition."

"That's right," agreed Lah-ma-Nah. "We have had an advantage here in Ur. We have a strong and visible patron god. Nannar-Sin can be seen every night. This helps the temple hold the attention and loyalty of the people, even if they aren't inclined to think too much."

"Yes," added Mahn-so-ni, "even though the palace and the temple are here together in the same compound and are supposed to work together, they also act as checks and balances on each other, to protect the people."

"But I thought the lugal was supposed to be the head of the temple too," objected Gart.

"Oh, you're right, Gart, in theory," said Lah-ma-Nah. "But evidently the lugals have varied a lot in what they made of that. Demmuzi seemed quite interested at first, especially after the new high priestess came. Now, of course, he can't stay interested in anything. Not much direction is coming out of the palace side of the compound these days. As for the temple side, except for the flurry about the snake, I don't see much there, either. They don't seem to have any real program. You know how the high priest is — and brother Shem-Ki." This last was directed to Mahn-so-ni, who smiled faintly and nodded.

"About the only one awake over there is Nin-ana-Me, the High Priestess," the physician explained to Gart. "She could shape them up, but they are too afraid of her. That's probably why she isn't here tonight."

"Why would anyone be afraid of her?" Gart asked quickly, then bit his lip. He hoped he hadn't shown too much interest here.

"Well, what they would say is — and this is not just a guess on my part —" continued Lah-ma-Nah, "'You better watch out for her. She may claim to represent Nin-Gal the feminine side of our patron god, but behind that lurks the bitch-goddess, Inanna. Before we know it, we will be sucked back into the old fertility religion; dancing and fornicating, and making sacrifices out in the grain fields.'"

"Instead of in a nice, well-regulated temple?" interrupted Mahn-so-ni.

"That's it, precisely." The physician's animated voice and gestures indicated this subject was very much alive for him. "Frankly, I don't buy it. I don't even think they really believe that themselves."

"Then why are they afraid of her?" asked Gart.

"I think she is just too much for them. She is too intense, too imaginative, and maybe the only one among them with a true calling for what she is doing. They are afraid of losing control."

"So she has to be careful not to scare them?" Gart asked.

"Indeed, she does," answered Lah-ma-Nah.

They lapsed into silence, waiting for the meeting to begin. By now Gart's initial shock about what he heard had subsided. He noticed that now he felt quite comfortable, as if he belonged there. These two men really seemed to be putting out for me, Gart thought to himself. Lah-ma-Nah scarcely knows me. Our only real link is that funny old guy, Man-to-Shi. Now that's an interesting thought!

The three men stretched and looked around the room. Several of the other members were fidgeting or pacing, seemingly annoyed with the delay. Colonel Alkohn was occupying himself by replacing the burning tapers.

Gart's unease was beginning to return. He felt he just had to say something.

"Well, I just can't imagine myself accepting an office, no matter how glorious, with the understanding that in just twelve years then.... Could you?" He looked searchingly at Mahn-so-ni.

Both older men looked at him but no one spoke. Mahn-so-ni was gazing over Gart's shoulder, now at his shoulder and now up at his eyes, evidently seeing him, yet looking beyond him. Gart had experienced that type of look before. But this was something more strange, more powerful. There was no locking onto these eyes. Gart's vision became blurry. Mahn-so-ni's stool seemed to sprout arms and a back, like a throne. A stick appeared in his hand. Now, it became a scepter!

"Well, Gart," he spoke deliberately, "I am quite certain that no one has ever asked me such a question, nor had it ever occurred to me." Then why did it effect me so? Mahn-so-ni asked himself. He suddenly felt lost. He wasn't exactly frightened, it was just that nothing looked familiar.

Gart glanced at Lah-ma-Nah who was looking at the two of them. He appeared to be very calmly taking in their conversation but giving no indication of what he thought.

The scattered group all turned at the sound of hurried footsteps in the entryway. It was Bruzi and a younger man whom Gart did not recognize.

"I hope we haven't delayed the meeting," said Bruzi, a bit out of breath. "We had some — uh — complications getting here. This is Na-tem-Na; my alternate member. He is well worth waiting for."

This man appeared to be about Gart's age. He was taller than average, lean and lithe. His faint, bemused smile seemed to indicate he was surprised to be there.

Immediately upon the arrival of the latecomers, Kre-eg signaled to a servant. The sound of hurriedly ascending footsteps was soon followed by the more ponderous but rapid descent of Ni-Pada-Dan. That august official, his hair a bit awry, went directly to the dais and gestured for Kre-eg to join him there, and for the others to bring themselves and the scattered stools back into formation. His initial expression of annoyance evaporated, and he gave a big sigh of relief.

"Sirs," the Lord Chamberlain began, "His Highness will not be joining us this evening, but he does send his greetings to the members of this council and does give us his permission to act on his behalf, 'for now,' as he puts it, on all matters of state we shall deem requiring our intervention. He also says he doubts it will do any good." The old fart! the Lord Chamberlain thought to himself. Surely this is the most frustrating lugal ten generations of my family have ever had to deal with. If he were evil, or even just mean, I would know what to do. But tomorrow he may be sweet reason, or not. We must get something into place here tonight. I have to get some recognition and more authority if the palace is to have any control at all.

"I will call this meeting to order," he resumed aloud, "although I want it to be understood that this body has been formed out of the concerns of many people and not just my own. In a few minutes I will turn the actual conduct of the meeting over to Captain Kre-eg, the commander of the Royal Bodyguard. I do not want anyone to feel that I am using my position to stifle discussion or promote my plans."

"If he has any," Mahn-so-ni whispered to Gart from the safety of their back benches.

Kre-eg stood up immediately. Before Ni-Pada-Dan was fully seated, Kre-eg had begun.

"Gentlemen, it is a great honor to serve you as chairman. First, I will ask the Lord Chamberlain to say just a few words about the history and purpose of this meeting for the sake of us younger members."

If Kre-eg was at all self-conscious about the contrived nature of his opening, Gart couldn't detect it. Ni-Pada-Dan was back onto his feet speaking in a smooth rapid manner that sounded to Gart much more like Kre-eg than anything he had heard from the mouth of the senior official.

"This committee is well based on custom and has met in times of crisis ever since the City Council became too big to function well. It last met twelve years ago prior to the selection of the new lugal. General Mem-el and I were there as alternate members.

"The composition of six members and six alternates is traditional. They form the auspicious number twelve. Customarily, the alternates speak only at the request of their full member and they vote only in his absence."

"Thank you, Your Excellency." Kre-eg was up again, perfectly on cue. "If there is no objection, we will proceed under the customary rules. Are there any opening statements or questions from the members? General Mem-el, sir?"

"Yes, I want to start off by saying a few positive things." The old soldier stood, slowly drawing his impressive frame up to full military posture. "I want you to know that I do agree to these meetings, but I don't see any emergency. I would like to point out that we have a well organized Guard, and plans to strengthen it are proceeding. We should have Colonel Bruzi tell us about that.

"There are always a few criminals around. We just need to get these ornery young bucks into the Guard and out of town, march them through the marshes for a few days and sweat the meanness out of them. A good safe fight would probably help, too. That's just human nature."

For the first time, the General paused and surveyed his audience. His gaze stopped at Colonel Alkohn who was seated to Gart's right. The Colonel's expression was serious, almost a scowl.

"I can see," said the old soldier, "that my alternate does not entirely agree. It would be only fair that we hear him out."

Before Alkohn could fully rise, Kre-eg held up his hand.

"First it would be proper for full members to have their turn if they wish," he said. "I recognize Ni-Zum-Ka."

Showing his teeth, that young pup, Alkohn was thinking as he settled back onto his seat. In spite of the slight affront to his pride, he admired Kre-eg's audacity.

The tall old priest rose smoothly. He, too, was looking very concerned.

"I wish I shared the general's confidence but I fear we have something more serious here than a few 'ornery young bucks.' We of the temple are noticing problems beyond hot weather and poor crops. Our tenants are using excuses to avoid paying rents due. They are downright insolent. Someone may be encouraging them in this. The devout seemed to be falling away from spiritual observances until the recent flurry about this sacred snake thing, and I give them no credit for that. Recently, there has been desecration of a number of the minor altars in the courtyard, and thievery and random destruction in the temple storehouses and shops. Something serious — fearful — is afoot."

Ni-Zum-Ka stopped speaking but he did not sit down.

"Was there something further?" Kre-eg prompted.

"Yes, yes there is!" he roused from his thoughts. "Where are the funds coming from for all these new arms and soldiers? We hope you are not expecting the temple treasury to pay for it. We get hit pretty hard every year. Many years ago, as a favor to the then lugal, we agreed to help with these disgraceful Lagash payments." Here the speaker stopped abruptly.

"I presume everyone here knows about that?" His survey of the audience revealed many knowing nods and two or three blank expressions. "Well, they should. At least this group should deal with it honestly." He sat down with emphasis.

"Thank you, sir. Did the colonel wish to speak now?" asked Kre-eg.

Alkohn rose slowly and stared for a moment in the direction of Kre-eg's belt buckle. He was weighing within himself the wisdom of being open with this group. He had no great confidence in the abilities of any of the members. But feeling a compulsion to say something, he began:

"I do not know if this is an emergency or not. However, I do take it very seriously, whatever this thing is. I have been asked to provide some night to night tactics and I find myself very puzzled and provoked. Just what the hell is happening here in our city? Maybe it's nothing, but it certainly seems like something is trying to happen."

Gart snorted loudly, then quickly feigned a coughing fit to cover his embarrassment as he felt the eyes of the assembly come to bear on him. Nin-ana-Me's favorite expression, he thought. Surely they can't be talking about the same thing. Or could they?

"Night after night," Alcohn continued, "we get reports of thefts and damage to property, of noisy assemblages, of shouted blasphemies and insults to the authorities, but when we get there, we only hear scurrying feet and find an occasional petty thief or drunken reveler. An invading army I can understand. Raiders and cattle thieves can be dealt with, but who are these people and what do they want? Who can help me to understand this thing?" The speaker remained standing. He was thinking, now I've done it! I made myself look weak in front of this strange collection of people!

Gart was so impressed by the earnestness and self-vulnerability in his commander's appeal he was not paying attention to his own actions. What should have been a very discrete finger signal and questioning look directed to Kre-eg was picked up by Alkohn.

"I am wondering if our chairman can help me here?" the speaker continued.

Oh shit, what's the matter with this country boy! Kre-eg was thinking as he flashed his famous smile at everyone, except Gart.

"What my esteemed alternate is reminding me of here," he finally began, "is that we have been observing a certain group of young men for some time. They are often seen in the canteens together, and seem to be intensely engaged in discussing something. Just what they are up to, we don't know." Kre-eg sounded irritated. "They appear to be a mix of various classes, trades, and tribes. They are cocky, brash, impudent, but I don't know that they have committed any crimes."

Alkohn raised a finger, as though to pursue the matter further, but Kre-eg shut him off, again.

"Thank you, Colonel, but I believe one of the members wishes to speak."

Shi-ten-Ku, the titular head of the City Council, had arisen and was awaiting their proper attention. Mahn-so-ni leaned over and whispered in Gart's ear.

"You will now hear from 'The Great Compromiser' and see how he got his name and job at City Council."

"Gentlemen, our Lord Chamberlain was very wise, indeed, in calling this council at this time. I, like the general, have great confidence in our present system's ability to continue to serve us."

As Shi-ten-Ku gained momentum, his voice became more melodious and his gestures more graceful. "However, I submit to you, that much of this city's problem is lack of visible leadership. I do understand that His Highness has been ill and that his illness has been mysterious and stubborn. Am I not right, Doctor?"

He looked at Lah-ma-Nah, whose wan smile and slight nod provided what little encouragement the speaker needed to continue.

"This leaves us all like a family without a father. If the people could just see him and feel his concern for them, I am sure we could lead them to realize just how fortunate we are to be here in Ur. Surely we can think of some occasion for celebration, display, parades and processions. Let us be active and not just accept these signs of distress."

There was no immediate response. Had they all been charmed or put to sleep by his melodic presentation?

A parade? Ni-Pada-Dan asked himself. Surely the old fool must be joking. What is there to celebrate when our whole society seems to be falling apart? No, wait, that may not be so stupid after all. It will give me a handle. I will draft a committee.

"Oh, I agree, something must be done." He sprang to his feet with enthusiasm. "Surely we can work something out. What do you think, Bruzi? Kre-eg? Doctor?"

"We do have a lot of green troops," said Bruzi. "They have never been on parade. It would give them something to work for — and Kre-eg, you need to shape up those Royal Bodyguard troopers." Bruzi could hear his own voice as if it were far off. What he was saying was all obviously true, but was he buying into a sham, just something to be doing when no one understood the problem?

"The household troops do need a change of routine," admitted Kre-eg.

"What about our lugal? Doctor, can we expect anything from him?" The Lord Chamberlain was now showing solid enthusiasm.

"That all depends. Some days, yes, something." Lah-ma-Nah's voice trailed off and was lost as the next person spoke.

"Everybody loves a party," said Ni-Zum-Ka. "Of course the last three Full Moon Festivals didn't bring in nearly what they cost us. This is different. The military can foot the bill here."

"If the chairman pleases, I will join him, Colonel Bruzi and our Chief Councilman, in arranging a large celebration in two or three weeks. That's enough business for one night." The Lord Chamberlain nodded at Kre-eg with more assertiveness than he had previously revealed.

"Then so be it. This meeting is adjourned," Kre-eg declared.

Mahn-so-ni was tugging at Gart's elbow.

"Do you want to go with me now?" he asked.

As they passed Kre-eg at the foot of the stairs, Gart gave him a little thump on the arm with his knuckles.

"You handled that right well, Mister Chairman."

"Yes, of course I did," Kre-eg answered loftily. "and as for you, Mister Alternate, in the future, the rule about not speaking until requested will include you sitting on your hands throughout the meeting. If you throw another surprise like tonight's at me, I will call on you to make a speech on the sex life of sheep."

Kre-eg could have been joking, but Gart knew he was not. Suddenly, he felt very tired. It had been a long day. The rush of energy was gone.

Tired as he was, Gart could not resist asking Mahn-so-ni one last question. They were passing the spot where they had seen Nam-Ku holding forth at the beginning of the evening.

"Sir, what is the connection between Nam-Ku and Ni-Pada-Dan? Are they related?"

"Related? Oh my, no! Not by blood," laughed the councilman. "And as for their relationship — hmmn? They are either the best of enemies or the worst of friends. They are quite involved in a business way. I guess it's business."

"Yes...?"

"Well, the story goes, that Ni-Pada-Dan, who is the descendent of a long line of councilors to the lugal, had always considered himself above things that bored him; the details of household finance — even the Royal Household. They were in bad shape, but there was no one to say *no* to him until the temple brought Brother Shem-Ki aboard to straighten things out. Shem-Ki, a hard-headed business man, was not impressed by the Lord Chamberlain's aristocratic background. As a result, Ni-Pada-Dan had to come up with much barley very fast or disgrace his family. He quickly found out that the only one in the city who had that much grain on hand was Nam-Ku. Of course, there was a price, and Dan has been paying ever since, in one way or another.

"But that's enough, Gart. You are a bad influence. You bring out the gossip in me."

Gart laughed. "We'll call it history. Thank you very much and good night."

As they parted ways, Gart muttered to himself, "This whole thing…pretty ridiculous…and stickier…trickier. What have I gotten into? Well feet, take me home, before I sleep in the street." And they did.

Leah had received word from Nin-ana-Me that her visitor had arrived. Her brother came bringing formal greetings from the king of Erech to Demmuzi, who had already granted him a brief audience. The prince had spent two nights at the observatory with Mer-luke and his assistants. He would depart late in the evening, as there would be a full moon and he preferred to travel at night.

Since Orson would be commander of the watch they could proceed with posting and placing the result of their long labors that very night. Leah and Sari had completed all of the copies on order. Orson had checked each one and declared them fit to travel. Nin-ana-Me and her brother would come by the apartment to pick up his copies on his way out of the city.

"They are coming now!" Leah went to the stair landing to greet them.

Nin-ana-Me and the man, whom she introduced as Prince An-Shan, came upstairs. His party of several men and donkeys remained in the street outside the courtyard.

The Prince did look a little like Nin-ana-Me, especially the broad forehead, but he was taller, slightly gray and leaner. He acknowledged the introductions in a preoccupied way and began to inspect one of the tablets awaiting him.

"Did you do this?" he looked at Leah, looking directly at her for the first time. "It is very well done!"

"Oh, I am merely the copyist," protested Leah, nicely blending pride and humility.

"There is nothing *mere* about it. This is fine work," he said. "I am also impressed with the writing style. Much is new here, but so logical, precise. It almost speaks to you."

"Our scribe, Orson, has great talent," said Nin-ana-Me.

The Prince continued to read. "I do have some questions," he said, "but you have obviously gone to considerable trouble and expense to compose and record this. You must have come to care a great deal for this city, these people."

After a moment of silence, Nin-ana-Me asked in a soft voice, "And the questions you mentioned?"

"Oh, just details." An-Shan searched the tablet again. "Here, at the last, it says 'the people of Nannar must *know* their grief.' Does that just mean understand it, or must they actually experience real suffering?"

Careful here! she thought. Is this poem really something about the stuff of everyday life, or am I about to burden two cities with ideas that apply only to me?

"Both formal thinking and direct experience are needed" she answered. "As I understand it, unless we speak out openly about the pain that we experience in life, we cannot use the message it brings to us. The wording is difficult here. The previous edition said, 'The people must see grief.' Orson has pointed out that this could be misunderstood."

The two tablets bound for Erech were now swaddled in cloth scraps from the tailor shop of Leah's father, then encased in a soft basket-bag withdrawn from Gart's newly acquired stock of trade goods. With a parting pat from Nin-ana-Me, the tablets were delivered to the Prince who, after proper, if restrained, nods to Leah and Gart, and a warm embrace for his sister, swiftly descended the stairs.

"This is the night?" Gart broke into Nin-ana-Me's moist-eyed reverie after what he considered a respectable pause.

"This is the night!" she answered with a bright smile.

The twelve final tablets had found their way to the courtyard hearth downstairs for the long baking process. Now there were ten.

"I will take with me the four copies I am to place inside the compound, if I may borrow another of your soft baskets, Gart. I will leave the four for the gates, plus the copies for myself and Orson with you. Someone will pick mine up tomorrow and bring you all your final pay. You can be sure that when the moon comes up, I will be thinking of all of you," she said.

The youthful sparkle in her eye and the hushed tones reminded Gart of the sworn conspiracies and secret meetings by the frog ponds of his boyhood.

It would be several hours before moonrise, and Leah urged Gart to rest with her before his adventures of the night. As the dusk lowered on the cooling city, Gart's eyelids lowered, too. His body would not allow a surrender to deep sleep, but a soft drowsiness comforted him.

The wind had shifted. He felt the welcome sea breeze through the narrow windows. With it came a familiar sound.

Tahh, tah, taahh.... Tahh, tah, tahh. Tah, tat, tat, tat, taahh.... The evening trumpet from the gate tower — caressing his brow, gently intermingling with his drowsy breathing. The horn was pleading, "Come inside now." But he could imagine the Prince and his little procession out beyond that gate, wending their way up river. Could they hear the horn calling? Would that sound go back with An-Shan and the tablets to Erech? Yes, it must. That sound, those words, verses — belong together, mustn't go too deep — sleep.

"Gart, Gart, wake up! Orson and the mason are here."

Gart cautiously descended the stairs, hanging onto the railing until he could shake himself awake. He had slept longer than he had intended. In the half light he could see Orson smiling and the mason, arranged for through Banarum, looking a little lost. Orson indicated the direction with a sweep of his free arm and they started off toward the north-east gate without speaking a word.

A few minutes later Gart was helping the mason select a good spot for the tablet to be cemented into the pillar just inside the gate, while Orson climbed the ladder of the watchtower to talk to the watchman. The light was much better now and Gart stepped back into a pool of moonlight. He could see Orson beckoning to him. He had climbed down from the watchtower to the runway along the top of the city wall. Once Gart reached the top of the wall and looked over the parapet, he understood why Orson had summoned him. The moon was just now rising from the marshes to the east. Tomorrow night would be the full moon festival, and Nannar was treating them to the splendors of his dress rehearsal.

"The old boy is really smiling on us tonight. That's a good omen," said Gart.

By the time they had reached the northwest gate, Nannar had lost a little of his girth, but the light seemed even better. As the mason didn't need his help, Gart climbed the watchtower with Orson. The watchman, an older man, was someone Gart had seen around the armory, but he did not know his name.

On noting the long copper trumpet in the corner of the tower, Gart said, "You must have been the one playing the gate call this evening. I could hear you from my house."

"Yes, Lieutenant. I played it tonight and most every night for the last ten years," he answered.

Gart looked off to the northwest where he could now see the first glint of the reflection of the moon on the Euphrates and thought of Prince An-Shan and his little caravan.

They reached the remaining gates without incident. Gart was pleased with his choice of masons. The tablets blended into the brick pillars and seemed to belong there. At each gate Gart collected dust from the area and rubbed it over the new mortar. It would take close inspection to suspect that the tablets were newly installed. They had now nearly completed the circuit of the wall, and Gart and the mason were free to go home. But since Orson was due to inspect the guard at the temple compound entrance, they chose to go slightly out of their way to accompany him.

"Whoa, what's this?" said Orson, as they rounded the corner of a building. The doors to the temple compound were standing wide open. No guards were in sight. "This is not right!" said Orson. "There should be two men here if the doors need to be open and one even if they are closed."

"Would you like to go home now?" Gart asked the mason. "Come to my house tomorrow evening and I will have your pay for you. We have to see about some things here."

The mason departed with a relieved, "Thank you, sir."

The two officers stepped into the moonlit compound. They found no guards inside the gate, but about seventy yards away, near the base of the ziggurat, was a cluster of people that began to scatter as they entered. Gart estimated there must be eight or nine of them. Two, who appeared to be carrying something, were going around the east corner toward the two ground-level temples, while the others dispersed toward the dairy pens and storehouses clustered around the north corner. No one came toward the gate.

"Let's follow those two with the bundles," Orson said.

They could see the two figures stop in front of the main altar on the northwest side of the temple of Nin-Gal, which faced, across some twenty yards of courtyard, the main altar of Nannar, now incorporated into that side of the ziggurat.

Meanwhile, Nannar had risen half way up the arch of the eastern sky. He seemed paler and more severe, yet flooded the little court with a cool radiance that reflected off of the whitewashed walls of both new and old temples, tempting the awestruck Gart to forget both danger and curiosity.

"This way," directed Orson in a faint whisper.

They skirted the northeast, then the northwest sides of the Royal Residence. They neither heard nor made any sound. They walked boldly toward the open-sided, thatched-roofed structure between the royal residence and the temple of Nin-Gal. This shelter was very familiar to Orson. It was the scribes' school where he had spent many years in perspiration and near despair. They were now in the shadow, and, if not invisible, at least obscure. By moving to the front of the building they moved within possible hearing range of the figures they were pursuing.

"Hey, don't we know those guys?" whispered Orson. "Yeah, that big fellow — oh, shit, it's Surbec. The little one, I can't see, but that basket with the cloth on it looks familiar.

"Yeah, yeah — it's got to be Bar-Shin. What the hell are they up to?" asked Gart.

The two young men placed the basket and two slender, elongated bundles on the ground directly in front of the Vessel of Containment, the large pottery urn that sat just in front of the altar. Surbec tiptoed to the urn and, shading his eyes with his hand, he stooped slightly to peer inside the vessel. He straightened up quickly. His whispered "Yesss!" was clearly audible to the observers. Bar-Shin gave a little leap of exultation, pumping one fist into the air, then bending over to opened his basket. He withdrew a dark, furry object.

"No! It's moving. It's a live animal!" Gart whispered.

"It's a mongoose," hissed Orson, muffling the whisper with his hand. "They are going for the snake. They must be crazy as hell."

Surbec rapped the urn with his knuckles, but jumped back, startled at the loud, sonorous "Bwannngg..." that resulted. Bar-Shin waved his companion off and pointed to one of the rolls on the ground. He returned the mongoose to the basket and unrolled the other bundle, which appeared to be a floor mat of rushes or grass. Surbec returned to the vessel, gingerly stirred it, using his rolled mat as a prod, and quickly stepped back. Within a few seconds, a hooded head appeared above the rim. It thrust in several directions, then disappeared.

"Damn, poke him again," said Bar-Shin, hardly bothering to whisper. "No! He's coming out! Get down here!"

In a sudden flurry of motion, Surbec leaped down the two low steps of the platform in front of the altar and unfurled his mat. Bar-Shin dropped his mat, took the mongoose out of the basket again and placed him on the ground, then quickly picked up his mat. The mats were evidently reinforced with a stick, on at least one edge, as the two men now held them up to form a funnel, flaring out from the basket.

During these activities, the snake had finished removing all of its eight-foot length from its earthenware bedroom. At first it moved slowly but gained momentum as it headed straight toward the three creatures and the strange structure before it.

"Sttt! Get him, boy!" urged Bar-Shin.

The mongoose was awake, alert and hemmed in on at least two sides. He must have known his business as the sleek little carnivore made an immediate frontal attack. The serpent, however, was still in motion and had not established a position. As a result, the glancing encounter in mid-air resulted in little damage. The mongoose regained his feet and began to circle the cobra, which was now coiling for full battle. The second attempt was a clear miss and brought the mongoose back to the neck of the funnel. His third leap may have nicked the snake at the base of the expanded hood, but the attacker's momentum took him well beyond the mat-walled arena, from whence, with great speed and wisdom, he fled to seek refuge in the direction of the altar and the urn.

"Come back and fight, you little bastard!" shrieked Bar-Shin, as he dropped his mat and went in hot pursuit. Spotting his quarry between the urn and the altar, the young man leaped to the capture, but with even less skill than his pet. Not only did he miss the mongoose but the urn overturned with a resounding clang, showering a few small chips on the frustrated young man as he sprawled down the steps.

"Oh, no! I'm bleeding, I'm bit! I'm snake-bit," whimpered Bar-Shin.

"Not this snake, she didn't," said Surbec. "She went that way." He pointed to the south corner of the temple of Nin-Gal, where Gart and Orson could see a rapidly receding black and wavy line.

"Hey, let's get out of here!" said the revived Bar-Shin. "Run!"

Only now, with their mute fascination broken, did Gart and Orson realize that there was a hubbub on the other side of the ziggurat. They could hear the bellowing of cattle, shouts and the sound of running feet.

"Us too," said Orson. "How are we going to explain this?"

"How were they going to explain this?" The question seemed even more complicated by the time Orson and Sari appeared at Gart's apartment the following evening. It was only then Gart heard the full story of what Orson had seen.

"Just after I left you, I found the night patrol. They were struggling with two prisoners whom they had just captured. These were all they had been able to detain from a small mob that had suddenly come running around the corner of the compound wall. I recognized none of the prisoners and they all pled ignorance, of course.

"The patrol sergeant gave them a few good lashes with the whip but that didn't change their story," Orson continued. "When I turned in my report to the senior watch officer I mentioned the unattended compound gates, noises inside and the people running outside the gate. I didn't say anything about your being with me or any of that stuff we saw inside. The watch commander didn't seem too interested. He blamed the temple personnel for the open gates and didn't pursue the matter."

"Why are you trying to protect Surbec and Bar-Shin?" Gart asked. "You...I mean we...could get into real trouble here."

Orson just shook his head silently, then finally said, "I don't know what those two were up to. I don't know who needs to know about it, or what they would do with such information if they had it. If we come forward we could be asked embarrassing questions about how we happened to be there. I think we should just wait and see if it all goes away."

Leah and Sari stopped their conversation and listened with concern to Orson's account. Now voices were audible downstairs and Sari went to investigate. It was Nin-ana-Me and her novice. They had come to pay Orson and his copyists as well as Gart and the mason. The payment was in temple tokens, which could draw grain from the temple stores or simply be used in barter. The Priestess emphasized that these came from her personal funds. Then she turned to Gart and asked:

"Did we pick a very good time, or a very bad time?"

"What do you mean, My Lady?" asked Gart cautiously.

"Well, I don't know what you know about it, but there was a major break-in and destruction of temple property last night. This must have been just after I had made my rounds distributing our new tablets. I don't know if anyone has even noticed them. The High Priest is outraged and everyone is very worried for their safety."

"Who do they think is responsible? Do you know any of the details?" asked Orson.

"Supposedly, they have two young men in custody, but they have said little that anyone can make sense of," answered Nin-ana-Me. "The temple dairy was ransacked. Several cows were slashed and two of them had their tails cut off. Storerooms, the temple record rooms, and the temple library were broken into, fodder and grain were strewn about, and clay tablets and tools were broken. A small fire was started, but it was quickly put out."

"Anything else?" asked Gart.

The woman paused a moment.

"Oh, yes, how could I forget!" She threw a sharply questioning look at Gart. Strange he should ask that, she thought, but she resumed her account. "On the other side of the ziggurat, at the altar of Nin-Gal, the Vessel of Containment was overturned and slightly damaged. The snake is gone. They say there is some blood.

Ni-Zum-Ka claims he has some 'objects of great interest' collected from the site, but he doesn't name them."

"Nothing has been said about the tablets?" asked Sari.

"Nothing. At least not yet," the Priestess answered.

No one seemed to know what else to say. Nin-ana-Me and her novice left and, shortly thereafter, Orson and Sari departed in a preoccupied jumble of murmurs and nods.

Two evenings after the night of the tablets the Regency Council met. Kre-eg called the meeting to order and immediately requested a report from Bruzi about the proposed parade and celebration which was now only a week away.

"I am pleased to report that preparations are well under way," Bruzi began. "There is a lot of enthusiasm among the troops and I am confident we can put on a good show, but I am a little unclear on a few points. Could some of the more senior members of the council...?" Here Bruzi spread open his hands and looked up, as though beseeching Ni-Pada-Dan in particular. "Could they just point out for me who it is we want to impress, and what points are we trying to make?"

After a brief pause, Ni-Zum-Ka, the Chief Priest, arose.

"Bruzi, I will try to answer you, but it will be a bit general and roundabout. Two nights ago the most recent of a series of impudent and outrageous attacks on us and our way of life occurred in the temple compound itself. This was no spontaneous outburst by hoodlums, as you can see by the following points:

"They took time to tempt the gatekeepers and get them drunk. There was a fairly large group of them, and they brought equipment with them, which fortunately, they left behind. Foremost among their mischief, they attacked the sacred snake at the altar of Nin-Gal, probably with a mongoose. This was a very shrewd move against a central symbol of our popular faith. What is worse, they evidently planned to replace one of our sacred writings..." the priest turned and stooped to confer with Mer-luke briefly. "...the classic *An Among Us; an Ode to Creation.* It was to be replaced by a subversive and threatening version.

"Fortunately for us, they badly miscalculated and were frightened off, leaving us not only our four original versions in various libraries and shrines, but also one copy of their substitute version in — of all places — a smelly mongoose basket. They may have realized that, by mistake, they had brought an unfired copy, which would tip us off. Otherwise the changes were subtle enough that they might have gone unnoticed.

"Now who are we dealing with here?" the priest continued. "It obviously included someone within the temple, or they would never have known those writings would have been on the altars that day." The old priest spoke with growing conviction.

"Is that the same as the tablet in the pillar just inside some of the city gates?" asked Shi-ten-Ku.

"I seldom go outside the city gates," said Ni-Zum-Ka, "so I do not recall. I think it is highly likely. As the title indicates, it is a very basic writing. Yes, yes, that must be it."

Gart was finding it difficult to follow Ni-Zum-Ka, then he noticed Mer-luke, who was glancing at the ceiling as if he were embarrassed.

"Bruzi," the priest continued, "I cannot entirely answer as to whom we will impress with military power, but I believe our enemy is within our walls, and I am determined to see that this rebellion is crushed. In this city there are only so many people with a captive mongoose, and certainly only a few scribes with the skills necessary to alter such documents, and I will find them!"

As Ni-Zum-Ka sat down, General Mem-el was already rising to speak. "My friend," he said, "that is a very interesting story you have to tell, and you come to some interesting conclusions. I am a little surprised to hear you so disturbed about the missing snake. I didn't think you were too fond of her."

"That is not the point," snapped the old priest. "Of course we don't worship snakes. We are a civilized people. At the most, the snake can be an omen, a reminder. For some people that may be helpful. The point is the harm intended, not the harm done."

"Oh, I see, no great loss, the snake, but I do join you in taking this matter seriously," said Mem-el. "Now this matter about the writings; threatening references, you say?"

"Yes."

"I don't mean to delay the council in this matter, but could we hear a little more about the threats?" asked the general.

Ni-Zum-Ka turned on his seat to confer with Mer-luke again before replying. "Well, for example, the revision ends by saying that the people of Nannar must see grief — or come to grief — something like that."

"And the original?" the interrogator continued.

"Oh, the original does mention the word 'grief,' but I have been assured it is in a different sense. It is not a threat." The High Priest's voice conveyed his annoyance.

"Are there other changes?" Mem-el persisted.

"Yes, yes, there are. No one major thing, but there are a number of changes. I don't feel it is appropriate to pursue that here. There was very definite tampering with the text."

"And you do see these textual changes as a danger and a concern to our fair city?" Mem-el had softened his tone to appease Ni-Zum-Ka.

"The spoken word can be the power that changes nations, and the written word can resound for generations." The old priest gathered himself up where he sat. Like a lion at bay, he seemed to gain strength from his utterances.

"Once again, very well spoken," said the old soldier. "What these marauders intended I do not know, but it does appear that, somehow they had in their possession a document entitled *Ode to An*, or was it *An Among Us*? This was on the precise evening a party, supposedly on a diplomatic mission of a vague nature, departed to return to Erech. Of course, you all know, Erech is the center of the now-languishing worship of their patron god: An. I shall say no more."

"Are you saying, sir, you think Erech has ambitions in this direction?" Bruzi asked in a very surprised tone.

"I didn't say that, Colonel," Mem-el answered, rising slowly and turning to face his audience. "You may say, 'Oh, Erech, she will continue up there, sleeping in the sun, dreaming of her distinguished past, as she has for one hundred and fifty years. She will continue her alliance with Umma, holding Lagash at bay, and therefore, she is our friend. But don't be so sure. Things change.

"Ambition makes strange friends. I urge you, continue to prepare this city for the dangers without and these minor matters here will fade away."

The general sat down as though he had carried the field.

As Shi-ten-Ku, the City Council President arose. Mahn-so-ni shared a faint smile and wink of anticipation with Gart.

"Mister Chairman, this is certainly a disquieting story. May I suggest that a show of civic unity and participation should send a warning to foreign meddlers, if there are such. I feel we should proceed with our plans for this celebration of — what was the title again?" Here the melodious one sought the eyes of Ni-Pada-Dan.

This old songbird has done me a great service, Ni-Pada-Dan was thinking as he got up to help him. At least we have some of the right people working together on something.

"Uhh — next week will be the twentieth anniversary, but the first official celebration, of the victory of Demuzzi-ki-ag over the invading armies of the king of the Amorites."

“Oh, yes, yes, it had escaped me for a moment.” To their surprise, Shi-ten-Ku seemed at a loss for words.

“As many of you will remember,” said Ni-Pada-Dan, continuing the rescue, “Demmuzi was merely our army commander at that time. It was the brilliant use of his forces that caught the Amorites as they were crossing the Euphrates in pursuit of retreating troops of our ally, Erech. The many prisoners captured were mercifully spared at Demmuzi’s insistence, and became the slaves that built our new ziggurat on top of a previous, much older temple. A few of those slaves are still living among us today. These were the events that won for him our eternal gratitude. It was eight years later that he agreed to become lugal.”

After a short pause, Kre-eg arose and scanned the group. All were quiet, except Bruzi and Na-tem-Na, who were engaged in a whispered conversation.

“Bruzi, you seem to be the one with the questions. Have they been answered?” Kre-eg asked, in a slightly cranky tone.

“Uhh, no, sir...uhh, I mean....” He was trying to reorient himself from the private conversation. Are these people able to look at any questions deeper than how to throw a party? Bruzi asked himself.

“I guess only part of my question has been answered. After the celebration, what then? I still don’t feel I know what the root of our problem is. Maybe this isn’t the place to ask what it means, but trouble is staring us in the face here. My kinsman and alternate, Na-tem-Na, is much better with words than I am. I would like him to speak to this.”

Kre-eg surveyed the group swiftly with an air that had become lofty and confident.

“There being no objection, please proceed, sir.”

The handsome young man rose smoothly to his feet and began without hesitation.

“Like Kre-eg and Gart, I may possibly know some of the people involved in the recent unrest. I do know people who might do rash deeds, though I don’t think of them as criminals. How are we to understand the discontent of these young people in a city that is supposed to be famous for its laws, its property rights and its safeguards against the abuse of royal power?"

The young patrician's pause seemed calculated. He was searching the faces before him to see if he had made contact.

"I fully agree," he continued, "that we need to be reminded of the history and traditions of our city. Those shared memories could help us to understand and to work together. I admit, I had never bothered to read *An Among Us: an Ode to Creation* until today, when I stopped at the city gate, wiped away the dust and took time to read it. I am no great scholar, but I found it surprisingly easy to read. However, what it might mean for me and for our city may take some thought."

Gart squirmed, his gut ached, his chest squeezed. This had all the makings of an enormous joke, but it was no joke. The thought of having to help keep such a complicated secret made him feel ill.

"I wonder," Na-tem-Na continued, "if these disturbances, this seeming insurrection, is a wake-up call to us from An, the God of Creation, or his grandson, Nannar, if you prefer. Is the God telling us to use our imaginations as Demmuzi did? Is he telling us that we need to build a higher level onto our society, as Demmuzi and others built up the ziggurat?" The silence was heavy, no one spoke or moved.

"Yes, let us parade," he resumed. "Let us remember, but to remember is not enough. Let us find out what these people are saying to us, or about us, that is not getting through. Are they just hungry, jealous, bored? Maybe not. In any case, that such disorder and quarreling among ourselves could happen here is shameful, grievous. We must keep looking!" He sat down abruptly. The group stirred, coughed, shuffled.

Finally, Kre-eg declared the meeting dismissed without further consultation. The parade was to go on.

Gart's route to the exit went by the spare but imposing figure of the Chief Priest, who laid a detaining hand on his arm.

"You know, Lieutenant — ah — Lieutenant..."

"Eber-Sin," Gart filled in.

"Ah, yes," Ni-Zum-Ka continued. "I have a feeling several of you younger men are being less forthcoming than you might be. Withholding identities, here, would be a poor idea. I have two once-thirsty guards whose lives depend on finding these criminals, and I can tell you they will be thorough."

"Oh, I do assure you, sir...," Gart's voice sounded too shrill to him. With conscious effort he lowered the pitch. "...And I will certainly keep my eyes open."

He was suddenly very much awake. Leaving Ni-Zum-Ka looking rather unsatisfied, Gart fled the royal compound and sought swift refuge — home.

CHAPTER EIGHT

Gart usually awoke an hour before sunrise, rested or not. Perhaps this was inherited from fifty generations of herdsmen always up with the sun to follow their flocks. This morning at least, he was thankful for a little time to collect his thoughts before he pushed off into the stream of humanity about to awaken beyond his door. As he breakfasted on leftover bread, dates and some barley gruel only slightly warmed on the gray coals of the dormant cooking fire, he tried to sort out the previous evening. Of course, he must warn Orson and Nin-ana-Me of this unbelievable turn of events, but what then?

When he arrived at Orson and Sari's apartment he found the door open, as usual. Orson promptly appeared, awake and dressed for the day. Gart tried his best to explain what he thought he had heard and understood the night before. He was not surprised that both Orson and Sari were having trouble following him.

"Let me get this straight," said Orson. "*An Among Us: an Ode to Creation,*" in its final form, is now part of our ancient sacred writings, even though its unknown author is still alive and 'among' us?"

"Right," said Gart. "And furthermore, the next to the last revision has become the one *after* the last edition and is the work of sneaky, blasphemous scoundrels who are an immediate menace to our faith and the security of our city!"

"Oh, my! Where did that come from?" asked the befuddled Sari. "What happens now?"

"It comes straight from the nether world as far as I am concerned," said Gart, suddenly aware of feelings of guilt and responsibility about what he must tell them next. "Now we have a high priest who is greatly vexed for reasons I only partly understand. He has all of his henchmen looking for one super-scribe and one mongoose lover, plus any stray rowdies they might identify."

Orson and Sari stared at him, still not quite comprehending.

"Oh, no," moaned Orson. "'Superscribe.' Oh, no! I'll bet that was what those old geezers were doing yesterday."

"What old geezers?" asked Sari.

"Two of the oldest scribes from the temple school were poking around the tablet room yesterday. The storage is mostly temple business records, but there are other records there, too, both for the priests and for the school. One of them must remember me from school days. He nodded to me," Orson continued.

"Could they recognize your work from what you do for Brother Shem-ki?" asked Gart.

"I don't know. Most of the accounting is pretty standard stuff, but once in a while I get bored and add some explanations or a flourish or two. If they were really suspicious, they might see a connection."

"If your style is the same as that on the supposedly 'ancient' tablets, how could they trace a 'recently altered' copy to you?" asked Sari.

"That makes sense, but people see what they want to," Orson said. "No well-schooled scribe would identify my style as very old, but if they were told it was by an authority, they might identify me as the one copying that style. Gart, wasn't Surbec supposed to destroy all of those old copies?"

"He certainly was. I made that clear. I don't understand why he would keep one. I'm sure he couldn't read it," Gart said. "It may all blow over, or it could be very serious if Ni-Zum-Ka's men question you."

Gart could feel Sari's stare. She had pressed her cheek against Orson's bare shoulder and continued to look at Gart. The pain in her eyes made him scramble for some remedy. Whoa, he thought, I'm already feeling guilty. Am I making matters worse by trying to manage everything?

It was Orson who asked the obvious question:

"Should I get out of sight, somehow, until it's clear how this is going to play out?"

Gart nodded in agreement.

"But where would I go?" Orson said. "I would be easy to find in the city and I have never been anywhere outside, except my parent's village and how would we explain my absence? I even have a part in the big parade next week."

"Most everyone does," said Gart. "And that may be in our favor. I doubt that they will bother us until after the celebration. Could you go out to your village, pretend you just came to invite your kin in to the parade, and see if that is a place you could hide? Failing that, I have an idea that is pretty drastic, but it would be good cover. If I can get you leave at the armory, you could get out of here right after the parade.

Gart had time to give his business at the stockyards only a brief inspection before going on to the armory. He was earlier than usual. He was surprised to find Bruzi already there, wandering among the shops and stock bins.

After a few minutes, Bruzi sidled up to Gart and said, "Say, aren't you one of the investors in the big boat that is supposed to go down east for more copper and ore? We are going to need a lot more metal before we are fully rearmed."

"Yes, I am, both myself and my kinsmen," answered Gart. "However, as yet, we are still short on funds and crew."

"How many more men do you need?"

"Two or three, I understand," said Gart.

"Well, we really need that copper," Bruzi continued. "I know one, maybe two, young men I believe I could convince to go. It would be good for them. Does it matter that they don't know much about sailing?"

"Well, I don't know…," Gart paused, then gave in to temptation. "How about mongooses? Do they know much about them?"

Bruzi's jaw dropped, then he rolled his eyes and sighed. "That was a weird meeting we had last night, wasn't it? How much and how do you know about mongooses, Gart?"

"I don't know much, but that is more than I would like to know." Gart replied. "I just happened to be in the wrong place at the right time. We may both know two or three people who need a trip for their health. If you can get two of them leave from the guard to go find copper, I will get busy on the rest of it."

"Agreed, agreed, gladly," the young colonel sighed with relief.

Gart quickly excused himself and headed straight for Mahn-so-ni's construction yard. Mahn-so-ni agreed that Orson would be well qualified to handle the business details and that the inexperienced "sailors" would just have to learn from the others as they went along. The financing of the mast and steering oar and part of the cargo remained a major problem.

"Let's face it, Gart, the only one hereabouts that would have that kind of resources available on short notice would be Nam-Ku. I hesitate to deal with him but let's go try."

Nam-Ku's grain warehouse and brewery were only a short walk from Mahn-so-ni's yards, so they were soon there. Nam-Ku listened patiently to their plight and proposal, questioning them in detail about their assets and needs. He did not inquire into why they were in such a hurry. For several minutes the three sat in silence, working through their calculations.

"Very well gentlemen, I think I can accommodate you. I believe I can get the timbers at your price, and I can probably find two hundred measures of barley here to complete your cargo. Just wait here a few minutes while I look into the details."

The two petitioners sat in uneasy silence as they waited for confirmation. They did not have to wait long. Nam-Ku returned with his smile undiminished.

"It's all arranged. Your men can pick up the timbers today and we could load the barley this afternoon, if you wish. For this service I would, of course, expect one-half of the profits."

There it was: the terms they had been dreading to hear. After a few moments of silently digesting these terms, Gart felt he must make some reply before he felt his full resentment.

"But, sir, if you did indeed get the timbers at the fair price, this would be twice your proportionate share."

"You are quite correct, young man." Nam-Ku was still smiling, if a bit condescending. "But, of course, not all portions are equal. That last part of any deal is the most important. It is a matter of timing you know." Nam-Ku continued to smile in silence, awaiting their next move. Finally he said, "Is it agreed then?"

The two nodded in resignation. Actually, it was no worse than they feared. They put their seals to the agreement and departed to get the blessing of Banarum and the other investors.

As they left the premises, Mahn-so-ni was experiencing the aftermath of his encounter with Nam-Ku. It was like a bad taste in his mouth. He turned to Gart.

"Is Kre-eg that stuck on himself, that greedy?"

"I don't know, sir. He scares me sometimes when he suddenly switches personalities. He doesn't have it organized like his old man, that's for sure. We may find out what he's really like, considering all the jobs he has somehow been appointed to."

Gart received word through Leah and Sari that Orson had gone, as suggested, to his ancestral village and returned, not having found a suitable place to hide. On the second afternoon after their visit to Nam-Ku, Gart heard that one of the young men in custody had died as a result of torture by the temple guards during questioning. The second man was still denying all knowledge of the matter. Indeed, he might know nothing, but what if he did, and talked?

Gart knew what he was proposing was risky and based on presuppositions, but he could think of no other course. It would have to be Orson's decision.

"I guess going to sea would be less dangerous," Orson agreed with obvious reluctance.

Sari hid her face and wept quietly.

Gart was feeling pangs of guilt about all the "great deals" he had been finding for Orson, but they must move quickly. The ship would have to be moved outside the walls before the mast could be installed. Departure was set for early morning three days hence, right after the parade.

Gart's concern for Orson was soon diffused by the preparations and growing public involvement in this parade. The plan was the soldiers would form up outside the city walls and follow the lugal and his group of chariots back across the bridge to the north gate. This would reenact Demmuzi's triumphant return after defeating the Amorites, twenty years previously.

They would need an audience, of course. At least Leah and her family and Sari would be there, and Jeme, certainly. It seemed to Gart everyone else would be in the parade. He calculated that there would be some five thousand men under arms of some sort. He could recall the spurt of energy he had felt when Bruzi's mosquito-bitten, mud-smeared expeditionary force had formed up and done eyes right as they crossed that bridge over the moat and, on into the North Gate. Oh, this would be so much grander!

Once the military entered the gate, they would be merged with the civilian part of the procession, units from each part to alternate. The column would double up inside the temple compound and march around the interior of the walls. Each of the fifty major gods in the Sumerian pantheon would be represented by an image born on a palanquin surrounded by a marching party of celebrants dressed in the appropriate color and, perhaps, carrying the symbolic plant or animal associated with that deity.

Such a massive undertaking would have been far beyond the temple staff's capacity to organize if Bruzi had not persuaded a reluctant Na-tem-Na to contact and recruit members of each of the fifty supposed original families. In most cases, there had long been a family association with a particular god. In some families, a quick adoption was necessary. Although Na-tem-Na strove to involve each of the families, he insisted his activities be kept quiet. He feared charges of class distinction would be a hindrance during the present unrest. Therefore, each family was to organize, using only the name of the patron god.

For those who were still left out, and many were, there was another chance. Each trade had its patron god and now, in the past week, long dormant guild organizations were resurrected in a festive frenzy of image making and the procurement of makeup and costumes. These units of tradesmen were trusted to join in at some appropriate time when the civilian column passed their quarter.

Once the lead chariots returned to the temple-palace compound, the king was to go to his balcony and review those following. The whole procedure would start in midafternoon, contrary to usual custom and convenience, because that was the earliest Lah-ma-Nah, the physician, felt he could have the king in a cooperative and presentable mood. All of this information about the parade came to Gart from Bruzi, who practically haunted him for progress reports and assurances regarding the ship's departure.

"We are finally on schedule, Colonel," Gart reassured him. "Has Bar-Shin agreed to go?"

"Yes, yes, gladly, if not gratefully. In fact, he seems quite taken by the idea. We will be glad if he has his next escapade out of the country. My father won't let him out of his sight, which is quite a change. Bar-Shin insists that Surbec go with him. I didn't tell him we were already planning that. I have the leaves for Surbec and Orson all approved."

"Maybe I would be better off not knowing, but how do those two young bucks explain what they were up to?" asked Gart.

"I'll be damned if I can understand what Bar-Shin is talking about. He won't talk to us that much, and when he does, it sounds like a bunch of bratty babble to me. Maybe my father and I are just too angry to listen. I'll give you a chance at him before they go. Maybe you can explain it to me."

"Hah!" said Gart. That was about as noncommittal as he could be, but his curiosity would not allow him to turn down the opportunity.

"They are a strange combination, Bar-Shin and Surbec, "Gart said. "I wonder how they got together?"

"Strange indeed," said Bruzi. "One is a homeless slave, ex-slave rather, who seems determined to make it in the system. He probably would, too, if he hadn't met my brother. Bar-Shin seems just as determined to lose all the things he didn't have to earn."

As they stood in silence for a few minutes Bruzi was thinking, maybe if I had stepped in — made the kid work like I had to — work with the system? Oh hell, I have no right.... He turned to go, then stopped suddenly.

"Oh, I almost forgot. You will need to change your parade plans. Kre-eg needs you in the first section. There is a serious problem with the chariots and we have agreed you are the one to handle it. You are to drive the second chariot."

"You have agreed! You and Kre-eg have agreed? It seems to me Captain Kre-eg, who has no direct responsibility for me, has been having an awful lot to say about my duties!"

"Gart, this is not Captain Kre-eg telling you. This is Colonel Bruzi telling you. In the parade you will be driving the second chariot."

"But what do I know about driving chariots? Why me?" Gart protested. "What's Kre-eg's problem, anyway?"

"'Why you' is because you are our local livestock expert. In addition, Kre-eg tells me you have a prolonged personal acquaintance with each of the four white asses in that chariot team.

The problem is they are all so ambitious they want to run over everyone in front of them. You might know something about that, too. Remember, *Lieutenant*, in the daytime you are military. Don't confuse that with your nighttime political activities.

Gart was aghast, dumbfounded. He knew it would take a while to digest all he had heard. Perhaps to lessen his embarrassment, he felt a stubborn streak arising.

"But my unit, I've — helped — put it together. It's not right a stranger should lead it!" Gart could see from Bruzi's stony glare he was doing himself no good.

"Lieutenant Eber-Sin, you will be driving that chariot anyway!"

Bruzi began to turn to go again. He was thinking, who is this, another Bar-shin? Well, I did assert some discipline this time.

"Kre-eg will expect you this afternoon," he said in a gruff but calmer voice.

The heat and stiffness began fading from the back of Gart's neck. Fading along with it was his dream of "Eyes right!" tromp, tromp, across the bridge. Now he had a familiar cool, tingling feeling. Driving a chariot! Four white onagers!

Yes, yes, his dream of months ago; he was driving a chariot for someone in the sky. But how could such a dream be connected to his real life?"

"Oh, Colonel Bruzi!"

The officer stopped, turned.

"Thank you very much, sir. I will be there." Then Gart flashed him a beatific smile.

That afternoon it did not take Gart long to locate some of the sources of Kre-eg's complaints. Except for three or four occasions in the past year when the onagers had joined informal maneuvers, they had had little training or exercise. In addition, the drivers, except for one, were inexperienced and out of practice. The animals needed their hooves trimmed and the proper control harness had been mislaid. It was little wonder the second chariot team tried to climb in and ride with Kre-eg on their first rehearsal.

The onagers pulled the two-wheeled chariots by pressing with their shoulders against a U-shaped yoke fitted under their neck and passing upward through holes bored in a crossbar that rode on top of their shoulders. The tongue of the chariot was suspended from this crossbar with a leather rope. The U-shaped yokes were stabilized by straps around the top of the front legs. This allowed for reasonable stops but backing up was impractical and retreat hazardous.

Guidance was by means of metal rings, in this case silver, welded into place after having been passed through perforations on each side of the upper lip of each onager. Rings from the right and rings from the left sides were joined by a series of straps and metal fasteners that could usually give some right to left control, but prompt stops or slowdowns were hard to achieve. Fortunately, Gart was able to locate the additional reins and straps which, when hooked to the halters, would allow a vigorous driver to haul the four noses down. After about two hours practice on this hot afternoon, drivers and onagers reached a solid agreement as to what was grounds for "slow" and "stop."

Gart's passenger on the second two-wheeled chariot was to be the army Commander-in-Chief, General Mem-el. To reduce the chance of dumping his distinguished cargo, Gart insisted the former driver and another stableman run alongside to grab halters, if necessary. They were to follow the royal chariot, which was larger. In addition to his driver, Kre-eg would ride to assist Demmuzi in his royal duties. The third chariot would follow with Ni-Zum-Ka and driver to serve witness to solidarity between temple and palace.

Gart stayed very late that evening working on the animals and equipment. He chuckled to himself when he found he was cleaning off some of the mud he and Jeme had applied to hide the silver ornaments of the halters during their trip to Larsa.

They would practice parading the next two mornings, then it would be time for the big show.

The rehearsals went well, and by midmorning on the day of the parade, Gart had mastered these new skills enough to feel somewhat at ease. Kre-eg seemed to be soaring to a level of good humor beyond anything Gart had seen in him before. Kre-eg had come outside the city gates and had stood smiling and patiently waiting while he watched Gart put the animals through their paces. Gart asked himself, is his personality improving or has he just caught parade fever like everyone else? He pulled his team to a stop a few yards from Kre-eg and asked:

"Tell me, Mister Chairman, why is it that everyone is suddenly so interested in this trumped-up celebration?"

"That's easy, Gart, BOREDOM, BOREDOM, and I think they miss the old fellow, their king. It's a pity he's the only one who is not interested at all. He just says, 'It won't help.' He doesn't even seem to remember it from one day to the next."

Gart got down from the chariot and handed the reigns back to the regular driver. He wanted to walk back with Kre-eg.

"Maybe you can explain something more to me about the parade, Kre-eg."

"Yes?"

"Well, I understand the six men with ram's horn trumpets in the very first rank, but who is that wild-looking man dressed in animal skins and carrying a stone ax who comes next — like he was leading the parade?"

"Oh, he is leading the parade," said Kre-eg. "In fact they call him Enkidu, 'The Wild Man.' I don't know why he's there, but it is an old custom every New Year and every other big occasion. I've never given it much thought."

By midafternoon the worst of the heat had dissipated. The sea breeze was beginning already, unusually early. "This must have been arranged by a committee of the gods," said Gart to his chariot crew. “After all, this is the first good party the gods, or at least their images, have been out to in a long time.”

A steady stream of humanity and hardware poured out of the north gate. The chariots and their teams had long been in place awaiting their important passengers, who would arrive by closed palanquins born by the Royal Bodyguard, once the traffic slowed down. Lines began to appear as the units formed up with their backs to the moat and the city wall. The chariots were to the west, farthest from the gate.

Gradually the shouted instructions and clang of equipment became a soft buzz and now a hush. Gart could see the three palanquins moving quickly across the bridge. Each was shrouded in blue cloth and born by eight sturdy guardsmen at a steady trot. They were flanked by the remainder of the Royal Bodyguard, their bronze short spears and burnished copper helmets gleaming in the afternoon sunlight.

The blue boxes were set down in front of their respective chariots. Ni-Zum-Ka and General Mem-el, erect and dressed in their finest, strode directly to their chariots. Demmuzi, in spite of helmet and battle sword, did not look very martial. Kre-eg’s hand on his elbow kept him trudging onwards and up into the lead chariot. The three curtained palanquins were moved quickly to the west where they were stacked out of the way.

At a sweeping wave of the arm from Kre-eg, the six trumpeters stationed at intervals in front of the formed units sounded three brief, undulating blasts: the call to arms. The trumpeters hurried with an exaggerated stride to the west to form the head of the returning column. From somewhere, perhaps the palanquins, the Wild Man appeared.

His costume was the same, but contrary to the erratic behavior Gart had observed at rehearsal, he stood erect, raised, then pumped his long cudgel in signal. With a bark from this strange figure, the first rank of trumpeters pivoted and moved out to start the review and return to the gate.

Gart suspected the Wild Man must be an officer with a heavy wig and painted up for what was a secret, if not exactly sacred, role.

Some twenty soldiers in two ranks, one from each of the units, all bearing pikes with colored streamers, wheeled into line. Next, a rank of four trumpeters sounded a loud, dissonant fanfare on their long copper instruments. Kre-eg's chariot moved out. As the royal conveyance passed in front of him, Gart saw Kre-eg bending sideways, pouring earnest advice into the king's ear.

Without any signal from him, Gart's team stepped forward to take their place in line, as if they had done it every day. Gart half-turned to give a feigned knowing nod to his passenger. The general smiled in warm appreciation. All chariots were now in motion. The Royal Bodyguard jingled with impatience, prancing at double-time in single file on each side of them.

They passed Colonel Alkohn and his pikemen. "DEMMUZI LUGAL! LUGAL! DEMMUZI LUGAL!... LUGAL," they roared in unison. By the second repetition, the sound was being reinforced by its own echo as it rolled back over the moat and reflected off of the city walls. For the first three choruses the old soldier's arm came up in a snappy response, but as each successive unit took up the words, the response became weaker. Kre-eg's side bends and exhortations were now needed for each marching unit, and the result was only a modest improvement each time.

Between bends, Kre-eg, either on behalf of his king or of his own high spirits, was acknowledging the roars with exuberant waves. Spearmen, archers, slingers, more pikemen, men with maces and cudgels, men with only staves, awaiting proper arms: unit after unit, thousands of men, but just one king. He was a bit faded, but their king no less. As the column neared the gate, each unit was a little less well armed. The ranks were less even, but the enthusiasm was greater.

Only when his chariot turned to cross the bridge did Gart realize he had passed his own unit, without even noticing!

As the column entered the narrow streets, it slowed. It all seemed different from what he had imagined when he day dreamed about marching at the head of his platoon. When he was learning to control his onagers, he had been too busy to think about what effect this parade might have on him. Now, the total experience of all the chariot rides of the past few days was fresh in memory. He was floating along, by the grace of these animals. He was higher up, out of the dust. He felt a part of *something* — something very large. Once more, he recalled brief snatches from his charioteer dream. He glanced out of the right corner of his eye. No, this was no shadowy figure to his right. It was quite substantial, even paunchy.

Suddenly, their audience was different. The ululations and chanting of the women caused Demmuzi to brighten up slightly and Kre-eg's waves became even wilder.

Between his bobs and exhortations to the king, the Royal Bodyguard Commander was getting in quite a few smiles and waves of recognition as he bowed to his left.

"BRAVO, DEMMUZI. BRAVO CAPTAIN KRE-EG! YEAH KREEG!"

What was this, a private cheering section? Was it Kre-eg's family? The brewery workers? No, it looked more like a group of temple women!

"YEAH, KREEG, 'ATTA BOY!"

"SHOW IT TO US, LOVER BOY!"

"BLOW ME A KISS, SWEETHEART"

Kre-eg was startled at first, but then he thought, there they are, like they said they would be; the whole *joy crew*. Bless their little pea brains, embarrassing, but — what the hell — do it in style!

He doffed his helmet and made a sweeping bow of acknowledgment. Unfortunately, the swinging helmet struck the driver a glancing blow on the back of his head, causing him to jerk the team, which now yawed sharply to one side. At the same time, the shift of weight of the passengers caused the car to tip up, nearly dumping the monarch into the street. Disaster was averted by a quick corrective shift and grab by Kre-eg. Demmuzi's clearly audible stream of well-articulated curses showed no trace of his previous lassitude.

The chariots were much closer together now, and in quieter moments, Gart could distinguish Kre-eg's voice.

"Can we straighten up a bit here, sir? Not much longer, sir." Kre-eg's hand had progressed from the lugal's elbow to a firm fistful of armpit. From his stance, Gart guessed that Kre-eg was bearing a good portion of the king's weight.

"I'll straighten *you* up, you smart ass young pup, when we get back to the barracks, I mean, palace," the old king wheezed.

"Big smile for the ladies now, sir," Kre-eg persisted.

"What the hell do I have to smile about?" Demmuzi continued to huff.

"They love their king. They have missed you, sir. Straighten up. Damn it, sir!"

"I sure as hell wouldn't miss you, Captain, if I had a donkey turd to throw at you right now!"

In front of the palace, Demmuzi fled his car with new found alacrity. After a reasonable time, His Majesty appeared on his balcony flanked by Ni-Pada-Dan and Lah-ma-Nah, who each tended an elbow while Kre-eg sat in the background and mopped his brow.

All three chariots drew up in line facing the two-story Royal Residence. The central window was unusually broad in comparison to the narrow slits that served the rest of the building, and most of the buildings in the city. However, it was barely wide enough to accommodate five people side by side. The late afternoon sun shone directly in, illuminating the review party to those below. After a few minutes, Demmuzi motioned for General Mem-el and Ni-Zum-Ka to join him.

As the high priest passed in front of his chariot, Gart's attention jumped to his plans for the next morning. Would Ni-Zum-Ka be mellowed or distracted by the celebration? Was he, Gart, subjecting his friends and Bar-Shin to unnecessary danger and trouble in fleeing an imagined peril? Was he flirting with treason by aiding fugitives? It was a little late to back out now. Men had already been promised double wages to load the ship right after the parade, before the serious beer drinking got underway.

At Gart's command, the chariots withdrew to make room for other units. They took up new positions against the wall, near the east gate of the compound, where they could watch the rest of the parade as it entered the plaza.

Through the gate they came, each block of soldiers in ranks interspersed between swirling blobs of noisy, costumed devotees-for-the-day dancing about a litter-born image and making a din with what must have been every drum, rattle and clangable metal object in the city. On and on they came, surely they would fill the entire plaza by the time the last units squeezed in. Already, temple personnel were planting large reed torches around the edges of the square. Daylight was beginning to fade. Gart was sorry Leah would miss this part, but he knew the decision to keep her out of the crowd had been necessary. She, her mother and Sari were to watch from the roof of a friend's house just outside the compound.

Gart was feeling the impact of the impressive display. He was sure he would long remember this vivid picture — the surge of emotion, activity and cooperation that had been released by such a casual calculation of a few men. What, if anything, would be the result? He felt too flooded to think, and his time for sleep would be brief tonight.

Because the night would be short for him, Gart passed up the after the parade parties, except for a bite to eat here and a wave there. He was early to bed, trusting to Leah and her now-crowded bladder to awaken him even earlier than his usual one hour before dawn.

He did sleep very deeply, and when he first felt Leah's hand on his shoulder, he was dreaming of ships and sandy shores. He was forced to choose between realities. His eyes began to focus and Leah's face, even more beautiful enhanced by the freckles of pregnancy, floated into view in the lamplight. Surely, this was where he belonged: home.

When he arrived at the ship, Gart found that most of the people were already there. Mahn-so-ni, Banarum and some other anxious investors were checking the inventory with Orson; barley, wheat, hides, baskets, rope, pottery and a selection of short swords, bows and arrows, hopefully far in excess of their needs, were all accounted for. In addition, ample provisions; skins of water and beer, dates and freshly baked bread were counted. The mast, boom and sail were aboard but not yet mounted. The new steering oar was in place.

Three of the night watch, who had been rewarded in advance, stood with torches and prepared to pull aside the floating grates that blocked the water gate connecting the inner lagoon with the outside canal system. The cargo was all accounted for, but the crew was still incomplete. Within a few minutes, a party of four could be seen turning the corner a hundred yards from the dock. Gart could make out Bruzi, Bar-shin, Surbec and a tall, spare old man, who, he presumed to be Bruzi and Bar-shin's father.

With the crew now aboard, Gart, Bruzi and Mahn-so-ni jumped on the ship to help pole the strange craft outside the walls. The older man remained on the dock, head bowed, arms behind him. Even with the mast down, the high-arched prow and stern of this fat envelope of reeds barely cleared the top of the gate. Once out the gate, they docked canalside to install the mast. While the captain, Mahn-so-ni and his workmen were busy, Bruzi and Gart got off. Bruzi motioned for Bar-shin to follow them. Surbec, without hesitating, was right behind.

Bruzi looked at Gart.

"Yes, I want them both," Gart answered the implied question.

"Well, little brother," said the colonel, laying his left hand on the smaller man's shoulder. "It may be some time before we meet again. I have one last — no, cancel that — one additional, request for you. You may remember Lieutenant Eber-Sin, Gart. You were introduced once. He is one of several people who have been busting their butts to make this possible for you, to provide you with a legitimate cover that might well save your lives. I think the least you owe him is an explanation of what you were trying to accomplish with this recent escapade."

The daylight was now sufficient for Gart to clearly see the straightening of posture and restrained twitch of the shoulder that caused Bruzi to remove his hand and step back.

Bar-shin's gaze moved slowly up Gart's frame and Gart watched the young man's expression shift slightly, from cautious restraint to a carefully restrained defiance.

"What is it, Lieutenant, that you think I — we — have done, and why, as an investor in this voyage, do you care about our motives?"

"As an investor, it doesn't matter, but as a citizen it does matter to me one young man has already died of torture and you have, unwittingly, placed a good friend of mine in peril." Gart could feel his anger rising, threatening to destroy all his plans for this conversation. This will never do! he lectured himself. He took a few deep breaths and somehow managed a rather sickly smile.

"What really got me interested was that night last week, when Orson and I watched — whatever it was the two of you were doing at the altar of Nin-Gal."

Gart had scored. Bar-shin's jaw softened. His gaze scattered. Surbec looked down in embarrassment.

"I really don't understand," said Gart. "Were you trying to overthrow the government? Do you have some personal gripe against the priests?"

"I — we — had no such grand ideas as overthrowing the government. And as for the priests, my complaints are not strictly personal. We were acting as a matter of principle, hoping to wake up a few people, including His Royal Numbness, Lugal Demmuzi. As for those naked idiots who prance up and down the ziggurat with their ceremonies and rigmarole.... I don't know if there's any hope for them. They are supposed to be so vulnerable to the needs of the gods. I don't know about that, but they surely don't seem to have any idea what their tenants and all the other hungry people need!"

Bar-shin had to stop for breath. His speech had become progressively more rapid and emphatic.

"His Royal Numbness, eh?" said Gart. "You don't seem to think much of our king."

"No, not that much, in spite of all the hoopla you people put on yesterday," replied the young rebel. "At least he has the decency to get sick. Maybe he understands more than we know."

Bar-shin had slowed down. His eyes and parted lips, indicated to Gart the young man was recalculating something. It even sounded like he might have a little empathy. Gart chose to proceed in a gentler tone:

"How would you expect our leaders, whom you describe as 'numb-heads,' to understand what you mean by what you have done? And what, exactly, do you want them to understand?"

"I...we want them to understand things are NOT all right here. For half the people in this city — the little people — life stinks!"

"So why didn't you just say so, instead of attacking some stupid snake in its urn or cutting off cows' tails in the middle of the night?" Gart asked. His patience was wearing thin.

"Lots of people have been saying the same things as we have, but who listens? Hey, if I remember right, Lieutenant, someone sent you a message down at the stockyards! Well, what did you make of that? What did you do about it?"

Gart looked at the speaker numbly. He was drowning in the torrent of words.

"We were thinking from the gut, I guess," Bar-shin said. "Now I see how it works. Attack the symbols and it gets to people on the gut level. Never mind that no two people will agree about the meaning of what we did, they will feel it all the same. If you add a little mystery, like we did, some people will remember, maybe even learn something."

Bar-shin looked at Gart, clear-eyed and calm, evidently satisfied with his own explanation.

Gart turned his gaze on Surbec.

"And as for you, my friend, what did you expect to get out of this?"

Surbec looked at the ground: no response. Gart had regained the offensive.

"Didn't we have an understanding you were to smash those tablets? Didn't we?" Gart demanded.

"Yes, but — " Surbec squirmed, twitching and narrowing his muscular shoulders, as if to slip out of a noose.

"You were throwing them away, anyhow!" Indignation had overcome Surbec's embarrassment. "What was the harm in letting my friend read one of them? I couldn't read it."

"Your friend?" Gart was trying for a touch of irony.

"Yes, he's my friend, and it wasn't because I saved his ass either!" Surbec snapped to stiff attention and said: "With all due respect, LIEUTENANT, SIR!"

It's not working; trying to shame or bully either one of these fellows, Gart thought. Maybe I should listen some more. He turned to Bar-shin again, but gently.

"That old, discarded tablet interested you, Bar-shin? What did you like about it?"

"Yes, it did interest me. I liked — the part – that went...." Bar-shin tossed back his head, eyes closed, evidently searching his memory while the slight circular motion of his right forearm sought the rhythm:

> "AN, in ancient times,
> Planted, — in secret,
> Date palms, in the garden
> East of mother Euphrates;
> A garden for his grandson
> Nannar-Sin — and
> His wife; — Nin-Gal.

The trees have flourished,
Delighting grandfather AN,
Who visits — from time to time.
Father Enlil, too,
But, the moon-couple
Walk about, there — every night."

Here Bar-shin stopped and touched the back of his head while he gazed out, beyond Gart, then resumed.

"Of all the gardens — and
Kinds of fruit-bearing trees,
In Enlil's earthly realm,
None were selected
As well as these.

The trunks are strong,
The leaves are broad,
Though worms bore
And beetles bite.

Centuries have passed,
Only now, can full bloom appear.
Still — perils await.

Again Bar-shin paused and glanced briefly at Gart, noting his befuddled expression.

Gart was thinking, how very strange, Nin-ana-Me's ode in Bar-shin's voice, as that voice resumed with crisp assurance:

Unless roots deeply drink,
The bitter, brackish waters
  of grief,
The fruit cannot mature,

And the birds, in their flight,
  cannot spread
Those small seeds,
  so vital, so inscribed,
To that quarter, North-West,
Where these waters rise."

Once more the recitation stopped, the speaker's brow furrowed with the effort of recall.

The last line kept echoing in Gart's mind. What was that last line about? Why had he never noticed it before?

"When this place has served our time,
And trunk and leaves
  are dust,
Birds will course their flight
  North-West.

The people of Ur
  need to know
  their grief.

Everyone was very quiet for quite some time.

"How did you ever get interested in this...ode?" Gart finally asked, still awed by the recitation.

"Well, I didn't learn it in school, that's for damned sure, in spite of what your High Priest might want you to believe. I learned it from the copy on the north gate pillar. I have always hung around there, so I know precisely when this 'ancient' document appeared on that pillar. I'm so interested because this author is saying the same thing we want to say, only much better. Mystery — symbols. Most people won't get it, because they have to work to understand it. The author is on to the same problem we are!"

"She is? Er...he is? The author, I mean." Gart was groping about — poise gone. "I guess I don't understand."

"Of course you understand, Lieutenant. It was you who just explained it to *me*. Without your grilling me, I wouldn't have thought about the timing. Isn't it amazing this 'ancient' wisdom should appear on the altar of Nin-Gal just minutes before we were to try to do a bad thing by leaving the wrong copy on that very altar? There was obviously a mighty *presence* at work there. I believe that you know much more about such things than you let on, Lieutenant."

Bar-shin began to walk to and fro, gradually slowing down as his posture relaxed. "I thank you, again, for helping me understand it."

"I helped you understand it? When?" Gart was having trouble following the young man's statements.

"Just now, your asking just the right questions pulled it together for me."

It must have been Enlil himself who whispered to the ship's captain this was the time to say, "We're ready now, climb aboard!"

"That's right, you land-bound mud daubers. Cast off. Let's go," Orson boomed out, testing his sailor's vocabulary.

Both the current and the land breeze caught them. The ship was moving without human effort. There were goodbye waves and brave smiles from all, even from Bar-shin. By the next day, they would be on the open sea.

Gart was surprised to feel the weight of Bruzi's arm across his shoulders, the slightest grip and then he was gone. Bruzi walked rapidly back through the gate to where the old man was waiting.

From the port, Gart went back to the apartment. Leah was surprised to see him.

"It's good to have you home. It seems I've hardly seen you in the daylight for weeks."

The two of them sat on the end of their bed, nuzzling quietly. It was getting uncomfortable for Leah to lie flat now. Gart was trying to give her his full attention but found his mind repeatedly straying.

"Can you rest now?" she asked.

"I'll probably rest better if I can talk about Bar-shin now — the young twerp. I felt compelled to talk to him personally, for some reason," said Gart. "Bruzi said he would arrange it. I don't know what I thought I was going to accomplish; straighten him out, I guess. Well, that wasn't quite the way it turned out. He turned me 'every way but loose,' as my dad used to say."

By this time, Gart was pacing back and forth in the limited space of the apartment. Brow furrowed, hands behind his back, he resumed his monologue. "I had supposed that bunch of young men were just trying to be defiant, insolent at best, that they really had given no thought to their actions. Bar-shin himself admits that they didn't understand what they were doing. They just did it."

"So what is so different about that?" asked Leah.

"Nothing," said Gart. "But now the kid is claiming to see a Grand Plan, or something. He puts himself on the same level as Nin-ana-Me, now that he has memorized her ode. He doesn't even know who she is!"

"He said that he is on the same level she is?"

"Well, no, but he claims they are talking about the same thing. They both talk about wanting to wake people up, although, come to think of it, she doesn't say it that way in the poem. They both seem to think things will start to happen if people wake up and look at...uhh...I guess you could say "*An Among Us.*" Improvement, progress, whatever! The twerp is all for 'justice now,' but Nin-ana-Me doesn't get so specific. She is more into the future. Bar-shin seems to think he is in the middle of a big deal, really playing some part in our destiny, just because they went out and trashed the temple one night!"

"Does Bar-shin say that?" Leah waited for Gart to calm down a bit.

"No, not in so many words, but it is implied. He talks about a *'Powerful Presence.'* Did you ever meet a *Powerful Presence?* Do you think that we — you and I — are important players in some big deal? The cheek of that spoiled brat!"

"He seems to have had quite an effect on you, Gart. That's unusual for you. I wonder why."

"That's right," he answered. "I wonder why, too."

"You seem embarrassed that you underestimated this 'twerp,'" said Leah. "But from what you have told me, you only met him once. I don't know just how you questioned him, but I doubt that you were rude. Why be ashamed of a little mistake?"

"That's all very true," said Gart. "In fact that is just the sort of thing I would usually tell myself, but there is something different here. I'm not exactly ashamed, just at a loss to explain my feelings.

"Somehow," Gart continued, "I feel my original ideas about him were right, at the time. It wasn't just that I needed to correct my opinion. It was Bar-shin. I could see him changing before my very eyes! Not only that, he was claiming that I was part of it. Then I thought, 'I can't take any credit for this. Where is this coming from?' It was spooky."

Several minutes passed in complete silence. Finally, Leah said:

"Tell me again, what were your original ideas?"

"I had seen him around, him and his mongoose — at least the basket. I had overheard some of his conversations at the food shop. He seemed intense, aggressive, quick in his movements, but maybe a little preoccupied. Later, when Bruzi introduced him, he seemed cocky, maybe a little breezy. It was that introduction that got several of us into some man talk about our fathers, most unusual for us to go into that very much."

As Gart paused, Leah was thinking, I had better not pursue this "man talk" business. Maybe I can turn the conversation back to Bar-shin.

"What did you hear about Bar-shin's father?"

"Bruzi was embarrassed and was trying to excuse his brother's brashness. He described their father as old, preoccupied, indulgent, but not very available, at least by the time Bar-shin came along," Gart answered without looking directly at her.

More silence. Once more Leah felt she should stay with the discussion of Bar-shin. “Did that change how you felt about the young man?” she asked.

“Probably, I’m not sure if I noticed. We got to talking.” Suddenly Gart felt impelled to stand up and walk, but he walked into a corner. He must escape! He headed for the door, thought better of it and returned to the wall, where he leaned on his crossed arms. Two huge sobs welled up from his chest and got away from him before he could choke them into a diminishing series of small whimpers.

“Now, where the hell did that come from?” he finally asked, peeking over his folded arms at Leah who came swiftly to his side. “I didn’t feel like that when Bruzi was talking. Why now? I’m getting soft in the head. I’m a hell of a big shot officer, I am. Don’t you dare tell anyone!”

Oh, careful here, Leah thought. “You always will be ‘a hell of an officer.’ I wouldn’t dream of telling,” she said.

“This is absolutely crazy!” said Gart after a few deep breaths had cleared the lump from his throat. “Our discussion didn’t get that deep. Sure, I miss Shelah, but he was a good father to me. He did what he could. He taught me a lot of things, he and Uncle Eb, both. I was well treated. How much does a boy — a man — have a right to expect from his father or anyone? You have to do some things for yourself!”

“Maybe this wasn’t just personal,” suggested Leah. “Maybe the sobs really belonged to Bar-shin and you were feeling his grief.”

“You give me an awful lot of credit,” Gart answered. “I don’t see myself as all that sympathetic. Besides, I didn’t even like him at first.”

“At first?”

“Well, after you struggle with someone long enough, it’s like they were family. Bar-shin will be O.K., if — when —they get back.”

How generous and wise of Gart, she was thinking. "Do you think Bar-shin was really needing something?" Leah asked. "After all, his father was there to see him off, wasn't he?"

"Oh, he came down to the dock, all right. He stood around for a while, but…"

"But…what?" she persisted.

"Well, when some of us jumped onto the ship to help pole it outside the walls, he stayed on the dock. I don't know if we should say he saw his son off or not," said Gart.

"I've just been trying to make a connection," he continued, "between Bar-shin's situation, and all this trouble we are having here, in Ur. Do we have a lot of people, maybe everybody, maybe even the officials, just doing dumb, stupid things, trashing the place, because they are mad or sad about something that is lacking, but they don't know what?"

"Maybe not," she said. "The poor people, the slaves and immigrants who are trying to make it, say they know what the trouble is. Just plain greed, meanness and bullying, that's what they say is the problem."

"Yeah, I know. That's what Bar-shin says, and he may be right, but most people don't think about it. They just blame the gods for everything."

"So, if everybody is doing dumb, stupid things due to some lack they haven't faced, what comes to mind — in your case, for example?" she asked. "I realize you say you were well taken care of." She was aware she risked offending her beleaguered husband.

"What comes to mind? Nothing in particular. Did you have an idea?"

"Well," she hesitated, "how about…that your father and uncle didn't get you into the hunter's brotherhood?"

"WHAT?" Gart sat up, as if stung by a bee. "What do you know about that? Women aren't supposed to know anything about that! I don't even know anything about it, myself! I'm not sure it even exists around here anymore! I have never mentioned that to you. Where did you get that idea?"

"You do talk in your sleep quite a bit," she said with a hint of amusement in her voice.

"That's not fair!" he pouted, but his words had a hollow ring. "No one likes to be left out," he finally admitted. "I truly don't know if the brotherhood exists any more, but I often wondered about it. I wondered about what Uncle Eb knew and if he found me lacking. At the same time, I knew it wouldn't be right for me. I could get excited hunting. I enjoy a dish of game. I know hunting is still important, but I couldn't devote myself to that, like some people do. That time has gone by."

"You don't think your father was involved?" she asked.

"I know he wasn't. He said as much. He was too much into taking care of animals to hunt unless he had to."

"But he would kill his own animals," Leah observed.

"If he couldn't get someone else to do it."

What a bind he must have been in, trying to coax something to live and then having to destroy it. Leah was so disturbed by this idea that her next question was just a play for time.

"Did he teach you all he knew about caring for animals?" she asked.

"No. Maybe he would have, but I was impatient. I knew somehow, that his thing wasn't for me. That's why I'm here, in the city, mixed up in such a mess. I wonder if I made a mistake. Maybe I should have stuck with the nanny goats."

She was not fooled by his self-deprecating joke. She had not heard that tone of voice before. In all their time together he had spoken little of Shelah. Had her husband been grieving in secret all along? As she thought she could hear

> "Unless roots deeply drink
> The bitter, brackish waters of grief,
> the fruit cannot mature."

I must find a way to stay on this subject, she thought.

"What didn't you learn from Shelah you wish you had?"

"Well — I don't think I have ever been asked a question like that before. But what I remember most was...just his way…maybe you could say 'how to brood.'"

"Brood? I don't understand," said Leah.

"The way I saw him being with the animals, especially if they were sick, or maybe if one was a runt or just little," said Gart. "He could just be there with them. He wouldn't say much or do much to them, other than a pat or a little nudge here and there. He would just stay there with them half the night sometimes. It seemed there was something just *so* clear between them, like he knew they could get it together and usually they would get well. I guess I was a little jealous of the animals."

"Shelah wouldn't stay with you like that?" Leah asked.

"I don't know," said Gart. "Maybe he would have, if he thought I needed it. I supposed I always seemed all right, so it didn't happen — so far as I recall."

"He didn't realize you wanted that?" she asked. She was hearing her words and remembering her own yearnings of not so long ago. That was a dumb question, she thought. Oh, how hard it is! Such a tearing feeling deep in her chest. How to answer, even when one hears the call?

"No, I don't know if he knew what I wanted, maybe it wasn't even that clear to me," Gart said.

"And you were afraid to ask?"

"Yes," he said. "I didn't know how to ask. Maybe I was afraid that if I got his full attention, I couldn't produce anything special. He seemed so strong and wise then. But at the same time, I think he was afraid, too."

"Why would he be afraid of a little boy?" she asked.

"Not of me, as a little boy," Gart said. "But, well, with an animal it's all so *now*. Maybe, with your child it's a lot different."

"It's so *now*?" she asked. "What do you mean?"

"With an animal, they won't live more than a few years. I don't know if animals understand that — or care. They have to live, right now. With your child it isn't just now. Your child links you with everything you are and have come from, and maybe to things you can't even imagine in the future. That could be scary, if you really see that."

"Did your father think of things like that?" Leah asked.

"Well, I just did," said Gart. "He must have sensed it, in some way. He was more restless with me. He would always find something to do. If we were doing something, making something, working with an animal, it seemed to take the pressure off. If we were just there together, something would start to build up, maybe an expectation of some sort. With an animal he could just wait.

He looked up at Leah, his gaze open and at peace.

"You have been very patient in listening to all this." He bent over and gave her a peck on the forehead.

"If I am about to be a father myself I had better shape up fast. Whatever I missed, I can pick it up myself. I must admit though, Mahn-so-ni has been a lot of help."

"Mahn-so-ni? Does he brood over you?" she asked.

"It's not that personal I'm sure. He seems to be brooding though, perhaps for the whole city. I am struck by how serious and thoughtful he has become. Enough of this about fathers!" Gart said in a lighter tone. "I do think a lot of people want the lugal to be big daddy. He can't do that for them. Even if he was well, and young, and had another twelve years, he couldn't fix everything."

Leah's calm and persistent questioning had had its effect. Gart's speech had slowed. The tenor of alarm and aggravation was gone. After a period of restful silence he said, "By the way, Leah, you never did answer my question about 'did you ever experience a 'powerful presence?'"

"I've been thinking about that," Leah paused. "Would you explain what you mean, or what you think Bar-shin meant when he said that?"

Gart sighed and thought a while longer. This was important. He shouldn't give her a hasty answer. His visitor the imaginary animal guide and the real jackal came to mind at once. Perhaps he could tell Leah about them but now they seemed trivial, though still pretty weird. The most they could do was give a hint or a nudge if someone was paying attention.

His next memory was of that first political meeting. In the silence after Mahn-so-ni's appeal it did seem that something was at work, bubbling with promise for the future. It seemed like it was felt by most of the people there. A lot of them were led into some action or other by that experience.

Was this what Bar-shin was talking about? Was he feeling called to do something in the same way Mahn-so-ni was? If so they surely went about it differently. Mahn-so-ni was thinking through every step. It was only after the fact that Bar-shin showed any sign of thinking. Back to himself. Could he answer his own question about feeling a "powerful presence?"

"Well, maybe once, outside of my dreams," he finally admitted to his waiting wife.

"Was that the night Nin-ana-Me was here? The night the writing was finished?"

"Yes, that was the time," Gart admitted.

"It's easier to feel it when she is around, isn't it?" asked Leah.

"Well, she is a pretty powerful presence herself. I admit that."

"That's not the same thing," objected Leah. "It is more than that. She affects it, but it is more than just her."

"Yes, I know," said Gart. "That night it seemed to be the whole situation, even the arrangement of the room and the people involved, not just what someone said or did, that made such a strong impression on me. I thought that something was complete. It seemed so perfect. But now, as I talk to you, I realize it's not over. That moment was like a summons to something else, not just a hint or a nudge, but a real summons."

"A summons? To what?" Leah asked.

"I'm...I'm not sure I can tell you right now," he said. Then he smiled.

"But surely you know. 'You are the one who explained it to me,'" he said, quoting Bar-shin. "You asked me the right questions."

"Mnnn...maybe so," she said as she got up and crossed the room. "But for now, I'll tend to feeding the fire and us," she said as she went to the door.

"No, wait a while," protested Gart. Her rounded figure framed by the door seemed aglow with life. "I'm not through."

Leah sat down on the bench and leaned her back against the wall. Gart knelt before her. He would have liked to lay his head on her lap, but since there was no lap left, he settled for the upper slope of her abdomen. He could hear a tiny heartbeat, faint and rapid, but very regular. As he was drowsing, he was thinking about how patiently Leah had questioned him.

"Leah, you continue to amaze me," he said. Then, turning his head to catch her eyes he said, "I am truly blessed by you; my hope and refuge in a very strange world." His voice trailed off and his gaze dropped.

She glanced up. The room had suddenly expanded, the walls no longer confining and their once-flimsy floor now as firm as the obvious truth of his recognition of her.

"Ummnnnn..." she finally said. "You seem to have gone far away."

"Yes, Leah, far away in my thoughts." After a few minutes he resumed, "Do you suppose someday...our children, or their children, will… 'course their flight northwest to where these waters rise?'"

"Oh!" he raised his head. Slowly a silly grin spread across his face. "I just got a definite *yes* kick in my ear."

CHAPTER NINE

It was now three days since the parade and two since the departure of the reed ship. Gart was wondering if the High Priest's investigators were still pursuing the mongoose mystery. He was not in the right circles to hear anything, although he did make it a point to pass by the city gates to see if the tablets were still there. They were, and at two gates student scribes had set up shop offering to read and interpret them for a fee. Somehow, he could not muster the courage to listen to their interpretation.

Surely it was too soon to assess the full result of the celebration, but Gart dutifully appeared at the appointed time and place when he was informed that "many and urgent matters" awaited the Regency Council's attention. Everyone was on time and the meeting started without delay.

Kre-eg and Ni-Pada-Dan congratulated all present for the work done on the celebration and both gave special recognition to Colonel Alkohn for the appearance and performance of his pikemen and to Na-tem-Na for his work in enlisting everyone of the major families in the event.

The Lord Chamberlain requested to speak and, after several minutes of striking thoughtful poses, he finally began:

"Gentlemen, it was a great party. The enthusiasm of the people was surprising. We showed off our army and our arms. We were able, at last, to show the people their king. How much we accomplished is hard to say. Some people had never seen their lugal, and now they have. Those who remember him from twenty years ago must have seen evidence of his decline. Those of us who see him every day were strongly reminded our lugal's term is near its end and we must begin making preparations to provide for a successor.

"Before we even begin this process, however, we should deal with General Mem-el's concerns that some of our disturbances here were the work of agents of a neighboring city; someone who might attack us. Do you have something further — General?"

"Yes indeed," responded the old warrior. "Much good work has been done by some of our people, even while others were celebrating. We are especially grateful to Captain Kre-eg, and others who have gathered information through business channels. I will ask Colonel Alkohn to present the findings."

"Sirs," the colonel began crisply, "we have tried to evaluate all of our near neighbors from a political as well as strictly military standpoint. We have looked at the likelihood of their attacking us, and the feasibility of our attacking them, if it should suit our purposes. We considered Eridu, Larsa, Erech, Lagash, Umma and Nippur.

"Eridu, to the south, is busily engaged in improving her irrigation system, and would hardly have the energy or the numbers to engage in adventures in this direction. We could subdue Eridu easily, but this would profit us little. The Assembly of Citizens probably would not agree to it because of family and business ties.

"Larsa, to our northwest, remains under the domination of Lagash, and must be considered together with that city, both as a possible aggressor and as an area for our expansion.

"Erech, to the west, remains a large old city with many resources. Their citizens probably consider themselves to be the dominant power in the area, whether we see it that way, or not. They remain in good trading contact with Ur and Umma. It is not clear whether they feel Lagash is an active threat. We base our ideas on the opinions stated by Prince An-Shan during his recent visit here. I personally am inclined to believe him. Whatever the reasons for his visit, I do not believe he was here for mischief, although the general was quite right in raising that question."

Colonel Alkohn gave a little bow of deference to his commander. "Nippur," he resumed, "continues to grow in wealth, size, and power but seems largely content with being recognized as the religious center of the world. It is quite distant and we need not fear Nippur at this time.

"It will come as no surprise to you," Alkohn took a deep breath and gathered himself up, as if for a final charge, "that Lagash remains both our major threat and our major opportunity."

There was a lengthy pause, at first silent then interspersed with murmurs among the members. Finally, Shi-ten-Ku posed the question.

"Colonel, I am puzzled. How do you see Lagash as an opportunity for us?"

Alkohn resumed his lecture in the same clear tone and regular cadence.

"Most of you are aware of the payments that have been made to Lagash, supposedly in secrecy, since before Demmuzi became lugal. However, he has done poorly in resisting their ever-increasing demands. If this were to be broken to the public, their reaction could be shame and anger at our weak government, or it could be directed into outrage and a thirst for Lagashi blood."

Bruzi raised a questioning finger. Alkohn yielded to him with a nod and a sigh of relief.

"We are properly concerned," Bruzi began, "not only with the facts of this scandal, but also with public reaction, as it seems likely this will soon become general knowledge. How was this secret kept so well over so many years?"

"It is not for me to say," Alkohn stated in a flat tone. "But there are stories that certain commercial interests, particularly those that control the barley market, have made it clear their arrangements were not to be interfered with. Some complainers have been subjected to threats."

Gart was watching the speaker, but noted a slight movement on the dais. Turning his gaze, he saw nothing different. Then it struck him as rather odd that Ni-Pada-Dan and Kre-eg were looking in such different directions, as if to avoid eye contact with each other and the audience. A glance at Mahn-so-ni drew a slight nod in response.

Alkohn resumed his strategic explanations:

"If this were properly framed, we could probably get the Assembly of Citizens to authorize marching against Lagash. Of course, if Lagash were seen as attacking us, the king, or this body, can simply go to war in self-defense!"

"But Colonel, how is this supposed to help us?" protested Shi-ten-Ku, who had now jumped to his feet. "We at the City Council have authorized increasing the army and buying arms, with the understanding that Lagash might be a threat to us. Now you are talking war. What we wanted was peace."

"Please, Councilman," said General Mem-el, who was now on his feet too. "If you had not interrupted, I am sure the colonel would have gone on to warn that war with Lagash would be a very serious matter. They are powerful and ambitious, and they seem to have settled their boundary dispute with Umma. They seem to be directing most of their commercial ambitions to the east and north. However, they have taken Larsa firmly in tow and are gradually eating their way into our treasury. It is still a mystery why they have sent several expeditions as far south as the Larsa-Ur border and then veered off to the northeast.

They certainly may be a further threat to us. The question is, should we simply wait and fight among our-selves, or should we look for an opportunity to rid ourselves of this oppressor and unite our citizens once more?"

The general's message hung in the air for some time. All three speakers, as well as Kre-eg, remained standing, their expressions very serious. The room seemed too warm, the air stale.

"I don't know, I just don't know." The City Council President was shaking his head as he sat down. "How is making war on Lagash going to unite us, except in the grave?"

Silence had prevailed for what seemed to Gart to be several painful minutes when Alkohn finally responded.

"Let me emphasize what General Mem-el has said," Alcohn began. "We do not see war with Lagash as a garden party, but for years we have endured increasing indignities. If we are to defeat them, at least without a fearful cost, we need some special advantage. I don't know just what, but we would need all the right breaks. However, we are the Regency Council and we are the ones who must act for the lugal now. We must look at both our perils and our opportunities."

"What sort of 'advantages' did you have in mind, Colonel?" Ni-Zum-Ka, the Chief Priest, spoke from his seat.

"Well, for example, Lagash seems to be having leadership problems also. We all know that the throne — *kingship* – is one of the one hundred *Mes* — divine principles given at the original creation. Am I not right, Your Excellency?"

The High Priest nodded a slightly suspicious assent.

"Lagash seems to feel called to reinvent the throne," continued Alkohn with one of his thin smiles. "You probably know that about twenty-five years ago the high priest of Lagash crossed the courtyard and assumed the throne.

"He may well have been the most qualified man, as he contended," the colonel continued. "He claimed he was simply returning to the good old ways when the priest was all powerful. But after one priest successor, the priests were back in the temple and a soldier was again on the throne. Now, I understand, they are trying something new. They have decided their leader is a god, and thus warrants total respect and obedience. It might take a while for this to be accepted. Could their confusion be our opportunity?"

"With all due respect, sir," Bruzi was on his feet, "we need more than a little confusion. We are ready to defend ourselves at any time, but we need several more months of training and a lot more arms before we would be able to mount a major expedition."

"I personally have no particular time in mind," Alkohn replied. "I do not know when Lagash will be ripe. I just hope Ur doesn't rot while we wait. Perhaps our priests can tell us if this is an auspicious time for us to go to war."

Mer-luke arose with a dry smile.

"By coincidence, or perhaps by grace of the gods, I asked the young priest who performed this morning's sacrifice to forecast regarding war and the City of Nannar. He told me that today's sheep liver warns us against foreign wars, but has favorable indications for defense. I might add, our study of the stars gives a very similar result."

After Mer-luke sat down, the audience began to stir about, murmuring and stretching to shake off some of the tension that had been building. Councilman Shi-ten-Ku indicated he would speak.

"Colonel Alkohn, can we do nothing to help ourselves, other than make war? What makes you fear Ur is going to rot?"

The colonel arose more slowly this time, beginning to show signs of fatigue.

"Those of you who still venture out on the streets at night," he began, "can smell the sweet-sour of that rot. You will notice a great many young men on the streets. It is common knowledge that when a youth feels the sap of his manhood rising, when he is ready to couple, he is also ready to fight. Let us be realistic. Unless we channel this energy to our benefit, it will destroy us."

Alkohn sat down abruptly, with a solid thump.

Mer-luke was now standing and looking annoyed. After a permissive nod from Ni-Zum-Ka, he said:

"If it please the council, Colonel Alkohn has very properly invited us to understand our situation in terms of eternal principles, the divine *mes*. I would like to point out that although *weapons* and *peace*, as well as *strife*, are on that list, *war* is not one of the eternal and necessary elements. Perhaps we should not yet despair."

The Lord Chamberlain now took the floor.

"Thank you Mer-luke. You are right, we must not despair, but war or no war, we have a very serious and complicated situation on our hands. At present we have a lugal who is not really a king, or at least not able to act as one. He has been ill, or possessed and gravely disabled for – how long is it now doctor?"

"It must be eight months now," Lah-ma-Nah answered.

"And is he getting any better?" Ni-Pada-Dan asked.

"Not really, sir. In fact, he's worse since the parade."

"How long should we say the city and its lands have shown signs of disturbance? Perhaps Ni-Zum-Ka has some records or observations about that," the Lord Chamberlain continued.

"We have noted drought and a mysterious decline in the health of plants, animals and men for about six months. Milk production is down considerably, and there seems to be an increase of irritability and quarreling in the surrounding countryside as well as crime and violence within the city. The concurrence of these conditions with the illness of the king has not escaped the notice of the general public," concluded the High Priest.

Ni-Pada-Dan remained on his feet, as though presiding.

"Dan," Mahn-so-ni addressed the Lord Chamberlain in his easy, informal way, "the inference here seems to be that the land suffers because of the illness of the king. I wonder, though, if we aren't the ones who are making Demmuzi sick?"

Ni-Pada-Dan appeared shocked and quite flustered.

"If…if you are suggesting our lugal has been deprived of good counsel, or...."

"No, no, Dan," Mahn-so-ni laughed. "No criticism was intended. It is the system I am concerned with. How could we expect any man to remain healthy for long, under these circumstances?"

"I guess I still don't understand what you mean." Dan replied.

"O.K.," Mahn-so-ni resumed, "We, the City Council of Fifty, elect someone lugal. It is usually an older man, usually a military leader of some sort. We give him a throne, but tell him not to feel too good about that, as he is only the tenant for the god. We tell him he is Commander-in-Chief but between emergencies the army falls apart. We tell him he is really the head of the temple, but the priests overwhelm him with rules about what he can and cannot do. In addition to this there is a law or a custom or something back there that says if he should survive for twelve years, he shall be strangled as the perfect love offering to Nannar. How could we expect a sane man to agree to such a position if he understood or to remain sane if he didn't?"

"Councilman — Councilman — please stop," implored Dan. I doubt that we have the collective wisdom, time, or energy here tonight to answer all your questions. Worse news yet, it is upon us to take some action without really understanding what ails our land. Lah-ma-Nah, when is Demmuzi's term actually up?"

"In about six months," the physician answered.

"I try to be a very practical man," said Bruzi as he stood up without bothering to ask permission. "Perhaps the gods have already narrowed the choices we can make. Alkohn is concerned that the city will bubble over soon, but I say, and the sheep's liver says, 'Not quite yet.' We will have to make do for a few months.

"In six months Demmuzi must go to his fate. I am sorry, Manz, if I sound the cold hearted soldier here, but we are talking about many lives. Surely, every lugal must know what he has agreed to. Right soon, we need to find a leader to replace him, someone qualified to lead and — yes — crazy enough to agree to it."

Ni-Zum-Ka rose to his feet as soon as Bruzi sat down. However, he waited silently to be recognized.

"There are some procedural problems here. I could go into the background of the many regulations that have been imposed on the *Me* of *kingship* in this city. However, to save time, I will state directly that the absolute prohibition against offering anything diseased or blemished as an offering to our god far outweighs any other consideration. I can assure you the priesthood will not allow the sacrifice of Demmuzi."

To Gart, the silence that followed the High Priest's pronouncement was denser, more oppressive, than the several that had preceded it. Most members sat staring at the floor or walls. Now a few pairs and trios began to murmur.

Ni-Pada-Dan had arisen, lost in thought and forgetting that he was claiming not to be presiding here. He was thinking: They are right, we must get a new leadership structure in place and Demmuzi can't help us with that.

"Yes?" He recognized Na-tem-Na without thought or ceremony.

"Sirs," began Na-tem-Na, "I hope this doesn't sound trivial but — well, I have been puzzled here when I hear 'lugal,' 'king,' 'His Majesty,' 'Demmuzi,' and so on. It seems that the same person may use all of these terms at various times. Is there a proper or preferred title?"

The audience squirmed, but Ni-Pada-Dan smiled warmly at the young man.

"It is not at all trivial. Your question points out how we have caught ourselves in a bind, trying to decide what kind of a leader we want. This problem has a long history. The person who knows the most about this is Lah-ma-Nah."

In response to the Lord Chamberlain's gesture, Lah-ma-Nah stood with a look of reluctance.

"Yes, there are some traditions regarding this subject and I do have some ideas of my own," he said. "I do wonder if this is the time to go into this at great length."

At this point a servant appeared at the door and gestured vigorously to the physician he was to go upstairs.

"It seems my feeling was correct, that I am not to speak now," he said as he half-ran through the room and up the stairs.

He was followed shortly by Ni-Pada-Dan. The remaining members milled about for several minutes. Kre-eg had just stood up, as if to make some disposition of the matter, when Dan reappeared.

"Gentlemen," the Lord Chamberlain spoke loudly, "His Majesty has just suffered another episode of dizziness and numbness on the left side of his body. This seems somewhat better now, but it will be some time before we know if it is serious. Under the circumstances, it would be best that we return in two days, ready to work on the situation as we find it then."

"Meeting adjourned!" said Kre-eg with obvious relief.

At last we have all agreed on something, he thought. In a few days a new leader, at least a temporary one, will be picked and I will be free from this dumb dance with Ni-Pada-Dan. This was beginning to get on my nerves.

As they streamed through the door, Kre-eg jostled Gart's elbow.

"Hey, fella, that wasn't too bad, was it?" Kre-eg asked. "It seemed like they would go on forever while we were in there, but actually, we're out earlier than I expected. Why don't you come along with me across the courtyard and have the temple ladies give you a deep message?"

"Hah!" Gart replied with a quick upward jerk of his head.

"It will do you good," Kre-eg persisted. "Your old lady must be getting big by now. She would probably appreciate your not needing to pester her!"

"I haven't heard any complaints," said Gart. "I would be surprised if Leah agreed with your idea. You will just have to bear the whole burden, Kre-eg."

"Hey, who knows what the ladies think?" Kre-eg dismissed the whole matter airily as he veered off across the compound.

As Gart turned his head to follow Kre-eg his eyes met Mahn-so-ni's. The councilman had been right behind them and his glance indicated he had heard their exchange.

"'Ol' Kre-eg, is as horny as ever," said Gart to cover his embarrassment.

"Horny, or something," said Mahn-so-ni. "At least, for some reason, he just keeps going at one thing or another, doesn't he?"

Gart nodded agreement as their ways parted.

As he walked home Gart wondered about Demmuzi's "dizzy spell." He felt a little dizzy himself. In his pride and excitement at being appointed to the Regency Council he had not dreamed the proceedings could be so murky, complicated and serious. Here he was in the middle of it but not in control of anything. Did any one of them know what they were doing? He had come to the city a skeptic, but he had never felt such grave and dreadful doubts. It would be good to talk it over with Leah, if she wasn't too sleepy.

As he climbed the familiar stairs he began to gain some sense of direction from the faint gleam of lamplight under the apartment door. As he quietly eased the door open, he stopped short. Leah was sitting motionless on the bench, the reflected lamplight glistening from tears on her cheeks.

"What in the world is wrong, Leah?" He dropped down on one knee to get a better look. "Don't you feel well? Are you having labor pains? Is the baby all right?"

"I just don't know," she answered. "It's like a black cloud over everything." She lowered her eyes to the table before her, seeing Nin-ana-Me sitting on this same bench several nights before, praying silently. Leah dared not do less this evening. Oh, Nin-gal, Oh, Nannar, she pleaded silently, let me be careful of my feelings of anger and frustration. Free me again from my sense of entrapment and let this be a time of new understanding. This man says that I am his hope and his refuge. Oh gentle, radiant couple of the night skies, grant that this man will continue to give me the nourishment I need and grant me the wisdom to allow it.

Finally she raised her eyes to meet Gart's anxious gaze. "Your getting hurt and all the troubles on the streets...the baby almost due, the problem of the tablets, the king, the talk or war...."

Gart got up and stepped across the room, pretending to stare out of their tiny windows for a while. He thought, as if things weren't bad enough, and now this. I could bawl, myself. He was immediately ashamed of his self-pity as he reviewed her list of concerns. She had them all, his worries and doubts, and was being a lot more honest in her feelings than he was. She must feel even more helpless than he did, hemmed in by this little room, her weaving and now heavy with child. He hadn't paid much attention to that.

He turned to her, his face flushed. "I get so saturated with this political stuff so I come home and dump on you and don't even notice what a fix it puts you in," he said in a hoarse voice. "You take it all in and gather it all up with great care. I think of just one thing at a time because I can bring it all home and talk about it. Maybe I expect you to cook it up for me."

He thought to himself, here I am again tonight with a whole basket of problems.

She waited, looking directly at him. Silence continued.

This is really hard, he thought. No, I can do it. I'm getting the hang of it. I can hold it in, but loosen up a little..., Wait a minute..., Then he exploded!

"It stinks, the whole damned mess! Talk, talk, talk, scheme, smirk and brag. Leadership, hell, now we have six leaders heading off in all directions — and their alternates are no better."

Leah's startled look made him back off. All his good intentions, he had blown it and unloaded on her again. "Oh, they all have a point, I guess," he said in partial retreat. "But who can ever put it together?"

After several minutes of silence, he began to chuckle.

"What? What?" She looked at him closely. There was such a glint in his eye that her heart skipped a beat.

"Well, this is really crazy," he said, looking embarrassed, "but is it possible that you and I, just being here together, gathering up all this stuff that is happening here in our city and holding it, just waiting, seeing it through lovers eyes...could have some importance, that it could make a difference?"

This man, she thought, how he frustrates and astounds me. He can seem to be so blindly practical and then he comes up with an understanding like this. With wide and radiant eyes, she held her arms open for him.

Their act of love, carried out with awkward care and great tenderness due to her advanced pregnancy, gave witness to their contract.

CHAPTER TEN

The following day, after he had made several minor trades at the stockyards, Gart proceeded to the armory, where he inspected and accepted new weapons and talked to two soldiers who had now chosen to join the full-time duty roster. During these activities he thought about the Regency Council meeting scheduled for that evening. When he tried to remember the meeting two evenings previous, the scenes, ideas and emotions were all scrambled up. When his attempts to sort them out failed to fall into any logical order he was left with the feeling he was the custodian of something that was to be carried with him just as it was, at least until the meeting tonight.

The meeting two nights ago had ended with almost every question left unsettled. If Demmuzi had not had a spell.... Well, no, that assembly was not ready to settle anything. By contrast, the sessions with Nin-ana-Me seemed to end so neatly wrapped up and in balance. He recalled his feeling that he had participated in something important without it involving his personal pride. Was there a skill to this? One he could use tonight?

The audience hall of the Royal Residence had begun to seem like home to Gart. The familiar faces drifted into the room gradually and settled into their habitual spots with little comment. Kre-eg opened the meeting by calling for a report from the Royal Physician.

"His Majesty seems to have recovered fairly well from his latest attack. This is one of five in the last two months. He has a mild weakness of his left leg, but this is hard to evaluate as he is not very active. He eats little, sleeps poorly and has periods of despondency and irritability."

The physicians tone was factual and tinged with fatigue.

"It would appear," said Kre-eg, "that the decisions we left unsettled two nights ago are upon us. The time for debate is over and we must push on. I wonder if Colonel. Alkohn or Colonel Bruzi have any further reports?"

Alkohn stood up abruptly.

"It seems our celebration is quickly being forgotten. There have been three small fires and several fights between gangs in the past two nights."

Bruzi spoke from his seat, "We continue to arm and train. We are a little more ready for war than we were two nights ago, if that is what must be."

Kre-eg conferred briefly with Ni-Pada-Dan before laying out the tasks of the evening.

"Most of us feel a sense of urgency to make at least some decisions on two or three key questions tonight. First, do we choose to solve the problem of violence by launching a foreign military action? Second, who will lead such an expedition and who will lead our city, and should that be one and the same person? Arising out of the second question, should this be a temporary appointment, or do we have the means and the will to select a new lugal now or in the near future?"

Councilman Shi-ten-Ku rose.

"Since we will need a leader, one man people can see and follow, whether there be war or peace, let us start there. We probably cannot wait for six months. What is possible without violating our law and customs?"

"I had hoped you could help us with that," said Ni-Pada-Dan. "The law states the lugal's term shall be twelve years. Trying to overthrow him during that term is prohibited by the God. If the lugal should die, the City Council is to elect a new one."

"That is the law," said Mahn-so-ni, "but what has been the practice?"

"The records are not that clear," answered the Lord Chamberlain, "but evidently all of the lugals, except six, in the last one hundred and twenty years have died within the twelve years. Probably some of those who died were ill or disabled at times but, lacking a crisis, their functions could have been carried out by others. There are lots of ways to duck and dodge but none of them seemed to work very well. Two appointed substitute kings for a day and sacrificed them, but those rulers never regained respect or control, and one appointed a substitute, a slave, who seized control and ruled very effectively for several years. The other three tried to ignore the whole thing but found their powers to rule weakened. They died within a few years of suicide or natural causes."

"The lugal is the one who must appoint the substitute? "Mahn-so-ni asked.

"Yes," said the Lord Chamberlain. He paced the dais for two turns before he faced the audience. "However, I am sure he could be assisted and encouraged."

"There is no precedent for simply electing a new lugal when the old one is alive?" asked Shi-ten-Ku.

"Not that I know of," said Ni-Pada-Dan. "In theory, it would be illegal."

"I believe we have enough background and discussion here," said General Mem-el. "Someone must be named to lead our soldiers very soon. Since it cannot be our lugal, some title must be devised. I know I am too old to campaign, but there are several younger military men in this very room who might qualify. I suggest this council pick someone within one month. I trust we have members here who can convince our lugal, and the City Council, to go along with the appointment of a substitute. Within six months, many things could change. We can make final decisions later."

Without hesitation, Kre-eg said, "All council members in favor, rise." All full members stood. The alternates humbly held their seats.

"That is some progress," said Kre-eg. "How can we settle the question whether we are or are not taking the field against Lagash?"

"Just a moment, Mister Chairman," Shi-ten-Ku said. "I object to being rushed into such a serious and foolhardy move. We have already heard that, lacking some special advantage, we have no assurance of victory over Lagash. I need to hear what such an advantage might be. I am sure the City Council and the Assembly of Citizens will be equally skeptical. In theory, only the Assembly has the right to declare war."

Kre-eg frowned at these objections but said nothing.

The high priest now arose, a mysterious smile on his face.

"Gentlemen, we may have something of interest here. It is quite a find, and you may not see immediately how it could help us. I would like Mer-luke to tell the story, but it is for your ears alone. If it has any value it must be kept as a strict secret for two or three months."

At a nod from Kre-eg, Gart went into the corridor and arranged to have the servants and guards posted out of hearing range. When he returned, Mer-luke was standing, waiting to begin.

"About three months ago, it was necessary to repair some brick-work in an antechamber on the ziggurat. This opened up a passageway into some storage areas in the observatory of the previous ziggurat, which were simply covered over during the most recent construction. Some of our students retrieved a number of instruments and records of calculations. They also found a large earthen jar containing many small identical tokens. We estimated that there were nearly two thousand of them. After careful study, we have determined each token represents one month and this collection and its associated calculations represent and attempt to predict an eclipse of the sun. We now believe it is possible to do this, and that such an event will occur here in about two and one-half months."

The speaker paused, searching for signs of comprehension by members of his audience.

When the High Priest spoke Bruzi usually preferred to retreat into his own fantasies. He scarcely noticed when Mer-luke took over. He was seeing his phantom troops lurking at swamp edge when he heard the word *eclipse*. Suddenly thick gray gloom descended into his fantasy. Moments later his men came charging out of the fog, triumphant and full of energy. This same energy pulled Bruzi to his feet and he suddenly realized he was standing in the chamber gesturing aggressively for attention.

"Eclipse of the moon, of course, but an eclipse of the sun? If this has a bearing on military matters, why have I never heard of it?" he asked.

"Perhaps it's because, by our calculations, it is one hundred and eighty years since it has happened here in Ur," Mer-luke answered. "There are few written records, and oral history is seldom precise. The stories tell of a rapid darkening often at midday, but not always. The sun disappears quickly and may be invisible for several minutes. The darkness is profound, but the sky is not totally black.

"As for the military significance; there is a story about an Amorite siege of Erech. This was about two hundred and fifty years ago. The invaders were breaching the walls when the high priest of Erech placed a curse on them. Within minutes the sun was swallowed up and the terrified Amorites fled. The people of Erech were equally surprised and frightened, but reaped a benefit from the experience. It would seem to me that if one army knew what to expect, even if they were told only minutes before, and the other army knew nothing, that might make quite a difference. What do you think, sir?"

The sound of voices gradually rose over several minutes as the members and alternates consulted their neighbors about the possible uses of this new information. Finally, Bruzi noticed that

Mer-luke was still standing, looking at him as if expecting an answer.

"I really don't know what I think about this idea. I do think that I wouldn't commit an army to battle on the basis of daydreams or interpretations of the stars," Bruzi said.

"You are absolutely right about that, Colonel Bruzi," said the astrologer. "Do not take any action based on our calculations that wouldn't be otherwise justified. I am really on the spot just by mentioning our ideas here. But how could I ignore the timing of this discovery? It raises the whole question of the concurrence of the paths of the heavenly bodies and the course of human affairs. Just thinking about putting such grand theories to the test with our own blood has filled me with dread. But each time I have tried to discard the idea, there has burst through the gloom an insistent conviction that says, This is it! Go with it!"

Both General Mem-el and Colonel Alkohn were on their feet.

"If I were to believe this," said the general, "even my imagination could get fired up. How can you predict such a thing?"

"I take no personal credit for this," said Mer-luke. "Two of my young assistants have correctly predicted the last two lunar eclipses. The dark day of the sun may require some different methods. We are handicapped because this darkening has been so rarely observed." He paused a moment then looked up, scattering a piercing look about the room. "It may be conceited of us," he said, "to presume a special message here for Ur...but if our patron, Nannar, has gone out of His way to prepare a special gift for us and we ignore it, the shame will ever be upon our heads."

"I find this a fascinating development," said Alkohn, breaking the lengthy silence. "Perhaps the heavens are encouraging us to do what must be done anyhow. We would want to be as sure as possible before we give this any weight. What further can you do to be more certain, and how precise do you think you can be?"

"One thing that would help us a great deal," said Mer-luke, "would be a better determination of times and dates from another point of observation. We would like to know if the story about the flight of the Amorites from Erech due to an eclipse refers to the one that was observed here one hundred eighty years ago, or was that a previous eclipse? It is possible the observatory in Erech may have records that would help us. Our present calculations indicate that the darkness will occur here in twelve weeks on the morning after the new moon and that it will most likely be about an hour before noon."

"Other than the observations from other cities, is there any way we could be more certain?" asked Bruzi.

"The only thing that occurs to me," said Mer-luke, "is the writings report that for twenty to thirty minutes before such an event, the star of Inanna was visible at midday. This would be a late warning, but if she is seen, we could be quite sure as to what would follow."

"We are very interested in what you have to say," said the general. "How can we help you get what you need."

"I and my assistants would be happy to go to Erech, Larsa, even Lagash, but the time is very short and we would need some men at arms for protection, some supplies and some excuse for going there that would not prematurely disclose our prediction, if it is supported by what we learn abroad."

"Excellent!" The old general gave a little jump in place as he threw up his forearms and chin. "It shall be done within a day! What do you say, gentleman, a junior officer and four men at arms, disguised as traders, of course?"

There was a general murmur of assent.

"What do you think, Colonel Bruzi? Should that officer be one of us?" the general asked.

"Well," said Bruzi, as he stood scratching his chin, "it would be very helpful in regard to secrecy, but that narrows it down to Lieutenant Eber-Sin and our chairman here. I know Gart's wife is expecting to give birth soon and he will probably have his mind on that, but I don't see why Captain El-Sheh, Kre-eg, couldn't go."

Gart was startled. His unborn child a factor in state policy? Bruzi had always seemed decent enough, but could he really be that aware or considerate? If Bruzi thought Gart was not attending to his duties, he would have told him directly! Did someone want to get Kre-eg out of town, or worse?

"Thank you, Bruzi, for volunteering the captain." Ni-Pada-Dan had sprung to his feet. "I would like to point out he is not under your direct command and he already has very important duties here at the Royal Residence, as well as on this council."

"Oh come now, Dan," said the chief priest, "he has an alternate. I am sure Gart could fill in at one or both of those jobs very well. I think Captain Kre-eg would do just fine as our diplomat. He has become well known for his charm and — dash."

"It is up to the general and the captain," the Lord Chamberlain said, biting off his words and throwing them over his shoulder as he sat down abruptly.

"Well, what is your reaction, Kre-eg?" The general said with enthusiasm.

Kre-eg did not answer, but sat down and turned to confer with Ni-Pada-Dan. After about two minutes the Lord Chamberlain arose to speak.

"I will speak on behalf of our chairman in this matter, as it would be unseemly for him to directly mention his requests." The expression on the speaker's face led Gart to wonder if he was having a pain somewhere.

"Our Commander of the Royal Bodyguard is pleased you have confidence in him. He would like to point out this mission could be rather complicated and each city will call for a different approach. If he is to represent the lugal and pretend the visit is simply returning the recent call of Prince An-Shan, which seems believable, he should carry the rank of colonel," Dan said.

Gart could hear the sharp intake of breath from Colonel Alkohn. The general's expression suddenly became grave. Bruzi was making faces at Gart, seeming to indicate he was not surprised. Ni-Pada-Dan had stooped to confer further. Now he resumed speaking.

"In addition, we of the Royal Household strongly suggest the Royal Bodyguard Commander should be a captain, as is customary."

Some members stirred but no one spoke. Everyone's eyes were on the deepening furrows of the general's brow.

"I hope, young man, you are not taking unfair advantage of my obvious enthusiasm for this project. I know we are asking you to risk your life. That is what soldiers do. I hope you will be as bold at seizing opportunities abroad as you are here."

"If it please the Council," Gart found himself on his feet, a cold sweat on his brow, "in defense of Captain— er-uhh — Kre-eg, it is true that on our recent embarrassing mission to deliver tribute, his rank placed him at quite a disadvantage when he had to face up to the Lagashi colonel. I was impressed with how Kre-eg managed. It was surely difficult. Just a little background here," he finished, lamely and sat down.

"Very well, thank you Gart. We do not have time to quibble," said Mem-el. "So, it will be Colonel Kre-eg-el-Sheh and Captain Gart-eber-Sin starting tomorrow. But let it be understood," he thundered, "these ranks are temporary! However, if this caper should really work, I promise they will be permanent." The old soldier finished with a chuckle of anticipation.

"Now, my soon-to-be colonel, what is your battle plan?" he continued.

Kre-eg stood, trying to mask his smile, then pivoted and strode the little dais as he calculated. "We will need donkeys…say…eight, provisions, trade goods and…baskets, lots of them. As mentioned, Erech should be easy: We are neighborly diplomats returning a courtesy call to their king and our friend, Prince An-Shan. We can be fairly open there. For Larsa we need trade goods, pottery, cloth, jewelry, dates. They will trade for anything. Lagash will be risky. There, we must break out our empty baskets. I'm certain that they know all about our poor crops here, so we go seeking a loan. We will dicker, but we might offer as much as two-to-one payback next year without being unbelievable."

"They would do that?" asked Shi-ten-Ku. "Bleed us for tribute and then loan it back to us?"

"At that rate of interest, certainly. Of course, not the temple or the king's men. These will be private lenders known to me," Kre-eg said.

"And of course, you plan to pay them back," said the councilman, tongue-in-cheek.

"Of course, sir, directly from their own royal coffers," Kre-eg answered.

"I am impressed with your quick answers," said Shi-ten-Ku. "You're a sly jackal, you are, a real trickster, but then your family is in banking."

"Very well," said the general, who seemed now to consider himself in charge, "can you be ready to go the day after tomorrow morning? Kre-eg? Mer-luke? Your assistants? Good!"

"General, if you please, sir," Na-tem-Na interrupted.

"Yes?"

"I feel I should go with them, if I may."

"So why do you feel you should go, young man?" asked Mem-el.

"It is just time — time for me to do something manly, go beyond our borders and do something for Ur."

"Well, you have convinced me, already," said the general. "What do you say, Kre-eg? Yes! Then, so be it. Now, Mr. Lord Chamberlain, are we to assume that Capt. Eber-Sin will take over all of Kre-eg's duties while he is gone, or do you wish other arrangements?"

"I am sure we can work it out as you suggested, General," said Ni-Pada-Dan, without much enthusiasm.

"Very well," Mem-el continued, "in the morning I will meet with Colonels Alcohn and Bruzi to begin specific planning on how we might impose our will on Lagash, with or without 'special assistance.' We have heard enough for one night."

"This meeting is dismissed," said Kre-eg without hesitation.

Gart struggled mightily to imagine himself presiding with such decisiveness. As he made his way toward the corridor Kre-eg grabbed him by the shoulder.

"They couldn't have picked two better men to promote. Right, commander? Come over here early in the morning and I'll show you the basics. Lah-ma-Nah can fill you in on Demmuzi."

Gart could only nod numbly and stumble home. He would have to tell Leah some of this tonight, but the rest would have to wait until he had thought it through himself.

The next morning, he arrived at the palace as early as he felt he dared, knowing Kre-eg's usual late hours. The guard at the entry said that Kre-eg was there and would be upstairs. Gart walked half the length of the upper corridor in the royal apartment without seeing or hearing anyone. Then he heard voices coming through the open door to the balcony which overlooked the king's central garden. He stopped just inside the balcony door.

"Oh, there you are, My Lady. I am in a hurry but I do have a bone to pick with you." There was no mistaking Kre-eg's voice.

"Really! I am surprised to hear that," Nin-ana-Me answered.

"I doubt you are all that surprised," he said. "A couple of your bully boys nearly threw me down the stairs at the House of Women last night."

"Oh, in that case, I may have heard something about it. How may I be of help?" she asked.

"To start with, you can let those guards know who they were dealing with." Kre-eg's voice was rising in pitch and volume.

"And with whom were they dealing?" she asked.

"With a *colonel* in his majesty's army, and the Chairman of the Regency Committee, that's who!" It sounded to Gart like Kre-eg was choking back a shout.

"Now, how could that be?" she said. "I heard they were dealing with some slightly drunk, very obnoxious young buck who was determined to have his way with whomever, wherever."

There was total silence for several seconds. When Kre-eg answered, his voice had dropped a register but had lost none of its intensity.

"I hope My Lady is quoting, in using such terms." he said.

"Precisely," she answered. "If we should be talking about the same person, I would like to point out that, even if you were intoxicated, you must have known you were over the border. One can hardly miss the two large jackals inlaid on the door pillars. Military rank has no bearing on the matter. You had no authorization to be there. The guards were merely doing their job."

"I don't care. They had no right to treat me with such disrespect." Kre-eg's previously ominous tones now seemed diluted with a slight whine.

"So what is the big friggin' deal? The stairway between the first and second level just meant I had to pay three times as much and be a little more polite. I can't imagine this 'boundary' of the third level is all that different."

"From what I hear from you and about you, I have no reason to believe that you could imagine that difference. I doubt you would want to know. Forget about it and stop trying to throw your weight around."

Her words practically crackled. Gart had never heard Nin-ana-Me speak with such crisp authority.

When Kre-eg resumed, his voice was in much better control.

"You're right. I can't imagine and I don't know. What, precisely, is the difference across that 'boundary'?"

"You said you were in a hurry," she said stiffly. "Are you really sure you want me to go into that?"

"I asked a civil question. I would like a complete answer," Kre-eg said, just as stiffly.

"Very well, *colonel*," she said. "I believe you are well acquitted with the first two levels of the House of Women. You know prostitution has been with us from the beginning. The temple attempts to regulate and segregate common prostitution, to reduce the disruption of family life. As you may have noticed, the first level is dedicated to those who simply want to relieve their tensions or to amuse themselves. As you have said, the second level differs little, except it asks more of the customer in cost and civility of conduct."

"Yes, yes. Now the third level," said Kre-eg.

"This is quite another matter," she continued. "This is a place where people come, or even live, for the purpose of engaging in rituals, including those that involve sexual acts."

"Why does anybody need to get involved in play acting about anything as natural as having sex?" asked Kre-eg.

"Ahh! Acting it is, indeed. Whether it is 'play' is a very good question."

"Enough word riddles," said Kre-eg. "Explain yourself."

"Ritual — is it play? Is it just going through motions for the simple pleasure of doing so or is it, as claimed, an actual participation in a drama extending beyond our time and place? I can't answer that for you. Personally, I think it could be either, depending on the attitude and preparation of the actor."

"I'll have to think about that one — but not today," said Kre-eg. His voice was lower, but his speech still brisk.

"You are leaving soon on a trip?" she asked.

"Yes, yes," he said.

"Into the countryside?"

"You might say that."

"Well, I doubt that your trip will take you back to a peasant's view of life, but you will be closer to the natural world than many of us city dwellers ever get. Perhaps, as you travel, you can think about some questions. Is it natural to live penned up behind city walls? Is there power in the rites still practiced in the countryside; libations, copulating in the fields to ensure fertility? When we move these to the city, to the temple, and stylize them, do we lose their power? Do we purify and elevate these earthy rites, or do they still include their dark and deathly perils?"

"I know that I asked for a complete answer," said Kre-eg, "but you are not giving me answers, just a bunch of questions that I have never heard of."

From the sound of footsteps on the shell-strewn garden path and the shift in direction of the voices, Gart judged the two speakers were now walking, together, back and forth under the balcony in front of him.

"I am guilty of taking advantage of your bad humor," said Nin-ana-Me. "I hope you are as uncomfortable with these questions as I am. They may not be answerable in words. That is why the men and women on the third level resort to ritual. No human authority or custom has recruited them. They come to seek meaning and to participate in strange and mysterious observances. One woman has told me that, at night on the ziggurat, she feels part of the whole drama. She is part of our earth-mother, Ki, thrusting her pelvis upward to meet Enlil's starry belly to generate times and civilizations yet unimagined."

"Enough!" said Kre-eg. "You are very poetic, but have mercy. The fourth level, quickly."

"You know those people," said the Priestess. "I am one of them. Our rituals are very public and fully approved by established custom, even the sexual ones. It is prescribed that those who participate publicly must give up their individual privacy in the service of bringing the people and the gods together. When the priest marches naked up the ziggurat, it is said to mean that he has left his personal pride behind."

"Well — harumph," Kre-eg finally said. "Interesting — if true. You sure do have your lecture down pat. BUT THAT DOESN"T EXCUSE THOSE THUGS OF YOURS! TREATING ME WITH SUCH DISRESPECT!" he shouted again.

"No matter what your conduct?" she asked.

"CONDUCT BE DAMNED!" he stormed. "Get off my back! You and your high falutin' theories. You're probably just a bunch of old witches trying to get yourselves back into power with fertility rites and all that shit! You want to rule the roost and scare people, just like they say they used to, before the priests got organized and put them in their place.

"The temple accepts prostitution and tries to bring some order to it," Kre-eg quoted. "What a crock of shit that is! It's a business, like any other, for the temple. Those dumb little gals are humping away every night just so the priests, or the building fund, can get fatter!"

"Be that as it may!" Nin-ana-Me retorted sharply, "at least we provide them with food and shelter and someone to care for them, to listen and comfort them while they are dying of childbirth or all sorts of nasty diseases. That is a hell of a lot more than their customers those high and mighty officers, those big-hearted business men, like your father, have ever done!"

The fury in her voice caused Gart to stop breathing for a few seconds.

"YOU LEAVE MY FATHER OUT OF THIS!" Kre-eg screamed.

"I would LOVE TO! What's the matter? Is it getting too crowded down on the second floor for the two of you?"

"THAT'S IT! YOU'VE GONE TOO FAR!" Kre-eg shouted.

The silence was like a blow in its suddenness. Gart stiffened. The foot-steps had stopped. He could hear nothing — except — now — Bzzt — Bzzzt — Bzzzt, the song of a hornet on the balcony. He eased forward. This was getting out of control! He would have to reveal himself and intervene. Now he could see Kre-eg's head and shoulders. His face was that of the storm god. He was leaning slightly forward, neck straight and gaze fixed. Gart could not see where his hands were, but those shoulders were drawn up.

"DON'T…YOU...DARE."

Her voice was coming from directly beneath Gart, heavy, solid, imperative. Suddenly, Kre-eg turned. Gart jumped back at the sound of pounding footsteps. There must be a stairway up from the garden. Gart was stepping backward as Kre-eg rushed through the balcony door and came to a sudden stop, his face livid.

"You heard, didn't you? Damn you!" said Kre-eg.

"Shhh!" Gart cautioned, thinking very fast, "you will disturb His Majesty!"

"Who the hell cares? The old fart never listens anyhow! Except... sometimes." Kre-eg's head had raised, his voice lowered. Gart turned to see the old monarch standing very erect, arms akimbo about twelve feet away, just into the hall from his chamber doorway. He was leveling an intense and stony gaze at the two of them.

Kre-eg, with Gart in pursuit, marched swiftly past the king without a sidewise glance. Gart noticed that Lah-ma-Nah had also appeared. About half-way down the front stairway, Kre-eg suddenly stopped and turned looking up to Gart, who was at the head of the stairs.

"Oh, yes, commander — well, talk to Dan and Lah-ma-Nah. They know everything to do. I have told the troops." Suddenly a smile began to slide halfway down Kre-eg's face. "Gutsy little broad, isn't she? I'll see you in a few weeks."

As Kre-eg pivoted and stamped on out the front entry, Gart could hear Lah-man-Nah's voice behind him.

"Shall we arrest him, Your Majesty? We can have his head chopped off, if you say!"

"Oh, no," His Majesty rumbled, "if he wasn't brash and feisty, he could never do the things that are being asked of him."

Gart had followed Kre-eg about five steps outside the entrance of the Royal Residence on his way to work. Then he remembered, he was already at work. He returned quickly and remounted the stairs. The lugal and Lah-ma-Nah were standing where he had left them.

"So you decided to come back, did you? That was a poor choice." said Demmuzi.

"I beg your pardon, sir," said Gart. "Yes, I am here for the day. I am Captain Gart-eber-Sin. I understand I am to be your new guard commander, at least for now."

"I know who you are, young man. 'At least for now,' huh? It sure didn't take your friend long to give up on this job."

"My friend, sir?" Gart asked.

"Yes, the great and charming Captain Kre-eg-el-Sheh. He is your friend isn't he?"

"Well — uh — I presume so. You could say that, yes," Gart stammered.

"You don't seem too certain, Captain. What's the matter, don't you stand by your friends when they are in trouble? Most people don't these days. Maybe they never did. The only friend I ever felt I could really trust was my body servant, and he was an Amorite slave. I trusted him, even after all the bad things we did to his countrymen," His Majesty droned on. "That doesn't make a damned bit of sense."

Gart noticed the odd tone of the king's harangue and its strange effect, or lack of effect, on him. Although the words were offensive, perhaps intrusive, they were delivered in a dull monotone tinged with pain and bitterness. Since the result seemed more like the recitation of a lesson, long committed to memory, than a personal attack, Gart did not feel threatened. He was reminded of his recruits hacking away resolutely with their practice swords which, of course, had no edge to them. He also noticed that the king's gaze, although aimed in his direction, didn't seem to focus anywhere. In spite of this, it was not a dull look. It seemed to Gart that there was still a little gleam of fire leaking out, peeping over the top of those hazel irises.

"Perhaps it is because your body servant knows you so well that you can trust each other," suggested Gart, hungry to hear a good word about someone.

"Hah!" said the king. "Knowing me, that would be the worst reason. I messed that up, too. He's gone. I freed him. Not fair that he should have to put up with me."

"And he left you, sir?"

"I had to practically drive him away. Now he is back home and we are both miserable, his wife remarried, his children not recognizing him."

"You know that, sir?" asked Gart.

"No, but it usually works that way," concluded Demmuzi.

Gart was glad for the silence that ensued. He glanced at Lah-ma-Nah for support but was met with only a gaze of forbearance that must have abandoned embarrassment, long ago.

"So, the captain, the other one — Kre-eg — what excuse did he dream up to get out of here and give the job to you?"

"Oh, no excuse, sir. The Council — er — rather, Colonel Bruzi felt Kre-eg was the logical one to provide an escort for some of the temple people to Erech, and other cities, on an urgent mission."

"I know that! Why are you telling me all this stuff?" said the king in a sudden burst of irritation.

Gart's jaw dropped in surprise. He was about to say, "But you just asked me," when his eye caught Lah-ma-Nah's signal to stop.

"Yes, sir," Gart said, meekly.

"So, Bruzi had mercy on him, got him out of here." Demmuzi resumed in his droning tone and plodding pace. "We are well rid of that Kre-eg. He only stayed half as long as Bruzi. He is twice as big a jerk as Bruzi and half the phony I have been."

Gart looked again to the physician for guidance, but when none was forthcoming, he knew he must wait.

"'The old fart never listens,' that's what he said about me. Well, that Kre-eg, he's the one who never listens. Unless...hey-yeah-heh-heh-eh."

Gart wondered if this sound was an attempt at laughter.

"Unless it was those last few statements that Nin-ana-Me laid on him down there, just now," the lugal resumed.

"It makes you feel better when you have someone to talk to?" asked Gart, continuing his efforts to turn this into a conversation.

"Nothing makes me feel better, but sometimes I have to talk. Because I am the king, you poor bastards are stuck with listening to me. My slave couldn't escape. The doctor here, maybe he can't escape, but he is pretty good at hiding. I get about half through talking and he hurries off to make me some willow bark tea. I think that's one cup for me and three cups for himself."

"All right, Your Majesty," Lah-ma-Nah finally interrupted. "It's time for your walk. It will be good for you. You know that. One of your guards will take you down to the garden."

"Royal Bodyguard! Hah! No one would bother to kill me, unless it was myself and I would probably foul that up, too. All right fellow," he said to the guard who was approaching at the physician's beckoning. "Hang up your weapon and let's go. I'm easy to handle."

As the two disappeared onto the balcony and down the stairs, Lah-ma-Nah chuckled quietly.

"Now you see why Kre-eg insisted the job deserves a promotion," he said.

"Yes, I do," agreed Gart. "Being a lieutenant is humbling enough in itself without this!"

"Courage, my friend," said the physician. "If you can hang on until this afternoon, you will see a totally different person. He's really a great soul. It has been a miserable eight months or so for him. I understand that there have been some bad times before, but never for this long."

Gart broke off the conversation because he could see the Lord Chamberlain coming into the entryway by the foot of the stairs. He explained to Ni-Pada-Dan that Kre-eg had departed in a hurry.

"I am told, sir, you understand everything that needs to be done here," said Gart.

Now here's a refreshing change, thought Ni-Pada-Dan. At least he has the good manners to use a little flattery. I might even enjoy a little rest from Kre-eg.

"Hah, indeed! Some days I understand too much — that can make me very unpopular," Dan replied. "But don't worry, I will give you the basic duties and we'll both hope for the best. You may know the Royal Bodyguard's function is to protect the king and his property in war and in peace. You may not have understood it is also important for the household troops to put on a good show; to make the king look good, to help people feel someone important is in charge here. I fear we have not done so well at this lately.

"Being a member of the bodyguard is supposed to be a great honor and brings higher pay. Unfortunately, there is a tendency for the members to get fat and sloppy. Captain Kre-eg was great buddies with the sergeants, but he didn't seem to care much about drill or inspections. His Majesty — well, you can see he hasn't been able to pay much attention to details lately. We really need to look better here, but you may have to proceed with a little caution. The sergeants can give a new officer a bad time if they want to."

At the Lord Chamberlain's suggestion, Gart requested and received a tour of the premises and an introduction to the guards on duty from the senior sergeant. This man, in his early forties, seemed rather bored and indifferent, but Gart surmised that the man was taking his measure. The sergeant had been in the same position and rank for ten years, and must have seen many commanders come and go.

"At what hours does the guard change, Sergeant?" Gart asked.

"At the sixth hour after noon and at daybreak, sir."

"I take it His Majesty inspects his guard in the evening then," said Gart.

"Oh, we don't do that, Captain. We have been — uh —skipping that since His Majesty hasn't been — uh — well."

"In that case, I will have to do the inspecting this evening. That seems a logical time for the entire unit to meet their new commander. Don't you think so, Sergeant?"

"Uhh — yes, sir. We will do what we can, sir."

Gart left the sergeant to poke about the workshops and storerooms of the royal residence on his own. The scurrying that he heard and the surprised looks he encountered from guards and household personnel told him inspections were unusual here.

By midafternoon Gart had to agree the Royal Bodyguard did not look very royal. Considering the numerous beer bellies, he wondered if the household troops would be capable of a real fight. It was true the last two commanders of this unit had received high and rapid promotions, but for the rest of the unit this assignment seemed to present no challenges.

The possibility of a war was looming larger and larger. Tradition would place the Royal Bodyguard at a prominent place on the battlefield. Was it his responsibility to prepare these men for war? If so, what lugal would they be protecting by then? He had been warned to proceed with caution. Evidently, it would take more than Ni-Pada-Dan's owl-eyed disapproval to get this unit into shape.

Gart had been wandering through the ground floor corridor and now he found himself in the garden of the central court. Immediately before him, about fifteen feet away, was Demmuzi seated on a bench staring at a gnarled old tree near the opposite wall of the garden. The tree must have been there for many lugals, and now it was struggling. Numerous branches were bare, others displayed yellow and tattered leaves. An occasional young sprout bravely presented a green and lustrous contrast. Perched on a bare branch was a bird of medium size. The wings and tail were dark, but the breast and head were a soft pearl-gray with a suggestion of tan. The bird was returning the monarch's regard with no evidence of special deference. As Gart followed the questioning twists and turns of the bird's head, he became aware the king was mimicking those movements with his head.

"Come over here, Captain," said Demmuzi, very softly. "I am conferring with my most trusted adviser. Did you understand what he just told me?"

"No, sir."

"He just told me that it was time for me to stop feeling sorry for myself, and to get on with my work. What do you think of that, Captain?"

"Very good, sir. I mean, there are a lot of us around here who could profit from that advice, sir."

"Now you see," the king resumed, "why he is my most trusted adviser. I suppose you would like me to review the bodyguard with you this evening? The bird told me that, too."

"Oh, yes sir! That would be very helpful." Gart was delighted.

In about an hour, Gart could see the guards congregating near the entryway. He sent one of the corridor guards to warn them that His Majesty, as well as their new commander, would be there to inspect them shortly. In spite of the warning, the men were not in good order some ten minutes later when they arrived at the front entrance. Lines were ragged, uniforms were not very uniform and some men were without their weapons. Stragglers were still arriving when Gart and the lugal had finished their silent inspection.

Quite by contrast to the slouching guardsmen, it seemed to Gart Demmuzi had grown, or at least straightened up, a good two inches in the past hour. He was still a little below average in height, but his broad frame, swarthy complexion, grizzled beard and now purposeful tread gave evidence of his previous bearing.

"Sergeant," Gart addressed the day commander, "what is the size of the bodyguard?"

"We are authorized forty men, sir, but we are five under strength at present."

"And how many men do you count here this evening?" Gart continued.

"Uhh — about thirty, I believe, Captain."

"That is what I count also," said Gart. "Where are the other five?"

"I would imagine that they are ill, Captain. I don't have word on that just yet," said the sergeant.

"I will expect to be present in the morning when you question those men," said Gart. "If we have an epidemic on our hands, I would want to bring it to the attention of the Royal Physician. I am sure you will send them word so these men do not keep us waiting in the morning."

"Yes, Captain. Of course, sir," said the sergeant sullenly.

"Sergeant Mag-sun," Demmuzi spoke for the first time, "I believe you have put on as much weight in the last six months as I have lost. You had better get that in control or we will cut your rations, and I don't want you giving the captain here a hard time. No funny business!"

"Oh no, sir, we would never do that!" The sergeant seemed quite surprised by the vigor of the king's speech.

"Most of you are too young to remember," Demmuzi continued, "but thirty years ago I was the new Royal Bodyguard Commander, so I know how that goes."

Gart and the king inspected the ranks once more, now that all the stragglers were in place. Gart resisted his temptation to get picky about their appearance, but before the king left Gart pushed the sergeant a little further.

"Sergeant," he said, "if the five missing men are fit for duty in the morning, I want you to give five other men the day off."

"The day off, sir? I don't understand."

"Only the day. They will report in the evening to Lieutenant Ramlil at the North Armory to join his unit in training exercises. Your men need to get back in touch with the active military units. I expect us to be prepared to take the field, if need be, in one month. You may dismiss your men."

Gart tried to sound as martial as Colonel Alkohn. It was a lot easier with a king to back him up. As he escorted Demmuzi into the palace and up the stairs, he saw no shuffle there.

"I liked the way you handled that, young man. You'll do all right here." The king chuckled. "I may just keep you. Maybe we can send that other fellow on a longer trip."

By the end of the second day on his new job, Gart was feeling more secure. Just being familiar with the premises and the faces of the people was helpful. He believed he had made a solid beginning with His Majesty. This was confirmed when the lugal appeared, without comment, for the second evening inspection ceremony.

Lah-ma-Nah had continued to be helpful and encouraging. Most of the household, even the Lord Chamberlain, who was not someone Gart could quickly warm up to, continued to be cordial. It would be some time before the power game between himself and the sergeants would be entirely settled, but Gart was hopeful.

The higher ration allowance that came with the commander's position was very welcome. It appeared futile to try to maintain an active business at the stockyards in the little time he had available. He would try to advise Mar-Ti, as best he could, and hope the lad could make a go of it. Time for neighborhood politics was also scarce now. Gart tried to remember names and extend greetings to his neighbors. If they knew his present job they would probably consider him an insider. That thought was unsettling. Did his unexpected promotion have to separate him from his fellows?

On the third day after Kre-eg's departure, Gart was speaking with Lah-ma-Nah at the entrance to the garden when Demmuzi entered from the opposite side. He walked toward them on the central path, but instead of sitting down at his usual place on the bench, he turned rather awkwardly to his right and approached the gnarled old tree. After a brief inspection, His Majesty broke off all of the little dead twigs that he could reach and pulverized them with his hands, allowing the debris to fall around the base of the tree. That task completed, he returned to the bench to take up his vigil.

"I don't know whether to give you the credit, Gart," said Lah-ma-Nah, "but our charge is eating better and getting civil earlier in the day."

"He is getting some very good advice," said Gart, pointing to the pearly breasted bird, who had just now arrived at his duty station.

"I had noticed," laughed the physician. "That bird has been a big help. As you may soon find, Commander, it is not true that His Majesty hates to talk. He *is* very selective about whom he trusts as listeners. You may be about to join the bird and me in that select circle."

As if on cue, Demmuzi turned to regard the two men in the shady corner.

"Come over here and join me, you two," he said.

As the two seated themselves on the ground in front of the king, Gart nodded at the bird and asked, "Is your advisor still nagging you about your work?"

"You know, he hasn't said a word about that," the lugal answered with a faint chuckle, "but work has been very much on my mind, so you are in for it, on that subject.

"That inspection of the bodyguard two — no, three days ago," the king continued, "that got me going again.

"There was something about it. 'Thirty years,' I said to myself. My first day as guard commander. I was so much like you, Eber-Sin — Gart, that is. I was a little younger, and just as eager, determined to make a go of it. If I've learned anything in those years that'll do you any good, I'd better get it together soon. That last spell I had got my attention. I know my time is getting short."

No one contradicted or tried to comfort him.

After a brief pause he continued. "The one thing I have never admitted to anyone is that I always had a sense that I was going to do something, or be someone, important. I don't know where I got the idea. Maybe my mother believed it, as mothers do. My father never said anything, one way or the other. Of course, he was often depressed. He was also drunk quite a bit, but he never said much, even then."

Here the speaker paused. He had cocked his head, gazing straight at Gart, but his thoughts were obviously far away.

With a sigh he resumed, "In any case, there was always that conviction, my secret that sustained me.

"By the second or third day as a captain and Commander of the Royal Bodyguard, I realized that that position was not nearly grand enough for whatever I was supposed to do. When circumstances placed me at the head of the army, just in time for us to sally forth and defeat the Amorites, who were falling back from a siege of Erech, I could not justify any great sense of accomplishment. I had simply plucked the fruit, ripe and waiting for us."

"That is not quite fair, Your Majesty," said Lah-ma-Nah. "By the accounts I have heard, you had made very shrewd preparations, posting runners and boatmen to keep our forces informed. Mem-el has said your tactics were brilliant."

"Believe what you will about the details," the king said. "Within a week I had become well known and rather wealthy, but the sense of elation lasted only a few days. In fact, within a month, I began to feel miserable, sleepless and gloomy. I recognized the pattern from my father, who was still alive at the time. I didn't want to think about what those feelings might mean, and it went away in a few days."

"You were able to enjoy your success then ?" asked Gart.

"In a way, I did," said Demmuzi. "I got a lot of attention for a while. Much of that was flattery, designed to serve those who served it up. When the army disbanded, I got the job as head of whatever was left. It was a good life. I got married and I was quite happy. Still, through it all, I was convinced that it hadn't happened yet. I hoped to have a son. Perhaps if I couldn't do *it*, whatever *it* was, I could pass the job on to him."

The speaker paused, heaved a sigh and resumed.

"The gods evidently willed otherwise and, for several years, my wife did not conceive. When she finally became pregnant, all seemed to go well."

Gart cleared his throat. He had no right to speak, but he could not entirely contain his impatience. He watched the lugal quietly twist a strand of his grizzled beard around his forefinger and then give it a sharp jerk.

"She was nearly to her time when she suddenly went into labor. She delivered a healthy daughter, but my wife continued to bleed and died within the hour."

"And your daughter, now?" Gart asked, a bit too quickly, trying not to think of Leah.

"She is all right, as far as I know," said Demmuzi. "She was raised by her mother's people. They didn't encourage me to come around much. I suppose they must have resented me over the loss of their daughter. They arranged my daughter's marriage to a wealthy man from Eridu after I became lugal. That is only a day or two's journey, but I rarely hear from her."

"You didn't remarry? There has been no one else?" Gart had waited a bit longer to pose this question. He feared he might be out of order, chatting with his king, as though he were some fellow traveler. He glanced at Lah-ma-Nah who smiled with what Gart interpreted as encouragement.

"No, I never remarried," Demmuzi said. "It was ten years after my wife's death when I became lugal, but I was still despondent when I agreed to it. It has been a strange life. The questions are all different and more numerous than I had imagined.

"As to there being anyone else, it would be best to say *no*."

The following morning, Gart arrived at the Royal Residence even earlier than usual, just to make sure all posts were manned and awake. He nodded silently to the guard at the main entryway and proceeded quietly through the lower hallway to the central garden. He paused at the garden entrance. He started a bit. There, seated on the familiar bench on the west side of the garden was, not Demmuzi, but a smaller, more slender figure clad in a gown of temple blue. Her head was covered with a cloth of the same color. By taking a step to the side, Gart was able to catch enough of her profile to confirm that it was Nin-ana-Me. She sat erect, immobile, apparently looking at the old tree, which was still in the shadow of the east wall.

What did she see there? Gart realized that his previous views of the tree had been dominated by the bird, or by Demmuzi's actions there. There was no bird now. Most of the dead twigs were gone. He had the impression this was a fruit tree, perhaps a tamarind, but he could see no fruit. For the first time he looked specifically at the tree itself. The trunk, as thick as a man's thigh, twisted upon itself, displaying several old stubs and shaggy lines of encrusted bark before it gave off a main branch at waist height. Three or four major forks, before its smaller divisions, were filled with the scattered, yellow-green tatter of leaves. Gart was beginning to feel himself drawn into an entrancing tunnel of leaves and branches, when a sudden eddy in the breeze stirred those leaves and brought him back to his post.

"Hello, Gart. You are here early this morning," said the blue clad figure. "I am usually gone before you arrive."

"Yes, my Lady," he said. "Do you come every morning?"

"I have for the past several months. I know His Majesty is always awake and usually not feeling well. Sometimes he wants to talk to someone, and at other times, not. I must say you seem to have made a favorable impression."

"I have been surprised he seems to want to talk to me. I guess he feels he has to pass on some of the things he has learned, and I am available."

"There is more to it than that," she said. "You are a good listener, as well as pretty sharp with the questions. He likes that. I wish you could have known him at his best. He was very kind to me when I first came here. He still is, as best he can be. When I first arrived, I was into playing the important foreign princess, but he knew that I was frightened. His tenderness in our ceremonial observances was something I did not expect. Those duties are long since delegated, but I will always be grateful."

The experience of that conversation followed Gart for several hours; the sound of her voice, low and even, and his own reaction to being so unexpectedly made privy to such personal thoughts. He searched in vain for one word to express how he felt. It never came, but it must have lain somewhere between *honored* and *confirmed.*

For the next two afternoons, Gart and Lah-ma-Nah waited in the shade of the inner balcony unheeded. His Majesty confined himself to consulting with the pearl-gray bird with the tan chest. These head bobbing conversations were brief, sporadic, serious. On the third afternoon, after seating himself, the king turned about and looked directly at them.

"Very well, Doctor, Commander. We are ready for you now."

The two men left the shade and sat at Demmuzi's feet as though resuming the conversation of three days previous.

"Is that a smile I detect beneath your beard, sir?" asked Lah-ma-Nah.

"Indeed it is, my friends. I have had a very good dream. I know you have been watching me and my councilor bird," the king continued. "We have reviewed a lot of history in the past two days. Much of it doesn't seem important now, but that does not mean that you will be spared from listening to some of it. The bird and I have discussed my long-held secret conviction of importance. Had my secret been found out earlier, I probably would have denied it." He threw his listeners an embarrassed little smile.

"After I became lugal, and I felt no different, I began searching for some grand project. Lugals were originally elected to lead the army in time of war. As the cities became larger, and war an ever present temptation, the job became a steady one. I had already won a war. I had no authority to launch a career of conquest, nor could I see any value in that. Instead of destroying, I considered building. But what? The walls were adequate. My predecessor had just completed a major enlargement of the ziggurat. My additions didn't amount to that much. The people are still admiring his work, and paying for it. Evidently, I had no great talent for diplomacy or intrigue, or I would have found a way to stop the secret and shameful payments to Lagash. In what realm was to be my calling?"

"Was that the subject of your dream, sir?" asked Gart. This was rash interruption and a venture arising out of sitting on the ground in the hot sun with ants biting his thighs and toes.

"Sometimes it is not so easy to say what the subject of a dream is. In spite of your frustration, I am not ready to describe it yet," said Demmuzi.

"Nothing so simple as building a temple or a monument would do," he resumed. "Maybe the gods intended that I do something more — uh — spiritual. The citizens of Ur have always taken precautions that their lugals not mistake themselves for gods, but could I cheat a little bit? When the previous Regency Council asked me to become lugal, they made only the slightest mention of the old stories of king sacrifice. I got the impression there would continue to be ways to evade it. To a despondent man in his mid-fifties, twelve years seemed a long reign. Recently, it occurred to me that by *not* evading the tradition, I might restore the sense of sacred obligation to my office, the sanctity it supposedly had in the beginning, before everyone began to think only of personal glory."

"Oh, sir — !" said Gart. He was neither able to remain silent nor to understand all that he was hearing.

"Now, it appears that even that is taken from me," the lugal continued. "There will be no glory for Demmuzi, a sick and damaged old man, certainly not fit for a sacrifice. What would Ur be giving up? And there is certainly little of my life left I would be denying myself."

"And yet you smile, sir," said Lah-ma-Nah.

"Yes, today I smile. The conviction remains with me, somehow, even as I wait for death, probably in some very ordinary form. How does a man proceed with a grand project under such circumstances? Doctor, recite for me again that passage, the one where Ut-Napishtim explains death to Gilgamesh."

"Again, sir? You know it doesn't solve anything."

"I know, maybe it is like my dream. It is not a direct answer to life's riddle, but it has its effect in another way. I like to hear it."

"As you wish, sir: When Gilgamesh was finally forced to face his own mortality, he sought counsel from Ut-Napishtim, that wise and ancient one who had survived the flood, told him:

'Nobody sees Death,
Nobody sees the face of Death,
Nobody hears the voice of Death.
Savage Death just cuts mankind down.
Sometimes we build a house,
sometimes we make a nest,

But then brothers divide it upon inheritance,
Sometimes there is hostility in the land,
But then the river rises and brings floodwater.
Dragonflies drift on the river,
Their faces look upon the face of the Sun.
But then suddenly there is nothing.
The sleeping and the dead
are just like each other,
Death's picture cannot be drawn.'"

"Yes — yesss." The old monarch gazed wistfully at the ground near the seated Gart. The tiny moving speck was an ant, one of Gart's tormentors who had abandoned that project and was now carrying a small bit of leaf away. "Under such circumstances, how might one proceed?" he whispered.

"If it please Your Highness," said Gart, very quietly, "perhaps by explaining your dream."

"You are as persistent as that ant," said Demmuzi, straightening up and focusing his gaze sharply at Gart. "I approve of that, but I can no more explain my dream than Ut-Napishtam could explain death. I will describe my dream, however, and you can make of it what you will.

"It seemed I was in a swamp or marshy place, near the city. I could not actually see my body, except perhaps my right hand. I could feel my muscles move as if my right arm was swinging a tool, something like a sword or a sickle, which was mowing down the tall rushes ahead of me. I was surprised that, although this was a marsh, I moved forward in an absolutely straight line and my feet remained on solid ground. I turned back to try to see the city, but I could not. I was struck by how straight the path was behind me. It faded into the distance and I could see no one, but as I turned to resume my work, I could hear the voices of several people, men and women, perhaps even a child. I knew they were coming down the path behind me, but I turned back to the north to resume working just as I woke up."

"Was the place familiar to you?" Lah-ma-Nah asked.

"It seemed north of the city, maybe a little west, but east of the present river channel. But there has been no swamp there in my time. It was drained and plowed long ago," said Demmuzi.

"And the path seemed to be going...?" said Gart.

"Hah! You can't trick me young man. I truly do not know where it was to end, but I felt very content that I had cut it as straight as I could, that far. It seemed to be following the river."

"North?" asked Gart.

"And a little west." said the king.

As Gart watched, the king's color seemed to fade and his attention wander. He slowly slumped forward on his bench.

"I am hot and tired. Get someone to help me to my bedchamber," he said.

CHAPTER ELEVEN

It was precisely two weeks after Kre-eg and Mer-luke had departed that the first word was received from them. Gart had just arrived at the Royal Residence that morning when he was approached by Ni-Pada-Dan.

"A messenger from Kre-eg arrived last evening. He reports all has gone well and the information they have received is very favorable. However, they have decided they should go on to Girisu, the capital city of Lagash. They were preparing to leave Larsa two days ago when our courier left them."

"The courier? Did one of the party return?" asked Gart.

"No, it was one of Nam-Ku's business people," Ni-Pada-Dan answered.

"Who else knows about this?" Gart asked.

"Only you and I, outside of the family," said the Lord Chamberlain who then bit his lip in annoyance. Was this the final fruit of his own financial bungling that Nam-Ku the Elamite was now referred to as *the family* in conversations at the palace?

"I thought you might be the logical one to inform the military, since you are now acting council chairman."

"Yes, yes, of course," Gart answered. A strange prickly sensation trickled slowly from the top of his head down to his knees. This was his first duty as "acting chairman." Messenger boy felt more comfortable, and that was how he must conduct himself now. Dare he call a meeting of the Council on his own, without consulting Dan first?

Yes, yes, he would!

Gart departed immediately to make the rounds of the military: Mem-el, Bruzi, Alkohn. He would send a courier to inform the other council members of the evening meeting. Fortunately, he found Mem-el first and was thus able to carry the general's authority and message to the other army members to appear at midday for military planning. They would use the Royal Audience Chamber, a much more pleasant setting than the crowded and noisy armories.

General Mem-el appeared promptly with three other senior officers. Bruzi and Alkohn followed shortly.

"You might as well sit in on this as much as you can, Commander," Mem-el said. "You are certainly going to be heavily involved here, considering your many jobs, temporary and otherwise."

The afternoon military planning session was long, tiresome and filled with spirited debate. Gart struggled to sustain an appropriate sense of gravity and foreboding during proceedings which were bound to have serious, perhaps deadly, consequences for them all. In spite of this belief and his fatigue, he found it hard to stay aloof from the enthusiasm of the senior officers. The news from Larsa had affected the old general like an elixir of youth. His big chance at last, perhaps, Gart thought.

Alkohn and Bruzi were not immune to the enthusiasm either, but they were much more realistic and pragmatic.

They both kept insisting on detailed planning, early assignment of duties, and plans to cover every imaginable failure. In his back row seat, Gart held his silence as his respect for the wisdom of these two officers grew.

The general seemed to extend himself to make Gart feel welcome. Both Bruzi and Alkohn had been rather aloof to him when he delivered the message that morning. He had wondered if his support of Kre-eg before the council during his brazen demands had offended his superiors. Now none of this seemed to matter. All of them were immersed in the challenge they had accepted.

At the end of the afternoon's work, General Mem-el dismissed the others, but called Gart aside to make certain that the plan and the requests of this group were ready for presentation to the Regency Council.

"Very well, Captain — Commander — Mister Chairman, how did you ever get so many jobs?" asked Mem-el.

"I always was greedy," said Gart, "but not that greedy. Now I will be a scribe, too. I'll scratch a few lines on this tablet to help me remember until this evening.

"The first goal," said the general, "is to convince Lagash to come and fight us at the precise time and place of our choosing."

"Is that possible?" asked Gart.

"Difficult, but possible," he answered. "They have a reputation for being proud, ambitious and overconfident, not unlike us. They may also be needing an excuse to relieve internal pressures, just as we do. My guess is that they are spoiling for a fight and a good, strong insult might bring them to our front door."

"That is where we want them?" Gart's voice rose with a slight quaver.

"Absolutely," said Mem-el. "First of all, we need them here to scare our own people into cooperating and exerting themselves in their own defense. Secondly, we have some special features to the lands to the north and east of us. That is the direction from which they must approach. As you know, the river protects us on the west. A few miles south of here it swings east and breaks up into the marshes that extend far to the north. That pretty well blocks any northeast approach."

"Yes, General."

"To the north we have irrigated farm land and a series of irrigation canals. It is across that area that any enemy must come. If we can draw up our army between the first and second canals north of the city, Lagash would need to assemble across the second canal to face us. We will have some portable bridges, as they may well have also, but the canal gives us a line and perhaps some time to parley."

"To parley, sir?"

"Yes, Captain, we may need considerable time to parley, not only to determine if our patron God will swallow the sun for us, but also to give our workmen time to cut the dams and flood the fields to their right rear and cut off their retreat. We also need time for our archers to move into range in their little boats among the rushes to the enemy's immediate rear. We will land a company of pikemen, by boat on the remaining causeway of dry land behind them."

"But what if they don't try to retreat, sir?"

"Then there will be one hell of a fight, my friend. We will have to fight twice as hard as they do, because it is our city that would be sacked if we lose."

"If it be the God's will that we do this thing, there is a lot to do in a very short time," said Gart. "Will you be leading us in the field?"

"No," the General answered. "If we are to believe our astrologers, we are being summoned by an extremely unusual opportunity. However, common sense tells me, this is not a call for personal glory. I have neither the reputation nor the personality to inspire our young warriors in battle, nor have I been able to impress the street mobs. It is better that a young man be appointed. We should decide, tonight, in order to invest him with some authority and bring him forward in the eyes of our people. He must become lugal; necessarily merely acting lugal, while Demmuzi lives."

It was now less than two hours before the full council meeting. Gart felt a need to get away from the Royal Residence, to clear his head, have something to eat and spend some time with Leah.

"You look very serious, my good sir," Leah said as she watched him eat.

"I am serious. It is serious," he said, staring at his plate.

"Is there going to be trouble?" she asked.

"Big trouble," he said. "The question is, trouble for whom? There will be a very important meeting in about an hour."

"Is there word from Kre-eg? Who will preside at the meeting?" she asked.

"Yes, we have word. It is going well. He should be back in a few days, if the Lagashis don't arrest him. I guess that means I am to preside tonight."

"Really!" she said, "I'm impressed. Who called the meeting?"

"I did," he said.

"Now I really am impressed," Leah said. "My husband rounding up the government of the city."

"You're impressed and I'm scared," said Gart, "but I don't see any path but straight ahead — through the swamp."

Gart returned to the Royal Residence in time to be well ahead of the other council members, thus he was surprised to see Mahn-so-ni entering the door just ahead of him. He followed the council-man into the audience chamber, otherwise empty, before Mahn-so-ni turned and recognized him.

"Oh, Gart, I had hoped to catch you alone before the meeting. Good news! The ship is back."

"So soon! Is everyone all right? Were they successful in their trading? Where are they?" Gart's rising voice revealed his delight, but he was having trouble dealing with one more unexpected set of problems.

"Yes, yes, everything, or almost everything, went better than we could have hoped for," said Mahn-so-ni. They did get to Dilmun and struck some good bargains, until the people there realized they were in serious need of copper and upped the prices. The ship is moored in a canal just beyond sight from the city. Orson wants to know if it is safe for them all to come into the harbor now."

"That's a very good question," answered Gart. "I am almost certain the incident at the temple has been forgotten by most people. I've heard nothing lately. Let me talk to Bruzi."

"They wouldn't come into the harbor basin until morning in any event," said Mahn-so-ni. "I'll send one of my sons out early with your decision."

Gart was glad to see Ni-Pada-Dan who was also early. He appeared to be in very good spirits and greeted Gart as "Mister Chair-man" and Mahn-so-ni as "Councilor."

"Perhaps, since our new presiding officer has acted so promptly and correctly in calling this meeting, we should work out the main points that must be settled this evening," Dan said.

"Of course!" Gart agreed, overruling a flash of apprehension about how to proceed with Ni-Pada-Dan sharing the dais.

"If we are to start a military action, we must have recognizable military leadership in the field. "I believe that same person should be named acting lugal. I have been informed General Mem-el agrees and he does not see himself in that role," said Dan.

"Who do you have in mind?" asked Mahn-so-ni.

"That is not for me to say, but the Regency Council must say, and quickly," Dan said

.

It took only a few minutes once the meeting began for Gart to forget his awkward feelings about presiding. Report followed report, and opinions flowed with little dissent. An alarmingly boyish enthusiasm carried them along while they made decisions of the utmost gravity. Only the city council president, Shi-ten-Ku and Ni-Zum-Ka, the chief priest, seemed to have serious reservations.

"I have two questions," said Shi-ten-Ku. "How can we be sure Lagash will not simply ignore us? Can we really insult them enough that they will walk blindly into our trap? I also wonder how we can create the hero we need on such short notice. I am not aware of any wave of popularity for anyone in particular."

"I also have a question," said the Chief Priest. "If things don't go all that well on the field, is the city to be left at the mercy of an enraged horde on our doorstep?"

"Those are all reasonable questions," said Ni-Pada-Dan. "I will respond to Shi-ten-Ku and ask General Mem-el to answer about our defenses. Each of these matters will take some careful planning, but I believe each can be resolved. General, please speak."

The old general rose quickly. "Of course there must be defensive planning as well as intrigue against the enemy. We must begin this immediately. We would retain some troops and a few officers within the city and man the walls with every available able-bodied citizen and gather all sorts of missiles. In addition, we must be prepared to block all of our city gates, while preserving a way to admit some of our own troops if the gods are not with us. This will require a good deal of labor and engineering. I ask Mahn-so-ni if he will head that project."

Mahn-so-ni, looking very serious and a bit pale, nodded assent.

"We must choose now!" Ni-Pada-Dan whispered harshly in Gart's ear.

"Gentlemen, without further delay, may we have your choices for acting lugal!" Gart's voice was clear and penetrating, but with a slight tremor at the end.

Two small, murmuring knots formed quickly, then hushed as General Mem-el arose.

"If the information we think we have about the eclipse holds fast, I believe we should proceed and our choice should be Colonel Kre-eg-el-Sheh."

From his standing position, Gart could see the faces of the entire assembly. Only Shi-ten-Ku and Ni-Zum-Ka showed any sign of surprise.

Shi-ten-Ku jumped up very quickly for a man of his age and girth. "I am amazed the General would suggest an officer with no actual experience in battle. I would feel much more confident marching under a seasoned commander like Colonel Alkohn."

"Thank you, sir," said Alkohn from his seat, "but I feel I will be much more valuable at the head of my pikemen. I am not suited to putting on a public show."

The response had been so quick and smoothly delivered it sounded rehearsed.

"I know Kre-eg — Colonel el-Sheh, is charming and flashy, but how are we going to build this into a hero men would be willing to follow into battle?" Shi-ten-Ku persisted.

"What if he refuses?" asked Gart, of no one in particular.

"No man would, or could, refuse such a duty," said the Lord Chamberlain in his most righteous manner. "We must have someone meet Kre-eg on his way back and delay him outside the city. He must prepare himself and we must prepare for a triumphal entry."

"And just what did he triumph over?" The City Council President was not going to concede, yet.

"Have you not heard. sir?" said Dan, throwing up his hands in mock surprise. "This brave young man, the son of one of our leading business men and the courageous commander of the Royal Bodyguard, discovered in the course of his duties a shameful secret, long hidden from the public by the corrupt and cowardly palace officials. For years our own government has been spending the public's resources to buy peace from the despised Lagashi. Having traveled abroad at great peril to establish the real truth, he returns now with the support of many, to seize power and redeem our honor!"

Gart's mouth hung open in amazement. He would never have imagined Dan to be capable of such dramatic gestures of indignation, arm flinging and finger wagging. Instinctively he turned to Mahn-so-ni to share his surprise and amusement but it suddenly became clear to him that this was more than a parody.

"He's not enjoying this much is he?" he whispered

"No," Mahn-so-ni whispered back. "This is as close to a public confession as he can manage. It's his little gift to us. Now we know he can look at reality. That will help."

Evidently some sense of this was coming through to the others as the initial chuckles soon faded into silence.

Finally, Lah-ma-Nah broke in, “That’s not fair to Demmuzi!”

“Nor is it entirely fair to his villainous Lord Chamberlain,” Dan finished with a bow. “None of that matters now. Heroes and victims, we are all in it together.”

As he straightened up, Ni-Pada-Dan looked directly at Gart with a hard and demanding squint that quickly made him realize that something was expected of him, so he blurted out as best he could, “Is there further discussion? Are there more names to be considered?”

Silence.

“Do you have any comments, Colonel Bruzi?” Gart asked.

At that moment Bruzi was thinking to himself, how did we wind up here? Everyone, myself included, has gone for flash and charm instead of experience.... What other way can we solve this? It’s hard to know.

“No, I have nothing to say,” he answered.

“Enough!” Dan’s whisper was harsh in Gart’s ear.

“Very well, lacking further objections I declare Colonel Kre-eg-el-Sheh is hereby appointed Acting Lugal for the city of Ur. The Regency Council has spoken.” Gart strove to make every word sound official. “We will recess for a few minutes while we reorganize the further business for the evening.”

The recess was for Gart’s benefit as much as anything. Kre-eg’s appointment was unexpected and unsettling to him. The men soon began to rise, stretch and mill around. Servants brought in beer and some cakes. Gart drew Bruzi aside.

“Did you know that the ship is back and waiting outside the city?” asked Gart.

“Yes, Mahn-so-ni told me as I came in,” Bruzi answered. “Is everyone all right?”

“Evidently they are. Do you think it’s safe for them to come back?”

"I should think so," answered Bruzi. "Here comes the man who could tell us, if we dared ask." Ni-Zum-Ka was coming directly toward them.

"Colonel Bruzi, who do you think might be put in charge of the forces defending our walls?" the old priest asked.

"That will be up to General Mem-el, sir," said Bruzi.

"I know that, but he seems so swept up in this project. I fear he will not give this matter much attention, and I know you could influence him. I do hope it will be in competent hands."

Ahh, here is my chance to mention Orson's name and watch his reaction, Bruzi thought.

"I imagine we will appoint one of the regular watch officers," he said. "Do you know Lieutenant Orson-til-Chah? He should be available?"

"Oh, yes, you mean the well-nourished fellow, the scribe?"

Bruzi nodded. He could detect nothing but polite interest in the priest's reaction.

"He seems to know the city very well. Somehow I would have more confidence in him. He is an educated man and a little older than most lieutenants," the old priest said.

Bruzi nodded again and Ni-Zum-Ka, seemingly satisfied, moved on to other conversations. Bruzi signaled Mahn-so-ni to join them.

"Bring them into the harbor in the morning," Bruzi said.

When Gart reconvened the session, it appeared that most of their agenda had already been settled informally. It was only necessary for General Mem-el to announce the prepared plan.

"I remember well the preparations Demmuzi made against the Amorites," said the General. "I will therefore immediately establish advanced outposts with regular couriers in all directions. I believe Captain Eber-Sin is the one to go out to meet our Acting Lugal and explain our strategy. We must not keep our new leader shivering by a campfire all night, so we will send tents, food and drink and establish a pavilion for the party to rest and refresh themselves. When the captain gives us the signal, we will send out the royal chariots, early in the morning, and recruit a crowd to welcome them in grand style by midmorning."

As he left the building following the meeting, Gart found himself, once more, in the company of Mahn-so-ni.

"Gart, you seemed very surprised Kre-eg was elected," said the councilman.

"I guess it's beginning to worry me to see so much power and responsibility placed on anyone as young and inexperienced —and flawed as Kre-eg."

"And placed on you also, to some extent?" asked Mahn-so-ni.

"Indeed," Gart said, startled to hear himself considered among the responsible.

The following morning, one of General Mem-el's couriers arrived with the news that two of Kre-eg's party would be home by midmorning. They had with them most of the donkeys and all of the barley borrowed in Girisu, the chief city of Lagash. The rest of the party had taken a detour south of Larsa and would spend another three days visiting certain places. The only one that the courier remembered was the temple farm near the northwest border. Gart was puzzled by this news but grateful for two more days to prepare his camp and his explanation for Kre-eg.

Gart located the pavilion in a vacant field about two hundred paces off of the main path from Larsa. This location was an hour's walk north of Ur. The most logical route from the temple farm came into the path just north of this point. Then he sent a courier to the farm with instructions to return as soon as Kre-eg's party was contacted. Kre-eg was to be told to look for a welcoming party at this location but nothing else. Early on the third day the courier returned. Kre-eg and his companions had spent the night at the farm and would arrive by late afternoon.

When the procession of five men and two donkeys was sighted, Gart went out alone to greet them. To his surprise, it was the wiry little astrologer, Mer-luke, who was setting the pace, and it was Kre-eg who was bringing up the rear. He was strolling along, hands behind his back with eyes downcast as though studying the tracks of those preceding him. He had never seen Kre-eg in such a posture. The contrast was so marked that Gart, at first transfixed, took the deepest breath he could remember. It was as if his whole world had expanded and a barrier between him and Kre-eg was gone.

"What is the story here, Captain?" Mer-luke asked. "We aren't to be allowed to enter the city tonight? I am weary and more than ready to be home." His tone was sharp and his glance piercing.

"Oh, I am very sorry, sir, I'm sure you are. This is a matter of state, which I will explain very shortly. We will try to make up for your inconvenience. Over there are four large tents with food, drink and soft beds, please take your ease and prepare for a special welcome in the morning. By the way, sir, were you able to confirm your theory?"

"Yes, yes, as far as possible, with our methods," said Mer-luke, brightening up. "The historical facts seem very solid. I only hope our calculations are as sound."

Kre-eg had pretended at first not to see Gart. He did not want to appear surprised by anything, but he had been startled when he glanced up from an unusual series of thoughts about his relationship with Gart to see that very person with both feet firmly planted in the field before him. It had not crossed his mind the "welcoming party" would be Gart, but now the strange appropriateness of that turned him back to his recent thoughts. He had always assumed he was the dominant one in the relationship. So why did he keep going back to Gart? What did he need that Gart had?

Gart's conversation with Mer-luke gave Kre-eg time to compose himself, if not to completely answer his own question. He approached the two in time to hear the end of their discussion.

He smiled at Gart but said nothing. The two of them followed the others to the tents.

"An affair of state, eh? That sounds pretty important," said Kre-eg. "Tell me, what this is about, oh my Commander."

"You are absolutely right there," said Gart. Kre-eg, of course, looked puzzled, as was intended. "I am indeed your Commander, now. You were named acting lugal four days ago."

Kre-eg turned and walked into the first tent. He slowly and deliberately sat down on one of the cushions on the reed matting of the floor before looking up at Gart. His expression was very serious.

"Surely, you are shitting me, sir," he said.

"No, this is no shit," Gart answered. "Perhaps I should say, 'the report is factual.' You may have your own opinion of those facts."

Kre-eg made no reply for several minutes, merely shaking his head from side to side.

"Well, at least my father should be happy," he finally said, "unless it was his doing in the first place. Perhaps not, though. He has been quite ill, recently."

After what seemed like several minutes of complete silence, during which Kre-eg stared fixedly at the mat before him, Gart brought another cushion and sat down nearby.

"Just what the hell is an 'acting lugal'? Can you tell me that?" Kre-eg asked.

"Why, I don't think anyone defined it precisely, other than — uh — the obvious," said Gart.

"I have heard of 'lugal,'" said Kre-eg. "That is supposed to be halfway between a real king and a battle chief; a temporary mediator between the God and men. I have heard of 'substitute lugal' which, at one time, was the poor wretch who was allowed a day or two of phony glory before he was offered as a sacrifice.

"Now you, my friend, as the Acting Convener of the Regency Council, should be able to say just what they expect from me and what authority I have, and for how long." Kre-eg's voice and expression had hardened progressively as he spoke.

"Well, I would say that we want someone up front to lead the troops with enthusiasm." Gart felt shamed into speaking with more authority than he felt.

"Like Enkidu, the wild man who leads the parades?" asked the weary Kre-eg.

"Well, yes, but with more brains," Gart answered. "Our 'Acting Lugal' also needs to impress our people, give them some enthusiasm and hope for the future. Someone young, who can be charming when he tries, like you. It is true that Mem-el, Alkohn, and the other officers are well along in planning the campaign, but there are many other matters that need an individual to make decisions."

"Like what?" asked Kre-eg.

"Well, just for example, it was mentioned that you would be the best one to plan how to challenge Lagash; how to stir them up enough to get them to come at us. The Council has begun to cautiously let the public know about our tribute to Lagash and they are giving you credit for 'discovering' this. That is true of course, in a way."

"This is far too serious a matter for personal vanity or timidity," said Kre-eg. "Do you see anyone else, any other way, at this point?"

"No, I…I come up with…nothing," Gart answered.

As they sat quietly, Kre-eg seemed very much present and also aware of Gart's presence, as though including him in his silent deliberations. Gart had never had quite this experience when he was with Kre-eg before.

Finally, Kre-eg spoke.

"What other news do you have for me? How is Demmuzi?"

"Just fair," said Gart. "He hasn't had any more strokes. He has gained a little strength, but the fight has gone out of him. He has been very kind to me, though."

"Is there anything else I should know?" Kre-eg asked.

"Oh, yes!" said Gart. "The ship is back from Dilmun, a very successful voyage, Orson and his crew are all healthy and very glad to be back."

"Even Bar-shin?" Kre-eg asked. "He must have mellowed since I knew him."

The silence resumed. Kre-eg seemed just as focused and even calmer than before, but Gart began to feel quite restless.

"I know I dropped quite a load on you, Kre-eg," said Gart, "but even before that when I first saw you coming on the road, it seemed something about you had changed."

"Maybe you're right," he answered. "This trip has been a very interesting experience for me. I had to spend quite a lot of time waiting on Mer-luke and his assistants. That gave me some time to think. It was fortunate we went first to Erech, where I spent several evenings with Prince An-Shan. I was very impressed with that man. He, in turn, it seems, is very impressed with the work and person of his sister, Nin-ana-Me. This all gave me some things to reconsider, including some subjects brought up during my last — uh — conference — with that lady, which you might recall."

"You spent your time waiting for Mer-luke and his men in all three cities?" asked Gart. "I can't imagine you waiting around for anyone."

"Well, I did wait, at least some of the time. I must be slowing down," Kre-eg said. It was time well spent, he was thinking to himself. Scenes of the people he had watched — just watched — and snatches of his reflections on his father and Demmuzi — both ill now, possibly near death — these came back to him now.

"Were the astrologers satisfied with what they found?" asked Gart.

"Yes, quite satisfied," Kre-eg answered. "Our records are the most detailed, but they were able to put together enough history to convince them that the eclipse of a hundred eighty years ago was seen in both Erech and Larsa. They would have settled for that, but I insisted that we go on to Girisu."

"For further confirmation?" asked Gart.

"Yes, and they found some, but I had other reasons also."

"Military reasons?"

"Yes, I guess so. I just needed to see what we were taking on," said Kre-eg.

"Is it foolhardy for us to challenge them?" asked Gart.

"It probably is, unless we have some very unusual circumstances working for us. If whatever powers there be can help us to get the new God-King of Lagash to make some rash decisions and come after us, we might defeat their army, strong as it looks."

"And take Girisu and their other cities?" asked Gart.

"I didn't say that," said Kre-eg.

Now just what did he mean by that? Gart was thinking. Well, it's late to belabor this. I should let Kre-eg rest.

The evening meal was somewhat delayed as the servants were slow in getting their cooking fires going. However, it was well worth waiting for. A sumptuous spread of roast waterfowl, fish poached in beer, wheat bread and a porridge of barley and lentils, several cheeses and apples and dates were consumed with great gusto and washed down with much beer and date wine. The travelers had been bathed and provided with fresh clothing by the servants. Other servants washed their soiled garments.

As the meal was being cleared, Gart debated with himself about questioning Kre-eg further regarding the meaning of his detour at the end of the trip.

"So Kre-eg took you on a little short cut to the northwest farm, and where else?" Gart addressed his question to Na-tem-Na to include the others in the conversation.

"We went to a place you know well," the young man answered. "I believe it is called Nafti Junction. We all enjoyed meeting your family, especially your Uncle Eb," Na-tem-Na continued, "but somehow I feel the special attraction for Kre-eg was something called a...."

"A horse!?" said Gart. "So, they still have him? Well, Kre-eg, did you give him another try?"

"Oh, no!" said Kre-eg, "There would be no honor in that, now. Evidently, I will always be remembered there for my first flight." I really have changed, he was thinking. That horse still interests me, but riding him wouldn't mean much in the world I am in tonight.

He got up and rummaged in the baggage piled nearby and returned with a small, flat basket of woven grass, which he handed to Gart.

"Here are some presents for you from your Uncle Eb. He said you would understand what they meant. The belt, however, is from Man-to-Shi. It's like the one I'm wearing."

Kre-eg sat down and stared silently at the embers in the small brazier before them. He was thinking of Man-to-Shi. "Captain, Captain of the Horses," the old man had called him this time. It had been a strange visit. The old man had been attentive. He had given no advice. So why do I feel like I have received something special, much more than a belt? he asked himself.

Gart took Kre-eg's withdrawal to mean that the conversation was concluded and thus he arose and left the tent, taking his basket and belt with him.

The travelers evidently slept early and well. They were already up, sitting around the cooking fire in the pre-dawn chill when he joined them. It would be some time before the chariots arrived, so Gart resumed his questioning.

"Kre-eg, what did you have in mind when you decided to take your party so far out of your way to see Man-to-Shi?" he asked.

"I felt compelled to see him again," Kre-eg said. "I didn't know exactly why then, but several lines of thought may have pulled me in that direction. The trip was challenging, but in the quiet periods I became rather awed by what we had set out to do. We are reaching back a hundred eighty years to reclaim an event to help us do some-thing that might possibly have effects extending even further into the future.

"I began to wonder: Were we, indeed, playing parts in some great drama, or were we just blindly going through motions. repeating the same old story? Gart, you may have…uh…overheard a similar conversation that I had with Nin-ana-Me just before I left."

"Yes, I must confess, I did," said Gart.

"Well, that lady said quite a few things about drama, ritual, acting and going through motions. She said the meaning of an action depended on the attitude and preparation of the actor. As we were walking through the countryside," Kre-eg continued, "I recalled her mentioning that I would be going out into the country. I also remembered the dramatic story of Man-to-Shi and the snake bitten bullock — how he had seized the moment and turned it into something else. Somehow, I just had to see him."

The chariots finally arrived and it was time to form up the "triumphant" procession. Gart chose to drive the second chariot once more. Mer-luke would ride with him, while Kre-eg made his bows from the lead chariot. The onagers and Gart were all much calmer this time. This parade seemed almost routine. When they reached the city gates, several hundred people were waiting, good enough for such short notice, good enough for their purpose. Gart had no trouble recognizing delegations from the temple, the military, Mahn-so-ni and sons. and the house of Nam-Ku. Jeme must have heard about the parade from Leah, and here he was, leading the stockyard hands in enthusiastic cheers.

Within hours of Kre-eg's return, the Royal Residence became a steady buzz of activity, which lasted late into the night. By the next evening, Mer-luke and his collective wizards had checked their calculations and reported that they found no reason to alter their prediction. That evening would be the winter solstice and, in precisely twenty-two days slightly before noon, Nannar, then at full strength though invisible at that time of day, would totally devour his offspring, the sun, to disgorge him after several minutes of darkness.

The astrologers were convinced enough to stake their reputations but perhaps not their lives on it. They again counseled that no policy be based solely on the precisely timed occurrence of this event.

General Mem-el remained the most enthusiastic about accepting this double challenge. Bruzi, Alkohn, Kre-eg and other senior officers were also intrigued but overwhelmed by all the details they must attend to in just three weeks.

It seemed to Gart he was suddenly the center of the whole enterprise. Although it was not clear that the Regency Council had any further function, or just whom the Royal Bodyguard was to guard, all the major players seemed to feel free to leave messages, questions, and requests in his care.

In addition to all of these considerations, Leah, who had been expected to deliver by now, was having only an occasional spell of false labor. Gart had been secretly plotting to send Leah and their baby with her mother to Nafti Junction in time to be out of harm's way, but he found himself struggling not only with Leah's reluctance to go, but also with his own conscience about using his secret information. If she did not deliver quickly, she would not be able to travel. He had hoped to summon his kinsmen to collect their profits from the returned ship and provide Leah with an escort. Now he was tempted to delay notifying them until the crisis was over.

Kre-eg moved into the Royal Residence immediately, occupying a room vacated by Lah-ma-Nah, who now resumed spending nights at his family residence. If Demmuzi noticed the increased activity and the lower level of attention he was getting, he made no mention of it. Gart extended his hours on duty again, both early and late. Usually he could spend some time at home at midday.

On the morning after the solstice, Gart noticed Nin-ana-Me and Kre-eg passing one-another in the upper hall. Their greetings were full and proper, if a bit formal. On the following morning, Gart was on his way to awaken Kre-eg, but found him waiting in the upper hall. As Gart approached, Nin-ana-Me came out of Dem-muzi's apartment.

"A little token for you from your brother, Prince An-Shan, who sends his greetings," said Kre-eg as he stepped forward.

"Oh, thank you, Colonel. I am happy both you and Orson are home safely," she said with a smile that included Gart as the two men departed.

"Kre-eg," Gart began, "the general wanted me to remind you the message to Lagash was up to you. Time is very short."

"Yes, yes, precisely," said Kre-eg. "I have given it some thought, but I want you to listen to it, content as well as form of address. There is also the question of timing and method of delivery."

"Let's go outside to talk about it," said Gart. "The plaza between the temples should be fairly deserted now."

"The sore point we should be able to use is this 'king-is-god' policy they have begun to push in Girisu. Their king, Dar-Azag, has been on the throne for about a year and a half," said Kre-eg.

He and Gart, in the course of their pacing, had just passed the place in front of the altar of Nin-Gal where the snake and the mongoose had met. That seemed long ago to Gart, but, in the full daylight, he thought he could see a slight stain on the limestone step, possibly from Bar-shin's scraped leg.

"I don't see why Lagash needs a god-king," Kre-eg continued. "I think all the priests and half of the people are either angry or skeptical. I would guess that Dar-Azag may be nervous about playing God; acting lugal is bad enough. Now listen to this, Gart. Will this get a rise out of him?

> TO HIS MAJESTY, DAR-AZAG, KING OF LAGASH:
>
> I, Kre-eg-el-Sheh, lugal of Ur and tenant of Nannar-Sin, patron of this city and Lord of all the night skies, must inform you of our Lord's extreme displeasure at those mortals, such as yourself, who play at being gods! Furthermore, Nannar has not forgotten the shameful tribute extracted by you from his tenants. Therefore, I shall lead the mighty men of Ur to wreak justice on your person and to ravage

> your land. You know you are powerless before a true god. Your only choice is, if you wish to spare your innocents and your holy places, you may appear before the walls of Ur with your armies and the unjust tribute of the past four years on the morning of the twenty third day after the solstice for a trial by combat of armies or by combat of champions. If you fail to appear we will be in your streets within two days.

"Is that strong enough?" asked Kre-eg. The acting lugal was nearly out of breath as his presentation had turned quite dramatic.

"This is it!" Gart said. "Once this message is in the hands of the officials of Lagash, there will be no turning back."

"Now you see why our great leaders left this job for me," Kre-eg said, wiping the perspiration from his brow.

For some while there was neither sound nor movement in the hot, deserted temple plaza. Kre-eg stared off into the mid-distance for a minute then moved his gaze to a tangential encounter with Gart. That look was long remembered by Gart. It reminded him of the desert; bleak and pristine. Finally Gart spoke:

"Feels pretty heavy and black?"

"Heavy, yes, but black? No, I don't feel that way. Let's get on with it," Kre-eg said brusquely. "Now we must ask ourselves, who would dare deliver this to Dar-Azag and when?"

"I have been thinking about that and I believe the answers to those questions are Bar-shin and in one week," said Gart.

"Now, you are the one who amazes me!" said Kre-eg. "Why do you think of Bar-shin, of all people, and what makes you think he could do this, or would do it? That sounds crazy to me."

"That is true," said Gart, "but I will stick by it. Something just reminded me of him. In fact, I have seen him daily lately. I have had Surbec, and several other men I trust, transferred to the Royal Bodyguard. Surbec and I have been after Bar-shin to sign on with us, too. He is resisting. He says he is no soldier but he keeps hanging around. I believe that he is well suited for this job."

"But he has relatives in Lagash! He is a malcontent!" protested Kre-eg. He isn't even a soldier, and you've invited him into the Royal Bodyguard? Isn't that a bit much, even if he is 'old family' and Bruzi's brother?"

"Yes, it is a bit much. That's what Bar-shin says too. I guess I have felt an urge to try to sponsor him since he got back and he is, to his credit, resisting me. He sees me as someone who has bought into a system that loves to rule and treats people like cattle, or just ignores them. He really makes me sweat on that one."

"I can follow all that," said Kre-eg, "and I easily recognized that attitude in Lagash. Are we that bad?"

"Maybe I'm kidding myself" Gart said, "but I think we are a little better. Our system is set up to try to balance power and humility. It sounds like Lagash has drifted away from that. I don't know if Bar-shin will see enough difference for him to risk his life, but I believe we have some people here who have hope and a vision of a future. If I understand your plans to spare Lagash, you are one of them and I think Bar-shin would agree.

"Are you speaking for him? This is a very serious decision, to entrust this task to anyone." Kre-eg looked sharply at Gart.

"No, I can't speak for him," Gart said. "If you want to talk to him, I suspect he is in the guards' quarters visiting Surbec."

Bar-shin answered them when they called his name at the door of the quarters. He came out blinking at the bright sunlight.

His expectant "Sirs?" was neither unfriendly nor deferential.

Gart was surprised to find his mouth dry. He felt obliged to open the negotiations, then he must leave it to Kre-eg.

"Are you still considering my offer?" he asked.

"Considering where you found me, I have to admit I am," Bar-shin said.

Kre-eg took a heavy look from Gart to mean he should proceed and handle the matter. "Gart has told me of your questions about joining his command," he said. "You have a right to be suspicious.

He could be just another one trying to use you by appearing to be your friend.

"Therefore, I can hardly ask you to do what I had in mind. It is so crazy and dangerous I dare not give it a noble name."

Kre-eg continued to look at Bar-shin in silence, each waiting on the other. Finally Kre-eg relaxed his stiff posture and Bar-shin relented.

"You can hardly dare ask me, but you know I'm very curious. Well, go ahead, ask."

"Very well, I shall, in a moment. You may know that I am just back from Lagash. You have relatives there. I would guess that you have visited there," Kre-eg said."

Bar-shin nodded.

"Within the year?" Kre-eg asked.

Another nod.

"You are quite a keen critic of how this city cares for its people. How did you find it in Girisu?" Kre-eg asked.

"Pphtt..." Bar-shin spat on the ground. "You know the answer to that. What are you getting at? What do you want me to do?"

This is it, Kre-eg thought, entrusting this to Bar-shin is one more wild gamble. He began:

"All signs indicate the Ur and Lagash are heading for a collision. Some of us have the task of trying to limit the damage. Maybe we could hope to even better ourselves in the long run, if we could turn Lagash from oppressor to ally. For that reason," Kre-eg took a deep breath, "I want you deliver a letter to Dar-Azag calling his god-king act for what it is, just one more attempt to use our people and his for selfish purposes. That should bring their army to our gates within weeks, if not days."

"You are CRAZY, sir!" After this sudden outburst, Bar-shin paused to collect himself. Then he launched into a rapid reply, delivered with clipped assurance. "It would take an alliance with the gods themselves for you to beat Lagash in the field. If you did, your troops would level their cities and you would have no ally left." He turned, as if to return to the guards quarters.

Not just crazy, Bar-shin was thinking, these young peacocks are as stupid as the old crop of so called officials. Don't they realize the power — and the temptation — they have just put in my hands? Dar-Azag will give me a palace and half of his harem for this if I play it right.

"We need an alliance with the gods you say," Kre-eg resumed, propelled by fear at the step they had just taken. "We are well aware of that…and we are proceeding with some very solid and unusual plans. It would be far better for everyone if you did not ask us to describe those plans further until you get back from Girisu."

Bar-shin stopped and turned around completely, a startled look on his face. It was as if he had been physically jerked upright by his sudden realization. These young peacocks are myself on a broader stage, and I am about to join them! Yes, I will be coming back from Girisu. He took two slow steps forward, as if to pass through the narrow space between Kre-eg and Gart. Instead he stopped, placing one hand firmly on the shoulder of each, not facing them, but staring at the surface of the plaza before him.

"Is there no turning back for Ur," he asked.

"No turning back," said Kre-eg.

"In that case...when do I leave? Am I going alone?" Bar-shin asked.

"Be ready to leave in three days," said Kre-eg. "My new seal should be ready then. That will give you two days on the road and a day or two to position yourselves at the Royal Court. I want the message to be given to the king in a public setting, then you get out of there. I want Na-tem-Na to go with you. He made some contacts at the Royal Court last week. That may be helpful." Here Kre-eg looked directly at Bar-shin and then to Gart.

"Are we all agreed?" asked Kre-eg.

"Yes, sir," they both whispered.

As Gart watched Bar-shin go out the temple gate he suddenly felt very small, as small as the day last year when he, Kre-eg and Orson watched from the river gate as the dark storm clouds covered the western horizon.

The following day, Gart found himself repeatedly pestering Kre-eg to clarify the new order in the household. In spite of Kre-eg's reluctant acceptance of his appointment, he showed no hesitation in asserting control.

"Just what is the job of the Regency Council now?" Gart asked. Kre-eg had motioned him to join the cluster of men, consisting of Ni-Pada-Dan, Mer-luke and Kre-eg, who had gathered at the entrance to the Royal Audience Chamber.

"As I see it," answered Kre-eg, "that council voted itself out of a job when they appointed me. That doesn't mean any of you will have any less work, just fewer meetings. Gart, I want to talk to you and Mer-luke in a few minutes.

While Kre-eg was gone, Gart asked Ni-Pada-Dan, "Is that right, sir? Does the acting lugal have to answer to anyone?"

The Lord Chamberlain squirmed, then made a jerking motion with his head, as though to dismiss the question.

"There is no real precedent here. We must all simply help him do the job we gave him to do, unless something goes horribly wrong."

When Kre-eg sat down with Mer-luke and Gart, he gave them only a brief glance, hoping to conceal how burdened he felt. Here I am, right in the middle of this wild situation, he thought. Can this be me, the wise guy, critic and foot dragger, about to tear the whole place apart? How did I get into this position? I'm not in control here. Am I supposed to be? But, we're on our way and I'm the one who has to steer. Now I have to put some crazy expectations on a lot of these people.

"We're making a huge presumption here," he said. "The idea that our supposed enemy will show up to meet our God, at a time we pick, is ridiculous — but too tempting to pass up. Mer-luke, how much leeway must we give you that day before you can tell us if we have special help or just a big fight?"

Now it was Mer-luke's turn to squirm.

"That is very, very difficult," he said. "We can't expect you to hold back two armies for more than a half an hour."

"I agree," said Kre-eg. "We need some way to distract them, to control their attention while we wait. Gart, that will be your job. I expect you to put on a good show."

"Me? Put on a show? What could I possibly know about that?" Gart's voice rose to a near shriek.

"The Commander of the Royal Bodyguard's job has always been mostly putting on a show. You should know that. You can come up with something," said Kre-eg. "Dream up something really wild. You have seen Man-to-Shi do some weird stuff."

"But I'm no shaman," complained Gart. "Besides, a shaman isn't a showman, an entertainer!"

"Well, not really," Kre-eg agreed. "but you'll be great. I have complete faith in you." He spoke with genuine conviction of mysterious origin. He grasped Gart's shoulder, ending the matter with a firm but gentle shake.

"My further concern," said Kre-eg, turning to Mer-luke, "is the precise moment of decision. Can one of you be at my side, right in my chariot on the field to say *'now'*?"

"That would be very hard," said Mer-luke. "To observe the sun without burning our eyes out, we really need our instruments, and they are bulky and located on the ziggurat."

"Runners could never reach us in time," said Kre-eg.

"No," Mer-luke agreed. "We would have to use some type of visible signal or trumpets. A breeze would put sound or smoke signals at risk. That leaves us with flags or flashing mirrors, which could be tricky. We would need some signal towers beyond the walls."

"That can be done," said Kre-eg. "I will send for Bruzi and Mem-el. We can use those mirrors to signal our unit commanders, especially the archers and pikemen in the marsh."

"How many men are we counting?" asked Gart.

"Mem-el says we can put thirty-five hundred armed men into our main force. They will assemble between the first and second canals to the north. We will have an additional five hundred archers in the swamp if we can find enough skiffs for them. That leaves about eight hundred on the walls, for reserve or defense, and about two hundred to cover our flanks to the southeast," Kre-eg said.

"One more thing," said Kre-eg, as they were all preparing to depart. "I do plan to call together all of the members of the former council in about a week to hear a final version of our plans. The message will be in Lagash by then and we will have patrols and couriers out."

That meeting was convened nine days after the winter solstice. It was just two weeks from *the* day, the day that would long be remembered as a most fateful one for their city. Gart was surprised to see Na-tem-Na enter the room. Kre-eg immediately called them to attention.

"Our messenger has just returned. Na-tem-Na, please report to the whole group. In this matter, we can't afford secrets among ourselves."

"Our God must be with us," said the young man. "I have just returned from Girisu. We were very fortunate. On the second night, we talked our way into the palace during a big banquet. We were able to get one of the servers to deliver a present from the new lugal of Ur directly into the king's hands while he was at table. We retreated to the door and did see him unwrap it. As instructed, we did not wait for any reply or reaction, but departed the palace and the city with very great speed. We know some merchants from Larsa who were in Girisu that night. Someone will get their report in a few days."

"Very well done," said Kre-eg. "General Mem-el, Colonel Bruzi, are we ready for them? What are we telling the rank and file to expect?"

"The armorers and smiths have been working day and night since our latest supply of metal arrived," said Bruzi. "We should have a good weapon in the hands of every trained man within two weeks, but with no time to spare."

"We will see to it we are ready," said Mem-el from his seat. "I would like Colonel Alkohn to explain how we are preparing the men."

Colonel Alkohn sprang to his feet immediately.

"We are now speaking to the troops openly about the tribute scandal. We are telling them of great dissatisfaction of our acting lugal and the officers in regard to that disgrace. We say there could be further trouble from Lagash, and now we are hinting it could be very soon. As you have noticed, our calculated day for the eclipse is during the week that we always celebrate the New Year. That is the one date that the old religion is allowed to show itself fully. As you know, that often results in a lot of drinking, copulating and general disorder. We are promoting the theory that Lagash knows about this and may be preparing to fall upon us at that time."

"Do you feel this strategy is working?" asked Mem-el.

"Fairly well," answered Alkohn. "They are training well, but we will need to build a fire under them when we step up our demands next week. I know the eclipse has to remain secret for many reasons, but how are we to handle that?"

At a nod from Kre-eg, Gart arose slowly, taking time to organize his report.

"I am preparing ten men from the Royal Bodyguard. They have only a slight hint at this point. They will be coached as to what to tell the junior officers, once the troops are in place. The ten will keep their eye on the signal tower. If they get a *go* signal, the officers should have a few minutes to tell all the men what to expect. During this time my ten men will advance toward the enemy and scream terrible, outlandish threats at them."

"Very well," said Alkohn. "That will require discipline and very good management. In the meantime, there is something else we must attend to. Starting next week, we will begin to appeal to our men's basic greed and savagery. We shall start to mention the wealth and pleasures of sacking Girisu and all of the other Lagashi towns."

"I see one problem with that, Colonel." Kre-eg cut him off quite abruptly. "There is to be no sack of Lagash."

Alkohn looked stunned. He looked back and forth between Kre-eg's face and the others several times before breaking the silence.

"I think you have missed the point, the whole idea. These are soldiers. At least SOME of us are soldiers. If we live, Lagash dies. That is how the game is played. That is what soldiering is about. That is their reward." The colonel's voice gradually progressed from patient explanation to confident assertion. His face turned from sallow to pink.

"I have other plans for Lagash," Kre-eg stated, matching the older man's assertiveness. "I have finally come to believe in this city, but if Ur is to be anything but a river port, if she is to burst into true flower, she must do more than burn and sack her neighbors. She will need both respect and support from the entire valley, or she will simply be the next victim in the cycle."

"So, now we have a statesman as lugal," said Alkohn with a tinge of sarcasm. "There are dreams of empire, perhaps?"

"I shall ignore your remarks for the moment, COLONEL," said Kre-eg. "But you are advised to be extremely careful."

The colonel made a little jump backward throwing up his hands in an expression of mock alarm.

"I do owe the others, at least a few words of explanation," Kre-eg resumed. "In regard to our handling of this great gift of forewarning, which we believe has been given us, what choice did we have? Three possible courses have occurred to me."

Gart straightened. Something sounded familiar about those last two phrases. Where did they come from?

"First of all" Kre-eg continued, "we could have said, 'Oh, this is just one of those weird things,' or, 'Oh, this is an evil omen, but don't think about it and it will go away.' To bury an encounter with our God, just as those records were put away and forgotten in the ziggurat, would have been a terrible waste.

"Second, we could simply say, 'How very lucky for us', and use it as our opportunity to rob, kill, rape and burn our neighbor, as has been the custom throughout the land of Sumer. After a few days, we would be sick, ashamed and hung over. Our sudden wealth would make us too lazy to work for a living. After we had finished fighting over the spoils, we could try to forget the whole thing as quickly as possible. This second possibility is what I think I just heard proposed here."

Kre-eg stood silent and poised, as if expecting a response.

"Yes...and your third course?" Alkohn obliged him, but his tone was still defiant, taunting.

"Yes, the third choice: I insist there must be a better way! We have a direct invitation from our God. A city that can raise such a ziggurat as ours can surely rise above mud-daubing savagery. Our patron God looks out across the entire land between the rivers every night. Surely, in this eclipse, He is trying to tell us something!"

The room was very silent. No one moved. Finally, Alkohn, still standing, appearing as transfixed as the rest of them, suddenly shook his head.

"And now we have a high priest as well as a statesman." His words remained defiant but their tone had lost its edge. "The City of Ur about to burst into bloom! Where do you get that kind of stuff?" The last statement came with a sneer, but there was a tinge of question also.

"After having walked the streets of Girisu and Larsa, I sought, and I have received, much very wise counsel." Kre-eg's voice was now showing a hard edge. "And I shall continue to do so."

"Rise above...rise above," the colonel was back in stride, a taunting sing song in his reply. "Hell, most of these clods we command don't know Nannar-Sin from a cow's teat. What are they going to rise above? If they don't get a chance to vent their meanness on our neighbors, they'll be back to killing each other within two weeks."

"We *shall* find a way. There will be no sack of Lagash." Kre-eg's voice was even but just as cold as Alkohn's.

"Now, Kre-eg," Alkohn's tone had switched to totally condescending, his facial expression transformed to that of a suffering but forbearing parent.

"I am YOUR HIGHNESS to you, Colonel."

"Your...Heigggugug!" — The colonel's choking sounds were no joke. His face had turned a deep scarlet. Finally with a rasping intake of breath, the colonel whispered, "Never! That is it! I have had enough. I was ungodly stupid to have gone along with this in the first place; naming some rich, spoiled young brat to be acting lugal, whatever that means! Dan, you said he could be managed! Well, manage him! The lot of you! Get him out of here! Don't just sit there like a bunch of dumb heads!"

But just sit there is what they all did. There was not a sound in the grand old chamber except the reverberating echoes of the colonel's shouts. After what seemed to Gart to be nearly a minute, the colonel began to move toward him and the door into the hallway.

"I can not believe this!" Alkohn huffed. "I'll take care of it myself. I'll have him out of here by nightfall, and the lot of you with him. My pikemen will dump you all in the swamp!" His voice rose to a near scream as he turned and shook his fist at the assembly.

Gart pursued Alkohn as he moved swiftly toward the front entrance.

"Guard! Stop that man! Don't let him out!" he shouted.

The outside guard moved quickly to bar the door and two others scrambled out of the entry guard room. Alkohn, seeing them, spun quickly, brushing by Gart before he could react and headed directly for the stairs. Gart saw him draw his dagger. He stopped briefly on the first step to shake it at the council members who were now crowding the audience room door.

"I know how to throw this whole thing back into the City Council, you bastards!" he shouted.

"He's going after Demmuzi!" Lah-ma-Nah yelled in the back.

"GUARDS!" Gart screamed again.

By now the upper hall guards were blocking the head of the stairs. Cornered, Alkohn turned again to retreat, but suddenly he launched himself into the air toward the knot of men at the bottom of the stairs. Among those men were three guards with their spears planted on the floor. Two of the spears penetrated deeply into his body, one in the upper abdomen, one in his chest. The wiry old officer grasped the rungs of the stairs, turned his eyes up to the ceiling and, after one prolonged shudder, became totally still.

One pillar of our temple has crumbled, Kre-eg thought as he surveyed the circle of faces frozen in dismay and disbelief.

Colonel Alkohn was buried before sundown the day following his death, after observances that were neither "quick and quiet," as suggested by Lah-ma-Nah, nor "full military honors," as requested by General. Mem-el. The body was moved to the City Council chambers that night. An honor guard from the Royal Bodyguard was posted. Gart instructed his men this was an accident and the details must remain secret for now. Bruzi took command of Alkohn's pikemen and they all escorted the body to the cemetery.

Gart settled for a few hours of troubled sleep before returning, at his usual early hour, to the Royal Residence. All the way there he wondered how much of last night's ruckus Demmuzi heard or understood.

As he reached the top of those fateful states he saw Kre-eg and Nin-ana-Me standing in the hallway. It appeared they had been speaking, but they fell silent as Gart approached. Uncertain about what was appropriate, he did not speak. Instead, he greeted Nin-ana-Me and then Kre-eg with an awkward gesture that started as a modest nod of the head, but then extended into a shallow bow. At this point, Lah-ma-Nah joined them, giving Gart an excuse to speak.

"How is His Highness taking the affair of the other evening, Doctor?" Gart asked.

"I wonder if he is even aware of it," Lah-ma-Nah said. "He is awake, but very weak and preoccupied this morning."

"Yes, very weak," Nin-ana-Me agreed.

The pall continued to hang heavily upon them and Nin-ana-Me decided to open the subject that was on their minds. She turned back to Lah-ma-Nah. "I was not well acquainted with Colonel Alkohn," she said. "Were you close to him?"

"I knew him only slightly," said Lah-ma-Nah.

For several minutes the group waited, eyes downcast. They began to stir as their time of observance seemed to complete itself and they quietly dispersed.

CHAPTER TWELVE

Late in the morning on the day following the burial of Alkohn, Gart was thinking about how silent Kre-eg had been throughout the previous day. His guess was that beneath the calm exterior his friend was deeply disturbed by what had occurred. Not only had they lost an able commander but Kre-eg must be wondering if his grand plan was credible. Perhaps it would help if he could get Kre-eg to talk out the details.

He was in search of him when he saw him with Nin-ana-Me seated on stools on the garden balcony at the end of the upper hall. They appeared to be engaged in earnest conversation but stopped as he drew near. Perhaps Gart's services were not needed but Kre-eg arose and came to meet him.

"Yes, Gart."

"I don't want to be a pest, but — well, Alkohn said if our troops didn't get into a good fight and...or bring home a lot of booty, they would fall right back to killing each other. Do we need to take that seriously?" Gart asked.

"I do take it seriously," Kre-eg answered, "and we are working on it." Kre-eg's nod toward the end of the hall seemed to indicate that *we* included Nin-ana-Me.

"Gart, if you will get to work on your plan to entertain the Lagashi army for a half hour or so, we will try to manage our own men for a few days afterward."

"Oh, no!" moaned Gart, remembering his task.

"By the way," said Kre-eg, "what was in the bundle from your Uncle Eb? I wonder if it might be something helpful."

"I'm ashamed to admit I forgot that! I put it aside and haven't even opened it," Gart said. "I'm going back home right now and will see what's in that bag. I need any help I can get." Although he had only the sketchiest idea what he would do with his own ghastly assignment, he was more worried about the even bigger job taken on by Kre-eg and Nin-ana-Me. He had just reached the front of the palace when that lady plucked him by the elbow.

"Gart, how is Leah? Surely she must be due."

"That's right. I am going home now to check on her. She was in false labor for several minutes last night. I pray that it will be tonight," said Gart.

"I want to be there. Can you send for me when you know that she is in labor? Do you need help? I could have my novice come and stay," she said.

"No, that won't be necessary. Between the neighbors and Leah's family, we have lots of help. I'll show one of Jeme's boys how to find you. Leah will be very pleased that you want to come."

Leah was sleeping when he got home. Her mother and cousin, who were in watchful attendance, reported that she had been uncomfortable all morning but had no true labor pains yet.

Gart searched quietly for the belt and the flat basket from Uncle Eb. When he opened the basket, he did not understand what he found there — at least not for a while. First, there was a strange, carefully crafted arrangement of feathers— which could only be falcon. After some trying he found it fitted over his shoulders, like a cape, but was very short. This garment, if it was such, was quite handsome. He had never seen anything like it. Next, he found a bone whistle, perhaps a bird call, and a small skin bag contained three fine arrow heads of obsidian. One was white, one black and one red. There was also a small but handsome obsidian knife with a horn handle. There were several little pots of what must be a scented body paint, black, white and red and also a gourd rattle and two objects, evidently whittled out of gazelle horns, that looked like nothing he could recognize, unless they represented tusks.

On a sudden hunch he fitted the slotted flat ends over his own upper teeth and, in so doing, nearly frightened his watching in-laws into leaving. There was a packet of gray, stringy moss and, on the bottom, an animal skin of some sort. He shook it out. It was nicely tanned and trimmed into a loincloth. The bluish gray mottled fur had been left on. It could only be — jackal.

What could this all mean? He could easily imagine Uncle Eb's smile as he prepared the basket, designing one more training exercise to sharpen his nephew's powers of deduction. Now a faint remembrance was stirring. He must have been very young. He seemed to recall half awakening from a nap and hearing something about "long-toothed-monster dancing." The voices were women, whispering and giggling. These things in the basket must be for secret initiation rites! The women were not supposed to know anything about those, but of course, they did. Why would Uncle Eb send these things to him?

Gart certainly would not qualify to be initiated into the Hunter's Brotherhood, at least not now. Suddenly, it came to him with clear conviction, Uncle Eb must be the last of the brotherhood. The boys still hunted, but it was no longer a way of life. These objects were being sent to the city, as everything seemed to flow to the city now. They were being sent to his care for some reason. Perhaps it was to remind him of his roots, roots that went back even to before his people became herdsmen. Yes, somehow these things must be intended for some strange and different initiation.

The days before *the day* were now strictly numbered. Gart had marked them as bright notches through the green bark of a willow wand which he carried with him by day and propped in the corner each night after wiping that day into the past, represented by the blank end of the wand, peeled and flattened by his knife.

When he arrived at the Royal Residence each morning, he usually found Kre-eg and Nin-ana-Me seated on their stools on the balcony above the inner garden. Later, he might see one or both of them sitting quietly with Demmuzi. The old lugal was now quite emaciated. He seemed to recognize everyone, but made no effort to converse. One day Bruzi came to see him when Gart and Kre-eg were both present.

"Learned a lot, those fellows," the sick man said. There were so many mumbles and head nods it was not entirely clear whom he was addressing. Gart felt the old king was speaking to Kre-eg and was signaling some degree of forgiveness.

On the few occasions Gart saw Mer-luke, he searched the astrologer's face with avid eye for any further news, but that gentleman would simply nod and duck his head as he moved on. The first indication Lagash was taking them seriously came through traders' channels. The price of grain had begun to climb progressively in Lagash, starting three days after Bar-shin and Na-tem-Na's hasty departure.

With one week to go, Bruzi began sending out patrols in strength to probe the entire area north, between the river and the marshes. They were soon encountering other patrols. These were Larsa's forces and, although they were quick to argue and threaten, they showed no desire to fight. Bruzi was convinced that were out there just to reconnoiter for Lagash.

The commanders received an unexpected gift of information just three days before *the day*. Somehow, Bar-shin had been able to convince his uncle and cousins to go to Erech, luring them with some exaggerated promises of business opportunities there. Messages from the uncle warned of an expedition being mounted in Girisu to march on Ur. The worry about being ignored was fading, but plenty of other doubts assailed Gart.

Temple personnel were actively preparing for the New Year celebration, which had now been declared to be due on the day after the big day.

Leah's pregnancy must have actually started later than they all estimated. It seemed she had been large with child forever. The baby remained active but not unusually so. It was during the early morning hours of the day just prior to "the big one" that her water broke and what promised to be honest labor began. By daybreak they were ready to send for Leah's mother and the midwife. As there were still long pauses between contractions, Gart decided to go to the Royal Residence early and return in a few hours. He was actually so early he could do little there. He left word of his plight with the sleepy guards and returned home. By mid-afternoon his mother-in-law told Gart to send for Nin-ana-Me.

Jeme's oldest son had been gone only a few minutes when he returned with the priestess.

"You have very swift messengers, Commander," she smiled at Gart. "To be truthful, I was on my way here when I recognized the boy's face and serious expression. I came to inform you personally that Demmuzi died about two hours ago."

"I am sad but not surprised," said Gart. "How did it happen?"

"He seemed to arouse from his sleep and said 'Yes, yes, that's the right direction.' Then he turned his face to the wall and it was over. Because of our present circumstances the temple staff will bury him this afternoon."

About an hour after Nin-ana-Me went upstairs, Gart and the men of the family assembled in the courtyard heard a lusty cry. Within minutes his beaming mother-in-law was on the upper landing.

"You have a son!" she cried.

Leah was disheveled and soaked with perspiration but not less radiant than the assembled women. Sari and the novice had arrived just in time.

Gart laughed with joy and amusement as he noticed Leah's glowing victory smile and compared it to the ruddy scowl of the black-haired little bundle pressed against her cheek.

"Our son, Gart, what shall he be called? Should we ask Nin-ana-Me for a special name?" Leah asked.

Leah's mother finished cleaning her grandson to her satisfaction, wrapped him in a woolen cloth and handed him to Gart. He handled the bundle gingerly. He was aware of the throng of beaming faces surrounding them, but his frowning, red-faced son seemed to be otherwise directed. Beyond his rough introduction to this world, what past, or what future, could this tiny person be protesting?

"We had not made a decision about a name," Gart answered. "Yes, I like that idea. My Lady, what should he be called?"

The Priestess thought for several minutes. Two or three smiles appeared, then faded. Finally, taking a deep breath she announced:

"His name shall be Peleg."

"What an unusual name," said Leah's mother. "I don't remember hearing it before."

"Does it have a special meaning, My Lady?" Leah asked.

"Ahh, I must be careful here," said Nin-ana-Me. "You must not be alarmed if some scholar tells you that it means 'split off from his people.'"

"I don't like that at all," said Leah with a frown.

"I understand," said the Priestess. "I think the proper interpretation is 'an off-shoot of his people.'"

"Is that better?" asked Gart. "And how do you see this fitting our son?"

"Oh, it is as much better as life is over death," said Nin-ana-Me. "You are an off-shoot from your tribe, Gart. You had to leave that place of your birth to come to the city to do things you had never dreamed of, but you are still connected in many ways. Surely, someday, the time of this city will have passed, and some of its people will need to move on, as you and I did. It may not be in your son's lifetime — but some of his descendants — yes, yes, that seems very right!"

Leah looked somewhat reassured.

"What do you think, Gart?"

"I am convinced," said Gart, very firmly. "Yes, he shall be called *Peleg*. We thank you, My Lady."

Gart did the best he could for the sudden influx of guests. Ordinarily the occasion would call for a sheep, maybe even a calf on his present salary. But Gart and most of his guests had now heard the army of Lagash was at that very hour setting up camp not more than a three hour journey to the north.

The expensive grape wine imported from upriver was soon exhausted and the local date wine was rapidly following, when Banarum, their landlord, appeared with beer and Orson with fresh baked bread and cheeses. By dark, everyone except Leah's mother had departed to pray or otherwise prepare for whatever was destined to play out in the next few days.

Gart was convinced it would only be by a sheer act of will anyone in the house would get any sleep that night. He was thankful he had completed his field preparations the day before Peleg's birth. The signal towers were all in place and ready to be levered up to their full height. His preparation tent with his materials, most of it from Uncle Eb, were next to the outermost tower and under guard. He had scarcely begun his checklist when he sank into a deep sleep.

He could hear a familiar voice and feel familiar hands shaking him. It seemed that he had to come back through a tunnel — months, years to reach them. The hands, of course, proved to be Leah's. The voice outside the door, once more, was that of An-Nam, the late colonel's orderly, who was now attached to Bruzi's household.

"Captain, Captain! Are you awake? I must know that before I leave."

Gart staggered out onto the stair landing and thanked the little man. He did not quite dare watch him descend the stairs and cross the courtyard. What if his master's ghost was with him?

Coming back into the apartment, Gart sat cross-legged on the floor and watched his son take his first meal. There was just enough of the dawn filtering down from the tiny windows that he could see Leah watching him. As the reality of this day overcame his sleepiness, Gart could feel the beauty of this moment begin to fade. He knew he must say something now.

"I know what you are thinking, Leah — and, no, I have no way of knowing if what is planned this day was necessary or if it will succeed. They didn't ask my opinion. It seems there is nothing to do but see it through."

"Will you be here to raise our son?" she asked.

"Yes, yes. Today is dangerous, but I feel confident I will be back," he answered. "And as for the secret I have shared with you, if the eclipse happens as predicted, that would convince me Kre-eg is taking us in the right direction."

"Will you be going to Lagash?" she asked.

"No, I don't foresee that."

"Nin-ana-Me told me quite a bit about the plans," Leah said. "She seemed convinced Kre-eg's terms will win Lagash over as an ally — that it will work — but...."

"Yes, but what?" he asked.

"When she left, she kissed me and the baby and said 'Goodbye,' it sounded so final. What do you think she meant by that?"

"I have no idea," said Gart. "If she was so enthused, you shouldn't take that 'goodbye' seriously. I do know that when I say goodbye, now, I mean until tonight or tomorrow." He kissed the two quickly and fled rapidly down the stairs.

At first, his walk toward the gate seemed indecently ordinary. The morning looked like any other, but soon the questions began to come. This enormous *thing* that was upon them and he, among thousands of others, was answering to that thing. Was "It" of the gods? Was "It" even a reality? Had anyone thought "it" out? If not, how did such a *thing* arise? Struggle, battle and death could at least be talked about, planned for. But this — this monster? Gart felt he was walking a line with awe and dread on one side and the horror of human stupidity on the other.

The sun was just coming up as Gart met his advanced party at the northeast gate. As they waited for a few stragglers Gart noticed Orson, who was collecting and deploying his defense forces just across the street. His expression was dour and downcast, most unlike Orson, even under such extreme circumstances. Gart crossed the street to speak to him.

"Are your all right, Ors?" he asked.

"I am in good health, if that is what you mean, but I sure as hell don't feel good about being up on that wall watching while you fellows are out there risking your hides," he said.

"I can understand that," said Gart after a brief pause. "But I sure feel good about having you up there to cover us if we have to head for the gate. Besides, if anybody survives today it should be you."

"What do you mean by that ridiculous remark?" Orson asked.

"You have a gift that will last and grow long after all the soldiers and politicians have turned to dust and blown away," said Gart.

If Orson had any protest he was prevented from stating it by the arrival of two of his subcommanders. After he had answered their questions, Orson stepped back across the street to where Gart stood and said:

"I want you to know that I hear you. I have been hearing all of you right along. I know that those swarms of wedge marks that fill my head are coming from some place. I don't know what to call it yet, but it is important and it has my full attention. Come back alive, Gart. I want to show you what I can do."

As Gart started to collect his party, he had a momentary feeling of release. He and Orson had met. Something was complete.

Gart had chosen twelve men from the Royal Bodyguard, including Sur-bec and Bar-shin, two of Mer-luke's assistants and four men from General. Mem-el's staff. They were to elevate and man the two external signal towers and be in position to relay messages to the unit commanders. As they crossed the bridge over the first canal, they could see the north harbor entrance to the city had been blocked with earth.

A crew had spent the night at the bridge over the second canal and was now preparing to pull it back. The second canal was about half full. Evidently, the water had already been shut off. The idea was to leave a muddy, but passable, barrier between the two armies. As Gart's party reached the second tower, they met a returning night patrol of six men, who affirmed the enemy was indeed out there. They had not begun to stir yet, two hours ago, when this patrol was relieved and told to return to the armory.

The patrol leader could only guess at the numbers, but there must be several thousand. They had at least six chariots and were carrying ladders and timbers, as though prepared to lay siege.

Gart's men were soon at work raising the flimsy observation and signal platforms an additional six feet, rotating their stilts onto the posts already in place. General Mem-el and Mer-luke would remain on the ziggurat. They would be able to see the entire battlefield. If their signal system worked as well as it promised, they should have a great advantage. If Lagash attacked too soon or outflanked them and took the towers, their advantage would be gone.

Soldiers and workmen spilled out of the gate in large numbers. The archers carried additional reed skiffs. Many boats were already in place at the edge of the marsh or on the small island several hundred yards out. A modest observation tower could be seen rising in that vicinity. Kre-eg and his chariots were to withhold their appearance until midmorning, if possible. All of Ur's units should be in place by then. It seemed unlikely that the Lagashi could mass large numbers before that time. If the enemy were, indeed, drawn into the area that had been so carefully prepared for them, the chariots of both sides would be virtually useless, except for show.

Couriers arrived every twenty minutes or so by the main, northern route. Gart did not dare stop them, but they indicated by waves and gestures action was coming after them. The water in the second canal continued to drop. The tower men reported they could now see the diverted waters beginning to creep across the fields on their left flank, toward the river. Pikemen moved into place in large, organized units. The big copper mirrors on the ziggurat and the gate tower winked at the field towers. Because of the low angle of the sun, the towers could not answer back effectively, but their rehearsals had indicated there would be no problem after midmorning.

The next courier came not by the main road but across the fields to the west. He stopped to catch his breath and to tell Gart a column of the enemy was on the road only a few minutes behind him. The tower men now reported that several of Ur's patrols were splashing through the shallow water in the fields to the west. No pursuers were visible, but evidently the road was blocked. Their mirror talk must be working! Or perhaps the enemy column was visible from the ziggurat. In any event, the stream of troops coming out of the gate broke into a brisk trot.

The crack of whips and the rumble of wheels told Gart the chariots were coming across the first bridge and the first part of their script, the part written by them alone, was complete.

Several senior officers arrived and established themselves near the bank of the emptied second canal about two hundred paces north and a little east of the second tower. They stuck several pikes into the ground, butt ends up with colored streamers attached. They had brought several wicker stools which they set in a crescent formation. They could only hope that the Lagashi officers would get the message "this is where we parley." Gart's tent was carried forward and erected about fifteen paces behind them. This was supposed to look like the pavilion of the commander or lugal, but that was not quite its function.

He had just ordered the last bridge timbers withdrawn when the first enemy soldiers appeared. Gart was surprised at how startled he felt. Only then did he truly appreciate he was one of thousands of men in a free fall, hurtling to their fate.

The Lagashi halted and began to spread out just out of bow range. Ur's units were still receiving stragglers, but were showing solid formations at their front.

"Come on, you beggars!" he whispered at the Lagashi soldiers. "Not too fast and not too slow! Turn left, damn it!"

Ur's archers had gotten the signal and had disappeared into the marsh. Kre-eg and his chariots were approaching. Soon they would turn right and pass in review in front of the troops.

The Lagashi troops initially extended in both directions, forcing a small mixed unit of Ur's archers and swordsmen to move down the canal bank to the west to cover them. Once the soldiers discovered the wet fields to the west they pulled back and all new arrivals turned left to face the massed formations of the defenders. A few soldiers scouted the edge of the swamp but without visible evidence of excitement.

At this point, Kre-eg and all of the chariots passed in front of their formed troops at a thunderous gallop.

"LUGAL!...LUGAL!" sounded loud and in perfect unison as the speeding cars passed each formation. Even without the city walls as a sounding board, the blast of sound was impressive.

Kre-eg stood at stiff attention as he tried to push away the sights and sounds without and the doubts and questions within. So many men on both sides, all tossing on waves of excitement and fervid righteousness, all drawn to this by a series of decisions that he dare not even think about now.

Gart eyed the slender shadows cast by the spear shafts planted at the parley site. It would be less than an hour before the predicted eclipse. What if it happened, but an hour early, or a day late?

The enemy had not yet shown any recognition of the parley process but Gart called his ten messengers together.

"Now is the time for the first instructions to be spread. When you say 'first instruction' to the commanders, they will let it be known we are expecting a special sign from the God and it may get very dark. The men must be utterly patient. Look to the signal towers directly for further instruction. A steady string of flashes for several minutes will say that it is likely to get dark. In that case, there will be fire arrows from the swamp. When those stop, the portable bridges must come forward to cross the mud. They must be prepared to fight, but if the Lagashi are frightened into giving up their arms they are to be captured alive, UNDER PAIN OF THE WRATH OF NANNAR! The officers know this, but remind them to start talking NOW!"

"And if we see no flashes from the towers?" asked one man.

"When the enemy begins to stir, our lugal will sound the trumpet. Hold fast until two volleys are delivered from our archers. We are to charge forward on the second trumpet."

Gart had turned to dismiss them, but stopped to add: "Remember! If it gets dark you must all run right up to the canal bank, sound your ram's horns and scream at them: 'THROW DOWN YOUR ARMS AND LIVE! NANNAR RULES HERE. HE WILL SWALLOW THE SUN AND SPIT FIRE ON YOU AND YOUR CITY. VENGENCE ON YOUR FAKE GOD-KING!'" he demonstrated in a muted shout. "This is very, very important!"

The Lagashi soldiers were still straggling in, but most of their units had drawn up solid fronts on the edge of the canal. Their officers eyed the mud and some were beckoning to porters to bring forward the poles and ladders. Some of the officers paced and gestured. A knot of officers collected opposite the banners planted by Ur. One of them, a tall, erect figure looked familiar to Gart. On closer inspection, Gart was certain. The tall one was the same colonel who had taken their tribute in Larsa.

As Gart walked to his tent, Kre-eg's chariot returned to the parley site. Looking at the glitter of the ascending sun on the thousands of burnished copper helmets and weapons on both sides of the canal, he suddenly feared that he might confuse them with the signal, if it came. When he turned to face the tower that fear was dissolved in one vivid flash. The tower man was hitting him right in the eye!

"Blink — blink — blink," almost as rapidly as one could bat his eyes. The flashes continued as agreed. Inanna had been sighted at midday! He must immediately enter his tent and get into costume.

Bar-shin was already in the tent. While they began their preparations they could hear the conversation at the canal bank. Kre-eg must have sent his chariot to the rear, as they heard it pass, while Kre-eg's voice could still be heard in front of the tent. Now there was another voice.

"You, with the chariot, you must have some authority. Let us settle this matter quickly. I'm tired of standing in the sun." The booming voice carried clearly across the canal.

"I am Kre-eg-el-Sheh, lugal of Ur. How do you propose to settle the matter?" Kre-eg answered. "Where is Dar-Azag?"

"He is at our camp and will greet you on your way back among the other slaves," the voice answered.

"You are no lugal, I know you!" another voice broke in. "Last year you were just a flunky, a lieutenant or something like that. You're a fake! Do you think you can play tricks on us?" It was definitely the voice of the colonel Gart had seen in Larsa.

"I am less of a fake than your Dar-Azag who sends you idiots to die for his trinkets. If you don't know enough to respect me, Colonel, I will soon introduce you to one who will take your breath away. How do you propose to settle this?"

"If we don't have to get our feet muddy, we might spare your lives. Put back your bridges, stack your arms and take us to your Royal Treasury. Do that now, or produce your champion, and we will take care of you later." The booming voice had resumed control of the conversation.

"I'm not ready yet," whispered Gart. "Bar-shin, peek out. Is it still flashing? Is it getting dark?"

"Yes, it's still flashing, but the sun seems quite bright to me," he answered.

"Oh, so you have brought a champion have you? Where is he?" Kre-eg asked.

"Right back there," said the voice. "Surely you can see that big man, with a sword as long as you are tall, walking back and forth. Where is yours? These were your terms. Don't tell us you forgot!"

"Oh, we have a champion all right," Kre-eg's voice continued, "but we thought you would all want to come and fight like men. Before you entrust your lives to that fat guy, you should know something. You claim to have a god-king. Our God is our champion, and if you insist, we will have our wizard summon him, starting NOW!"

"A wizard? Is that what I am? Is this what a wizard looks like?" Gart whispered.

"Oh, yes, sir! It must be," Bar-shin answered, obviously very impressed. "Look!" He held up the small copper mirror.

Staring out of the mirror was the wildest face Gart had ever seen. His head was covered with a disheveled wig fashioned from moss. Much of his face was hidden by a beard of similar material. Most of his body was painted black, except for heavy white streaks over his bones, crudely outlining a skeleton. His garments were a loincloth; the jackal skin, held up by his bullock-hide belt, and the little feather cape covering his shoulders. Around his neck had been placed a necklace with a small whitened skull flanked by a half dozen limb bones about the length of his hand. His ankles would now jingle with bells. In one hand he held a red gourd rattle and in the other a small flat drum. His face, where visible, was painted stark white, except for a thin red line around each eye and down his chin. There was a red triangle on the forehead of the skull.

An initial silence greeted Kre-eg's announcement of the "wizard." Then laughter rumbled across the canal.

"You have no wizard! You have no champion. You're stalling, for some reason. Do you think we are just out of the swamp, like you people?" This was the colonel again.

"OUR WIZARD WILL SUMMON THE GOD — NOW!" Kreeg's shout was a bit strained.

As Bar-shin held the curtain aside, Gart ran out the door and landed in a broad based crouch. Slowly, he raised up slightly and began to circle and prance. His efforts were greeted initially with a shriek of laughter from across the canal. This quickly died down, as the onlookers began to take in the details of this apparition.

Only fleetingly aware of the converging eyes upon him, Gart was saturated with awe and dread, but surprisingly, he felt limbs and torso fill with a surge of power. He made brief obeisance to the four quarters. In so doing he saw the tower— still blinking — and the sky — still bright. His fellow officers quickly drew aside, giving him full access to the canal bank and the army of Lagash.

Gart began a series of preplanned traverses in front of the enemy officers. The not-quite-mincing-steps, the not-quite-bobbing trunk movements were a mixture of Man-to-Shi and the wild-man parade marshal. At the end of each traverse he would raise hands and head to implore the skies, strike the drum with the rattle, moan, shriek and reverse his direction. His gait soon synchronized with the flashing mirrors.

Blink — blink — blink — step. Blink — blink — blink— step. Then he realized he did not actually have to look at the tower. The reflection of the flashes sent to him were reflecting off of the copper helmets of the Lagashi officers. If he did not look down frequently, the blinking made him dizzy. Now he could see that the flashes were striking the haughty colonel right in the face.

Blink — blink — blink — step.

Blink — blink — blink — step.

How long could he keep this up? He was getting closer and closer to the canal bank. He looked up. Was he getting dizzy or was the sky beginning to darken?

Suddenly, there was a crash just across the canal. The colonel, and all of his equipment, had hit the ground and was threshing about!

Lagashi officers were running in all directions, some pointing at the colonel, some shading their eyes to look up to the sky.

"It's the falling sickness," someone shouted. "Look at the pink froth on his mouth!"

"It's the hand of the moon god!" a new voice shouted.

"Shut up! Don't panic! He's had these before!" This was the booming voice again.

"YOU don't panic! You old fool! We've walked into a trap!"

"What's happening? It's getting dark!" shouted another voice.

"That's Nannar-Sin's sickness. This is his city and that's no wizard! That's a real demon!" The second officer was nearly screaming.

"That's the demon deputy of the moon god! Let's get out of here!" Another voice rose above the babble.

The flashes had stopped. It was, indeed, getting darker, but as he tossed back his head to do a leaping pivot, Gart could still see some blue — but with stars now! A flaming arrow passed above him, arcing toward the swamp. It seemed his feet never touched the ground again. The sound of the rattle striking the little drum continued, but where were his arms? The gloom rapidly deepened.

"Run! Head for the swamp!" The voices sounded far away. A cascade of fiery arrows arched out of the swamp and total pandemonium broke loose on the other side of the canal.

Thump — thump — turn — twist. A true demon? The hand of the God? What had happened to his arms and legs? Was the God sucking him up into the blackness? Wave after wave of cold prickles coursed up his back. Had he blundered into something too awesome for a mortal to bear?

It must have been an hour or more later when Gart realized he was sitting on the folded tent that was now back under the signal tower. Bar-shin was scrubbing the paint off of his face with the remnants of his wig. He was shivering and praying —to Enlil — to Nannar — to Nin-Gal — to grandfather An. He was giving thanks and asking forgiveness of every godly name he could remember.

Slowly, he began to reorder his memories of the intervening time; the swiftly deepening dusk, the second cascade of fire arrows from the swamp followed by the sounding of many ram's horns, an orderly rush of troops over the little bridges. He must not have actually lost consciousness at all.

The nearby canal bridge was back in place and all sorts of traffic streamed in both directions. Long files of frightened, defeated soldiers, roped together and stripped of everything but their loincloths, were headed north. They were under guard by swordsmen who were bossy enough, but seemed oddly quiet. Other small groups, mostly officers who had been disarmed but not stripped, were headed, under heavy guard, toward the city gate. Along the edge of the marsh there appeared to be some bodies. A few wounded from both sides were being assisted off the field by their fellows. Strings of donkeys arrived from the city. Three of Ur's chariots approached, loaded with discarded arms. Now the tower men reported that a column of captured chariots and pack animals was coming in from the north. The troops from the island must have taken the Lagashi camp.

The fourth chariot contained Kre-eg, along with some Lagashi arms. The onagers halted at the base of the tower and Kre-eg got down. He stood silently looking down at his bedraggled, still paint-smeared friend for some time before he finally said:

"Let me tell you, young man, you scared the hell out of me."

Gart arose slowly to face him.

"Let me tell you, I'm not even sure that was me out there. That was really.... Oh, man, I don't even want to talk about it."

Kre-eg stepped forward and embraced his friend for the first time. He stepped back, raising his arms in dismay as the three of them burst into laughter. Kre-eg had been imprinted across the chest with Gart's skeleton paint.

"Climb in, Gart, let's go home in style," Kre-eg pointed to the waiting chariot.

The streams of soldiers, porters and prisoners parted to allow the prancing onagers to pass. Cheers rose for the dusty, paint smeared pair as they passed, but to Gart they seemed muffled and unimportant. Everyone was very busy or preoccupied.

Here was another chariot ride, but Gart was too muddled to take much notice. He was still not even sure where his legs were. He sought to support himself by grasping the rim on the front of the lurching chariot. The scene rolled by, but he could only attend to his memory of enormous, black space extending in all directions. As his fear mellowed into wonder and fascination he began to question how it could be that such a tiny creature as he could find himself in the middle of such a cataclysm. How dare he think he was in the center of it all? But there it was. The darkened vault of the heavens fixed in his mind's eye did not move. He knew it wouldn't.

Just before they reached the inner canal bridge, Kre-eg signaled his driver to turn off to the right and to go up the canal bank toward the river.

"We had better get this paint and dirt off, or you will scare your wife and baby, and I will scandalize the Lord Chamberlain," Kre-eg said, as he motioned for a stop. The two plunged into the water without testing it and Gart was sharply reminded by the chill that he still had a body.

"Who was it that wanted to go swimming about a hundred years ago?" yelled Kre-eg, as he scrubbed himself vigorously with mud.

"That was you, damn it, and that was only a year and a half ago, damn it!" said Gart through chattering teeth. "That was summer then. If I had had any sense, I would have gone swimming in that flood and skipped all those meetings."

The two squatted naked among the reeds to dry off. The afternoon sun was quite warm and showed no after-effects from being swallowed by the moon only a few hours before.

"I feel almost human again," said Gart.

"It's a good thing you do," answered Kre-eg. "We still have the trickiest part ahead of us. I will need a *daemon* deputy tomorrow, as much as we did today."

"Oh, no!" moaned Gart, not comprehending. *Daemon* deputy? *Demon* deputy? He didn't even want to know if there was a difference. "What's left to do, other than the clean up, and the New Year celebration?" he asked, sensing immediately his question was a feeble attempt to stop a world that just kept coming at him faster than he could handle.

Kre-eg remained silent for several minutes, although he continued to look directly at Gart.

"Why are prisoners going both ways?" Gart finally asked. He was not comfortable waiting for Kre-eg to answer his question.

"We have to do this just exactly right," Kre-eg said. "If we are to get respect and cooperation from Lagash and all of our neighbors, we have to do it absolutely right."

"But what is it that we must do 'exactly right'?"

"We are sending half of our army to Lagash, escorting most of their men home. They are defeated and disarmed but it is necessary that we save them from humiliation by making it clear that they were defeated by the God. When their people see our armed soldiers and their disarmed men in their streets, and when they see all that gold and silver on its way back to Ur, we will have their attention. If they saw the eclipse too, we shouldn't have trouble from them for a long time," Kre-eg said.

"I'm still pretty shaken up from today," he added.

"As am I," said Gart.

"But it seems very clear to me," Kre-eg continued, "if we fail to use this gift from the God to change people's thinking — that would be a terrible waste. What we have done so far is nothing.

We must do something more, something wildly extra-ordinary, to mark this day so it has some meaning to our people."

Gart found himself growing uneasy again about what he was hearing. "Something really, wildly extraordinary?"

"You must have given this a lot of careful thought, Kre-eg," Gart said.

"It's not just my idea," said Kre-eg as they remounted the chariot.

"You have a great career ahead of you as a politician and statesman," said Gart.

"I don't think so," Kre-eg replied, in a tone so crisp Gart was startled.

As he strode from the chariot into his home courtyard, Gart felt a sudden wave of dread. This faded quickly as he mounted those familiar stairs. Before the last step, a lusty cry reassured him about at least one family member. Leah's beaming face made it two. Whatever the source of his dark premonition, it wasn't in this house.

It was still quite dark and rather chilly when Gart left the apartment the morning after the eclipse. He was aware of a sense of urgency he struggled to understand as his legs carried him automatically toward the Royal Residence. He was surprised at the number of people in the streets at this hour. Was he late? Had something gone wrong? Had there been a counterattack?

As he entered the gate to the temple compound, the lighted torches on the ziggurat, and in the courtyard, reminded him that the rites of the New Year would shortly begin. Entering the Royal Residence, he also found an unusual number of torches and lamps burning in the lower hall and in the audience chamber. Just inside the entrance to the room, Kre-eg sat quietly on a stool on the low speaker's dais. Looking about the chamber, Gart saw no one else.

Kre-eg indicated, by a small hand signal, that Gart was to join him. But when Gart had seated himself, Kre-eg continued his silence, looking at Gart but without further sign of recognition. The sense of dread that Gart had felt so strongly when he left Kre-eg the previous evening began to come back.

"'The trickiest part remains.' You mean today?" Gart asked.

"Yes — yes — today."

"The troops will be in or near Girisu by tonight," said Gart. "To take a city without a battle, and without sacking it, is unheard of. Are you afraid that will get out of hand?"

"Oh, no, that is not the problem," said Kre-eg, now fully present. "Bruzi is a believer. He can see the long range benefit and he has good control of his troops. We made a point of not sending so many of our men that they would be overconfident and get out of hand. The tricky part is to catch this tide of emotion, even add to it, so new horizons are opened up right away. Never before has there been such an opportunity."

"You mean the New Year? You plan to use the ritual in some special way?" asked Gart.

"Yes, yes! It is decided," said Kre-eg with a sudden violent shake of his head and shoulders, as though once more coming out of a daze. "That is what ritual is for. It makes people—some people — see differently; remember, establish something.

Gart's uneasiness grew. "You said, yesterday, that we must do something 'wildly extraordinary,'" he said.

"Yes...yes, only human sacrifice will do. We must make the strongest statement possible. We must show that it is not that we do not dare to take human life, but that we have taken the care to not plunder and murder, that we did that knowingly—deliberately and for a good reason."

Gart felt numbness surround his mouth and extend downward into his shoulders. His struggle was not even on the level of belief or. disbelief at this point. He simply must stay focused, not be overwhelmed, keep talking.

"Do you really think you can change human nature – the order of things?" Gart could hear his own voice, but it sounded wooden, far off.

"Human nature? Yes, even that." Kre-eg's voice was suddenly warm and assured. "If I wasn't convinced we can change the order of things, at least a little, I wouldn't go to such extremes."

The numbness had not left Gart's face. He wasn't sure he wanted it to. He began to look at Kre-eg with suspicion. Had this man, who had such disdain for god-kings and not much respect for any authority, gone too far?

"Wouldn't this be contradictory? Confusing? Sacrificing prisoners so it will be remembered that some were spared?" His voice still sounded flat, distant. "Sacrificing prisoners is nothing new."

"Oh, we're not talking about prisoners," Kre-eg's voice rose. There was almost a suggestion of a chuckle. "Those prisoners can go home, as soon as we get our gold and soldiers back. We have volunteers."

"Volunteers? Who would believe such a thing? Everyone would think that they had been duped or were possessed." Gart was now fully alert and beginning to feel annoyed.

"Perhaps, but I think not," Kre-eg said serenely. "What if it were their lugal and the High Priestess who volunteered?"

"WHAT? You have gone absolutely mad! Both of you!" Gart shrieked.

"Perhaps. But I think not. Perhaps, I have gone absolutely sane." Kre-eg's answer was firm and direct.

Gart stood up suddenly and walked toward the rear of the room, as though to flee the situation. Then he stopped and turned slowly. He must be alert. He must be very, very careful with a man in this state of mind. His initial wave of fear and surprise was slowly turning to anger. He must control that.

"Somehow, Kre-eg, after all of your brilliant work, you have fallen into some very serious errors in thinking. This must not happen. As your friend I cannot allow it. When and how did you make this decision?"

"First of all," said Kre-eg as he jumped up, straightening himself to his full height, "let's get this straight. You cannot prevent this. I'm the lugal and I don't owe you any explanations."

In the momentary but tense silence that followed, Gart stared at the fine tremors in Kre-eg's eyelids. Was he extremely angry or was that a twinkle he was holding back?

"However," said Kre-eg, breaking into a smile, "I do want you to understand, completely. In fact, if this is to work, we need at least someone to completely understand. You are our best chance. Go ahead. Ask your questions."

Glad for another chance, Gart said; "All right, Kre-eg, how and when did you decide to do this?"

"I don't feel that I had much to do with deciding this at all," said Kre-eg. "I didn't ask for any part of this situation. I feel absolutely and powerfully thrown into this. What I must do has, fortunately, only been shown to me bit by bit. You must know, Gart. You must feel as thrown into my life as I do!"

Gart could not deny having such an experience, but he must not start agreeing with anyone in Kre-eg's condition.

"You have been *thrown* before," he said as the picture of the bucking horse flashed across his mind. "There are still plenty of places you can get off! Does Ni-Zum-Ka know about this? As chief priest, is he going to allow this?"

"He didn't bat an eye. It was almost as if he were expecting it," said Kre-eg. "As for getting off, I am quite sure that I don't want to. I like this ride. I feel free for the first time in my life."

Gart stared at him numbly, struggling to make sense of what he was hearing. A very brief flash of his chariot dream came to mind. Was this "free" feeling the same kind of flying?

"Oh, I have given 'getting off' plenty of thought," Kre-eg resumed.

"You had better think again, real quick!" Gart snapped. "What I mean is — what have you considered?" Kre-eg's fierce look told him that not one bit of control had been ceded.

"Well," said Kre-eg, "'three possible courses came to mind.' Does that sound familiar to you, Gart? This is not Man-to-Shi talking. These are my own thoughts."

Gart nodded slightly, acknowledging the association.

"The first course that occurs to one," Kre-eg seemed as calm and detached as a lecturer who knew some abstract subject by heart, "is to simply resign this acting lugal thing and to settle down, get married, raise a family, sell beer, get fat and old. I had never accepted my life was going to be like that. In my family I haven't known any lasting commitment or close personal relationship and, until recently at least, I wasn't attracted to the role of householder.

"The second course might be to get myself elected the real lugal and compete with all the other rulers of the past, and all of those now trying their hand in our neighboring cities. Since few take that old twelve-year limit seriously these days, some way could be found around that. I admit that appeals to me a little more — but not much."

Here, Kre-eg paused and paced the little dais where they had been sitting.

"It is the third course that fascinates me." he said. "Who else has had a life so complete — for his capacities —and also a chance to end it with meaning and honor at just the moment of ripening; to shed the body not just to be forever young in memory, but as a marker to remind people that life extends beyond their city walls, their personal ambitions, even their bodies."

The luster in Kre-eg's eyes startled Gart and he realized he had been lulled, snared, by the dramatic explanation. Surely this must be madness, but he would make one more appeal to reason.

"What makes you think this will mean anything to anyone, Kre-eg? Why won't they just remember you as another ruler who went too far too fast and couldn't handle it?" Gart asked.

"Ahh, that is quite right," Kre-eg continued, unperturbed. "We found this to be the most difficult part. It is just sorting itself out right now and is beyond our control. The survival of this marker, this stela, depends on other persons including, to some extent, on you, Gart. It is important we reach an understanding."

We? Ahh… Nin-ana-Me, yes, that's who! He had been so focused on Kre-eg he had not even begun to try to understand the role of the Priestess in this folly. He had gotten nowhere trying to reason with Kre-eg. If he was to save his friend's life, he must attack now, use any tactic.

"Nin-ana-Me! of course! She's the one who has led you into all this! She sure fooled me. I never thought she could do something like this. If she could fool me, you must have been easy, with your weakness for women." Was that a flush he saw on Kre-eg's cheeks? Better pour it on. This might be the right track.

"I never paid any attention to that talk about 'watch out for the all-devouring fertility religion.' I thought we were beyond all that. I thought Nin-ana-Me was on an entirely different level. I suspected the two of you had something going, but I never thought it would kill you! Kill you both! She's going down and taking you with her. Wake up, man. Wake up and knock some sense into your head. Knock some sense into her head, too. We need you — need you both. Kre-eg, how could you change so much?" Gart sobbed as he collapsed onto his stool and hid his face in his hands.

What could he try now? In his mind's eye he saw Colonel Alkohn flying down the stairs. Oh, how welcome those impaling spears must have been, if he were as frustrated and in the grip of his convictions as Gart felt now. But Alkohn had been wrong. Brave, sincere — but wrong.

He was aware Kre-eg was standing by his side. He felt a light hand on his shoulder.

"You never disappoint me, Gart. That was a wonderful try, but you don't get the main idea, and even you may know that you are wrong — wrong — wrong."

"How do you mean, 'wrong'?" Gart asked in a flat tone. He leaned over to wipe his nose on his kilt.

"Wrong about Nin-ana-Me talking me into anything. We arrived at our decisions independently. Maybe that's not quite true in my case. She really gave me a jolt and I have been working it through since my last trip began. When I say I love this woman, don't confuse that in any way with my habits and opinions up to the last few months. This is not like anything you would know about. No, — I can't say that, I don't know what your experience of love is, but she really got through to me and I have discovered things about myself that I hardly recognized.

"You were wrong if you thought that our decisions were based on the fertility religion. We can't go back to that now. We mustn't forget we have it in our background, but that does not explain the extreme importance of Nin-ana-Me joining me in this act. Her participation can demonstrate the power unfolding in this particular sacrifice. It is not just crazy thinking by a man who flew too high. There is more involved here than one person's thinking, man or woman," Kre-eg concluded.

"I'm sorry," Gart said. "After all of your explaining, I still don't see why this is the only way, or even the best way, for either of you."

"If I were to stay here, become lugal, circumvent the old tradition of term limits, and use the sparing of Lagash as the foundation of a bigger empire, it would just be more of the same. It would be very logical and forgettable. Nothing new would have been established.

"If I am no longer here, the sparing of Lagash can stand alone and be remembered in itself. That could be a seed for something new. It's much more likely to take hold if nourished by the grief and sorrow of the people over a loss that they can feel; something that doesn't fit their usual ideas of success," Kre-eg said.

"But will people understand?" Gart asked. "It's completely unreasonable."

"Most will not understand, but I am betting you can, and perhaps a few others. My work is over, but yours will take much longer. The drama of our leaving today will help you, Gart. You are the one who can remind people to listen for their own call. Surely they won't be called to show care in the same way. Today's circumstances? Never again. But others will be called to care, to serve the God in other ways."

"I still can't quite believe what I'm hearing," Gart shook his head stubbornly. "It's not something I would in any way have expected from you."

"And for good reason," Kre-eg said. "My character and my background hardly support it. This is not all my doing. I have had help from others, including you, my dancing daemon. Could anyone explain your conversion into a magician simply out of loyalty to me, when I had done little to deserve it?"

"I still see the hand of Nin-ana-Me here," said Gart. "I can follow — if with difficulty — your explanation, but why should she join you?"

"Like myself," Kre-eg answered. "Her work is done and she must get out of the way for it to endure. I know about her authorship of that 'ancient' ode. That writing has taken its own course, a surprising one. If its human author becomes known, as could easily happen if she remains in office, its power will be diminished."

"Umphh," Gart grunted. This was not so much in resistance as a signal that he was considering this further explanation.

"Don't you see, Gart, it is by the combined efforts of the God and men that the armies of Ur have prevailed. It is awe that has propelled them. The armies of Lagash have submitted without undue humiliation. Who could expect them to resist a god who swallows the sun? Here is a miraculous invitation for something new to enter in.

"Soon this city will need you, Gart. Mahn-so-ni will make a great lugal, yes, even a great king. Bruzi will make a great commander-in-chief, but they will need you. With your help, they will learn how to avoid flying too high."

"What do you want me to do?" Gart's voice, deliberate, wooden, echoed in the empty audience chamber.

"I'll explain that in a little while. I have some things to do. Perhaps there are some things you need to attend to before the rites begin. I will meet you back here in a half an hour," Kre-eg said, as they walked to the foot of the stairs.

Gart turned and walked swiftly out the front entrance. He wanted to leave the scene, clear his head. But he could feel the pull of habit and duty as his course veered off to the left and delivered him, all too soon, to the rear entrance. Surely he must have some business there in the servant's quarters and storerooms. Suddenly, he found himself at the entrance to the inner garden.

There, once more, on the Demmuzi bench, was Nin-ana-Me, clothed in a full gown of sky blue. Her head and shoulders were covered by a shawl of similar color but of a slightly deeper hue. At her waist gleamed the golden buckle of a belt woven of leather thongs. She appeared to be studying the tree with the same patient regard that both she and Demmuzi had previously shown. Gart searched the branches, but could see no bird.

The Priestess arose and approached the tree in the way the old king often had. She seemed to be studying the ground, scuffing around the exposed roots with her sandal toe. She repeated the process on the other side, then in front. Was this some kind of ceremony, perhaps in honor of Demmuzi? Was she simply trying to distract herself from the course she had chosen?

She crouched, lightly touching the rough bark on each side of the old trunk with her hands. Gart's hands tingled in memory of a rough texture he had also tested. She stood, running her hands over the main branches, her fingers lightly touching the partially healed wounds of recent pruning. Next, she circled around behind the tree. Something had caught her attention. Gart moved several steps to his right, along the wall, to see what it was. It was a nest! He had never seen that before. He watched her exploring fingers trace a line. The darker twigs of an old nest had obviously received a recent addition. Was that the work of the same old bird, or another generation with wider ambitions?

She looked up through the new shoots and old branches, squinting at the brightening light. Gart pictured the intricate pattern of sky that she must be viewing. How often had he done the same as a boy in the groves along the river? He marveled at how vividly he was sharing her experience, just by watching, without a word spoken.

She turned and walked back to the bench. She must have been aware of his presence right along, although she had given no sign. She stood waiting for him to pass in front of her on his way back to the audience hall.

"Goodbye, Gart," she said.

"Goodbye, My Lady," he answered quickly, moving on just as rapidly, away from the level gaze of those gray eyes, flecked with gold.

The details of Kre-eg's further instructions to Gart in the audience chamber were overwhelmed by the events that necessarily grew out of them. In later times, Gart's only specific remembrance was hearing Kre-eg say:

"Yes, Gart. I *have* changed, but Nin-ana-Me and I are not the only ones who will be stepping over their old limits and into a new realm today."

That strange statement was to stand out like a stela in Gart's memory. Throughout the many years that followed, no other day was to compare with the pain and drama of that day. It marked his entry into an entirely new understanding and form of striving. Yes, his work did, indeed, take much longer. Those words of Kre-eg's were kept in service due to the uncanniness of the call of care which Gart experienced in that chamber — a call coming, not from Kre-eg's explanations or personal appeals, nor any other external source, but from within himself; a call contradicting all of his ordinary habits of thinking.

By midmorning, Gart was on the fourth level of the ziggurat, on the east side of the four step-like tiers of limestone. Here was the

Bed-Chamber of Nannar. Also in the party of seven were Ni-Zum-Ka, two younger priests, and three of the Royal Bodyguard. A low stone altar had been newly erected. It was flanked by two conical stacks of recently captured arms. A double line of captured helmets marked the north border of the area. Gart could not see, but had been told, that there was now an exact counterpart on the west side of the bed chamber, except that the flanking cones there were not arms, but the more usual offerings of grains and fruits. His counterpart in the other party was an officer chosen by lot.

At the appointed time, Gart and his counterpart were to assist the priests as directed. The volunteer victims were to be strangled, so their bodies could be returned to mother Ki as unblemished as possible. The bodies would be buried as rapidly as possible, before their light should fade. No libations they, not spilled upon the earth to sink in formless dissolution, but, in death, *beings still*, interred, incorporated, bringing their *above* to the *below.*

The Rite of Renewal for the New Year would ordinarily have been held at dawn, like the less important, monthly renewal rites. Because of the unusual circumstances and the expanded proceedings, the beginning of the ceremony had been delayed until midmorning. If there were no delays, the sacrifice would be completed at the same hour that the eclipse had occurred the previous day. It was obligatory, Gart had been told, the Rite of Renewal at the New Year be performed by the lugal and the High Priestess. The monthly rites could be, and usually were, delegated to others.

A flurry of activity around the entrance to the Royal Residence suggested the ceremonies were about to begin. Gart could not see the House of Women to the west but there were some eddies in the crowd there. He could see a great deal more. Not only had he never attended a ritual on this level, he had never been so high above the earth. He could see hills across the Euphrates and, on the near bank, fields and marsh and the main road to the north, now deserted. The people were still swarming in through the main gate to the compound. Never had he seen so many people at one glance, not at the parade, not even on the battlefield. If what he had felt yesterday was the gaze of a thousand eyes — could he bear this?

The ram's horns sounded. The four stairways to the north quickly cleared. The knots of attendants surrounding the lugal and the chief priestess were only half-way across the courtyard when the first celebrants began the ascent. There was a rank of four priests, all totally naked, for humility, each bearing a basket of earth on his shoulders. These baskets had just arrived, each from some far part of the four quarters of the realm of Ur. This loose earth, properly mixed, would form the marital bed for the New Year Rite of Renewal.

Six steps below the priests, followed the trumpeters, one rank of rams horns, then one rank of copper trumpets, followed by more ram's horns and more trumpets. They did not march directly upwards, but walked the length of each step as the long line of marchers and counter-marchers moved higher. The trumpeters were followed by men bearing bundles of captured arms and alternating ranks of women bearing sheaves of grain reserved for the occasion. The effigies of the major gods moved in, litter-born, from the smaller shrines surrounding the compound. The images and their escorts soon turned aside to stop at the level assigned according to that god's traditional rank.

The parties of the two chief celebrants approached the fourth level. Their accompanying attendants filed off to the sides as the waiting new attendants walked with slow and deliberate steps toward the center from their respective altars to stand briefly with the couple. Gart, who was at the head of his column, stopped just as the two turned to face each other.

It was very quiet.

A bird called, high pitched and far away.

In this, the moment that endured the most vividly for Gart, he saw in Nin-ana-Me's gaze the full power of the immanence he had glimpsed in audience hall and writing sessions. In Kre-eg's wide eyes and clear visage he saw an abandonment of self — not reckless — in her safekeeping. The coming cost of their gift unreckoned, they turned again to face the blue doors. Kre-eg bent slightly to slip a supporting forearm under that of his partner.

"My strong right arm," she said to him as she turned her left hand and fingers downward to form an airy dome on his proffered palm.

"My great treasure and the arch of heaven," he returned her gaze.

It was in this manner that the couple walked through the open blue doors of the bedchamber of the God. Those doors closed slowly behind them.

How is time measured? By actions? By thoughts? By the coming and going of the sun?

Kre-eg descended the four limestone steps from the east door. Through that door, light from the open west door could be seen within the dim chamber. Kre-eg approached the stack of arms. There he left his cloak, scepter and breast-plate of gold and lapis lazuli. He laid down the helmet which he had carried in his left hand. When he turned and walked directly to Gart, he was clad only in a loincloth held by a thong. In his right hand was a belt familiar to Gart. It was just like his!

"Commander, come. Do your duty." The whisper was harsh, urgent.

"Mercy, Kre-eg, I can't do this!" Gart whispered back. His knees shook. "To voluntarily and with a *will*" he recited to himself. He frantically scanned his memory to support himself in what was happening. "Give up some valuable possession — in search of a greater good, but without any guarantee —" he continued to whisper. Now he closed his lips lest he be heard. He could foresee Kre-eg's young body on the stone altar. The sight of that body would be engraved in thousands of minds, but Gart alone would sense the personal loss as he, himself, offered up his own carefully built sense of who he was by entering into this act.

"Yes, you can!" Kre-eg's searing whisper insisted. "You will be amazed at what you can do! Only you know how to lead a lame bullock across the river!"

Just like a sheep, a goat, a bag of grain...don't think. Do what you must. As Kre-eg knelt, elbows on the altar, Gart straddled him, braced his shaky knees against warm flanks. As the loop of the belt passed over the head, Gart's hand brushed the tip of that long bony nose.

Does the bow realize what is launched from its string? How high the arc, how long the flight? Perhaps later, but at that moment of transforming power, sharp blends with dull and fills... everything. So it is also with the arms of men. Sinew and bone spring and bend in action and then... relax. The deed is done. Let the keening begin. Let bitter tears of grief wash the courtyard and cleanse the heart.

Once more a fierce and fiery Utu ascends the vault of the sky and reaches his zenith, his unrelenting rays undamped by any experience of yesterday.

At the water's edge,
a squadron of dragon-flies
  ...slowly ascends
 ... in staggered line.
Their wings scatter the sunlight…
    into sparkles of magenta and gold,
until their faces...look upon...
   ...the face of the sun
and all are lifted by a passing zephyr
  ...from the sea
and suddenly propelled …
  ...along the river bank...northwest.

EPILOGUE

"Grandfather, what is an Aiperu?"

"Why, where did you hear that word?" the old man laughed.

"One of the boys in the town called me that today. I don't think it was meant as a compliment."

"Oh, we are called that sometimes," his grandfather said. "You are probably right about the boy's intentions, but his understanding of the word is probably as bad as his pronunciation. He should have pronounced it EBER-U, and you should only be honored to be known as a descendent of Eber who was Lord Chamberlain to two of the most famous kings of Ur. Some of his descendants held high offices until recently, in fact."

"I've heard that story," the boy said, "but I have a question I never dared ask."

"Surely you dare ask me. What is it?"

"Well, if our family was so great, what did we do to get banished so that we are here, freezing our shins, in these drafty tents out in the fields? Why is it that we have to pay rent to that stupid little king in Haran?"

"Oh, we're not banished. We did nothing disgraceful. In fact, it was probably because of the power and wealth of our family we were called — I was called — to go back to the quiet and hardships of the desert."

"What do you mean, you were called, Grandfather? Who called you?"

"Well, let us just say that *El* passed by the city one day and ruffled the waters of the west basin in such a way that I understood He meant for us to leave that place," the old man explained.

"I've never heard you talk about anything like that," the boy said, quite surprised.

"Oh, I wasn't the first to be called away from that city. Your forefather, Peleg, went back to the shepherds and spent many years wandering with them before he was persuaded to come back to succeed his father as Lord Chamberlain. He must have needed to get away from the city, as I did, to try to make sense of all the things that have happened there. When we repeat the same old mistakes and don't remember, don't take responsibility for what we have learned, life goes around in a circle and we lose our taste for it. In Ur there were too many people and too many gods," he said.

"But why must we go to the desert?" the boy asked.

"Everyone knows that plants grow and flower and bring forth fruit," the grandfather resumed, "but it's only in the desert there is space and time enough that we can recognize those processes within ourselves. Only when there is time for awe do we take the trouble to put what we have seen into words and establish them in memory."

The boy looked somewhat skeptical and soon returned to his concerns. "But if wandering in the desert is supposed to help us, if we are walking in the ways of our god, El, why do people attack us, call us names like *Aiperu* and say we are shiftless and don't have any roots?" he asked.

"Be patient with them, young man. How could strangers know we weren't the usual marauding thieves and robbers. They can't see our roots because our roots are not here. They are not in the soil of this land or any other. Our roots are inside us."

"'Inside us'? Do you mean in our memories? Our imagination?" the boy asked.

"Yes, you have the right idea." the old man said. "But there is more to it than that. We have learned — some of us — how to hold these memories in reverence, to brood over them until we understand the choices we can make."

The boy seemed a little more convinced but, not knowing what to say about inward roots, he fell back on his own experience.

"I don't remember Ur. I was just a little baby when we left, but I always imagine her as a high and wonderful city shining in the sun."

"Your imagination is certainly more agreeable than my memories," Grandfather said. "When we left there I was convinced it was sinking into the swamp. Even the ziggurat was showing signs of wear and neglect. Indeed there was a time, and not so long ago, when Ur was a shining example for all of Sumer. Her kings were wise and just and their reigns were long. All of the crafts and sciences were in full bloom. Everything seemed to fit into its place: metal craft, the design of buildings, weaving, the building of chariots and boats and writing —yes, that was probably the heart of the matter there — writing. But that was all in the times of Peleg and his son Rue and those things have faded. It's up to us to bring what we can of those times with us to new lands. These are new times."

"I've heard lots of those stories, but I don't remember much about Eber. Was he a hero, Grandfather? Was he the one who conquered the other cities and made the whole land of Sumer rich?"

"No, I wouldn't call him a hero, at least not in the usual sense. He wasn't a mighty warrior, nor a lawgiver, nor a poet as such, but he is to be honored for cutting a path for us. Eber's task was to remember and to remind and advise. By doing that, he preserved the lives and the works of the kings and the poet that he so loved."

"'Cut a path for us?' Do you mean Eber is helping us even when most people don't recognize his name?" the boy asked.

"That's right. Indeed, the king Eber loved the most had the shortest reign of all and no monuments to him are to be seen. That king did subdue certain cities but is most remembered for what he learned about himself. Our storytellers often miss the point of their tale as they try to keep it exciting.

"You and I should remind those story tellers not to leave things out because neither that nameless king, nor Eber, nor any of us, was ever unnecessary. We are all leaves and branches on the tree of life. When we tend to those inward roots that we have been talking about, we all have our job to do in our time."

"And the poet, Grandfather, who was that?"

"The poet? Her writings are lost, but the joy of her life and work lives on in the stories that Eber first told. You probably have never heard those tales, but it would be good to save some stories until you are a little older. Remind your father or uncle to tell them when they think the time is right. I'll speak to them about it tonight, before you leave."

"But surely you're coming with us? I couldn't leave you behind," the boy protested."

"No, I'm too old to travel so far. I'll stay here with your cousins."

"But you're our leader, Grandfather!"

"No longer. This is as far as I can go. It's your uncle's dream that will be leading you on south, perhaps even to the shores of the western sea."

"But will you be all right here, in this place, with my cousins? I've never felt at home here."

"And rightly so, my son, but the trees of Haran also have leaves and I am content to be one of them."